Bolivar

By Jamie Edmundson

THE WEAPON TAKERS SAGA
TORIC'S DAGGER
BOLIVAR'S SWORD

BOOK TWO OF
THE WEAPON TAKERS SAGA

BOLIVAR'S SWORD

JAMIE EDMUNDSON

Rarn
Publishing

Bolivar's Sword
Book Two of The Weapon Takers Saga
Copyright © 2018 by Jamie Edmundson. All rights reserved.
First Edition: 2018

Rarn
Publishing

ISBN 978-1-912221-03-5

Author website jamieedmundson.com
Author newsletter http://eepurl.com/cvEqgP

Cover: Streetlight Graphics

For Mum

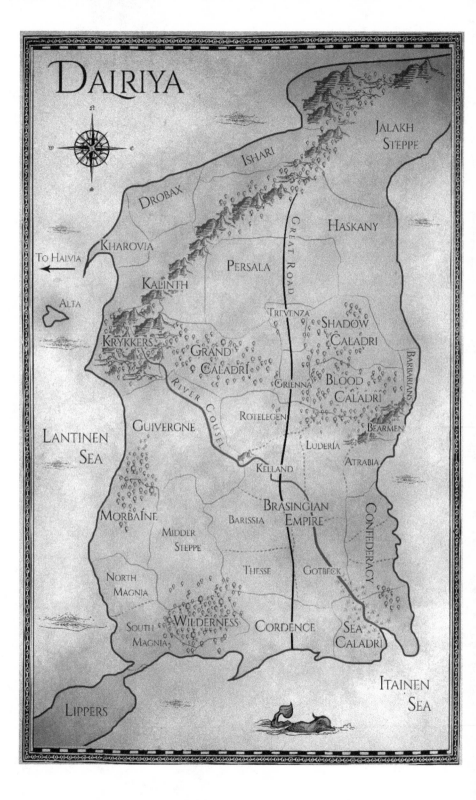

Dramatis Personae

South Magnians
Soren, a wizard
Belwynn, Soren's sister
Herin, a mercenary
Clarin, Herin's brother
Farred, a nobleman of Middian descent
Gyrmund, Farred's friend, an explorer

Edgar, Prince of South Magnia
Leofwin, Edgar's bodyguard
Brictwin, Edgar's bodyguard
Ealdnoth, Edgar's court wizard
Wilchard, Edgar's chief steward
Burstan, a captain in the army
Anulf, a soldier
Morlin, a soldier
Ulf, a smith
Ragulf, a standard bearer

North Magnians
Elana, a priestess of Madria

Cerdda, Prince of North Magnia
Ashere, Cerdda's younger brother
Mette, Cerdda's mother
Elfled, Cerdda's sister
Irmgard, Cerdda's wife

Middians
Brock, a tribal chief
Frayne, a tribal chief

Cordentines
Glanna, King of Cordence
Rosmont, a Cordentine ambassador

Barissians
Dirk, a priest of Madria

Emeric, Duke of Barissia
Gervase Salvinus, a mercenary leader
Curtis, a soldier

Kellish
Moneva, a mercenary

Baldwin, Duke of Kelland, Emperor of Brasingia
Hannelore, Empress of Brasingia
Walter, Baldwin's younger brother, Marshal of the Empire
Rainer, Baldwin's chamberlain
Decker, Archbishop of Kelland
Gustav the Hawk, Archmage of the Empire
Lord Kass, a nobleman

Rotelegen
Jeremias, Duke of Rotelegen
Adalheid, Duchess of Rotelegen, his mother
Veit, a scout
Rudy, a prisoner in Samir Durg
Jurgen, a prisoner in Samir Durg

Other Brasingians

Arne, Duke of Luderia

Godfrey, Archbishop of Gotbeck

Coen, Duke of Thesse

Lord Emmett, a Thessian nobleman

Guivergnais

Nicolas, King of Guivergne

Bastien, Duke of Morbaine

Russell, Bastien's man

Kalinthians

Theron, Count of Erisina, Knight of Kalinth

Evander, Theron's squire

Sebastian, Count of Melion, Knight of Kalinth

Alpin, Sebastian's squire

Galenos, Grand Master of the Knights of Kalinth

Tycho, Knight of Kalinth, Theron's friend

Remigius, Knight of Kalinth, Sebastian's friend

Euthymius, Knight of Kalinth

Philon, Knight of Kalinth

Leontios, Knight of Kalinth

Nestor, a smith

Jonas, King of Kalinth

Irina, Queen of Kalinth

Straton, eldest son of Jonas

Dorian, second son of Jonas

Diodorus, Count of Korenandi

Haskans

Shira, Queen of Haskany, member of the Council of Seven

Koren, Shira's uncle

Persaleians

Pentas, a wizard
Cyprian, a prisoner in Samir Durg
Zared, a prisoner in Samir Durg

Krykkers

Kaved, a mercenary
Rabigar, an exile

Torinac, a chief
Maragin, a chief
Guremar, a chief
Hakonin, a chief
Stenk, a young warrior
Porimin, an historian

Caladri

Dorjan, King of the Shadow Caladri

Isharites

Erkindrix, Lord of Ishari
Arioc, King of Haskany, member of the Council of Seven
Siavash, High Priest of Ishari, member of the Council of Seven
Nexodore, a wizard, member of the Council of Seven
Ardashir, a wizard, member of the Council of Seven
Tirano, a wizard, serving Emeric of Barissia
Roshanak, a wizard, lieutenant of Shira
Mehrab, a wizard, lieutenant of Shira
Babak, Arioc's servant

Other

Vamak, a Dog-man
Tamir, a Barbarian chieftain

Prologue

S IAVASH PAUSED OUTSIDE THE PRIVATE chambers of Lord Erkindrix, a thrill of anticipation coursing through his body.

To be invited here was a rare honour, even for him. Ordinarily, Erkindrix only held meetings in his Throne Room, or the Council Chamber. The private chambers were only accessed by those servants who tended to his physical needs. They were nameless, nugatory creatures, who no doubt saw him at his most vulnerable and repulsive. Siavash didn't dwell on that.

No. Siavash, High Priest of the Order of Diis, member of the Council of Seven, didn't thrill at the thought of sharing an enclosed space with Erkindrix and his decaying, putrid body. He craved proximity with a God. For Diis himself, the mightiest deity of all, inhabited the body of Erkindrix. His eyes rolled beneath the Lord of Ishari's. His words could, at times, be heard through the reedy voice of his vessel.

Siavash entered the room. The stink of Erkindrix knifed through the cloying perfumes which were used to mask it. The Lord of Ishari lay prone on his bed. He had yet to regain strength enough to stand since the attack on Edeleny. Ishari had won a great victory against the Grand Caladri, but at a price. Scores of their magi lay dead, scores more had been pushed into madness by the confrontation.

'What news?' asked Erkindrix through a gargle of saliva.

Siavash approached the bed. He felt the presence of Diis—powerful, malevolent. It was as if his God, crushed inside the tiny, wizened frame of an old man, cast a shadow the size of a mountain. Siavash felt the primeval fear of encountering such a being; he felt the ecstasy of proximity to such power. Instinctively, he dropped to his knees.

'I can report that most of the lands of the Caladri are being taken with no resistance. The only exception is to the south, where a faction has organised a military defence, supported by some surviving magi. It is not a significant threat, but they are able to use the terrain to their advantage.'

1

'Good.'

Siavash prepared to deliver the bad news. He would enjoy the telling, but he had to be careful not to let Erkindrix see it. The Lord of Ishari's relationship with Arioc was a close one, and Siavash knew that he always had to tread carefully on such territory.

'Unfortunately, when our forces reached Onella's Temple, Her Staff was missing.'

'Missing?' Erkindrix spluttered.

'I should say, taken. It is unclear by whom, or where. But King Arioc has captured some prisoners whom he believes can reveal that information.'

'Inept,' Erkindrix barked, 'to allow such a thing.'

Siavash smiled inwardly.

'What other news?'

'Queen Shira's force has crossed into the Empire. Given her victory over the Rotelegen army, she should not take long to complete the conquest.'

Calling Arioc's bitch a Queen never fails to stick in my throat, he added to himself.

Erkindrix grunted. With what looked like some effort, he pushed himself up into a sitting position. 'The weapons,' he hissed. 'The threat from these weapons should not be underestimated. Nexodore has failed to deliver them, now Arioc fails me.'

Siavash almost volunteered then. To gain these weapons would be a trifling task, and yet give him success where the dread Nexodore and Arioc had both failed. But to leave Samir Durg, to leave his Master and his God, when he enjoyed such unrivalled proximity; that could be a dangerous mistake.

'Send Pentas,' said Erkindrix. 'He must retrieve them.'

Siavash's lip curled up into a sneer at the mention of the name.

'What?' demanded Erkindrix.

'A human? He can't be trusted with such a task,' he replied with distaste.

'Then who?'

Me? No. I must play a cautious game. My place is here, at the centre; at the very heart of power.

'You are right, My Lord. I will instruct Pentas. I will make sure that he understands the importance of these weapons.'

I

STRANGERS

THE LIGHT OF MORNING FORCED Belwynn to open her eyes. Her mind gradually returned the events of yesterday to her consciousness. Splitting up from her brother Soren and the others, Belwynn had joined Elana, Dirk and Rabigar in a search for Onella's Staff. They had found it in the Temple, Elana seemingly guided to its location. The wizard Pentas had then teleported them away from danger. They had travelled a long distance under his spell, and once they had stopped, felt exhausted and ill. They had fallen asleep pretty much where Pentas' magic had dropped them, too tired to prepare a fire or even to eat a cold supper.

Belwynn pushed herself up into a sitting position, rubbing her head which banged with pain. She looked around. Pentas had seemingly dropped them halfway up a hill. The trees which had surrounded them in the forest of the Grand Caladri were sparser here, while the ground beneath them was rocky; large chunks of stone littered the landscape about them.

Elana and Dirk were still asleep a few yards away. Rabigar wasn't there. Belwynn supposed that he had gone to collect firewood or search for food. Her stomach grumbled at the thought.

So, Soren and the others had not made it. Perhaps Pentas had failed to reach them in time? They could be dead. A feeling of dread stabbed at Belwynn's insides. She tried to reach her brother.

Soren. Soren?

A few moments of silence passed, but then there was a response.

Belwynn? Is that you?

It was Soren and he was alive. It was not easy to pick up what he was saying though. There was some kind of interference—more than the distance that separated them.

Yes, it's me, Belwynn replied. *Where are you?*

Captured...must be careful. We defended the entrance to the Temple, but Arioc himself came for us. We're all alive, but they caught us. They're taking us north, to Ishari or Haskany. They've got wizards monitoring me...must be careful.

There was a pause. Soren's voice was thin, and Belwynn's ability to pick up what he was saying varied, as if he were putting his hand over his mouth and taking it away again. Belwynn had experienced something similar once before, when her brother was with Delyth, the marsh witch.

Where are you? Soren continued. *Did you get the staff?*

Yes, we've got it. Pentas, the wizard with the red eyes, found us in the Temple. He told us we had to escape. He teleported us away. I don't know where we are, but we're safe. He said he would look for you—

Thank Toric you're safe. It must have been too late for him to get to us. You must get the weapons to safety. Contact me again tomorrow when you've found out where you are. But we'll have to keep it brief. It's dangerous. Goodbye Belwynn.

Bye Soren, Belwynn answered.

She wanted to cry. Her brother and the others had been captured by Arioc and the Isharites. There was no way of knowing what would happen to them and she had no way to help—she didn't even know where she was. She suddenly felt tired and alone. Gripping her head in her hands, she wiped away a tear that had started to fall with her palm. She had to control herself. She was in charge now. She would have to be strong.

A noise to her left made her turn sharply. It was Rabigar. He marched over and opened his arms, a pile of tree branches dropping on to the floor. He yanked at his belt and held up a brace of squirrels.

'Breakfast,' he declared.

Belwynn forced a smile. 'Thank you, Rabigar. I've just spoken to Soren. He and the others were captured by Arioc. He said that they're all alive and being transported northwards.'

Rabigar nodded. 'I think that's about the best we could hope for. If they're being transported north, it means that Arioc wants them alive. He would have killed them otherwise. I'm sorry if that's not much comfort.'

'No, it's fine. I know it could have been much worse. It's just that the prospect of rescuing them is so daunting—we don't even know where we are!'

'Not entirely true,' replied Rabigar. 'I got a clear look at the stars last night. Pentas sent us in a north-westerly direction. I reckon we're on the border between the Grand Caladri and Kalinth. Now, we'll have to be careful. By all accounts the King of Kalinth is nothing more than a puppet of Erkindrix these days. But we're not far from my homeland. If we make it there, the weapons will be safe. Then we can work out what to do about your brother and the others.'

That Rabigar had a plan, even if somewhat vague, was something for Belwynn to hang on to for now. He was taking the initiative, and Belwynn was grateful for that.

'First things first, though,' Rabigar continued. 'We'll get breakfast ready and try to wake those two up.'

They did not get far that day. The exhaustion caused by the events in Edeleny had not left their bodies. Dirk, in particular, was not well. He walked on in grim silence, as if all his concentration and energy were needed just to put one foot in front of the other. Belwynn gave him Onella's Staff to lean on across the difficult terrain. Although Rabigar seemed to think that they were in Kalinth, the landscape in this region seemed to be a combination of the forests of the Grand Caladri, and the hilly country of the Krykkers. When Belwynn complained about this, Rabigar would point to the distant mountains to the south-west and claim that *they* were real hills, not these. Occasionally, when they crested a hill, they would get a glimpse of the Plain of Kalinth stretching away to the north, and though Belwynn disagreed with the Krykker that such a view made the climb worthwhile, she had to admit that it was a fine sight.

What they really missed were horses. On various mounts, they had travelled over half the length of Dalriya in the past two weeks. By comparison, walking pace seemed slow and laborious. Belwynn suspected that they had barely covered ten miles when they stopped to make their camp for the night.

When she woke the next morning, Rabigar had again been the first up. A small fire was already burning and chestnuts were being slowly cooked.

'Are those edible?' asked Belwynn suspiciously.

'Yes. Sweet chestnuts. Horse chestnuts are the poisonous ones. Here,' he said, pointing at them. 'They have a little tail on the bottom. That's how you tell you've got the right kind.'

He sounded more than a little pleased with himself.

'I've been thinking about our position,' Rabigar informed her as she sat up. 'There is a trading town called Korkis, it should be about five miles west of here. I know it quite well. It picks up trade between Kalinth, the Krykkers, and occasionally the Grand Caladri as well. We could do with picking up some supplies and utensils. If I'm right, we should get there by lunchtime.'

Belwynn nodded. She was happy for Rabigar to make the decisions for now. Last night she and Soren had a very brief conversation, partly because he was worried they would be caught, partly because neither had anything new to say. Her brother and her friends were still being transported northwards. Part of her wanted to turn around and follow, but Soren insisted that she find a secure place for the two weapons before she did anything else.

'Then what?' she asked Rabigar, leaning over to the fire to inspect breakfast.

He pointed out a couple. 'When the shell splits, they're ready.'

Belwynn grabbed one. It was hot, too hot for her fingers, and she juggled it around in the air before letting it drop into her lap. She sucked on her fingers to cool them down. Rabigar looked on with a disappointed expression on his face.

'Then we head south-west for my homeland. I don't know what kind of reception I will get. But at the very least they will keep the Dagger and Staff safe. They may do more to help.'

He paused, studying her face, as if unsure whether to continue. 'I've mentioned this to Elana already. The Krykkers have another of these weapons. In our Great Meeting Chamber, in the mountain of Kerejus. Bolivar's Great Sword, which he used in the Battle of Alta.'

Belwynn nodded. She wondered why Rabigar hadn't mentioned this before. She could tell that a part of him still had a loyalty towards his people, despite his years of exile. No doubt this sword was a great treasure.

'How many years is it since you left?' she asked.

Rabigar seemed to think about it.

'Thirty. And then some.'

'Do you ever miss it?'

'I will always miss my home.'

It was said with such feeling that it stopped Belwynn from asking her next question. *Why* was he exiled? But Rabigar knew her thoughts.

'You're curious to know what happened?' he asked her.

She shrugged. 'A little.'

'I will not tell you, Belwynn. It is no disrespect to you: it is a question of honour to me. It is a matter for my people only—not a story to be discussed by others. I have kept it to myself for all these thirty and more years. That is a long time. But I would have you understand one thing. I was a very different man then than I am now.'

6

His gaze drifted to the mountains of his homeland and a faraway look came to his face.

When Elana and Dirk were ready, they set off for the town of Korkis. They walked mostly in silence, everyone seemingly content in their own thoughts. For Belwynn, though, the morning walk began to make her feel lonely. She missed her brother. But she also missed the sharp asides of Herin, and Clarin's calm, protective presence. She had come to value her three current companions, but was not close to any one of them. Belwynn began to dwell on her captured friends. She wanted to try to talk with Soren again, but since it could be dangerous for him, she resisted.

It was a long morning, made worse by grey clouds that blew in and deposited a constant drizzle; but by midday they were on a path heading towards Korkis. The town had been built on top of a hill, and as they got closer they could make out a wooden palisade encircling it. As they made their way up, Belwynn could make out the individual wooden stakes, buried into the ground and sharpened at the tip to make an effective barrier against an attacking force. The entrance to the town was through a formidable looking wooden gate, perhaps fifteen feet high, from where defenders could fire down at the enemy.

Today, the gate was wide open and there was a single guard on duty, who looked out at their approach with a lazy expression.

'We're here to buy some basic provisions,' Rabigar shouted up.

The guard simply waved a hand to let them through, seemingly more than used to strangers arriving.

Once through the gate, there was an open plaza. A log built road led straight ahead towards the centre of the town. Wooden built shops and stalls were positioned on either side. A statue of a knight on horseback marked the central square. Because they had arrived at midday, the town was quite busy.

'The number of people here makes it safer for us,' said Rabigar, speaking under his breath as the four of them began to mingle with the crowd. 'But there's no point in staying any longer than we have to. I'll get the cooking utensils, clothes and any other extras we need if you three get the food. We'll meet up by the statue.'

Belwynn, Elana and Dirk soon found that oats were the most plentiful crop in this region. However, prices were still high, and Belwynn noticed that a number of the shoppers in Korkis looked hungry, prepared to buy damp bags of oats or old, shrivelled looking vegetables that in happier times wouldn't have been sold in the first place. As they moved from stall to stall, Belwynn picked up on the problems the merchants were encountering: trade from Haskany and Persala had all but dried up since Ishari had taken control; the produce which did arrive was mostly smuggled out. Very little arrived over the mountain routes from the Krykkers, while nothing came in from the Grand Caladri at all. There were even problems within Kalinth. A dispute between King Jonas and the Knights of Kalinth, along with rumours of Drobax raids, discouraged people from travelling too far.

After surveying the choice that was available, they agreed on what to buy. Oats could form the basis of a gruel, quick to prepare and full of energy, if rather dull to eat. They were able to supplement this with beans and vegetables, especially cabbage. A number of stalls sold pickled cabbage in clay jars, which would stay edible for weeks.

They found themselves fully supplied with food and waiting by the statue for Rabigar to return with the more complicated items. A number of armed guards walked about in twos and threes, dressed in brown leather with a spear and shield motif sewn on to their front jackets. Belwynn noticed how the people in the town shuffled out of the way at their approach and tried to avoid eye contact. The guards would sometimes stop off at a stall to help themselves to some of the food, while the stallholders looked away as if they hadn't noticed. All in all, there was an unsettling atmosphere in the town. It seemed to Belwynn that with less to go round, the bullies of the community were making sure that they didn't go hungry. Elana and Dirk seemed to sense it too. They were both very quiet and huddled down by the statue, as if the smaller they made themselves, the less they would be noticed.

Suddenly there was a disturbance a few stalls away from where Belwynn was standing. A young child was struggling in the grasp of a stall-holder. Peering over, Belwynn could see that it was a girl with close-cropped hair, perhaps about the age of seven. She was thin and hungry looking, but still seemed to think that she had a chance of escaping from her captor.

'Caught her trying to nick a loaf,' the stall-holder was saying to the surrounding crowd.

A couple of guardsmen appeared at the scene. One of them held out a hand. The baker wordlessly passed the child over. The guard gripped her wrist hard. She continued to struggle, but the guard struck her across the face with the outside of a gloved hand. The girl stopped struggling and now had tears in her eyes, looking around with a fearful expression.

'We know how to deal with thieves,' said the guard in a voice designed to carry across the crowd which had now stopped what it was doing to look.

Belwynn had seen and heard enough. She didn't think through her actions. Some part of her mind propelled her body towards the confrontation in the street. As she approached their space, the group turned to look at her. The baker frowned at her. The young girl looked up nervously. The two guards stared stony-faced.

'I will pay for her bread,' suggested Belwynn reasonably. 'I don't think she's a thief. Just a hungry child.'

Almost as the last syllable left her mouth, the rest of Belwynn's brain caught up with her actions. This was not clever. The second guard hefted a long spear, pointing the metal end in her direction.

'We don't have strangers coming here telling us what to do. We have town laws to respect.'

Some in the crowd murmured their agreement. The guard, perhaps emboldened by this, gestured at Belwynn's waist where her sword was belted.

'Drop your sword to the ground. You're under arrest.'

Belwynn expected no justice from these men.

'No,' she said. Instead she drew it out, stepping back slightly to give herself room for a swing.

At this gesture, there was a sudden rush of movement and noise. The stallholders and shoppers moved away from the confrontation, some gasping in shock at the turn of events. At the same time two groups moved to join them. Three guards who had also been patrolling the centre of town moved over to support the first two. Meanwhile, Dirk and Elana moved over to join Belwynn. Dirk looked ill, but at least he carried a short sword. Elana had no weapon at all.

'Back off,' said Dirk in a cool voice.

The guardsmen smiled, their dirty teeth bared in delight at the sudden sport they were being given. All five now had weapons out, two of them holding spears with a reach far greater than the swords held by Elana and Dirk. They began to move towards Belwynn and the others.

'Kill them,' shouted one of the guards, his eyes staring at Belwynn as he said it.

'Try to leave the women alive!' suggested another, to the laughs of his comrades.

They did not take the threat from Belwynn and Dirk seriously, and why should they? Belwynn might show them she knew how to fight. Dirk could probably draw on his last reserves of strength if he had to. But they were outnumbered by bigger and stronger men. Belwynn wished that Elana and Dirk hadn't come over to help. They would have been more use staying out of the fight. At least, she thought to herself, the little girl had been forgotten. Belwynn could not see her anywhere. No doubt she had slipped away by now.

Belwynn held her sword out in front of her and edged backwards. Behind her, Dirk and Elana also retreated. The guardsmen fanned out so that they could attack from the sides. Someone came at her from behind and to the right—another guardsman sneaking up on them?

'Rabigar is here,' said Elana.

Belwynn was glad she did, because she was just in the process of taking a swing at the Krykker.

'Don't worry,' he whispered as he walked by.

Rabigar put himself in-between Belwynn and the guardsmen. His sword was in one hand.

'We're leaving,' he informed them in a matter of fact voice. 'Let us go and there will be no bloodshed.'

The guardsmen sniggered.

'We want bloodshed,' said one of them. 'Yours.'

To the guards, Rabigar's arrival didn't change their superiority and control of the situation. Rabigar's eye patch perhaps seemed to suggest he was no real threat to these soldiers. But Belwynn knew better. They might have a chance to escape now.

Rabigar was moving at some speed towards the guardsman who had shouted out.

'You want my blood?' he shouted, almost roaring a challenge.

Rabigar reached the guard before the others could react. Once in range, the guard let out a roar of his own and swung a club in a descending arc towards the Krykker's chest area. Rabigar blocked the strike up high and then spun into the remaining space. In the same motion, he swung his blade up into the undefended neck of the guard, the sharpened point slicing through the jugular vein. As Rabigar retreated, he was sprayed by a squirt of blood, the guard sinking to his knees before toppling over. Screams erupted all around them, as the crowds which had been watching the confrontation turned and fled. The four remaining guardsmen suddenly looked worried. Rabigar turned around.

'Dirk, you lead us towards the far end of the town. I know a way out. Belwynn, we're walking backwards to put off anyone from following. Elana, you're guiding our steps. Let's go, as quick as we can.'

II

PURSUIT

BELWYNN KNEW HOW LUCKY SHE was that Rabigar knew an alternative exit from Korkis. The trading town was in chaos after the confrontation she had started in the central square, but its soldiers were organised enough to close the gates to prevent an escape.

Rabigar led Belwynn, Elana and Dirk through a maze of side streets. Following them all the way were two of the town guards. They were wary enough of Rabigar not to challenge them directly, but they made sure not to let them out of their sight. Doubtless they planned to corner them until reinforcements arrived.

The guards hadn't bargained on Rabigar's knowledge of the town.

They arrived in an alley. Rabigar led them on, but they soon stopped at a dead end. Ahead of them were the wooden stakes of the town walls, driven in too deep to lift out with any ease. The two guards stood at the top of the alley, holding their prey in, but reluctant to move any further. One of them began shouting out their location to anyone who would listen. It wouldn't be long before they attracted the right attention.

Rabigar approached the wall. He kicked at it. A section swung open. It was attached with hinges to the rest of the wall, effectively opening as a gate with a space large enough for one person to fit through. It had been constructed well, invisible except to those who knew to look for it.

Rabigar stepped one foot over onto the grassy hill outside the town wall.

'I'm glad that's still there,' said Rabigar, grinning at the others. He turned around and climbed right through. Belwynn, Elana and Dirk quickly followed and they were all outside by the time the two guards reached the gate themselves.

Rabigar led them away from the town, making for a wooded area about a mile to the north. For a moment Belwynn thought they were safe, but the guards were not giving up so easily. Korkis seemed to be an independent and military minded town. The soldiers were not about to let them escape unpunished. The two guards had soon attracted the attention of their colleagues manning the northern gate tower, to the west of the postern gate. By the time Belwynn and the others had reached the outskirts of the wooded cover Rabigar was leading them to, a force of about a dozen soldiers had set out from the town to chase them down. There was no doubt that the men of Korkis could see them.

When they entered the tree line, Belwynn glanced back once more. A single rider had now joined the men on foot. He would be able to eat up the distance between them, and ensure that the soldiers wouldn't lose their quarry. She shared a glance with Rabigar.

'I think they've got a couple of dogs as well,' he said, his head cocked upwards, suggesting he had heard rather than seen their presence.

They pressed on into the wood. It felt a little safer once they were out of sight from the soldiers, but Belwynn knew that their pursuers would have no problems following their trail.

Rabigar looked upwards. 'Less than two hours until it gets dark. Then they'll have to stop. A night out in the cold might persuade them to give up the chase. We've got to keep going.'

Dirk and Elana nodded in agreement at his words, but they didn't seem particularly reassured by them.

Belwynn felt terrible that they were in this position because of her actions. 'I'm sorry,' she said. 'If I had just kept out of it we wouldn't be in this mess. It was stupid.'

'No-one blames you,' said Elana, gripping her shoulder. 'You acted bravely, for that young girl.'

'Maybe, but there are more important things. I should have been thinking about the weapons, about Soren—'

'No,' said Elana. 'You did the right thing.'

Elana sounded like she meant what she said. It made Belwynn feel better.

It wasn't long afterwards that they heard the barking of dogs behind them, indicating that their trail had been found and their pursuers had entered the woods. They were travelling as fast as they could, but Dirk was still unwell and they had been walking almost all day. The soldiers would be stronger and faster. They had to make it to nightfall.

They marched on, Rabigar trying to find a passable route through the trees. The sound of the soldiers and the dogs behind spurred them on. Rather than following directly behind them, they seemed to have fanned out to the left.

'Cutting us off from the deeper part of the wood,' said Rabigar grimly in explanation.

Belwynn gave him a worried look.

He shrugged his shoulders as if it didn't matter. 'They want to push us out into open ground. If they want to waste time doing that, it's fine by me.'

Gradually, but inevitably, they were getting closer. An hour passed in this way, Belwynn and the others trying to maintain the ever-diminishing gap which would keep them safe. Meanwhile, the Korkis soldiers continued to herd them in a north-easterly direction. The sun moved lower and lower in the sky and the light began to go. Soon it would disappear altogether and they would have to stop.

Belwynn heard a horse's hooves behind them. She turned around, grabbing the hilt of her sword. The horseman from Korkis was a hundred yards behind them. He had moved ahead of his other comrades and was alone. Rabigar moved towards him, sword in hand, to stand in front of the others.

The horseman moved a bit closer and then stopped, eyeing up his opposition. He was a young man, perhaps just into his twenties. He drew a sword from his belt.

'I've found you,' he said, smiling at the idea. 'The others aren't far behind. Turn yourselves in now.'

'Why?' asked Rabigar. 'Scared of spending the night out in the woods?'

'You're the one who should be scared,' the soldier retorted hotly. 'Give up now, or I'll finish you off myself!'

'Go ahead and try,' replied Rabigar calmly. 'I could do with that horse after I slit your throat.'

Rabigar's bravado seemed to pay off. The soldier looked at him uneasily. He did not seem entirely comfortable on the horse and had no doubt heard that Rabigar was a dangerous opponent.

'Maybe I'll just wait here for the others,' said the soldier. He cupped his hands to his mouth. 'Over here,' he shouted.

A surge of panic ran through Belwynn's body.

'We're going,' said Rabigar, maintaining his steady voice. 'Belwynn, you lead the way. I'll stay behind in case he tries anything,' he said loudly.

Belwynn nodded. She led them off in the same direction they had been going. Elana and Dirk followed behind while Rabigar brought up the rear, his one eye on the mounted soldier. After a while the soldier urged his horse on and followed behind, all the time keeping a safe distance from Rabigar. Every now and again he would shout out to the other soldiers, who would shout back in return. These new tactics were certainly scaring her, but Belwynn realised that they were using them in desperation. There was little light left and the other soldiers were too far away to reach them tonight.

Another half an hour passed. Then Rabigar suddenly turned and ran at the soldier who had been following them, his sword ready to strike. For a moment, the soldier seemed unsure whether to take on the Krykker or retreat. He decided on the latter, turning his horse around and giving it a hurried kick, urging it away. Rabigar stopped and let him go. Once a safe distance away again, the soldier turned around in his saddle.

'See you in the morning,' he crowed, before continuing until out of sight.

Rabigar made them carry on walking until he was sure that their pursuers had stopped for the night. He threw his bag down to the floor, making a jingling sound as his new cookery items hit the ground.

'Well, I'm not going to start cooking *now*,' said Rabigar. 'I don't know whether to leave these things behind in the morning. How did you three get on with food?' he asked.

'We haven't got much that tastes good raw,' replied Dirk. 'Dried oats, vegetables...'

'Get that pickled cabbage out,' suggested Belwynn. 'It will taste alright and then we can leave the jars behind.'

Belwynn forced herself to eat the food so that she would have enough energy for tomorrow. She could hear noise from the other camp, less than a mile away, and it set her on edge. For all they knew there could be soldiers out in the trees right now, watching them.

Rabigar insisted that the other three get to sleep and that he would keep watch all night.

Belwynn was too tired to argue. She considered contacting Soren. But what could she say, except to blurt out the danger they were in? That wouldn't help them one bit, and it would only add to her brother's worries.

She lay down, desperate for rest. But her mind was reeling and couldn't switch off, and the hard ground was uncomfortable. She wept then, silent tears of frustration at the events of the last few days.

15

Elana appeared next to her. Without saying a word, the priestess put her hands to her shoulders, then to her neck, and on to the top of her head. Belwynn lay still. She felt her body let go of some of its tension.

'Is this magic?' she asked drowsily. She had witnessed Elana's healing abilities more than once over the last few weeks; not least on Dirk, as he lay close to death in the lands of the Blood Caladri. He had killed the dread sorcerer Nexodore with Toric's Dagger, though had paid a heavy price for it with internal damage that not even Elana could fully heal. But Belwynn had never seen Elana use her powers for something as trivial as this. 'I have no injury that needs to be healed,' she added.

Her question went unanswered, and she drifted into sleep.

Rabigar woke them while it was still dark. Belwynn still felt exhausted, and her muscles ached, but within minutes she was ready to go. They agreed to leave their non-essential items at the camp, so that they did not have to carry them. Rabigar left his new pots and pans.

'Maybe they'll be happy when they pick this lot up and forget about us,' he suggested.

Belwynn doubted that. They were only a matter of minutes behind them, and the mounted soldier knew exactly where they were.

They headed north, scraping their way through the trees in the dark. By sunrise, the force from Korkis was after them again. They soon heard the barking of the dogs to the west, and again Rabigar was forced to head eastwards to evade them. Belwynn couldn't help wondering whether Gyrmund would have been able to get them out of this situation. The tracker had led them through the Wilderness, with its dangerous vossi inhabitants. Rabigar was doing the best he could, but the men from Korkis were gaining on them.

As they moved further east, the trees became more and more sparse. They had reached the plain of Kalinth. No more woodland to hide in, just rolling open countryside.

They had no choice but to press on, despite feeling more exposed. It seemed to be mainly sheep country in this area. They marched uphill through a field covered in sheep dung. They reached a thick hedge which stretched away in either direction as far as the eye could see. Rabigar heaved himself over a gate into the next field. The sound of shouting reached them from the direction of the woodland. They had been spotted. There were still about a dozen soldiers, just emerging from the trees. One of the soldiers had two hounds held on leashes. His arm was held out in front of him as they pulled forwards. The horseman who had found them the previous evening accompanied them. They waved their weapons in the air in triumph at seeing their quarry.

Belwynn bolted over the gate. Elana and Dirk quickly followed. Rabigar looked around. There was nowhere to hide. He decided to take them in the same direction, gently rising uphill in an easterly direction, perhaps in the hope that there would be some rescue for them on the other side.

They reached the crest of the hill which gave them something of a vantage point. The woodland lay to the west of them. To the south and east was more grassland, divided up by the local farmers with hedges or stone walls. Some had sheep in, most lay empty. Some distance to the east Belwynn could make out a set of buildings which was probably a farmstead, but it was too far to reach in time. To the north, the plains briefly dipped low, before rising again to a point slightly higher than their own. Behind them, the soldiers from Korkis had almost reached the gate into their field. They were five minutes behind.

Rabigar pointed north. 'This way,' he said.

Belwynn almost refused. She was tired and scared, and Rabigar was dragging them onwards with no hope of escape. Elana and Dirk wordlessly followed him and Belwynn found herself doing the same.

They began to jog, taking advantage of the downward slope and trying to put some distance between themselves and the soldiers. A series of shouts and whoops rose up behind them. As she ran, Belwynn could now make out some of the words shouted at them. She heard the phrase 'slit your throat,' more than once, but most frightening was the excited barking of the two dogs.

They reached the bottom of the hill and began moving uphill again, slowing to a tired walk. Belwynn used the staff she carried to push herself along. She heard a noise behind her and knew it must be the horseman again. She turned around to see him approach them at a gentle canter. She drew her sword but kept on walking.

'Where are you going?' he laughed at them cruelly. 'There's nowhere to hide here.'

The only answer he got was the panting of breath as Belwynn and the others tried to push themselves up the hill. Dirk was slowing alarmingly. He

17

stopped to cough. It wracked his body and he gasped for breath which would not come. Belwynn thought he was going to collapse there and then, but Elana supported an elbow and the attack eventually passed. Dirk leaned over and whispered something to Elana, but she angrily refused and dragged him onwards.

The horseman came in close behind Belwynn, sword drawn. She was forced to stop and hold her sword in front of her to protect herself. A cheer went up from the rest of the soldiers, about two minutes behind them. Rabigar came back to stand next to her.

'Carry on, Belwynn,' he said, 'I'll keep them busy here for a while.'

'I may as well stay with you,' she answered.

'No,' said Rabigar, pushing her away.

Belwynn turned away, tears in her eyes. She looked upwards to where Elana and Dirk were still struggling above them. She saw something strange up above. Belwynn wiped the tears away from her eyes on her sleeve so that she could see more clearly. At the top of the hill sat two men. One was clearly a knight of Kalinth. He wore gleaming armour which sparkled in the sun and was dressed lavishly, in sea blue with a gold trim. He rode a huge warhorse, decorated in the same colours. Next to him sat what must be his squire, riding a palfrey and dressed in simple brown leather. He was carrying two huge lances. Their presence somehow didn't seem real, like an out of place and bizarre addition to a nightmare, that lets you know you are dreaming.

Belwynn gathered her senses. 'Help!' she cried up towards the knight in desperation, stumbling up towards him as she called out. 'We are being attacked! Please help us!'

The knight turned to his companion and said something, holding out his hand. The squire passed him one of the lances. It had a blue and gold flag attached which snapped in the breeze. The knight kneaded his mount forwards, down the hill. He reached Elana and Dirk.

'Move on up, there,' Belwynn heard him say in a clear voice. 'My squire will look after you.'

The knight reached Belwynn. He wore no helmet, and looked at her with dark brown eyes, framed with mid-length, chestnut brown hair.

'Please help us!' implored Belwynn. He nodded to her. 'Please carry on up the hill, My Lady,' he said.

The knight rode on. Belwynn turned around. The horseman from Korkis sat open mouthed as the knight descended the hill, stopping next to Rabigar. But the soldiers from Korkis now arrived on the spot. They looked at the new intruder fiercely, in no mood to let him interrupt their sport.

'My name is Theron, Count of Erisina. What business goes on here?'

'These men are trying to kill us!' shouted Belwynn down the hill, knowing that she sounded hysterical, but unable to control herself.

'These four killed a man yesterday in Korkis,' one of the soldiers spoke up. 'We're placing them under arrest.'

'I killed a man in self-defence,' stated Rabigar calmly. 'There is no law or justice in Korkis,' he added.

'Liar! You're gonna pay, Krykker! And this dandy ain't gonna help you.'

The soldiers laughed roughly at the comment and began to edge forward.

'These are the lands of my uncle, Sebastian of Melion,' said Theron, his voice rising in anger. 'Not the lands of Korkis. He directs the law here. These four will face justice at *his* court. I am prepared to escort some of you there to put forward your case.'

'Put forward our case?' said a soldier in disbelief. 'We've tracked these for a day. They're gonna get their justice now. I suggest you get out of our fucking way!'

Theron wheeled his horse around. 'So be it,' he said over his shoulder and pushed his horse back up the hill.

Belwynn felt as if she had been physically struck. This knight had given her hope of an escape and had then ridden away. Rabigar backed up the hill towards her as the soldiers began to move forwards, spreading out in a row with grins splitting their faces. There was less than a hundred meters between the group of soldiers and Rabigar and Belwynn, who were now standing side by side again.

The soldiers approached but then stopped and looked past Belwynn and Rabigar up the hill. Belwynn heard a rumbling noise and turned to look behind her. Count Theron had not departed the scene, but had moved back up the hill in order to charge back down it at the enemy. He had gathered considerable pace and was heading directly for them, with one hand on the reins and the other gripping his lance, held up at ear level.

The soldiers from Korkis were unsure what to do. If Theron and his horse struck one of them it would most likely be deadly, but surely then the rest of them could finish the knight off. They waved their weapons ahead of them, hoping to ward off the charging knight. Theron rode past Belwynn and Rabigar, now at some speed. His horse thundered forwards and he locked onto an enemy, the end of the lance targeting one of the soldiers. His aim was accurate and the lance went straight for the chest of one of the soldiers. The target saw it coming but was unable to get away in time. He twisted his body to one side but the lance struck just below the armpit and embedded deep into his body. The momentum of the charge delivered a huge amount of power into the strike and sent the soldier spinning into the air as Theron let go of the lance.

Theron veered his mount to the right, avoiding the line of soldiers. He drew his sword and headed toward the mounted soldier who had followed and tormented Belwynn and the others. He was sitting positioned slightly apart from the rest of his comrades. Theron's mount sidestepped around the young soldier, who had gone pale with fear. Theron made several quick feints towards the soldier with his sword. He eventually got a response when the soldier swung his own sword out to block one of the feints. Theron pulled out of the way and then swung his sword back again, smacking the flat of the blade across the soldier's chest. The shock and impact of Theron's strike caused the soldier to lose his balance and he toppled backwards off the horse, which bolted away.

By this time the other soldiers of Korkis had caught up with the combat. Theron dug his heels in and pushed his mount away with seconds to spare. A couple of the soldiers tried to chase after him but they soon looked absurd as Theron's horse pranced away from them, seemingly able to move in any direction. Theron moved back up towards the top of the slope. The soldiers looked unsure about how they should cope with the manoeuvrability of this new enemy. Belwynn could hear them discussing what they should do about the knight. They had all but ignored Rabigar and herself, who started to back away up the slope to join Elana and Dirk.

Theron claimed the second lance from his squire. Meanwhile, the Korkis soldiers had decided on their approach. They began to march up towards Theron in a closely packed line. The two soldiers who had been attacked by the knight remained sprawled on the ground behind them. As they drew closer, the dog handler released his two hounds, which both headed straight for Theron. They soon reached the knight and his mount. One of them kept a safe distance and barked at them but the other moved in closer, trying to nip at the horse. Theron's mount leapt up on its hind legs and kicked out in front of it. The kick connected soundly with the hound, which went flying up in the air and landed in a heap. The second dog continued to bark but did not seem willing to get any closer.

Theron made a second charge down the slope, his lance tucked under his right armpit. He charged straight at the centre of the group of soldiers, who stopped their march to defend themselves. Theron veered away at the last minute, to the left. He passed by the line of soldiers and buried his lance into the midriff of the soldier at the end of the line. There was a loud cracking sound at the moment of impact, and Theron rode on, leaving a lance buried in yet another soldier.

Dirk appeared at Belwynn's shoulder, accompanied by Theron's squire. He was just a boy, perhaps fifteen years old. But he had his sword drawn. The young squire motioned down the hill with his weapon.

'Let's give them something else to think about,' he suggested.

Belwynn turned her head to look at Rabigar. He shrugged his shoulders, and began to march towards the enemy. The other three marched alongside him. Theron pulled his horse around to Belwynn's left, threatening to attack from a different angle.

The odds of the confrontation had been evened up. It was originally ten soldiers and two dogs against four tired runaways, only one of whom was a real fighter. It was now seven versus five, but the five included a deadly horseman and the seven had lost three comrades already. The morale of the soldiers broke. They weren't prepared to shed more blood.

'I'm out of here,' one of them was saying.

One of the soldiers tried to rally the others, arguing that they could still win.

'You're free to go,' Theron called over. 'We won't pursue you. Enough lives have been taken here.'

That was it. The soldiers walked away at speed, desperate to get away from the encounter. The horseman had recovered enough from his fall to go with them. With only the occasional look over the shoulder to check they weren't being followed, the men from Korkis began to disappear from view. Belwynn realised that she had been standing still for some time, as the mixture of physical exhaustion and drop in adrenaline left her in a torpor.

Elana had joined them and was seeing to Dirk, who was sitting on the floor, looking deathly pale. Theron was seeing to his horse, making sure that the stallion had not received any injuries. He looked up from his inspection.

''Vander, check the bodies, see if they live. If not, see if they have anything useful on them. Then we'll have to bury them.'

Theron's squire nodded and did as he was told, moving from one body to the next, closely inspecting the items he found but discarding most.

'They're dead,' he declared in a steady voice.

Theron looked up. 'Right. Better get this over with,' he sighed.

This man has killed many times before, Belwynn thought to herself, as she watched the knight and squire work. Still, they were going to give the soldiers from Korkis a proper burial.

'I'll help,' she said, walking over to where the corpses lay.

Theron turned to look at her and frowned.

'This is no job for a lady,' he said.

'It's no job for anyone,' replied Belwynn. 'But it's a job that needs to be done.'

III

TO PROTECT AND SERVE

FARRED LOOKED AROUND THE HALL of his new house, somewhat bewildered. He wondered whose home it had been, just a few days ago. A wealthy family, judging by its size and location. They had taken virtually everything with them, leaving the place bare and sad looking. His weapons, armour and saddle bags lay in a pile next to the hearth—on a warm summer evening such as this there was no need for a fire, though he was tempted to light one just to bring some life to the room. He wasn't quite sure what to do with himself, so that when the knock came on the door he felt a sense of relief.

He opened the door to find a prince and a war chief standing outside. The chieftain, Brock, had the rich, brown skin colour of the Middian people, while the prince's skin was lighter in tone, reflecting his mixed Middian-Magnian parentage. Ashere, styled prince, though in fact the younger brother of Cerdda, the ruler of North Magnia, gave a sly grin.

'What's your house like?' he asked.

Wordlessly, Farred waved them in so they could inspect it for themselves.

'Nice,' commented the Prince.

'I don't like them,' growled Brock, folding his arms.

Brock was the leader of a tribe on the Midder Steppe, a people whose Farred's own family were descended from, though they had long ago given their allegiance to the Magnian crown. His family had become settled farmers and landowners, whereas the Middian tribes of the Steppe still followed their traditional nomadic way of life. And they didn't live in houses.

'What if these houses fall down on top of us in the middle of the night?' he demanded, staring up at the ceiling suspiciously.

'Do you have this to yourself?' asked Ashere, avoiding returning to a topic of conversation with Brock that they had already endured several times.

'Yes.'

'Are your men well quartered?'

'I've left that to Burstan,' Farred said.

Ashere raised an eyebrow.

Farred smiled. 'He can be a pain in the arse. But in truth, he's a good organiser. More suited to barking out orders than me.'

Ashere nodded. 'Shall we go?'

They exited into a street in Guslar, the capital of the northern duchy of Rotelegen. It was a grim city, largely empty of life and full of ghosts since the defeat of Duke Ellard's army four days prior. Most of the citizens had now fled south, fearing the approach of the Isharite army which had crossed into the Empire.

The exodus meant that it had not been difficult to find enough space in the city to house the Southern army they had led here. Farred had been given command of two thousand South Magnians by Prince Edgar. Brock led another two thousand from his own tribe, funded by King Glanna of Cordence. Finally, Ashere had brought the same number of North Magnians, and had assumed overall leadership of the combined force.

The street was full of the sounds of soldiers shouting and carrying on, but as the three men made their way into the centre of Guslar, that noise soon faded and the city became eerily quiet.

The street they followed ran dead straight, bisected at regular intervals by crossroads.

'I've never seen a city built like this before,' Farred murmured, thinking of the disorganised warrens of streets usually found in the towns of Magnia.

'The Persaleians founded Guslar,' said Ashere. 'All their cities are built to the same layout. Which means that if we follow this street we'll arrive at the central plaza.'

Brock shook his head and muttered something to himself, making clear his aversion to the urban environment.

Farred, however, admired the precision. Sure enough, ahead of them the street opened onto a huge open space. Spaced regularly around this plaza were other streets leading off in all directions. Inside the plaza was common land, which Farred supposed was used for markets and public gatherings. A few buildings were located here, the largest in size being a cathedral and castle, the latter of which belonged to the dukes of Rotelegen. It was Brasingian in style, with high stone walls and towers. And it was to the castle they headed.

Much of the city of Guslar lay abandoned, but its castle was still occupied. As they approached the gates they were waved through, expected guests of the

Duchess. Farred met eyes with some of the soldiers on guard duty as he entered the castle bailey. They stared coldly back. *Hardly a warm welcome*, he considered, *for foreigners come to fight on your behalf.*

They were wined and dined at Guslar Castle, given prominent places at the top table.

Ordinarily, Farred would have relished the role of honoured guest. But the mood was sombre, and the food basic. These were people making ready to leave their home. The new duke, Jeremias, was still a boy. He did his best to play the host, but it was a role he had clearly never attempted before, and he had no conversation. He sat, white-faced and barely eating, clearly wishing he were somewhere else. He had lost his father and brothers only a few days ago, and his new responsibility clearly weighed heavily on his young shoulders.

His mother, the Duchess Adalheid, still lived, and she was a stern woman. Her hair, dark but greying, was pulled back from a face heavy with lines. Her eyes, small and brown, regarded them without warmth. Farred wondered how stern she had been before her husband led an army of men, including her sons, to their destruction. Maybe she had smiled and laughed a lot before that. Now, it looked like she would never smile again.

Adalheid explained, exhaustively, how she had sent most of the people of Guslar south, along the Great Road to Essenberg. She was keen to give them every detail. It seemed to Farred that it was partly to demonstrate her ability to fill her late husband's shoes, partly to share the burden of leadership with strangers.

'Those who can fight and ride still serve the duchy,' she said. 'I am sending them into the countryside, where the people are often ignorant of the threat which faces them, or too stubborn to leave. The message they carry is stark. Everyone in Rotelegen must evacuate. The duchy has been given up to the enemy. Emperor Baldwin's point of defence is Burkhard Castle. No help is going to come.'

The Duchess made only a token effort to hide her bitterness regarding Baldwin's perceived lack of action, and the other diners clearly agreed with her assessment.

Prince Ashere made a sympathetic face. In truth, Farred knew full well that Ashere agreed with Baldwin's decisions. Moreover, the suggestion that no help was forthcoming was offensive. Hadn't all three of them led thousands of men here? And hadn't they been asked to fight the Isharite army, to cover the Rotelegen retreat?

'I wanted to ask a favour,' Farred began after a pause. 'None of us know the territory here and it would be an immense help if you could assign some local men to us, to act as guides.'

Adalheid raised an eyebrow at the request, turning her eyes to the men at the table. One of them gave a brief nod.

'I will send a man over to you tonight,' she said.

'Thank you.'

The meal continued, and not once did Adalheid ask after their men, offer them any further aid, or express a single word of gratitude.

Farred felt a sense of relief when Ashere had excused them soon after the end of the meal, citing the need to supervise their soldiers. In truth, the Rotelegen looked equally relieved to see them go.

'Thank Toric that's over,' Farred exhaled as they retraced their steps through Guslar back to their new quarters.

'It's a sorry mess to have a woman and young boy lead this tribe,' commented Brock.

'It's a shame,' said Ashere. 'Duke Ellard was perhaps the most respected soldier in the Empire. Baldwin needs all the experience he can get.'

'You have to give Adalheid her due, though,' Farred argued. 'Who would envy her position?'

'Agreed,' said Ashere. 'Well, here we are back at your new abode, Farred. Have a good night.'

Farred said his farewells and once more found himself alone in the hall of his new house. The same feeling of not knowing what to do with himself came over him. The room was just as bare as before, except someone had been in and left a small pile of firewood by the hearth.

'It could get chilly tonight,' Farred said out loud, and knelt by the hearth to arrange a fire.

He stood back to admire his work, but then hesitated before lighting it. There was a knock at the door.

Upon opening it, he found Ashere waiting there, a half smile playing on the Prince's lips.

'Come in,' said Farred.

'Up to much?'

'No. I was debating whether I should light a fire,' he said, gesturing at the hearth.

'Hmm,' said Ashere, examining it.

There was a silence. Farred turned to meet his eyes. The Prince held his gaze.

'I could keep you warm tonight,' said Ashere.

They led four thousand soldiers north-west from Guslar on their first mission. They had left when it was still dark. After two hours, the sun had risen and they were in position, a few miles to the west of where they expected the Isharite army to be.

They had acquired the services of Veit, a local man who knew the land well enough to act as a scout. While the main force waited, Veit led Farred, Ashere and Brock eastwards. The general of the Isharite army was Shira, Queen of Haskany. Ashere expected her to send out small war bands from her main army, to raid the surrounding territory and look out for enemy forces. He was hoping to find and intercept one of these bands.

It did not take them long.

Veit led them up a hill to a vantage point overlooking the Great Road. It looked like it was alive, a giant worm wriggling across the landscape. The numbers moving south along the road were mind numbing, and they stretched back as far as the eye could see—the soldiers at the front were miles ahead of those at the rear.

They looked to see if any smaller units were heading in their direction. From their position, they could see three units all heading westward, to separate destinations.

'They move across the land in a brazen manner,' growled Brock. 'As if they own it.'

'This army has seen no opposition since it broke through the defences on the northern border,' said Ashere. 'And they act as if they don't expect to see any more. It is time to change that.'

Farred looked at the nearest unit. He estimated its size at no less than two hundred soldiers.

'Where are they headed?' he asked Veit, pointing at the group.

'There is a village in that direction,' he replied.

'How far from here?'

'Three miles.'

'Could we get there before them?'

Veit considered the question. 'They're much closer than our forces. Even though they're on foot, they're probably going to get there first.'

'A shame,' said Farred, frustrated.

'But we won't be far behind?' asked Ashere, interested.

'Nope,' Veit replied. 'A matter of minutes, I would say.'

Ashere nodded. 'Instead of intercepting them on the way, we will have to get to the village as soon as possible.'

He looked at Farred and Brock for confirmation and they both nodded, a fierce grin emerging on the Middian's face which spread to the rest of the group.

'I will take the main force,' Ashere continued, 'and head directly for the village. Farred, you take your men and circle around, entering from the same direction as the enemy and blocking off a retreat. Brock will hold onto five hundred of his Middians and act as a reserve force, looking out for trouble.'

On the outskirts of the village, Farred and his men waited in silence, their breath visible in the cold morning air. The anticipation of battle throbbed in Farred's chest. The sensation moved outward from there to his gut and throat, threatening to make him physically sick. He could see the same kind of tension in the faces of the men around him. They had to wait a while longer yet.

When they could hear Ashere's attack, they would move in. Not before, because the enemy force in the village was too large for his men to handle alone.

Then they heard voices on the wind. Everyone looked at each other, but especially at Farred. Farred waited. More voices. They sounded like shouts. Then the clang of metal on metal.

'We go!' shouted Farred.

Farred slowly led his force along the dirt road. At first, they passed open fields on both sides, but then they began to find the odd hut. Each building they passed, and any other cover, had to be inspected carefully. However small, there was the chance of an ambush. The enemy could be armed with bows and arrows. Farred wasn't going to get caught out on his first military engagement.

The sound of fighting drew closer, yet they could see nothing. He could see the tension on the faces of his soldiers. Farred knew his troops wanted to release it and go charging in, because that was how he felt.

'Steady,' he said in a loud voice. 'We're nearly there.'

They rode on, approaching a row of mud and wood built dwellings on the right-hand side which marked the beginning of the village proper. Then they saw it. Standing outside the door of the second hut, staring back at them. These raiders weren't Haskan troops. They were Drobax.

It was like a monster from a children's story. Half-naked, with grey skin, spindly limbs, sharp nails and teeth and black, beady eyes. The eyes of the Drobax bulged with fear as it realised how many mounted soldiers were heading its way. It dived back into the house, shouting something unintelligible, presumably in its own language. There were likely more of them inside.

That was when Farred lost control.

He shouted something out aloud and then he was riding straight for the house, many of his men with him. Realising that they couldn't ride inside, Farred and those with him began to dismount. It soon became a disorganised mess, as soldiers handed the reins of their mounts over to comrades to hold.

Any kind of counter-attack would have caught them out. The Drobax, however, had stayed inside.

Farred approached. He peered through a crack between the door and the wall and could make out a few figures inside, weapons held at the ready. They favoured their chances inside rather than out.

One of his soldiers shouted a war cry and ran for the door. Farred and many others followed behind. One of the Drobax thrust out a spear into the doorway, but Farred's men were half expecting it and blocked the weapon down.

Then they were in. Farred had to squeeze into the small house as the Magnians crammed in, eager to meet the enemy. It was dark and cramped inside the hut. It was difficult to make out the enemy and all but impossible to swing a sword properly. Shouts and screams filled Farred's ears. A figure leapt out of the shadows to his left. It struck at the soldier standing next to Farred. The soldier, though surprised, was able to block the attack. Farred used his sword to punch the Drobax, smashing his hilt into its face. The force of the strike sent it over backwards and it was then pounced on as his men jumped in to deliver a death strike.

Taking a breath, Farred looked around. The fight was over already. About a dozen bodies lay on the floor. Some were Drobax, others dead villagers. None of his men seemed injured.

'Sir!' said a soldier, part of a group huddled over a body in the far corner.

Farred walked over and the group parted to let him see.

It was a woman. She was naked but alive. She stared up at him with wild eyes. Suddenly Farred realised what had happened here. The Drobax had killed the men but stayed in the hut to rape the woman. He felt sick at the thought. He couldn't begin to think what this woman had gone through. His men were standing around unsure what to do.

'Get some bloody clothes on her!' shouted Farred. 'Anulf, Morlin. You're assigned to protect her until I get back.'

Farred marched out of the house to see what was happening. His soldiers had started to enter the other houses on the row, but they seemed to be re-emerging without having found anything.

Farred needed to restore discipline. He began to bark out orders. He left a hundred of his troops at the huts with the horses, then led the rest ahead on foot.

They half walked and half jogged into the village, the road slowly rising uphill where they could see the church spire, which was located near the centre of the village.

The noise of fighting got closer. Then the chaos began again.

More Drobax were found. They were in isolated groups, and they dived into buildings when encountered. Farred sent groups of soldiers to deal with them while he continued to march towards the centre of the village, making sure that each building was fully searched along the way.

They crested the top of the slope and looked down on the scene below. Ashere's larger force was mopping up the last of the opposition. The last point of resistance was at the village inn on the left, where a large group of North Magnians were forcing their way in. Despite already having huge numerical superiority, many of Farred's soldiers couldn't be prevented from running over to join in.

As Farred walked down the road, Ashere rode up to meet him. He dismounted and they clasped hands.

'What happened to your horse?' asked the Prince.

'Oh...we left them behind,' said Farred, smiling ruefully. 'We didn't meet much resistance. What about you?'

'When we got here the villagers had locked themselves inside the church. Most of the Drobax were out in the open trying to force their way in. They fought back viciously, didn't run away. Once the main group was dealt with we had to start searching everywhere else.'

'Good. I'm glad there are some survivors,' said Farred, his mind going back to the poor woman they had found.

Ashere nodded.

'What are we going to do with them?' Farred asked.

Ashere shrugged. 'Nothing.'

'But some will be wounded. They should be taken back to Guslar. More Drobax might come—'

'Farred. It's not our job to take these people to safety. That's what the Rotelegen soldiers are doing. We'll tell them what happened here when we get the chance. But our job is to take on this army, to try to buy a little time for Baldwin and Jeremias to get ready. We need to make another strike now. I can't afford to have part of our forces wandering about escorting civilians all over the place. We need to stay united.'

Farred could see the sense of what Ashere said from a military perspective. But he still found it difficult. They had just rescued these villagers, and now the Prince proposed to abandon them to their fate again?

'Very well,' he replied. 'But I'm sending some of my troops back with a woman we found.'

Farred could feel his jaw sticking out, daring Ashere to disagree. The Prince of North Magnia grimaced.

'So be it, Farred,' he said. 'They're your soldiers after all. You're a stubborn man,' he said, shaking his head.

Farred couldn't tell whether he was annoyed or amused. Perhaps both.

'Right,' said Ashere, 'gather your men. When we're finished here we need to meet up with Brock. We're moving out.'

IV

THE WAVES AT THE SHORE

B ELWYNN WAS IN A BED. SHE sat up with a start. Where was she? As her muddled brain tried to think, the chase through the woods came back to jolt her. She felt sick at the memory. They had been chased out of the woods, across some fields—she had thought they would all be killed. Then Count Theron had arrived.

After that it was a bit of a blur, as if a part of Belwynn's mind had turned off in order to recover from the trauma. Theron and his squire, Evander, had escorted them to the home of his uncle, Sebastian of Melion. Belwynn had felt safe in the company of the knight, a feeling she hadn't had since their stay with the Blood Caladri. Theron offered his mount for Belwynn to ride, but she knew that though he might protest, Dirk could walk no farther. He was bundled on top of the warhorse and soon fell asleep.

Theron had asked them why they had been chased from Korkis. Belwynn was able to answer this truthfully, telling him about the encounter with the soldiers and her intervention to help the little girl. The knight seemed to admire Belwynn's actions and muttered darkly of developments in Korkis and elsewhere in Kalinth. When his questions began to range further, Belwynn's answers became much vaguer. The fear of revealing too much information, along with her general tiredness, left her virtually monosyllabic.

Theron had been too polite to press the matter, but Belwynn knew that this morning she would have to give a better performance. Uncle Sebastian would doubtless be present as well, she thought sourly. They had arrived so late and so exhausted last night, that Theron had ensured that they were found rooms immediately—she had yet to meet her host.

Belwynn pushed away the bed covers, and swung her legs over the side of the bed, where they landed on a soft rug. They had all been given well-appointed rooms in Sebastian's house, which Theron had called Sernea. It was a fortified structure with strong stone walls that served as the headquarters of the estate. The steward had originally arranged for Elana and Belwynn to share the same room, but the priestess had insisted on looking after Dirk during the night, so Belwynn had been given the luxury of a room to herself.

Opposite her was an empty bed, where new clothes had been laid out for her. She dressed quickly, since it was chilly without the covers.

Her room was sparsely decorated and was clearly designed for defence as much as for comfort. The two outside walls each had an arrow loop, where archers could be positioned. These wedge-shaped openings allowed the archer to target a wide angle, while the slit in the wall gave good protection. Belwynn peered out of the loop which faced the front of the house. An archer stationed here could cover the track which led up to the main gate. There was no gatehouse, and the house could not withstand a sustained attack from an armed force. It was designed to afford protection from minor threats, such as anything Korkis might offer. And that was good enough for Belwynn.

Her thoughts turned to her brother.

Soren? Can you hear me?

Belwynn? How are you?

Soren's voice sounded unclear once more, as if distorted by some barrier.

Fine.

She paused to think. Was it worth the trouble of telling Soren about the events in Korkis when she was now safe? She decided not.

We're still in Kalinth. We're at the home of a knight. How are you?

No change here. I don't want to talk for too long. Contact me tomorrow, Belwynn. And stay safe.

That was it? She desperately wanted to talk to her brother, and had to stop herself from replying. She stood in the room, fighting to control her emotions. An overwhelming sense of feeling lost overcame Belwynn then. Her parents were dead, both taken from her too soon. She had always leaned on her brother for support, for purpose. His goals had become her goals. And now he was gone too. She was in the middle of a strange country. And she didn't know what to do.

'Deal with it, Belwynn,' she told herself out loud.

She gave herself some time, taking some deep breaths. She stretched, forcing her body to wake up.

What should I do first?, she asked herself.

She suddenly realised how hungry she was. She felt like she hadn't eaten in days. She left her tower room and took the stairs down, looking for the kitchen where she expected to find breakfast.

It did not take her long to find it, the smell of hot porridge drawing her to the right place. The kitchen was warm and inviting. A huge pot hung in the fireplace and a number of people were stood around it, chatting quietly while they had their breakfast, no doubt after their early morning chores. Belwynn didn't recognise anyone and entered a bit hesitantly.

'Porridge, love?' asked an older woman, perhaps a cook, with an encouraging smile.

'Yes please,' Belwynn replied, her stomach rumbling.

She was handed a bowl and spoon and the cook ladled the steaming breakfast into it.

'Honey?' asked a younger woman, maybe a maid at the house. A pot of honey was being passed around the group and Belwynn took the dipper and let the honey drip into the bowl. Wasting no more time she began to tuck in, blowing on the hot porridge to stop it burning her mouth.

The staff at the house were pleasant enough, but Belwynn was glad when Rabigar wandered into the kitchen and took a bowl of porridge for himself. They found a corner to stand in out of the way while they ate.

'How are you?' he asked.

'Fine. I slept well enough and this food should sort me out. Thank you for taking charge back there. I didn't think we were going to make it—' she began, getting a lump in her throat and leaving the statement there.

'We weren't, until the knight showed up. We owe him our lives, but we need to be a bit careful. We don't know who they are.'

Belwynn thought that they needed all the help they could get, but she nodded along.

When they had finished, their bowls were taken and shortly afterwards a familiar face entered the kitchen and approached them.

'Evander, isn't it?' asked Belwynn, recognising Theron's squire.

The lad smiled, seemingly pleased that she had remembered his name.

'Yes, that's right. My lords would like to speak with you now. I've been asked to fetch you.'

'I see. Have our other two friends come down, yet?' asked Belwynn.

Evander looked over at the servants, who shook their heads.

'Would it be possible to bring their breakfast up to their room?' she enquired.

'Of course,' said the woman who had served her.

Evander led Belwynn and Rabigar back upstairs to a small room that appeared to be Sebastian's private study. He had a shelf of books, a desk and a few chairs. Theron and Sebastian were seated, deep in conversation, but stood up to greet them.

Theron walked over with a warm smile.

'Ah, how are you?' he said. The knight gripped Rabigar in a handshake and gave him a slap on the shoulder.

'My lady,' he said to Belwynn, taking her by the hand and lightly touching his lips to it.

'We're much better, thank you,' answered Rabigar. 'But Elana and Dirk are tired, we suggested they stay in their room.'

'Of course,' said Sebastian. 'From hearing Theron's account, I assume that you both must be tired, too. We are going on a hunt shortly but I insist that you stay and get some rest today. My people will see to you.'

Sebastian of Melion was a tall and handsome man, his hair still dark despite middle age. His face was welcoming but seemed rather care worn.

'This is the Lady Belwynn,' said Theron, 'and Rabigar, a skilled Krykker warrior by my reckoning.'

'Good to meet you, please take a seat,' said Sebastian, gesturing to the chairs.

They all sat down.

'Welcome to Sernea, my house,' began Sebastian. 'Please, anything you need, just ask someone and it will be provided. Now. Here in Kalinth we are rather cut off from events elsewhere in Dalriya. This is something which I deeply regret and is largely because of difficulties within our kingdom. So, when foreigners arrive out of the blue, I hope you will understand I am eager to share news. Theron has told me what happened to you in Korkis, and there is no need to explain that episode to me. You are quite safe here. Unfortunately, Kalinth has become a rather dangerous place for travellers recently. And you are a rather...can I say, out of the ordinary group of travellers?'

Belwynn smiled and nodded at the comment. It was all very polite, but Sebastian had managed to get straight to the point nonetheless.

'Now, now, uncle,' said Theron, smiling at Belwynn in a conspiratorial way, 'before you subject your guests to an interrogation, it is perhaps incumbent upon us to explain *why* our kingdom is a dangerous place for travellers. It is a disgrace for which we should apologise a thousand times over in shame before we begin to ask whats and wherefores to visitors in our land.'

Theron said the words in good humour but Belwynn could clearly see the passion that lay behind them.

Sebastian smiled thinly at his nephew's outburst but was clearly not impressed by it.

'Theron, this is not the moment to start discussing politics.'

'Politics? That is a strange word to use when our country and its people are on the brink of ruin and subjugation!'

It was now Sebastian's turn to bristle with passion.

'Are you saying that I don't care?'

Theron reached a hand over to rest on the older man's forearm.

'No. I apologise uncle. I know that isn't true. I just get so...frustrated.'

Sebastian grunted and turned his attention back to Belwynn and Rabigar. He looked embarrassed that he had argued with his nephew in front of them, but set his jaw firmly and continued.

'It is incumbent upon me to ask strangers in my lands what their business is.'

'We have travelled from the Empire,' began Rabigar.

'Up the Great Road?' demanded Sebastian, sounding astonished.

A Drobax army had passed down the Great Road. The idea of the four of them travelling up it sounded ludicrous.

'Not quite,' explained Belwynn. 'We came via the Grand Caladri.'

'The Grand Caladri?' responded Sebastian, sounding no less surprised. 'I've never heard of humans entering their lands before.'

The count looked at them, eager for an explanation. Rabigar and Belwynn shared a look. Making up a story seemed pointless.

'I'm afraid we have grave news for you,' said Rabigar. 'We were in Edeleny four days ago. It was invaded by Arioc and his forces. I fear the whole realm is taken.'

'Invaded?' gasped Theron. 'How?'

'They used magic.'

'I haven't heard of this,' said Sebastian, seemingly in disbelief.

'Why would you have?' asked Theron.

'We saw it with our own eyes,' said Rabigar firmly, in a voice that left no doubt.

'How did you escape?' asked Theron.

'Magic, again,' replied Rabigar. 'A wizard, by the name of Pentas, teleported us out.'

'He got some of us out,' added Belwynn. 'But the rest of our group were captured. Arioc has taken them prisoner...' Suddenly, Belwynn felt herself breaking down. Her voice wobbled and tears began to stream down her face.

Pull yourself together, she demanded.

'My brother, Soren, is one of them...'

Again, she couldn't finish speaking, her voice sounding hysterical. It was like listening to some other person in the room talking, rather than herself. She looked at the sympathetic faces of the two counts looking at her and she felt totally embarrassed. She wiped her nose on the back of her hand, imagining what a state she must look like.

'I'm sorry,' she blubbered, and decided to stop talking.

'Not at all,' said Sebastian, somewhat awkwardly. 'You have experienced an awful few days, there is no need to apologise whatsoever. Excuse me if I am a little shocked by what you are telling me.'

'And please,' said Theron, reaching over and holding her hand lightly, 'understand that as knights we will do whatever we can to get your brother back.'

'Thank you,' whispered Belwynn.

'You haven't explained, I have to say,' Sebastian added, 'what exactly you were doing in Edeleny in the first place.'

There was a silence. Rabigar looked over to Belwynn with a raised eyebrow, as if seeking permission to tell more. She nodded her acquiescence.

'I suppose,' said Rabigar, 'we were there to get a staff.'

'A staff?' said Theron. 'The staff Belwynn was carrying yesterday? Why is that so important?'

Rabigar puffed out his cheeks. 'This isn't a short story. It begins in Magnia, about three weeks ago...'

***

At last, Shira could see the outskirts of Guslar for herself.

Despite the resounding success over Duke Ellard and his forces, the progress of her army had been frustratingly slow. This was primarily because she had agreed that a large force of Drobax should be in the van of the army to deal with any resistance. They were far less effective than the well drilled Haskan soldiers, but were totally expendable. Indeed, despite considerable deaths, her advisers indicated that there had been no significant depreciation in the numbers of Drobax in her army. No-one knew exactly how many there were, not even to the nearest tens of thousands. Such calculations were complicated, she had learned, by the Drobax army repopulating as it went along, so that while many might die every day, many infants would be born. Only a small proportion of these might be expected to live, but even so, that left hundreds who would.

All of which meant that, while Shira's army had begun its march south days before Arioc's forces had even assembled, he had now successfully conquered the lands of the Grand Caladri, while she had only made a small inroad into Imperial territory. The resistance offered by the enemy had been tiny but had succeeded in slowing down her army. Still, it was a totally futile gesture. The Drobax she commanded were like the waves lapping at the shore. Endless. Infinite. Relentless. You could wade into the sea, slash and hack at it with all your might if you wished, but it would avail you none.

Shira beckoned over her Uncle Koren, the man who had taught her how to fight and who she trusted the most. She pointed in the direction of Guslar.

'How far?'

'Apparently, a couple of miles to the main part of the city. No more than thirty minutes, certainly.'

'I want to lead the force in. We'll take Haskans only.'

Koren furrowed his brow. He was a logical thinker, a tough realist, carefully weighing up the possible and ignoring the impossible. Shira had huge respect for him, though found him humourless and dull company.

'You shouldn't go. There may be some resistance, enough to put you in danger, but not enough to justify your presence.'

'I'm bored, uncle. That's my justification. And it's an order.'

Koren turned away and began organising a force, though Shira knew full well that every time she disagreed with him it rankled. She called over Roshanak, the Isharite who oversaw the Drobax forces.

'I'm going to lead the force into Guslar. I will billet all the Haskan forces in the town but I don't want a single Drobax there. Can you organise a suitable overnight location elsewhere?'

'Of course. Anything else?'

'When you've done what you need to, come to Guslar yourself and we'll meet there tonight.'

Roshanak nodded courteously and began giving out orders. It was not long before the huge army began going its separate ways. The Haskan forces, relatively small in number, began heading towards the capital of Rotelegen, with Shira and Koren in charge of the mounted regiment who would attack the town. The Drobax were herded west of Guslar where they would spend another night in the open. Shira felt a flush of relief that she would be free of their stink and repugnant presence for a night. Excited, she called out the order to advance before all her soldiers were fully lined up, and pressed on at the head of her forces.

As they rode, the countryside of Rotelegen began to merge into the city of Guslar. At first, they passed unremarkable looking dwellings, but the walls of the city soon took shape ahead of them. The main gates, guarding the northern entrance to the city, were closed; but there was no sign of any guards on the walls.

Shira and Koren pulled up at a safe distance. Her mounted soldiers milled about ahead of the gates, gradually daring to get closer and closer, but there was still no sign of defenders. Eventually a couple of the more daring individuals dismounted and gave the gates a good push, but they were locked in place.

'Up there!' one of the soldiers shouted, pointing up at the battlements above the gate. Shira, along with everyone else, strained to see movement, but she couldn't make anything out.

'I'm sure I saw something move,' argued the soldier defensively, as his comrades began to question the sighting.

A wagon pulled up and Koren began barking out orders, as the contents of the vehicle were unloaded and assembled. A battering ram, that most straightforward of siege weapons, was soon made ready and volunteers quickly emerged to grab a hand grip.

'I've not seen them so quick to put themselves forward before,' Shira said to her uncle with a smile. Taking hold of the ram usually made you a target for the enemy. This time, however, there did not seem to be an enemy.

'Swing!' commanded Koren.

The ram, made of an oak log but encased with metal at the tip, was attached by ropes to an overhead beam. The men raised it backwards before swinging it at the target, using the energy created to make a stronger impact. A dull thud echoed around the walls but the gates remained solid. However, after a few more strikes, and with the men starting to find a rhythm, the splintering and cracking of wood could be heard.

Suddenly, a missile came down from overhead and one of the men working the ram was sent to the ground.

'Arrows!' was the fearful shout and the soldiers looked up at the walls. Those who had bows began firing upwards until Koren shouted at them to desist. No enemy was visible. The unfortunate victim of the attack was dragged over for Shira to inspect. It had actually been a short spear which had been hurled from the battlements, hitting the man in the chest and killing him.

'Restart the ram!' demanded Koren, shouting at the top of his voice.

The men quickly returned to their task, but now some of the other soldiers had their sights trained on the walls in case of a repeat attack. None came, and the gates made a horrible ripping noise. The ram had twisted one the gate on the left in on itself. The men were then able to push open the other gate, and Guslar was open to the invaders at the loss of only one life.

Shira nudged her horse forward and peered into the town, but it seemed completely deserted. While the spear thrower on the wall was a warning that this was not entirely true, it seemed that there was no longer any genuine military presence left in Guslar. Still, Shira was not going to take anything for granted.

'We're going in to take the town! Keep discipline and stick with your unit at all times. Anyone who disobeys will be fed to the Drobax!' Shira raised her sword in the air. 'For Haskany!'

With that, she manoeuvred her horse past the gates and led her force towards the centre of town. The central square was dominated by two buildings—the castle of the duke, and the cathedral of the bishop. But each road leading in was lined with the tall, well built houses of the nobility and merchant class—men who had grown rich on the trade coming up and down the Great Road.

Shira led her forces to the two targets. As they approached down the main street, missiles came in from the houses on either side. Shira reacted to the first signs of organised resistance by waving units of her men into the houses to clear them out. She continued herself, taking half of the remaining force towards the doors of the cathedral while her uncle took on the castle. The doors were locked shut, and arrows were fired down at them from the thin windows of the building. The Haskan soldiers were quick to overwhelm the defenders though, firing arrows and stones at the windows to push back the defence. Then, the ram was quickly brought back into operation.

This time, the going was slower than at the city walls. There were clearly a significant number of people taking refuge inside the building, and they had barricaded the doors. Minutes went by and the ram seemed to be having little impact.

Shira took some time to look over at the castle. Koren's forces had got into the building, but the fighting was still ongoing.

She ordered fire arrows to be shot into the cathedral, in the hope that it would cause a distraction to the defenders. The tactic seemed to have some effect, as the battering ram started to rattle the doors. Then, one of the doors fell over towards the attackers, the hinges and locks shattered by the ram. With whoops of excitement the Haskans headed for the opening, ripping out the tables and benches blocking their way into the cathedral. The defenders stabbed out with their spears and threw whatever missiles they had to hand. Several Haskans were hit, and had to be dragged away from the fight by their comrades. But the blood lust was up, and more soldiers took their place.

Shira was one of them, and the presence of their queen gave even more impetus to the Haskan attackers. Their superior weight of numbers started to tell and they slowly pushed themselves forwards. Shira, in the middle of a scrum, made sure she held onto her sword and shield, kept relaxed, and kept her breathing even. The movement forwards gathered pace, and suddenly Shira found herself heaved into the central part of the cathedral. She peered around her, letting her eyes get accustomed to the darker environment. She picked out the enemy and they were not so many as she had expected. Many were women and children. It confirmed her earlier suspicions that the Emperor had given up Guslar, and pulled his forces out.

Ready, Shira led her men into the attack. She feinted at a defender armed with a spear, drawing in the thrust which she sidestepped, and then flicked her blade along the shaft of the spear, cutting the fingers off the hand of her enemy and forcing him to drop his weapon. He retreated to the far wall, and already, it had moved from a fight to a slaughter. Shira led the work, not shirking to cut down her share of victims. It was the women who disgusted her the most. Crying out for mercy, or asking for their children to be spared. Grown women who still thought some tears would save them, who hadn't armed themselves to fight for what they wanted. Shira felt no remorse at ending their lives: useless, overgrown children who had no chance of survival in this world.

The work was soon over. The blood of the defenders was splattered up the walls of the cathedral. Shira's soldiers checked to see if anyone survived, perhaps playing dead. They then took anything they valued from the corpses.

Shira called over one of the men.

'Find my captains, ask them to meet me in here as soon as possible.'

She raised her voice so that those in the cathedral could hear.

'Fan out from here in your units, check the remaining parts of the town for any survivors. Then find somewhere to sleep for the night, but stay together. We must be vigilant. The Imperial forces are still at large, they may counter-attack.'

She made a point of watching the soldiers go, so that they reconnected with their units under her stern gaze. After they had left she looked about her. Wandering over to the far side of the cathedral, she found some chairs and busied herself with setting them up, one for her and three for her captains. She took a seat and waited.

Koren was first. She gestured to a seat and he sat down in that stiff, formal way she associated with all old soldiers.

'Any news?' she asked.

'The castle is taken,' Koren looked around the cathedral dispassionately. 'Probably more in here than there.'

'Really?' replied Shira, surprised. 'Trusting their gods more than their rulers?'

Koren shook his head. 'Baldwin must have organised a full evacuation days ago. The people left here are those who refused to go. Those in the castle weren't his servants, they were...squatters. Oh, and before Baldwin's forces left, they poisoned the water supply. I've sent orders round for the men not to drink or eat anything they find.'

'Poisoned the water?' came a voice from the doors. 'What a dirty trick.'

Shira's other captains entered the cathedral, both of them Isharites. While Koren was in charge of the Haskan troops, Roshanak was in charge of the Drobax—or, at least, in charge of the Isharites who controlled the Drobax. When Shira had been assigned control of the army she had some initial curiosity about how this was done, but as time had gone on, she decided she did not want or need to know. The Drobax seemed to behave like mindless animals in a lot of ways, but the Isharites had somehow trained them to follow strict orders, so that they could behave like a military force of sorts.

Mehrab, meanwhile, led the magi assigned by Erkindrix to Shira's army. While they had contributed absolutely nothing so far, he still managed to take a superior tone, as if he were actually in charge. The thought that he might be, made Shira dislike him even more.

'Well, you've chosen a lovely venue,' he continued, waving his arms around the cathedral interior, the walls smeared in red blood. There was something rather comical in the way he did it, but Shira kept her lips tight and gestured to the chairs she had prepared for them. Both took a seat.

'So, I take it there's little of value left?' asked Mehrab.

'No,' replied Shira. 'I was hoping for some treats for our soldiers. Loot. Even some nice food. It's good for morale. But I don't think we'll find anything.'

'We caught them by surprise, and got lucky when Ellard over-committed himself and attacked us the second time,' commented Koren. 'But since then, to give him credit, Baldwin has done well. Slowed us down long enough to strip out the duchy and deny us any sustenance. I don't think we'll find anything 'til we get to Burkhard Castle.'

'How will that affect supplies?' asked Mehrab.

'We're still getting enough provisions to feed the Haskans,' answered Shira, 'but it means no spare food for the Drobax. How are things with them?' she asked Roshanak.

'We've settled them, their camp begins about a mile away from the city. As for the food issue, I still don't see any major depletion in our numbers. I will tell you if that changes.'

'In which case, our objective is still secure,' commented Mehrab.

And that is it, thought Shira. When she had been given this command, she had seen it as her chance to shine. But the nature of the task didn't allow it. There were no genuine strategic decisions to take. She was just taking the Drobax to the Empire, whereupon they would destroy it. While Arioc would be winning praise and support for his daring invasion of the Grand Caladri, Shira was simply expected to succeed. Indeed, it was unthinkable that she wouldn't.

Koren was looking at her, perhaps reading her mind. Shira had seen a chance to escape Arioc, but even hundreds of miles away, she was still in his clutches.

V

OF WIVES AND WAR

IN THE COURTYARD OF SERNEA, Belwynn sat on her horse and waited. Her friends Rabigar, Dirk and Elana were also seated and ready to go. They looked healthier and happier from having spent three nights at Sebastian's home. Some colour had returned to their faces, though Dirk still had his racking cough, and was clearly in need of more permanent rest.

Belwynn suddenly felt a wave of sadness flow over her and she gripped the reins of her mount as she fought it away. Dirk had lost his health. Rabigar an eye. Belwynn's twin brother Soren, and her closest friends Clarin and Herin, were captured by the Isharites, facing only Toric knew what kind of torments over the coming days. What price had already been paid, and was yet to be paid, for getting involved in this? The only thing keeping her going was a feeling that they were making progress. *A journey somewhere always feels like progress*, Belwynn considered—*assuming, that is, that you do eventually leave.*

Also seated on their mounts in the courtyard were the Counts Sebastian, Theron, and twenty of Sebastian's retainers. They had been trying to set off on the road to the High Tower, the seat of the Knights of Kalinth, for some time. So far, they had failed. Just as they seemed ready, a servant would rush out from the house and load up some forgotten provisions. Or one of Sebastian's soldiers would clamber off their horse and sheepishly run back in on some unnamed errand, returning to the sound of gibes and curses from his comrades. Even Sebastian himself was at it, remembering some gift to be presented to someone or other, but he couldn't quite remember where he had placed it for safekeeping. Belwynn and her friends looked on somewhat bemused—they had so few possessions, that they were hardly going to forget anything.

Sebastian seemed a little ill at ease, anxious even, and it appeared to be rubbing off on those around him. Not Theron, however, who seemed to be taking great delight in the proceedings, and laughing heartily at each delay. It made Belwynn wonder whether Sebastian had ever had a wife. She thought things might be running a bit more smoothly if he did.

When, at last, they did get going, Theron fell in with Belwynn and began chatting in his easy way, pointing out local landmarks. In truth, Belwynn found the area around Sernea to be quite monotonous; a hard and dry landscape, very different to the lush farmland of home. She listened politely, enjoying his company, but turned the conversation to matters of more interest to her.

'I was wondering, Theron, about Sebastian. I was thinking this morning that he does not have a wife...has he ever?'

'No, never. The Knights of Kalinth do not take wives.'

'Oh, I didn't know that,' Belwynn was taken aback by the news. 'So, you are sworn to be chaste?'

'Well, I didn't say that, did I?' responded Theron, giving Belwynn a look. She wasn't sure if he was trying to make her blush, but having spent so much time in the company of Herin and Clarin, it took a lot to make Belwynn blush.

'So why can't you take wives?'

'It makes us better soldiers. Men with wives have their heads cluttered with other things. Usually money.'

Belwynn made a face at him but let him continue.

'Men with children have other priorities, are wary of risking their lives—rightly, of course. When you become a knight, you join the Order. Your brothers in the Order are your family. You have to be prepared to give your life for it.'

'I can understand that. But to never have children?'

'Not never. Not for most men. Most knights serve for a limited time only, often ten years. Then, if you want to leave, you are given some land, and you can find a wife. And raise some boys to be knights!'

This prospect seemed to please Theron and he had a big beaming smile on his face.

'But Sebastian has served for more than ten years, hasn't he?'

'Yes. Those who choose to rise high in the Order, the commanders and officers, must stay in the Order. Those are the men who devote their whole lives to the Knights. By doing so, they win the respect of the soldiers.'

'So how important is Sebastian in the Order?'

Theron shifted in his seat, suddenly looking more serious about things.

'In influence, my uncle is second only to the Grand Master, Galenos. But more popular than he is.'

'Why?'

'Galenos continues to follow a policy of absolute loyalty to King Jonas. The King has made a peace with the Isharites, and has forbidden any military action against them. The most cowardly, cynical act I've ever witnessed.'

'You disagree with Galenos?'

'Of course I do. The Knights of Kalinth are sworn to protect the people, but most of them are standing by while raiding parties from Kharovia and elsewhere pillage, burn and rape with impunity. The king's own soldiers do nothing, but sit whimpering behind their walls—'

'I see,' said Belwynn. 'And you?'

Theron looked around him, in case anyone was listening. 'Can I trust you, Belwynn?'

'Of course.'

'I and others of my comrades have been forced to take action. We go by the name of the Kalinthian Defence League. We ride out and intercept the war bands when possible. But we are few in number. And we must keep our identities secret. People suspect that the League is made up of knights, but if our identities were discovered we would be expelled from the Order.'

'Does Sebastian know?'

'He knows alright. We've had plenty of arguments over it. But he's the one who can change things, not me. And I think what you told us yesterday about the power of Ishari, the weapons, what's happened to the Caladri—all of that—that might have done more to persuade him than all the arguments I've tried. The fact that we're all going to the High Tower today is a start. We need to be prepared for a confrontation.'

Oh Gods, thought Belwynn. *As if we are not in enough trouble. I seem to have started a civil war.*

***

Farred was exhausted. But equally, he felt lucky to be alive, as he always did after a raid.

Ashere liked to vary the time when they attacked the army of Ishari, to maintain the element of surprise. This last time, he had chosen sunrise. They had never done this before, mainly because it meant travelling through the night from their base to reach the enemy, a manoeuvre with so many difficulties it was usually avoided. However, Ashere's forces, made up of his own North Magnians, Farred's South Magnians, and the Middians under the leadership of Brock, had united into an effective and disciplined force under his leadership. They were also much more confident about the terrain, having traversed the borderlands of Kelland and Rotelegen many times now.

This time, Ashere had taken Farred and about seven hundred men to the enemy camp. Farred, like most, had not got any sleep before they set out, nerves getting the better of him. They then had a long, protracted journey north in the dark, trying to locate the enemy camp without being identified themselves. Usually, Ashere targeted the Haskan soldiers in these raids. This was because they had things worth destroying: supplies, horses, transport. This time, however, they approached the Drobax.

The sun had risen enough for them to be seen as they approached. But, unlike the Haskan positions, the Isharite generals rarely set up watches over the Drobax. They didn't seem to see the point, and had a general disregard for the well-being of these monsters. So, as Ashere led the charge, there were no warning calls, and the Drobax were still asleep, mostly lying on the cold floor with no protection from the elements.

Farred felt the usual surge of excitement as they swept in on horseback. The attack provoked chaos as the Drobax, waking from their stupor, ran in all directions, and were slow to organise an ordered resistance. They killed freely for minutes, until Ashere ordered the retreat. He was wary of his small force getting caught, and so they sped away again.

Turning round in his saddle, Farred could see the bodies and the blood left behind. But the Drobax who remained seemed unconcerned. They would march as normal today, and inch their way closer to the imperial forces in Burkhard Castle. It made him wonder what they were doing. The futility of it. The other soldiers seemed to share his mood, and it was a quiet and sombre journey back to the base.

When they got there, Ashere ordered an evacuation. The enemy were getting too close, he judged. They were going to relocate to Burkhard Castle.

Ashere made sure that he rested his forces, rarely taking the same man on two raids in a row. He was scrupulously fair about this. The only exception was himself. He had led every single attack. If Farred was exhausted, he wondered how the Prince kept going. The effects on his body were clear to see. He had always been a striking figure, with jet black hair and light brown skin, that seemed to glow with health. But now he seemed permanently drained of colour, with hollowed eye sockets. Like a ghost. The men liked this. They admired him but also feared him, whispering about supernatural powers. They liked to think that this dark prince brought fear to the enemy.

The emotions Farred felt as he came within sight of the Empire's mightiest fortress, he knew were shared by the rest of the soldiers. They were tired but more united than they had been before they left. They felt overwhelmed at the numbers of their enemies, but proud of what they had achieved.

The two giant outcrops that formed Burkhard Castle loomed ever larger until they reached the small settlement at the foot of the castle. It was noticeably busier since they had left for Rotelegen, with soldiers from different parts of the Empire now stationed in separate camps. Tradesmen had arrived to set up shop, since wherever there are soldiers, there are goods needed, and money to spend. They even rode past what appeared to be a makeshift brothel, a wooden hut outside of which two women called out to the men as they passed, offering a night to remember.

But the space set aside for the Magnian forces when they had first arrived had been kept for them, and the men returned to their old tents. Furthermore, plenty of food and drink had been provided, much more than the sparse rations they had been living off over the last few days. Ashere was informed by an official that the castle had been told of their arrival, and that someone would come down to meet them. Farred looked up at the battlements on top of the nearest outcrop. It looked like a tiny toy castle had been placed there, precariously, by a giant child; and that it might, at any time, slide off the edge.

As the soldiers prepared their camp fires, and the smell of roasting meat filled the air, Farred and Brock waited with the Prince for a messenger to arrive. Eventually, Brock gave a whistle. He had caught sight of a group of half a dozen men making their way down the path. Farred looked over at the group and got something of a shock.

'It's Baldwin himself.'

Wearing a chain mail vest, the Emperor came marching over towards them, flanked by his most powerful allies. Walter, his younger brother and Marshal of the Empire, whose job it was to organise the defence of the fortress. Arne, his father-in-law, and Duke of Luderia, who had brought his own contingent of soldiers with him to the castle, second only to Baldwin's in size. Rainer the Chamberlain, chief administrator, and the man entrusted with the Emperor's money. And finally, Gustav the Archmage, known as 'the Hawk', who seemed, to Farred, to walk as if he were the one who was really in charge.

Ashere walked over to meet them and gestured for Farred and Brock to follow.

Baldwin beamed as the two groups met and grasped Ashere on each arm, in a kind of half-hug.

'Prince Ashere, my Empire owes you a debt of gratitude I hope one day to repay. You have done far more than I could have hoped for,' Baldwin said earnestly, nodding at Farred and Brock as he delivered the words. 'I trust your men are settled well?'

'Yes, thank you, Your Majesty. You have been most generous with your supplies.'

'Please, Baldwin will do. I will need to catch you up on some developments. You and your two lieutenants have got rooms in the castle. Eventually we'll get your men up there as well.' Baldwin clasped Ashere on the shoulder and began leading him up the path.

'I hope you will notice that we have been using the time you have bought us well. Our defences are now much improved.'

As they began heading up the path Farred fell in with Walter. The Marshal began to point out the improvements he had made to the fortress, no doubt picking out the same features Baldwin was explaining to Ashere. Since this was the only path up either of the two huge rocks that constituted the fortress, it was the obvious point of attack for the enemy.

Walter had built a series of wooden gates along the path, each a foot thick and bound with metal, which could be used to stop attackers. In addition, ledges had been constructed along the path which wound its way around the rock above them. This allowed defenders to rain down missiles directly over the heads of attackers, and yet remain safe. The combination of the gates, and the height advantage provided by the ledge, was murderous, and trying to attack them seemed suicidal. Despite being well aware of the size of the force that Ishari was about to deploy here, Farred felt a little more confident that they could be stopped.

Although Rainer had taken them up when they had first arrived at Burkhard, a week ago, Farred was no less impressed by the defences the second time round. They took the left-hand path as they approached the summit, Farred smiling as he recalled that the middle and right paths led nowhere—just another way to bottle up the enemy. As they reached the top of the crag, Farred could see that the walls and five towers of the Duke's Keep had been heightened and strengthened. Baldwin led them across the stone bridge to the larger castle atop the other rock, known as the Emperor's Keep.

In the main hall, the Emperor and Prince sat down in a corner, intent on their own conversation, ignoring everyone else. Farred got a sense, perhaps, of why Baldwin was so keen to talk with Ashere. The weight of leadership and responsibility must have lain heavily on him. Ashere was one of the few men who could talk to him as something of an equal.

Walter gestured for Farred and Brock to follow him. He led them to the far tower and up the stairs until they were at the top of the battlements.

'This is the best view from the castle,' said the Marshal, resting his elbows on the wall and leaning out. He pointed to the east. 'You can see the Great Road for miles in either direction. To the south, the lands of the Empire. Mostly undefended. To the north, the horde will be heading down this road. They could go on past. But they won't.' Walter turned to look at them. 'You've seen their army. And you've seen this castle.' He looked at them, his eyes asking an unsaid question.

Farred and Brock looked at each other.

'We'll kill many,' said Brock.

A flicker of pain crossed the Marshal's face. He looked at Farred, who tried to choose the right words.

'You've done well, Walter. I think you'll hold out for a long time.'

He nodded, a resigned look now on his face. 'I see. Thanks for your honesty. Then we'll kill as many as we can and hold out for as long as we can.'

A brief silence fell on them, since there was nothing much more that could be said on that topic. Walter turned back to look out from the battlements. He pointed again, this time south down the Great Road.

'That's why I brought you both up here,' he said, allowing himself a small smile.

Farred looked out over the battlements into the distance. At first, he saw nothing. Then, as his eyes focused on the monotonous terrain, he saw movement. The Great Road was moving.

'An army,' he said.

Brock moved over to the wall and peered over.

'Who is it?' asked the Middian.

'The army of Gotbeck,' replied Walter. 'Archbishop Godfrey is leading them himself. There's at least another ten thousand men on top of what we've already got.'

'That's more Drobax we'll kill then,' remarked Brock with a serious expression.

'I think we'll hold out for a while longer now,' added Farred, keeping a straight face.

'Well, you two are delightful company,' responded Walter, frowning balefully. 'We'll have to do this again sometime. I can't wait to tell my brother the good news.'

Walter invited Farred and Brock to Baldwin's war council. In the Emperor's Hall, a table had been laid out with food. To either side of Baldwin, who was positioned at the head of the table, sat the dukes, the men who controlled one of the seven duchies of the Empire: Arne, Duke of Luderia; Godfrey, Archbishop of Gotbeck; Jeremias, the new Duke of Rotelegen, who was accompanied by his mother, Adalheid, the widow of Duke Ellard. Prince Ashere and Walter were positioned after them. Farred and Brock were at the opposite end of the table to Baldwin, seated with his advisers, Rainer and Gustav the Hawk.

'The spread of these foul ideas has been like a fire in dry woods,' intoned Godfrey, his voice deep and compelling. 'A contagion of the soul which will not lose hold. Even when I arrived with my forces to restore order, men and women, often of the labouring class, whom I have always felt to have been the most sensible and level headed of our peoples, chose to die in futile resistance; leaving their children orphaned, rather than submit to my authority. And I have been far more forgiving, far more ready to accept false recantations and weak compromises, than I would ordinarily have done, because I was only too aware of my duties here, to defend the Empire from another, far greater threat. I hope you understand, Baldwin, that for me to have left Gotbeck in such a chaotic state, taking my forces with me, would have done far more harm than this delay in reaching Burkhard.'

Farred was just about following the Archbishop's story, which centred on a religious revolt he had felt forced to put down before leaving his duchy. However, he had a tendency not only to speak in long sentences, but also to deliver them in what Farred supposed to be his sermon voice; loud, booming, and talking to his audience as if they were stupid. Most of the others at the table had polite faces on, but Farred also detected a certain amount of discomfort with the subject matter under the surface.

'I quite understand the predicament you have been in, Godfrey,' began Baldwin. 'Do you have any suspicions on the origins of these teachings?'

'More than suspicions, Your Majesty. It is quite clear that preachers from the Confederacy have been behind it. What is more, they have clearly been allowed to come and go across the border without the authorities there interfering. In my opinion they have even encouraged it. They have certainly been as difficult and unhelpful as they could have been, when they know very well about the great enemy that threatens Brasingia. I understand in present circumstances there is little that we can do, but if the situation were different, I would be advocating an aggressive response against them.'

'I see. Well, the Confederacy has ever been a thorn in our side. I don't need to remind you of the endless problems they caused my late father, the Gods rest his soul. But, as you say, that will have to wait for another time. I am keen to hear everything you know about our southern duchies. Emeric in Barissia is in open revolt. Coen in Thesse claims that he is unable to spare any troops because of this.'

'Well, Your Majesty,' began Godfrey, 'all my sources, which of course are principally from trusted men in the Church, indicate that everything Coen is telling us is the truth. Emeric seems to have access to huge wealth, presumably via Ishari, and has used it to amass a large army. Coen's forces are significantly smaller, but are able to shadow his movements, and so far, the Barissians seem unwilling to make a move. Of course, now that my own army has left Gotbeck, the situation in the south has changed. The Barissians don't have to worry about a second front any longer. I would think it only a matter of time until Emeric moves against Coen. He will plan to neutralise Thesse, and then turn against our sparsely defended duchies.'

Although Godfrey liked the sound of his own voice, his face looked suitably grim, and he did not appear to be enjoying what he said. 'In truth, Baldwin, he must surely be intending to move on Essenberg when he can, and claim your imperial throne for himself.'

'Well, Godfrey,' said Duke Arne, 'no doubt you're right, but the man is a fool. Surely he must see that it will only be at the whim of Ishari that he holds it.'

'Ambition can easily cloud a man's judgement,' interjected Duchess Adalheid. 'When Baldwin was elected Emperor, my husband accepted the decision and gave him his full support.'

Baldwin bent his head in acknowledgement.

'But most men can't do that,' Adalheid continued. 'Emeric will have been festering over it ever since, believe me.'

'Well,' said Baldwin, 'I have as much to fear as any man from Emeric, since I have left my family in Essenberg. That said, we cannot afford to worry about it now. A threat of far greater proportions will be with us soon. Prince Ashere, what was your estimate of the arrival of the Isharite army?'

'Your Majesty, the full army will arrive in three to four days' time. It is slow moving due to the Drobax. It is possible that they will send Haskan units faster than that.'

'Who leads it?' asked Godfrey.

'Gustav?' asked Baldwin, indicating that the mage should field the question.

'Shira, Queen of Haskany,' began the wizard.

'Arioc's slut?' interrupted the Archbishop.

Gustav inclined his head towards the Archbishop, presumably in confirmation of the statement. 'She has with her an uncle,' he continued, 'who is an experienced general, and a coterie of Isharite sorcerers. So, although she herself lacks experience, and Arioc is not with them, I think we need to expect strong leadership.'

'Walter,' said Baldwin, 'what needs to be done?'

'The defences are almost ready. Now that Your Grace's soldiers have arrived,' continued the Marshal, indicating Archbishop Godfrey, 'they will need to be accommodated in the castle, along with all the other fighting men still outside. We also need to ensure that any non-combatants leave for the South.'

'We can lead one more sortie out,' said Ashere. It was half statement but also half question, since he turned to Farred and Brock for confirmation. Farred and Brock looked at each other and then nodded their consent.

'I don't expect you to do that,' replied Baldwin. 'You and your soldiers have already done us a great service. Now that you are here I intend to keep you in reserve. It is time for others to risk their lives. My own men can go if you need more time, Walter.'

'I would request one final sortie, Your Majesty,' said Ashere. 'Then I would feel that I have done my job to the best of my ability. After that, I would be happy to be deployed as you see fit.'

Baldwin looked at the Prince and nodded. 'Very well. If you put it like that I must grant you your request. Please ask my brother to provide you with whatever resources you need, Prince Ashere.'

Farred felt a shudder go down his spine at the exchange. For some reason, he wished Ashere had not volunteered them. But it was done.

VI

TWO TOWERS

THE HIGH TOWER OF THE KNIGHTS of Kalinth was not what Belwynn had expected. The knights seemed to her to be a sober, disciplined group of men. They dedicated themselves to a military life, forgoing a family. They lived in a tough landscape of hills and moorland. So, to find that their Tower was an elegant folly, with its thin walls and slim, tall spires, totally useless as a defensive structure, was a surprise.

'It's very pretty,' said Belwynn as they crested a hill and she got her first full look at it.

'Yes, it is,' said Theron, smiling sweetly at it like you might smile at your favourite aunt or uncle.

'It's not very formidable looking, though. It's not going to intimidate your enemies.'

Theron kept smiling. 'True enough, but we have the Fortress of Chalios as our defensive bastion, should the need arise. The High Tower is a much more pleasant place for the Order to meet. Most everywhere else in Kalinth is bleak and imposing,' he said and looked Belwynn in the eyes. 'So when you have something delicate and beautiful, you treasure it all the more.'

Belwynn looked away and they rode on in silence, eating up the distance to the Tower, until they were dismounting and organising the stabling of the horses. Theron boasted that the stables at the High Tower were the largest in Dalriya, and a number of grooms descended on them, ensuring that all the horses were marked up with Sebastian's coat of arms, a simple blue shield with one red chevron, before leading them off to what looked like a maze of buildings.

The importance of the High Tower to the knights had led to the growth of a town around it, with shops and guest houses providing services to the knights and their entourages. Apart from the horses, accommodation for humans in the Tower was confined to knights only, so Evander was sent off to book lodgings for himself, Belwynn and the others, while Sebastian's retainers and servants organised themselves separately.

'Come, now the boring arrangements have been made, let me show you the Tower,' said Theron, gesturing all four of them to the grand entrance.

Again, no real effort had been made to make the entrance defensible. It was approached by a set of polished, grey marble steps, with a six-pillared portico above it. The entrance itself was wide enough for the five of them to walk through side by side. Ahead of them was a wall, dominated by a huge embroidery depicting a battle scene, where knights on horseback were charging at an army of Drobax. Theron took them to the right, then a right angle turn to the left brought them into a large hallway. Various people were milling about here, while others leaned against walls chatting. Some were dressed in all their knightly finery; others were servants who worked in the Tower.

'In there,' said Theron, pointing to the room on the right, 'is the chapel. Only knights may enter; that is where we are inducted into the Order. Opposite,' he said, waving to the left, 'are the kitchens and stairs leading up to the sleeping quarters. But I wanted to show you the Great Hall.'

Theron led them ahead to the formidable oak doors of the hall. Each was flanked by a giant marble statue. On the right, a white mounted knight, his horse risen on its hind legs, was thrusting his lance ahead of him. On the left a fearsome green dragon, on its hind legs in a similar pose to the horse, reached out with its clawed and scaled front legs.

Theron pushed at one of the doors which was already slightly ajar, and with a bit of a creak it opened wide enough for them to slip through. Belwynn was first struck by the height of the room; the ceiling was a good twenty feet high, and was decorated with painted murals. Servants were coming and going through a door which connected into the kitchens, preparing for the evening meal. At the other end of the room was a raised dais.

The rest of the room was taken up with round tables. In front of the dais was the largest and grandest, and the other tables radiated out from it, like the spokes of a wheel. Belwynn had never seen a set up like it. The halls she had been in were almost always set up in a horseshoe shape, with most people sitting on benches. The nearer you were to the top of the horseshoe, the more honoured you were by the host.

'The round tables denote equality?' she asked.

'Yes,' replied Theron, 'of a sort. The idea is that all the knights are brothers, and in that sense, are equals. But everyone wants to be seated as near to the main table as possible. You can't avoid human nature.'

On their way out, heading down the hallway, a huge shout rang out and another knight came bounding over towards them. Theron let out a similar cry and the two men embraced in a big bear hug.

Theron turned to the others.

'This is Tycho, my best friend. Tycho, these are new friends I have made. It's rather a long story. Belwynn, Elana, Rabigar and Dirk.'

Tycho was of a similar age to Theron, but of a darker complexion. Even standing next to Theron, Belwynn could see that he was heavily muscled, with a broad chest, huge shoulders, and a thick neck. He had a friendly, open face and he shook each of them by the hand, Belwynn's hand disappearing into his when it was her turn.

'Well, sometime soon you'll have to tell me the story. Is it true that your cousin is here?'

'Yes...' Theron began, but his attention was diverted. 'Evander! Over here!' he shouted, interrupting himself.

The young squire, who was making his way over to them anyway, hurried a bit faster.

'Lord Tycho,' he said in greeting to the other knight.

Tycho gave him a whack on the shoulder which sent a shudder down the young man's body, but he seemed to be expecting it, and continued unfazed.

'I have secured our accommodation, my lord,' he said to Theron. 'Good rooms at the Green Dragon.'

'Excellent. Well done, 'Vander,' Theron replied.

'Well, I think we should go there now,' said Belwynn, sensing that Theron needed to get away and discuss politics with his friend. 'Thank you for showing us the Tower, Lord Theron.'

They said their goodbyes, and followed Evander away from the Tower and into the town. The town had clearly grown up next to the Tower in a completely disorganised fashion, and Belwynn found herself concentrating hard on remembering the route, as Evander navigated the twists and turns. Solid stone buildings stood next to temporary shacks built of untreated wood, and the paths narrowed and widened at random, so that at one minute they would all be walking side by side, the next in single file, as they squeezed their way past people coming in the opposite direction.

As well as grocers feeding the knights and their entourages, they walked past farriers and blacksmiths, who seemed to be making a good living.

A bellow of pain erupted from one of the smithies, followed by a scream. They hurried over. Outside they found a smith on his knees with a splinter of metal sticking out of his neck. Blood was pouring from the wound. A small crowd had already gathered around him.

'Careful!' cautioned one of them, as the smith fumbled at his neck with big, grimy fingers. 'You might make it worse!'

'Let me deal with this!' demanded Elana, making her way over to the man. Belwynn and the others followed her.

'It might have hit his jugular,' murmured Rabigar as they took a closer look.

Belwynn looked around at the crowd for resistance, but they seemed willing enough for Elana to tend to the man.

'Who are you?' demanded the smith, wild eyed with fear.

'Calm down and let me have a look,' replied Elana, going down onto her knees so that she was at the same height as her patient. She had a look at the injury, and then used one finger to put some light pressure on the neck below the wound, which reduced the flow of blood.

'My name's Elana,' she said, calmly. 'What's yours?'

'Nestor. Can you get it out? I was hammering iron and a bit flew off. Is it bad?'

'Don't worry, I'll get it out.'

Elana placed the fingers of her other hand around the injury and closed her eyes in concentration. Nothing seemed to happen at first, but the blood flow started to reduce further. Then, she carefully placed a thumb and forefinger on Nestor's neck where the piece of metal had entered. She gripped the end of the metal with her other hand and slowly pulled it out. The crowd, which was growing in size, gasped as she removed it and placed it onto the ground beside her. She kept her hand over his neck for a while longer and then removed it. The injury was still visible but it had stopped bleeding, as if the internal damage had been healed.

'There,' Elana said. 'It should be fine now, but you need to take the rest of the day off and rest—no physical activity. Protect the wound from any damage.'

'Thank you,' said the smith, getting gingerly to his feet and then pulling up Elana with him. 'Thank you,' he repeated, enfolding her in a hug. 'You saved my life. Please, let me pay you.'

'No,' responded Elana, frowning, 'I don't need payment.'

'Then take something from my store, please, anything you want.'

But other members of the crowd were now moving in, asking Elana what she had done, and how. Rabigar approached Nestor and took him to one side, no doubt discussing their shared trade, if not the accident itself. Belwynn shared a look with the young Evander, who was staring open mouthed at what he had just witnessed. She gave him a brief smile and shrugged. Something told her that this story was going to get retold. A lot.

***

It had been a hellish journey since they had been captured in the lands of the Grand Caladri. Moneva had been kept away from the others. She had her hands tied the whole time, and had to ride on the same horse as an Isharite. They had taken it in turns to ride with her, their arms wrapped around her from behind as they held the reins of the horse, squeezing her more than necessary, gripping her with their knees. Their breath was heavy on the back of her neck. Sometimes they would hold the reins one handed and rest the other on her thigh. It was all Moneva could do to stop herself screaming out and fighting. But she knew that was what they wanted. So instead she kept quiet, didn't react, and gave them as little pleasure as she could.

The treatment handed out to Herin, Clarin and Gyrmund was no better. They would get kicked and slapped about regularly. Some days they would eat, others not. They sat on a cart most of the time, but at other times the Isharites might decide that one of them should walk. They would tie their hands to a rope connected to the cart. If they tripped they would get dragged along until they regained their feet. Their captors laughed a little when this happened, but most of the time showed no interest in them.

Soren, meanwhile, was kept in his box the whole time. A special group of Isharites had watch over him and his box, which had been placed on a second cart away from the others. Moneva had never seen them open it to let some air in, or give him anything to drink.

When they stopped for rests they would manhandle her off the horse, and dump her on the ground. But they made sure that she got enough food and water. She would always sit away from the others but sometimes near enough that she could take surreptitious glances to see how they looked. She knew better than to do more than that. Gyrmund didn't. The first time he had started to call over to her. Herin quickly shoved an elbow into his ribs so that it came out as a meaningless yell. The Isharites walked over and kicked him. Moneva stared at the floor, a lump in her throat, praying that he wouldn't be so stupid again. He wasn't.

Most often she sat alone while a group of them would eat and stare at her, talking amongst themselves with their leery faces trained on her. One would say something and the others would all laugh, staring at her all the more fiercely. She repeatedly asked herself why they didn't rape her, why they stopped short of any direct sexual contact. She assumed that Arioc had given the order, and that they were too scared to break it. But she didn't know that. He wasn't with them, and she hadn't seen him since the day of their capture. So, she said nothing, didn't react, or draw any kind of attention to herself. She behaved the same way day after day, in the hope that if she did, they would leave her alone again; and surely, eventually, they would get where they were going, and the journey would end. She deliberately didn't think about what would happen then.

It had been obvious to Moneva that they had been travelling northwards, and that the lands of Ishari were the most likely destination. But her geography was pretty poor, and anyway, those lands were steeped in mystery, since few people had been there and returned to tell the tale.

There were signs of permanent habitation. They travelled on proper roads, and she saw grazing animals in the distance. But no buildings, and no other travellers.

Then a huge fortress emerged on the horizon, growing bigger as they approached. Moneva had seen nothing like it before. It hadn't been sited on any significant geographical position. The surrounding land was flat and featureless. It was as if it had been dropped down in this location from the skies. Its walls were three times as high as any she had ever seen before, with huge circular towers in the corners. A huge wall extended out in either direction from the fortress proper as far as the eye could see, presumably enclosing a vast complex. The most remarkable thing was the colour. It was not just the dark jet colour of the stone; but that the walls, when touched by the pale sun above, glimmered and sparkled, as if infused with some dark magic, which, thought Moneva, was entirely possible. The whole effect was to suggest that crossing to the other side of the immense wall would take you into a new, unknown world, somehow separate from the rest of Dalriya.

As Moneva began to wonder what they would find behind that wall, her rider steered the horse away from the rest of the convoy. One other rider joined them. It was all done in seconds, with no talking or farewells to their comrades. They were making their way directly towards the fortress, along a gravel road, while the rest of the convoy headed in a more north easterly direction, presumably to some other part of the complex. She turned back in her seat. She made eye contact with Gyrmund and Herin who were staring in her direction. Clarin seemed to be slumped asleep on the cart. She then turned around again.

The two riders seemed to be in a hurry. They trotted their mounts over towards the huge metal plated gates which were the main entrance to the fortress. As they neared, Moneva realised that the glimmer of the walls came from crystals which had somehow been embedded amongst the black stone of the wall. When opened, the gates would be big enough for ten cavalrymen to ride through abreast. Above them, about ten feet up, a small, square section of the metal gate swung open with a squeak, large enough for a head to pop through. The head belonged to an Isharite soldier, and a brief conversation ensued. Moneva still found the language incomprehensible, and they talked fast, but she did notice both her captors and the fortress guard use the word 'Arioc'. It was impossible to tell how the conversation went, since their faces showed no emotion that she could read. After a short time, the head poked back inside, and the metal window was slammed shut.

They waited outside. Moneva's body gave an involuntary shudder. Her rider noticed and said something to his comrade on the other horse, before putting his arms around her chest and giving her a hug. Both of them laughed. Moneva stared straight ahead at the gates, trying to keep her breathing steady. Shortly, another squeaking and grating noise preceded a door being opened. Like last time, it wasn't either of the main gates. Instead someone had opened a smaller door that had been built into the main gate. Moneva had not noticed it before.

Once opened, the two riders manoeuvred through the gate. Six feet ahead of them was another length of wall. Any attackers who made it through the gate would, at this point, find themselves trapped between the two walls which ran parallel to each other. She got a brief glimpse of the inside of the outer wall, which was a complex of stairs and platforms leading all the way to the top. It seemed lightly manned at the moment, but could clearly hold many fighters if necessary. Before she could take in more they were off, turning left and moving between the two walls until they headed through a gap in the wall on their right. They continued straight ahead for a while before some more zigzagging brought them to the entrance to one of the huge towers that Moneva had seen from a distance. One guard stood sentry. The two riders dismounted and one of them lifted Moneva from the horse. After a brief conversation with the guard they were admitted in.

The entrance room was sparsely furnished. A closed wooden door faced them. Instead, the soldiers gripped Moneva's upper arms and guided her towards the set of stone steps. They were steep, twisting stairs, winding their way up to the next floor of the tower. Moneva's legs felt stiff from all the horse riding, and she had trouble with her balance on the first few steps with her hands still tied. But the two men then gripped each arm and part shoved, part lifted her up the stairs, so that she had to quickly move her feet to find the stairs to avoid being dragged up.

They arrived at a wooden door leading to the rooms on the second floor. One of the soldiers banged on the door roughly. Then, without waiting very long, banged again. The door was unlocked and opened from the inside. Another Isharite stood in the doorway. He glared sternly at each of them, showing no surprise that Moneva was standing in front of him. He began questioning the two men. He seemed older, or at least superior, to the other two. But it was hard to tell. He had the same dark colouring as the rest of the Isharites and his faced showed no obvious signs of age.

Making a strange clicking noise with his mouth, he waved his hands at the two men to bring her in. Moneva was propelled into the room. Even though she knew how big the tower was, the room seemed huge. It was expensively furnished with handcrafted bookshelves, soft Haskan rugs, a wardrobe, and scattered with other strange objects she had never seen before. Three doors led off from this room, all closed. There didn't seem to be anyone else in.

'Welcome to Lord Arioc's chambers,' said the man easily. 'I am Babak.'

Moneva made an involuntary gasp, both because she had not heard anyone speak Dalriyan for days, and because of where she was.

He paced over to one of the doors and opened it.

'You will be staying in here until he returns,' Babak informed Moneva casually, his accent thick, emphasising the consonants.

Making the same clicking noise at the two soldiers who had brought Moneva here, he waved an arm at the room. Grabbing Moneva by the arms once more, they propelled her into the room, which was much smaller, and dominated by a four-poster bed. The men didn't stop, and before she realised what was happening they had thrown her unceremoniously onto the bed. She picked herself up to the sound of their laughter. Both men were staring at her, one of them licking his lips. But, to her relief, they turned around and sauntered out of the room.

Babak appeared at the doorway. He looked at her but said nothing and closed the door, staying on the other side. She heard the click of the door being locked. Moneva was alone for the first time in a week. And she began to cry—big, heaving sobs, which she hid by pressing her face into the mattress of the bed.

VII

FRIENDS AND ENEMIES

THE WARM SPELL THEY HAD BEEN enjoying in Magnia showed no signs of stopping, though there was enough of a breeze to make travelling comfortable. Edgar, accompanied by a small entourage, approached Wincandon, the lair of his enemy. Cerdda, Prince of North Magnia.

At least, that's what Magnian history recorded: two families, bitter rivals who ruled a divided country. But recent events had questioned that old narrative. South and North had united against a much more serious enemy. They had come together to form an army, led by Cerdda's brother, Ashere. This army would now be active, helping to defend the Brasingian Empire from Ishari. And here, in Wincandon, they would perhaps achieve even more.

Wincandon was a small agricultural estate, surrounded by the lush Magnian countryside. But it was owned by the royal family of North Magnia and here, in Cerdda's hall, a Conference of the South was to be held.

Edgar nudged his horse onwards into the village. Orderly, well maintained houses sat either side of a dirt track that led to the hall, visible in the distance. To his right, just beyond the houses, the gentle tinkling of a stream provided some background noise. Looking across, he saw a large, vertical waterwheel that dominated the skyline. A watermill had been built on the near bank, providing the villagers with the power to grind their grains into flour.

When they reached the hall, Cerdda was waiting for him outside. Edgar dismounted as servants arrived to take away the horses. Cerdda approached and they embraced.

'You found us, then?' he asked.

Edgar nodded. 'We made good time. Some hall you have here,' he added, taking in the size of the building before them. It was larger, by a distance, than any hall in South Magnia.

'Yes. This is where we spent our childhood—I have fond memories of the place. I have enlarged it since. It's a place to get away. For family time. Talking of which, you must come in and meet them.'

Edgar followed Cerdda into the hall. It was light and airy inside. Groups of armed men had claimed different parts of the hall for their own, talking amongst themselves while servants brought them food and drink. They made their way towards the back of the hall. Edgar noticed some familiar faces on the way. He nodded to Frayne, the Middian chieftain who had participated in the Conference that Edgar had hosted some two weeks past. His presence was a good sign that the Middians might be willing to raise more soldiers.

A set of wooden stairs zigzagged its way up one wall to a second floor. The two princes took the stairs. Half way up, Edgar could hear female voices talking above them. The stairs opened into a large reception room. An unlit fireplace dominated the opposite wall. In between, there was a table, with trays of food and wine glasses atop it. Half a dozen chairs were positioned around it, with rugs and cushions scattered on the floor. To the right, three doors led off from the room, presumably bedrooms.

Three women were in the room, all working with needle and thread, which they put down when the two of them entered.

Now that he was here, Edgar felt hesitant. He wasn't used to female company. He had grown up an only child, and his relationship with his mother had always been somewhat distant, more so since the death of his father, and his inheritance of the throne. More than that, however, the people in this room had been enemies of his family in the civil war. He wasn't at all sure how they would react to him.

'Edgar, may I introduce the three most important people in my life. My mother, Lady Mette,' Cerdda began.

'*Please*, Cerdda,' said Mette, standing, 'Mette will do. It is a pleasure to finally meet you, Edgar.'

More than once, Edgar's father had emphasised how beautiful Mette was, and he could now see for himself. She had a deep brown skin tone with large, almond shaped eyes, framed by straight, jet black hair. Edgar moved to take her hand. Instead, Mette opened her arms and embraced him.

Releasing him, she took over the introductions.

'This is my lovely daughter-in-law, Irmgard,' she said.

Irmgard, Cerdda's wife, was a handsome woman with more typical Magnian looks. She was tall and slender, brown hair hanging loose to her swan-like neck. She seemed more reserved than her mother-in-law, allowing Edgar to take her hand and plant a kiss.

'And Elfled, my daughter,' finished Mette.

Turning to Cerdda's sister, Edgar found himself looking at the most attractive woman he had seen in his life. Elfled had inherited her mother's dark brown eyes and dark hair. Her hair was curly, however, falling in ringlets about her face. Her skin, like her brother's, was a golden-brown colour.

'Hello Edgar,' said Elfled, embracing him just like her mother had.

Edgar froze. The closeness of her, the smell of her, threatened to overwhelm his senses. His mind went blank and refused to work properly. When she withdrew, he became conscious that he had been speaking, but had no idea what he had said. He looked around at the faces in the room. No-one was making a face as if he had said anything stupid, but he suspected that they might all be too polite to let him know if he had.

'Is your mother well?' enquired Mette.

'Yes,' Edgar replied, recovering. 'I visited with her a few weeks ago. She is very content.'

'I am so happy that we have got the chance to meet you at last,' said Mette. 'You will both be very busy today, and it is not a time to dwell on the past. But I wanted to let you know, Edgar. I have never felt any resentment towards you. My husband and your father ended up on different sides in the civil war. Bradda believed that he could no longer support King Alfrith. Your father decided that he must. But there was never any personal animosity between them. Your father acted with honour in everything he did. So have you. I am proud that you and Cerdda have started to build bridges. It is time to put the past behind us.'

'Do you two have time to stay awhile and have a drink with us?' asked Elfled. 'We have some Cordentine red. It might help you get through the evening.'

'I don't know,' said Cerdda. 'We have more guests arriving, and—'

'Yes,' said Edgar, interrupting. He found himself a seat on one of the chairs. The only way he was leaving, he had decided, was if he was dragged out by a demon.

Edgar rubbed his eyes. He was struggling to stay focused on the discussion at hand. He had, perhaps, had one glass of wine too many. Lord Rosmont, representing King Glanna of Cordence, was demanding chapter and verse on what he would be getting for his master's money. As with the earlier force sent to the Empire under the leadership of Prince Ashere and Farred, the Cordentines had not been persuaded to supply their own soldiers, but were prepared to bankroll others. Edgar accepted that it was necessary for them to make sure that nobody ran off with their money. But since most of Glanna's money would be going elsewhere, Edgar found it hard to stay interested.

Instead, his mind kept returning to Elfled, Cerdda's sister. There was something about her. He couldn't keep his eyes off her when she was in the room, and kept thinking about her when she was gone.

Making his excuses, Edgar left the negotiating table. The conversation continued without him. He headed out of Cerdda's hall and took a few deep breaths of fresh air. It was a warm summer evening, and he felt a fleeting sense of disappointment that he wasn't getting to enjoy it.

Still, he had to take pleasure in the fact that they were close to achieving something very important. Wincandon was an ordinary estate in North Magnia but, in Edgar's view, it was the setting for something extraordinary. No one he had talked to could recall a treaty with signatories from so many nations. As well as South and North Magnia, led by himself and Cerdda, there was Frayne, a chieftain from the Midder Steppe, who had offered to recruit soldiers so long as someone else would pay their wages; Russell, representing Duke Bastien of Morbaine, who could not formally commit soldiers without the authority of King Nicolas of Guivergne, but was negotiating on other sources of aid; Lord Emmett, representing Duke Coen of Thesse, who, with the backing of Emperor Baldwin, was requesting aid against the traitor, Emeric of Barissia; and finally, Lord Rosmont, who had authority to commit Cordence to the war. They were close to signing a full treaty and declaration of war, on both Ishari and Barissia—and, crucially, to committing to another army, even larger than the one they had sent to Brasingia.

Edgar wandered away from the hall towards the southern end of the village. He stopped at the mill pond, a pleasant spot dominated by a large willow tree. Some of the yellow catkins had fallen onto the surface, and were twirling around in the breeze. Beneath the surface, sinewy eels patrolled their underwater kingdom, wriggling into view and away again.

'Penny for your thoughts?' said a female voice.

Edgar turned around sharply. He had assumed that he was alone and his heart beat fast as he peered at the shaded end of the pond. Emerging from under the willow tree, Elfled, Cerdda's sister, walked towards him. He met her half way, keen to take the chance to spend some time with her alone.

'Well?' she asked him.

'It was getting a bit boring in there,' replied Edgar.

'Going that well, then?'

'No, it's not going badly. Just slowly,' said Edgar, looking around them. 'Sometimes I crave a bit of peace and quiet.'

'Oh. Well, I can't share that sentiment. I get more than my share of peace and quiet.'

Edgar looked at her quizzically.

'That's the life of a princess,' she explained. 'Over protected, spending your days sewing and reading. Excluded from important meetings,' she said pointedly, making Edgar feel a bit embarrassed. 'Until you get married off to some stranger twice your age.'

'Right. I'd never really thought about it before. No sister, you see.'

Elfled laughed.

'And what's so funny?'

'I was thinking to myself, what a shame for you, being an only child. It's the strangest thing. When I was growing up you were the devil. Sitting on my family's throne, dripping in the blood of innocents. I happily hated you: a childish, unthinking kind of hate. But now I've met you, I can't hate you anymore. You're so fair and...*reasonable*.'

'I'm not always that reasonable.'

'Come on Edgar, you were emoting with a spoilt princess about her not having any work to do!'

Edgar laughed. 'I suppose so. Anyway, it's made me very happy to have befriended you and Cerdda.'

'I think it's a really important thing that you are both doing today.'

'Yes. Although we're hardly going to make an impact on Ishari's forces.'

'Maybe. I didn't mean just the war, though. Nobody would have predicted North and South Magnia working so closely together, even a year ago. It's an important step towards uniting our country again.'

'Union? That's a long way off.'

'Is it? Cerdda and Irmgard love each other very much. But they haven't had children after years of marriage.'

'Ashere?'

Elfled's mouth gave a twitch of a smile.

'I doubt that my brother Ashere will have any children.'

Of course, that left Elfled herself, but Edgar knew that if he pursued that avenue he would end up going bright red and tongue tied.

'Well then, maybe it is possible,' he murmured.

'It is. Don't you think Magnia should be one country again?'

'Yes. Of course I do.'

Elfled seemed pleased with that response. 'So, what's left to sort out in there?' she asked, nodding in the direction of Cerdda's hall.

'Well, we're yet to agree on the objective of intervention in the Empire. We want to keep Essenberg out of Emeric's hands. Anything more than that would be over-stretching our resources in my opinion. The other main sticking points are money, as usual, and leadership of the force we send.'

Elfled sighed. 'Hardly sticking points. Sometimes I think you should let the women sort these things out, it'd be done in half an hour. The money is just like buying something from the market: you haggle and meet in the middle. As for who is in charge, it should be the complete opposite. No compromises. Who would you trust the most to do the job? Make sure it's them.'

Edgar smiled. 'Maybe you should go back in there instead of me and sort them all out.'

'Who *would* you be happiest with in charge?' Elfled persisted.

'Well, it would be unfair to ask Cerdda to go when his brother led the first force.'

Elfled nodded. 'So?'

'Me.'

'I agree,' said Elfled, with a shy smile.

Edgar let out a big breath as he came to terms with the idea. It would mean being absent from South Magnia for a long time, a move not without its dangers. He had no military experience to speak of, either. But at the same time, it felt right. The force they would raise needed someone with his status to take overall command. It also meant that he would keep control of things.

'Well. Looks like I might be going to Brasingia.'

Elfled looked at him solemnly. 'Good luck, Edgar.'

***

Soren? Soren!?

Nothing. Belwynn had been trying to contact him for a day now. She knew that something was wrong.

She didn't know what to do. Opening the door of her room at the Green Dragon, she stumbled out into the corridor. She crashed into someone coming the other way. Elana.

'Belwynn, what's the matter? Is it Soren?'

Belwynn tried to say something but instead burst into tears. Elana put her arm around her and directed her back into the room.

'Sorry, Elana. I'm embarrassing myself all the time at the moment.'

'No, you're not. Don't be silly. You still can't talk to him?'

'No. I don't know why,' said Belwynn, then paused for breath. 'Well there's one obvious reason. He's dead.'

'You don't know that, Belwynn. Why have they kept him alive for a week, transporting him somewhere, only to kill him? How do you feel? Do you feel he is dead or alive?'

'I don't know, Elana! I can't speak to him; I can't sense his presence.'

'So we don't know what's happened, Belwynn. Don't give in to despair yet.'

Belwynn took a steadying breath. 'You're right. But I need to do something about it. I can't just sit around here anymore being useless.'

'We will do something, Belwynn. We'll do something here, in Kalinth, first. I know that we're supposed to be here, and that what we do will be important. Can you have patience a while longer?'

Belwynn wiped her eyes. 'I don't have a choice, do I?'

Elana shook her head. 'Not that I can see. Look, why don't we go to the Tower, and see if there's any news?'

Belwynn nodded. 'Alright.'

'First, I need to check on the other two.'

Belwynn went with Elana to the room across the corridor which Rabigar and Dirk shared. Belwynn looked away as Elana lifted Rabigar's patch and inspected his eye; or, at least, where his eye used to be. Taken from him by Emeric's jailers in Coldeberg Castle, it was a wound that could have killed him had Elana not been there to treat it.

'It's still looking good,' she told him.

She then moved on to Dirk. He didn't look well. Placing her hands at various places, she moved around his body, murmuring prayers to her goddess,

Madria. When she had finished, he seemed to Belwynn to look visibly better, his skin losing the grey tinge it had before.

'We're going to go to the Tower. Either of you fancy a walk?'

'No thanks,' said Dirk. 'I think I'll rest up here.'

'I'll take you there,' said Rabigar. 'I've a mind to visit with our new friend, Nestor the smith. I think he could do with an extra pair of hands.'

Belwynn smiled to herself. It looked like Nestor was going to get some extra help whether he needed it or not. They said their goodbyes to Dirk and left. The visit made Belwynn realise how much Elana had been doing in recent days, looking after the victims of two serious attacks. She felt guilty about leaving it all to the priestess, while she remained absorbed with her own troubles. She had even heaped those on to Elana as well as everything else.

'How is Dirk doing?' she asked Elana.

'He's not recovering. The injuries are too severe. I'm keeping him alive, but...'

Elana trailed off, perhaps struggling with her own emotions.

The news made Belwynn go cold. She had assumed that Dirk would make a recovery in the end. But if even Elana couldn't properly heal him, what hope was there?

'I'm sorry,' said Belwynn, feeling like she should say something else, but knowing that whatever she said would be inadequate.

'Thank you,' said Elana. 'I am trying to help him find peace with his situation. Madria helps him.'

They headed down into the main lounge of the Green Dragon. Its dark interior and smell of ale, familiar to virtually every inn Belwynn had visited, was not appealing this morning, and she felt much better once they got out into sunlight and fresh air.

They began making their way through the maze of streets towards the High Tower. They had not gone far when they heard a shout.

'There she is!'

Swinging round, Belwynn saw a group of half a dozen women gesturing towards Elana. Elana waited as the group headed towards them. As they got closer one of their number held out a small bundle of blankets towards Elana. It was a small girl.

'My child, she is sick,' pleaded the woman, her eyes raw with emotion. 'We don't know what to do.'

Elana looked at Belwynn, as if to say sorry.

'Don't worry. I'll be fine on my own,' said Belwynn.

'Are you sure?'

'Of course.'

'I'll stay with Elana,' said Rabigar. 'Just in case.'

Belwynn watched the women lead Elana and Rabigar off down a side street. At that moment, she envied Elana her talent, God-given or not. It allowed her to be useful.

Belwynn continued alone. The atmosphere in the town felt safe enough for her not to worry. The fact that there was a palace full of armed knights no doubt had something to do with it. As she approached the Tower, she noted the complete absence of security. It seemed that anybody could walk in, yet nobody who was unwelcome tried to.

Belwynn walked up the colonnaded steps leading to the Tower entrance, and she noticed someone looking in her direction. It was Tycho, the friend Theron had introduced to her when they had first arrived. He was in conversation with two other knights, both about the same age as him. He said his goodbyes to them and they headed off together away from the Tower. Tycho smiled and walked over.

'Lady Belwynn, a pleasure to meet you again.' He gestured at the two departing knights. 'Just sending for reinforcements,' he said and then looked at her with a frown as if he wasn't sure whether that was information he should have revealed.

Belwynn pretended she hadn't heard. 'I was hoping to see Theron or Sebastian?'

'Right, I'll take you up. They're in a meeting together.'

'Oh. I've come at a bad time?'

'No, no, just a small meeting—an *unofficial* meeting,' he said mysteriously.

Belwynn wasn't convinced that Tycho was cut out for cloak and dagger politics.

He led Belwynn through the Tower entrance and into the main hallway. Instead of going straight on towards the Great Hall, they veered off to the left and through a doorway. Straight ahead Belwynn could hear the sounds and smell the aromas of the kitchens. Tycho led her to a set of stairs that took them to the next floor.

'These are the chambers of the knights,' he commented as he led her down a corridor. 'They are allocated to us when we visit the Tower,' he added.

They passed door after door. Compared to the splendour of the Tower elsewhere, the living quarters seemed sparse and cramped.

'The rooms look very small,' she commented.

'Yes, but big enough for one man to store his possessions and to sleep.'

They moved further up the corridor, and Tycho rapped on one of the doors. There was a shout from inside and he opened the door. Sebastian, Theron and a third man whom Belwynn did not recognise were seated inside, on a bed and two chairs.

'Hello, Belwynn,' said Sebastian, standing up. 'This is my good friend, Remi.'

Remi looked to be of a similar age to Sebastian. He was a big man with a big black beard which was flecked with grey. Remi gestured at them. 'Come in, come in,' he said, indicating that it was his room.

'I'm not intruding?' checked Belwynn, squeezing in but finding nowhere suitable to sit.

'No,' said Sebastian. 'We need to talk to you anyway. I should have come to see you before, but I've only recently come out of my meeting with Galenos.'

Sebastian's tone of voice suggested that the meeting had not gone well. They shuffled onto the bed to make room for Belwynn and Tycho on the two chairs.

'I explained to him that I had changed my position on King Jonas,' Sebastian continued. 'That I thought it was our duty as an Order to intervene. I used some of the information you have given us, about Ishari aggression,' he said, looking at Belwynn, 'and all the other arguments, including our responsibilities to the people.

'I thought that I could persuade him. But he wasn't interested in persuasion or debate. He just repeated his position, that the Order should remain loyal to the King of Kalinth. In every situation. He didn't engage with me at all,' Sebastian shook his head, evidently still bemused by his lack of success. 'I didn't get anywhere.'

It seemed as if the energy and drive had all been sapped out of Sebastian by the setback.

'The man's an idiot, that's the problem,' said Remi darkly.

Sebastian shook his head as if to stop his friend's tirade, but the other knight raised his hand and pressed on.

'And he's surrounded himself with idiots. Men like Euthymius. He listens to them more than the rest of us now. They spend too much time in this Tower, and not enough in the real world.'

'I think he felt like I was challenging him,' said Sebastian dolefully. 'That I was being disloyal. I'm afraid that he now sees me as an enemy.'

'I'm sorry for you, uncle,' said Theron, 'but I'm not surprised. This is how our Order has been run for years now. Anyone with a different opinion to the leadership is cast as a traitor. It is weakness. Galenos is old and weak and doesn't want to confront the truth. In fact, he would rather turn on his own brothers than do that. And it is our country and our people who have been suffering for it. Weak leadership from the knights and from the royal court. It is killing our land.'

They were stark words and delivered without Theron's usual good humour. It left the room quiet and still as the words were digested and their implications, which had been left unsaid, hovered in the air.

'I think we need to think ahead carefully from now on,' said Remi. 'Starting with the feast tonight. We can't afford to be naive: if Euthymius and his allies now see some of us as enemies, they may be on the attack.'

Belwynn swallowed, and after a moment's hesitation, piped up. 'I was thinking. I would like to go to the celebrations tonight. I would like to sing.'

The four knights in the room all looked at her with the same expression.

'You want to sing?' asked Theron after an uncomfortable pause.

She smiled reassuringly, her first proper smile of the day. 'Let me sing tonight, Theron. It will help. Trust me.'

Belwynn had had enough of feeling useless. It was time for her to do something.

***

It was a strange day for the middle of summer. It felt more like one of those winter days, grey and wet, when the sun never really appears, and the day never gets going, offering a half-hearted interruption to the night before retreating again. A non-event of a day.

The weather doesn't help things, Farred thought to himself, *but we have other problems.* The force led by Prince Ashere had been unable to make contact with the Isharite army since setting out from Burkhard Castle over six hours ago. A big bank of fog to the west slowed down the scouting parties who struck off in that direction, so that long after the other groups had returned to report their findings, the army had to sit and wait for the western party. The most recent group had yet to return at all.

He sensed the mood of the soldiers, much more negative and frustrated than they had ever been before, and he understood it. Upon arriving at Burkhard they had received a warm welcome. They had all felt satisfied at a job well done, and they had mentally prepared for the next stage of the conflict. Leaving again so soon, and heading back out against the huge and seemingly invincible enemy army, left them feeling flat and fed up. The prince had asked Farred and Brock to bring only half of their men, but even those more willing amongst them didn't really want to be here.

Ashere sat astride his horse a few feet in front of his army, gazing into the distance. He seemed not to notice or care about the morale of his soldiers. Farred wasn't sure whether it was an act or not. His aloofness and intensity had been a strength until now, but today it didn't seem to be working so well.

Farred nudged his horse forwards. His eyes met with Brock's, and the Middian pulled in alongside him, before they walked their horses up to Ashere's.

'They're still not fucking back yet,' said Ashere by way of greeting, still looking into the far distance.

'When they do get back,' replied Farred, 'I think we should call it a day. We can always go out again tomorrow.'

'Maybe,' said Ashere.

'Definitely,' responded Brock. 'Even if we do find the bastards, we have to engage, withdraw, and make it back to the castle. We've run out of time.'

'Yes,' said Ashere in an absent-minded way.

Silence.

'Ashere?' demanded Farred, getting exasperated.

Ashere finally looked at them both.

'I'm sorry. I just don't get it. They should be here. We should have found them by now. I'm missing something...'

Ashere's voice trailed off. He then cocked his head slightly to one side.

'What's that noise?'

Farred didn't hear anything. But Ashere obviously had, so he concentrated harder. Then his ears tuned in. A rumbling sound. Farred realised that it had been going on for a while now, in the background. It seemed to be coming from the west. Then suddenly, in a flash, it came to him.

'Form up!' he yelled at the top of his voice, stretching his arm out to the west.

The South Magnians he commanded stared back in shock at the sudden explosion of volume. But Ashere and Brock, coming to the same realisation as him, shouted the same command, and so their small, mounted army started to wheel in the direction of the noise.

It was the fog. The Isharites had been here all along, hidden by the mists, no doubt engineered by their magicians. Farred cursed himself. They had got so used to attacking the unsuspecting Drobax that they had got casual about the threat posed by the magic wielding Isharites. This time, the Isharites had set their trap, waiting for Ashere's approach, eager to get their revenge.

The rumbling noise got louder, and Farred began to make out fast approaching figures on horseback coming through the mist. The Haskan cavalry. His adrenaline kicked in, his mouth went dry. They had no idea how many they were up against. He turned to look at Ashere for guidance. The Prince was standing up in his stirrups. He raised his sword in the air.

'Charge!' he bellowed.

Shouts rang out all around as the soldiers dug their heels into the sides of their stallions, trying to build up acceleration as fast as possible to meet the oncoming attack. Ashere's mount sprinted ahead and Farred urged his horse after it, trying to keep pace and not lose sight of him in the enveloping fog.

In a matter of seconds, they had engaged with the enemy, who came hurtling through the mists towards them, shouting their own war cries. These were Haskan soldiers, disciplined and well-armed fighters, not the Drobax they had got used to. Some of them held lances tucked under their armpits which they waved in his direction, trying to unseat him before continuing past to get at the ranks behind. They were like ghosts, flitting into view and then disappearing into the mist again. Farred knew that they would carve right through his force, and then they would be able to wheel around and approach from the rear, surrounding them.

A mounted Haskan soldier came at him with a sword. Farred pulled at his mount's reins so that the beast sidestepped away, and he twisted in the saddle to avoid the blow. But the Haskan wasn't giving up and returned for another go. This time Farred met the blow with his own sword. They held position for a while, each trying to push the other back while their stallions buffeted each other. The Haskan twisted his wrist and scraped his sword down the length of Farred's blade, aiming to chop off his fingers. But Farred was prepared for that. In one fluid motion, he pulled his sword away and then swung it back with all his strength towards his opponent's neck. The Haskan managed to put his sword in the way just in time, but the sudden movement and the strength of Farred's stroke caused him to lose his balance in the saddle and he tumbled backwards. One foot came out of its stirrup and he spiralled onto the floor.

Farred saw movement out of the corner of his eye, and he turned just in time to see Ashere's mount going down. The Prince was surrounded by three Isharites, their crystal swords still managing to glint in amongst the tendrils of mist. Farred looked around him but no support was in sight. They had got separated from Brock and the rest of their comrades, and the fog made it impossible to see where they were.

Farred knew he had to act fast, and urged his mount straight at the group. Ashere was on his feet and still had his sword in his hand. The three Isharites circled warily, not least because the prince's horse was still alive and writhing on the floor, kicking out with its legs. They realised that Farred was bearing down on them just in time and turned to meet him. He was unable to slow the pace of his charge, and the nearest soldier evaded him and swung out his sword. Farred sensed his mount take the impact, and he slid his feet out of the stirrups just before it collapsed under him. Their momentum carried them into one of the Isharites and they became a swirling mass of bodies until Farred was thrown off to the side. He landed badly and was too winded at first to move.

Forcing himself up, Farred grabbed his sword and looked around. The Isharite he had crashed into was trapped under his horse, not moving. Farred stabbed down to make sure he was dead.

He turned around, looking for Ashere. He forced his body to return to the location where Ashere had been brought down.

Peering through the mist, he saw the familiar figure of the Prince. Ashere was staring ahead, a vacant, far away expression on his face. At his feet lay the bodies of his two assailants. Ashere made eye contact with Farred. Something broke. He dropped his sword to the floor, and his legs buckled underneath him. Farred rushed over and knelt over him. Turning him gently onto his back, he saw a large wound where a blow had pierced his armour. The prince had fallen unconscious but was still breathing.

Farred stood up and looked around. He could hear fighting going on but it was some distance away. He presumed that they had ended up behind the enemy's lines. He tried to fight down the panic and think clearly, but his predicament seemed hopeless.

He heard the rider approaching before he saw him. Brandishing his sword, he stood in front of Ashere's prone body and waited.

It was Burstan.

Quickly taking in the situation, his captain dismounted.

'Let's get him on the horse,' he said gruffly.

Farred had never been so pleased to see anyone in his life, but couldn't find any words. In silence, they grabbed Ashere's limbs and, with Burstan murmuring soothingly to his horse, hoisted him up and laid him on his front ahead of the saddle, with his legs and arms dangling over the sides. Farred wasn't sure if it was the best position, but hoped that it might put pressure on the wound and stop the blood loss.

'Get him out of here,' said Burstan, gesturing at the horse.

Farred looked at him in disbelief.

'I'm not getting on there. You get him out of here.'

The captain shook his head.

'Burstan, that's an order.'

Burstan turned his back on Farred.

'I'm going back to be with the men,' he said over his shoulder. 'He's your responsibility, Farred.'

Burstan walked away.

'Burstan, get back here!' hissed Farred at the departing figure, but it ignored him and disappeared into the mist, so that he was alone with Ashere again.

Swearing, Farred clambered into the saddle. A sharp pain in his back told him that his fall had done some damage, but his immediate concern was escape. Assuming that they had charged to the west, and that Burstan and the sound of fighting were over to the east, Farred turned his new mount to the south and hurried away.

Once he had escaped the sound of fighting Farred relaxed a little. He thought of his men back there—those who were still alive would be surrounded by the enemy. He thought of Burstan returning to the fight. But it did no good to dwell on it, and he pushed those thoughts away.

As the nervous minutes ticked by and became first one hour, then two, Farred began to accept that he had escaped. He checked Ashere's pulse every now and again. He was still alive but showed no signs of consciousness. Farred knew that he had to get him back to the castle as soon as possible.

He thought that anyone else who had escaped would be well ahead of him, since his mount was slowed down with two riders, but after a while he caught up with other escapees. Two Middians shared a horse, and explained that they had both escaped, but one of their mounts had pulled up lame. A North Magnian gave a huge smile of relief to learn that his prince was still alive. Later on, they caught up with an injured South Magnian who looked almost as grateful to see Farred. It seemed that more had got away than Farred had feared. He supposed that the fog might have helped. But despite that, they all knew that many of their friends were dead. They travelled in silence, all nursing the same kind of soldier's guilt that their comrades were dead and dying on the battlefield, while they were running away.

By the time they reached the outskirts of Burkhard Castle, the sun was going down, officially giving up on the most miserable day Farred had ever experienced. A party of Brasingian soldiers found them as they approached. They took Ashere away and led Farred, now totally exhausted, up to the Duke's Keep, where the other survivors had been gathered in the main hall. They were bedding down for the night but got up again to greet Farred and the other latecomers. It was a strained greeting, sombre in mood, and yet with genuine pleasure to see others who had escaped. He was grabbed in a big bear hug, and there was Brock standing before him.

'I heard about Ashere. At least you got him out of there.'

'It was Burstan. He gave me his horse—'

'You look terrible. Try to get some sleep.'

Farred nodded. His body was desperate to lie down. Brock guided him over to some bedding and a blanket. Farred turned to him.

'Burstan? I don't suppose...'

Brock shook his head.

No. It was a stupid question. Burstan, like so many others, was dead.

VIII

DOGS AND DRAGONS

BLOOD WELLED INSIDE THE GLOVE of Gyrmund's right hand. He tucked it under his armpit in what he knew was a vain attempt to stop the flow. But he had no way to bandage it up, and he could not stop working. He continued to hack at the walls of the mine with the axe, now held in his left hand. His muscles ached each time he raised his arm, and each time he smashed it into the wall. But the Isharites who controlled the mine had made it quite clear that whoever gathered the smallest amount of diatine crystals would be executed at the end of the shift.

Gyrmund excavated the patch of crystals he had exposed further, chipping away the rock that encased it. The crystal itself, he knew, was incredibly strong. If he missed a stroke and the blade hit the crystal, it wouldn't chip or crack: the danger was to the axe blade.

One further blow and the crystals came free. He breathed a sigh of relief. That, surely, put him in the clear. He looked up and down the underground tunnel. Torches placed along the walls cast enough light to see what was in front of him, but not beyond his little area of light. He could not see any of the guards so he took the opportunity to have a rest while he could.

Time was impossible to measure down in the mine. It was his first day, but it felt like he had been down there for a week. *The end of the shift must surely come soon*, he persuaded himself. They had been given nothing to eat or drink since breakfast. The oxygen down in the tunnel wasn't sufficient to fill his lungs, and with the heat, cramped conditions, and hard, physical work, he had felt like he was going to faint more than once. He held his right hand up in the air to try to slow the bleeding.

After a while he heard footsteps from down the tunnel. One of the guards was approaching. As he came into sight Gyrmund bent down and carefully picked up the chunk of crystals, placing it in the wheeled metal box which he would take back up to the surface. The guard kept watching so Gyrmund began hammering at a fresh patch of wall, making sure he put enough effort in to keep the guard happy. Bored, the guard moved on. After he was sure he had gone out of earshot, Gyrmund stopped again.

Eventually the sound of whistles blew throughout the mine. The other miners began heading to the exit tunnel, and so Gyrmund fell in with them, dragging along his box, and making sure that none of the others filched any of his crystals. He looked at what they had collected. Some had more than him but some had less. He knew that he would have a physical edge over many of the miners, because the conditions down here would clearly take their toll on those who had been here longest. But he had worried that they would have the advantage of experience. In the end, he had done enough.

As they reached the exit tunnel, the miners had to crawl on their hands and knees to get out, hauling their precious cargo with them. The walls pressed in on Gyrmund. He tried to keep his breathing steady. The truth was he couldn't stand the confined space, but if he began to think about where he was he would lose control.

After Moneva had been led away towards the fortress at Samir Durg, their Isharite captors had led them further along the wall until they approached one of the towers that were spaced along it. They had reached their destination, and unpleasant thoughts had begun to enter Gyrmund's mind. His sense of foreboding had risen further when Soren, still enclosed in his box, had been led away elsewhere. Gyrmund had exchanged nervous glances with Herin and Clarin. They didn't need to say it but they were all thinking the same thing: was this the time when their captors decided to kill them? And if not, what did they intend to do with them?

In the end, it was nothing much. They had been shoved in a room on the ground floor of the tower and left. All day and all night they had sat in a cold room, with nothing to do but wonder about their fate. Even Herin and Clarin had been quiet. There was, in truth, little to say. They had dozed away the time. It had felt terrible, but it had been easier than being trapped underground all day. Gyrmund would now have grabbed the chance to be allowed to go back to that room in the tower.

It was not until this morning that, still with no explanation, they had been led to the crystal mines, and turned over to the guards who ran the mines with slave labour. One of the reasons they had been kept alive had at least become clear. Strong men were needed to man the mines, especially since the attrition rate was so high. In a brief welcoming speech, it had been made clear to them that at least one miner was killed at the end of each shift to ensure that they all worked as hard as possible. As Gyrmund made it to the last stage of the journey up to the surface, he was about to find out if that was true.

The route up to ground level was the same as the route down he had taken this morning. The miners crammed into a rickety metal lift and a pulley system was used to raise it to the surface. At the mine entrance a pack of mules were taking the weight, and by walking from one end of the yard to the other they pulled up the ropes attached to the lift. The ropes strained and squeaked as Gyrmund and the other miners shuddered and jolted their way to the surface. When Gyrmund shoved himself out of the lift and took a proper, full breath of air into his lungs, a wave of emotion came over him and he had to stop himself from crying.

He noticed that the other miners were handing in their specially made protective gloves to one of the guards. He waited his turn and handed his over. The guard looked at the ripped gloves and at Gyrmund's bleeding hand. With no warning the guard struck him hard across the face, muttering angrily in words that Gyrmund didn't understand. Gyrmund turned away quickly, fighting to control himself so that he didn't strike back.

He noticed Herin and Clarin standing next to each other a few feet away, and walked over to them. They must have come out on an earlier lift. They had placed their boxes of crystals in front of them and had joined a loose semicircle of miners that was forming opposite a group of Isharite guards, who were observing the activities with apparent boredom at the far end of the yard. Gyrmund joined in the line next to Clarin. Both brothers had mean looks on their faces, and Gyrmund felt grateful that he was in with them rather than on his own.

'What the hell did you do to your hand?' asked Herin, leaning over to look at him with a disgusted expression on his face.

Gyrmund assumed that it was meant as a rhetorical question.

Clarin peered into his box.

'I got more than you,' he said, looking inordinately pleased with himself.

They waited for a while and then, gradually, the atmosphere changed and there was a quiet hush. The guards were walking along the semi-circle, looking at how much each miner had brought out. One of the miners was pulled out into the middle of the yard. He was grinning and almost laughing to himself hysterically. It was horrible to watch.

The guards emptied his box onto the ground. There was next to nothing in there. It was as if he had slept all day. But Gyrmund thought he understood. He had just given up.

He was pulled over to a tall wooden post with a horizontal bar at the top. A piece of rope was fetched over and a noose placed around his neck. He was still grinning manically. Gyrmund looked at the expressions on the faces of the other miners. They suggested that what they were seeing was the normal procedure. Herin and Clarin looked on impassively. The rope was fed through a metal hook attached to the bar, and then three guards pulled on it, dragging the unfortunate victim up by the neck. He hardly fought it. By the time they had finished and were winding the rope around some hooks half way up the post to keep him hanging there, he was already dead.

The guards began shouting and Gyrmund and the other two followed the lead of the other miners. The individual boxes of diatine crystals were emptied into larger containers, and then the boxes were carefully stacked along the wall of the yard for the next day. The miners were then led out of the mine yard along a path, presumably towards their sleeping quarters.

They walked through open, unused land, but they were still behind the main walled enclosure which was visible in the gloom ahead of them.

The path took them to a large, fenced area. They were led through a flimsy looking gate. There were no buildings, suggesting that they were supposed to sleep in the open air. The idea was bearable in this weather, but would surely see them all off in the winter.

The guards stayed inside with them. Herin and Clarin marched over to the far side and Gyrmund kept close to them, looking at the height of the fencing and imagining escape. They stopped and stared out through the fence in the direction of the main fortress, too far away to be visible.

'I'm surprised they don't get escape attempts over this fence,' said Gyrmund. 'I know we're still behind the wall, but—'

Herin frowned at him and nodded over to their left, the section of the area closest to the wall. And Gyrmund saw them. Pits. Big metal grates at ground level covered the entrance which was why he had missed them. Only the handles stuck up slightly. They were kept underground during the night. He looked around at the guards and the miners who were pacing up and down. They were being given a bit of time above ground before being sent down.

Gyrmund shook his head, panic rising in him.

'No,' he hissed, 'I can't do it. I can't do this.'

Herin turned on him angrily.

'You'll have to do it. We do it until we get the chance to escape.'

'How do we do that?'

'I don't know yet. But I'm not going to die in this shithole. I'm going to get out of here. So, Gyrmund, you're gonna go down into that pit, you're gonna work in the mine tomorrow, and you're gonna keep on doing it until the day comes when we get out of here.'

Gyrmund nodded. He hated Herin at that moment. He hated him because he was being so much stronger than he was. Lost in the wild somewhere he would have coped with: no, he would have been in his element. But this was not something he was coping with. He needed Herin and Clarin to get through it. He didn't like it, but there it was.

A group of guards made for the pit grates. They unlocked them and pulled them open, the metal landing on the floor with a clang. The other guards began shouting at the miners and rounding them up. Herin and Clarin made straight for the pit entrance, and Gyrmund followed them.

It was a six foot drop down into the pit. The walls had sconces attached, and the guards lit them, shedding a dim, flickering glow along the straight lines of the pit, and creating shadows which danced along the walls. One end of the pit stank of faeces and urine, so they made their way towards the other end.

Herin chose a position for them at the far end of the pit, and all three leaned against the wall and watched as the pit filled up with the other miners. The men who found themselves in this stinking pit were from all over Dalriya.

The greatest number were humans from the east of Dalriya, commonly referred to as Barbarians. Gyrmund had visited there himself, and learned that they did not refer to themselves by that name. There were, in fact, over fifty different tribes, each with their own name and traditions, all independent of each other. They had never been united and had no wish to be, but lived out a tough existence, farming and foraging on difficult land. Over the past year the forces of Ishari had been gradually subduing these tribes, and many of the men folk had clearly ended up here.

Gyrmund had learned that this campaign had been successful, and that Ishari had moved south into the lands of the Bear-men. This was confirmed by the presence of one of them at the opposite end of the pit, where the prisoners made their toilet. It was crouched down against a wall, seemingly oblivious to the smell. Although he was well travelled, Gyrmund had never seen one before. In most respects, it was human-like, but larger in every way, with huge, powerful shoulders. Bigger than Clarin or any human Gyrmund had met. A huge mop of dirty hair and a scruffy beard covered most of its face. But they didn't completely disguise the huge, powerful jaws that protruded out from its face. Certainly, nobody was getting too close to it.

Gyrmund had spoken to fellow travellers about the Bear-men, and knew that they avoided all contact with other races. If humans entered their territory they would usually disappear. They had their own language, impossible to understand. Gyrmund wondered how they had persuaded it to go down the mine in the first place.

In addition, there were a few prisoners from other lands. Gyrmund could identify some Persaleians, who had likely been captured defending against the recent invasion; and Gyrmund studied two men in quiet conversation who had taken up position on the opposite wall to them. They had Brasingian moustaches, though how they came to be here wasn't obvious.

As Gyrmund was considering going over to introduce himself the dungeon fell silent.

'Who are they?' asked Clarin, glancing over to the other end of the pit.

Gyrmund took a quick look. Five creatures were heading in their direction.

'Dog-men,' he replied, recognising them as a race who lived in the north, and who had long ago come under the control of Ishari. They were known as fearsome fighters, built like humans but generally taller and stronger, their bodies covered in fur, and with a muzzle full of sharp teeth.

'Don't know what they're doing down here,' Gyrmund added. 'They usually fight for Ishari.'

'Punishment. For ill-discipline of some kind,' said Herin. 'Be very careful with them,' he advised, emphasising each word.

The five Dog-men walked slowly up the centre of the pit, eyeing the prisoners around them, who all looked away and avoided eye contact. The one in front was the biggest, a great beast of a creature, whose muscles rippled as it walked along, and whose black eyes stared out with hatred and aggression. The other four flanked it, walking slightly to the side and behind, signifying it as the leader. Inevitably, it led the group to the three newcomers. It walked up to Clarin, who happened to be standing in the middle of the three of them, perhaps because it saw him as the main threat. The others stood two to each side, so that they stood in a straight line of five facing Gyrmund and the others, black eyes staring and muzzles twisted into snarls. Gyrmund took a quick glance at Clarin and Herin, and was impressed at how relaxed and unflustered they looked; he did his best to do the same.

'Where are you from?' demanded the leader, its voice incredibly loud so that it rang out around the pit. It was shoving its muzzle into Clarin's face, but the rank smell still carried over to Gyrmund.

'Got caught in Brasingia,' said Clarin casually, as if it happened to him all the time.

'Well, you're in your worst nightmare now,' said the Dog-man, pulling back his lips into what Gyrmund guessed must be a smile, but looked like a snarl. The other four pulled the same kind of face as if a great joke had been made.

Clarin nodded in agreement. 'It's a shithole alright.'

The comment displeased the Dog-man, who clearly wanted to see fear on Clarin's face.

'And I'm Vamak, the tormentor in chief,' he added, turning around to look at his four allies, 'we're in charge down here. If we don't like someone we make their existence so miserable they beg to go back down the mines.'

'I understand,' said Clarin.

Gyrmund could not help but be impressed by Clarin. He answered the Dog-man politely enough, and did nothing to provoke him, but at the same time his body language suggested that he was unaffected by the intimidation. Vamak clearly found this unsatisfactory, and felt the need to assert his authority further, but didn't seem sure how to deal with it. Then, suddenly, he raised a hand, revealing a vicious looking set of claws at the end of his fingers with which he gestured at Clarin.

'You'd better understand or you won't live long. Here, this will help your memory,' he said, and, with a quick flick, scraped one of the claws along Clarin's cheek. Blood instantly welled along the wound. Clarin started forward but Herin quickly put one arm across his chest, shoving him back against the wall. Vamak looked at Herin, then Clarin, before throwing his head into the air and laughing—a sadistic bark of a laugh. The others followed suit and Vamak took a good look around the pit, making sure that everyone in it had learned the lesson.

'I'm in charge down here,' he shouted loudly, so that the whole pit could hear him. 'The Isharites don't let me kill new ones,' he said, speaking now just to Gyrmund, Herin and Clarin. 'They like to get their full use out of you first. But in a few days' time I'll be free to do what I want with you.'

They then moved away, taking up position at the end of the pit farthest away from the toilet. This area had been left free for them by the other prisoners, and this was clearly part of the process of establishing a pecking order.

Gyrmund looked over at the other two. Clarin stared straight ahead, still struggling to stop himself going straight after Vamak. Herin turned around to face his brother and Gyrmund, putting his back to the Dog-men.

'Well, now we have our first objective to work on,' he murmured. 'How to take down that son of a bitch.'

***

'Lady Belwynn? They are ready for you now.'

Belwynn felt a fresh burst of nerves.

While the Knights of Kalinth had been celebrating their feast of Saint Stephen in the Great Hall of the High Tower, she had been waiting in the kitchens until they were ready to hear her sing. She had spoken a little to the kitchen maids at first, but they were clearly very busy catering for so many knights at once, and so she had sat there with little to do but watch them, go over the song in her head, worry about it, and wonder why she had ever suggested it in the first place.

Now that it was time to go, she had to see it through. Evander led her out of the kitchen to the Great Hall. Most halls in Dalriya had a harp to provide music in the evenings, but the harp she had been given to play by the Order was the most beautiful she had ever seen, made from alder wood, and with golden strings. When she had given it a test, it played as good as it looked. That gave her a bit of confidence.

The room went quieter as the assembled knights watched her being led to the dais. It felt like a very long walk. She got herself settled on a chair while Evander positioned the harp for her. He then departed the dais and left her alone. All eyes were now fixed on her, and the room had gone completely quiet.

Theron stood up from his position at one of the tables near the middle of the room, though not at the large, central table where the highest ranked knights were seated.

'Introducing the Lady Belwynn of Magnia,' he boomed into the silence. Belwynn thought he slightly slurred the words, and noticed that a lot of wine had been flowing during the feast. Maybe that was no bad thing.

Belwynn located Sebastian at the central table. Two seats to his left, Theron had told her, would be Galenos. She checked that the man sitting there fitted the description she had been given. Yes. Straight back, closely cropped grey hair, clean-shaven, and an aquiline nose.

'Grand Master Galenos,' began Belwynn, making eye contact with him before looking around the room, her voice ringing out clearly around the hall, 'Knights of Kalinth. I am honoured to be given the chance to perform for you tonight. I intend to perform a song which I learned when I was very young, but instantly fell in love with. It was a song about a place called Kalinth. At the time, I fancied it was a pretend, fairy tale land. When I was older, and knew better, I used to dream of visiting Kalinth to see its knights for myself. And, finally, here I am. The song I will sing is called Stephen and the Green Dragon.'

There was polite applause and mild cheering from the audience once Belwynn had finished speaking. She had hoped for something more when she introduced the song, Stephen and the Dragon being the best loved story of the knights. It was a different kind of atmosphere to any other hall she had been to. She had to hope that she could have the same effect on this audience as she usually did.

'In Chalios there dwelt the beast
That wrecked our land from west to east
No king nor duke nor count had fay
To seek the dragon out to slay

No spells nor rich man's wealth had he
But Stephen had his bravery
No men to fight for him had he
But Stephen had his chivalry'

Belwynn looked over at her audience, many mouthing the familiar words themselves. Some stared at her, already captivated by her voice. She knew the lyrics of the song had a crucial role to play in their plan. She glanced at Galenos, watching on with a frown. Did he suspect?

'So long the people of the land cried out
For saviour with no fear or doubt
'Til one young knight swore 'It shall be me
To end this monster's tyranny'

No spells nor rich man's wealth had he
But Stephen had his bravery
No men to fight for him had he
But Stephen had his chivalry'

Some of her audience were now entering the trance like state Belwynn could induce with her voice. Galenos and his entourage were looking around the hall, suspicion on their faces. But it was too late to stop her now.

When Belwynn finished the song, with the dragon slain, many of the knights jumped to their feet to applaud. Theron, Tycho and their allies were prominent at first, but others in the room followed their lead. After the applause ended some sat back down again but others stayed on their feet.

'A lesson for the Order,' shouted Tycho, gesturing with one arm at Belwynn. 'The Knights of Kalinth were founded to confront and fight evil. Ishari is our dragon. Yet here we are cowering in the High Tower, while they grow in strength and infect our kingdom with their poison.'

Tycho moved his arm along until it pointed directly at Galenos. If he felt fear, he showed none. Belwynn suspected that he wasn't the kind of man who did.

'Our Grand Master has failed us!' he declared.

An intake of breath followed this statement and then there was shouting from all over the room, some for and others against, but nobody could properly be heard, until Euthymius pushed his chair out and stood up to confront Tycho. He pointed straight back at the young knight.

'Treason!' he shouted, his voice slightly hysterical. 'Tycho attacks our Grand Master and our King! Does your oath of loyalty mean nothing to you,

Tycho? We are the Knights of Kalinth, and we are sworn to obey! But you and your allies have made a habit of defying orders!'

'No!' shouted Theron, who was already on his feet. 'We are speaking for our Order. We are sworn to protect our kingdom and our people! They must come before loyalty to any one man.'

Theron's argument seemed to take everyone assembled by surprise. Belwynn could see many of the knights frowning as they tried to grapple with the contradictory statements offered by Euthymius and Theron. Into the moment of silence Remi struck home.

'Sebastian! Lord Sebastian must speak!' he demanded.

Other knights, prepared by Theron in advance, joined in the call.

'Sebastian! Sebastian!'

All eyes turned to him, even those of Euthymius and Galenos. The Grand Master seemed uncertain, almost in shock at the unexpected attack he was facing. Sebastian looked at him for a moment. Then, slowly and deliberately, he stood up and looked out at the room. He took his time before he spoke, to make sure that everyone was listening.

'I have come to the decision that our Order can no longer ignore the threat to our kingdom. It is with regret that I say Grand Master Galenos has failed to show proper leadership in recent months. I am therefore submitting myself to replace him as Grand Master.'

The Great Hall erupted in uproar. Belwynn surveyed the scene. Theron and his allies, plus those knights who had been persuaded by her song and who agreed with what they had done, were certainly making the most noise, cheering Sebastian's name. A smaller group were hostile and shouting back, calling Sebastian a traitor. The majority of the knights, those not on either side, were looking around in bewilderment.

Overall, Belwynn believed that it had worked. It had certainly gone to plan, though she feared it had been a bit too slick. It must have been obvious to some that it was a deliberate ambush, as well organised and thoroughly planned as a military campaign. Those knights caught in the middle might blame Theron and Sebastian for dividing their Order. But Belwynn believed that most of them would support Sebastian in the end.

Evander appeared at her side to lead her away. The Great Hall was chaotic and, fearing it might even erupt into violence, Belwynn was quick to leave the dais. Turning around, she took one final look at the central table. She saw

Galenos, white as a sheet, and suddenly looking much older. She saw Sebastian, sombre and serious looking, with his head slightly bowed. While all around them both, younger men jostled and shouted and jeered. Belwynn had made her impact in Kalinth. But at that moment she did not feel proud.

IX

IN ARIOC'S CHAMBERS

MONEVA HAD NOW SPENT A DAY and two nights in the bedroom in Arioc's chambers. The only contact she had was with Babak, the man whose job seemed to be looking after the rooms. He brought her meals. He was polite enough. He showed her another tiny room off the main chamber, which was a toilet with a hole in the floor. Other than that, he left her alone.

During the day, he left the chambers to run unspecified errands for a few hours. He locked the door behind him with a key. Moneva considered trying to escape. When he returned, she considered attacking him and taking the key. That would have been easy enough. But she knew that trying to escape from the tower, and then the fortress, would be next to impossible, so she didn't try. That was why she had been given the relative freedom she had, rather than being locked in a dungeon somewhere.

Deep down she knew why she had been taken here.

Moneva felt like she understood men. She had inhabited the world of men for as long as she could remember. She had no memory of her mother, who had died when Moneva was two. Her father was a kind enough man, but not an attentive parent. When he died from a fever she was still only ten, an only child with no income. She was not completely alone, but led a transitory existence, staying with various family, friends and neighbours. She spent increasing amounts of time on the streets of Essenberg, getting involved in petty crime. That was how she came to meet Max.

Max, it turned out, was a ruthless crime lord. But to Moneva, he was kind, complimentary, and, above all, interested in her. A father figure. He was like that with all the children, always having time for them. It wasn't an act. Not completely. But he began to show special interest in Moneva. She was better than the other kids: quicker to learn, sharp witted, and more hard working. Also, she was a girl, and that gave her a special edge. He could send her to spy on people, run special errands for him, and people wouldn't suspect her.

Jamie Edmundson

After a period of transition Moneva left her old ties, and immersed herself in Max's world. She devoted herself to learning the trade, just as if she had been apprenticed to a cloth maker or a dyer. She wanted to please Max, and any small praise or acknowledgement from him was enough—was all she wanted. As she got older and stronger, she was taught to fight and to kill, just like the boys. Max insisted that she was given equal treatment, not spared anything because she was a girl. She never asked to be. Despite her age and her gender, she became a respected member of the unit. People knew that she was completely loyal to Max, and that he trusted her completely. More than anyone else. That made her powerful—even feared.

But things changed when Moneva stopped being a girl and started to become a woman. Max began to flirt with her. It was innocent enough at first, but gradually got more serious, and Moneva was very flattered by it. She was young and naive and thrilled when Max paid her any kind of attention. Eventually they became lovers. Looking back, older and wiser, Moneva realised that she had never wanted that. She had wanted a father. But she had wanted to please Max, and had felt grateful for what he had done.

Their relationship lasted a few more years. Max became increasingly controlling and possessive of her. But, in a strange way, by making Moneva his lover, he had begun the process of losing her. Their relationship became more equal. Whereas before Moneva had idolised Max, she now started to challenge what he did or said, to stick up for herself. He wanted her to remain unquestioningly loyal and compliant. In the end, she walked out on him and on his business. But she couldn't entirely regret that part of her life. She had been given the skills to make a living, and to look after herself in a dangerous world.

Alone in Arioc's bedchamber, Moneva found herself returning again and again to that period of her life. A part of her knew that she was preparing herself for what was to come.

Despite that, when Arioc did arrive she still went into shock. One moment he was not there, the next he was. He was shouting at Babak in the rough language of the Isharites, apparently issuing one angry demand or order after the other. Moneva sat in the bedchamber, looking at the door which stood between her and the King of Haskany, trying to keep calm. Eventually the shouting stopped and was replaced with more subdued murmurs, though she could not make out what was being said.

94

The door swung open and Arioc was standing there, looking at her. To Moneva, he had the sort of expression someone has when they have put aside a treat for later, forgotten about it, and then rediscovered it. He had a very expressive face, and made no attempt to hide his thoughts, but then, Moneva acknowledged to herself, why would he?

Arioc held out one hand in a formal way, almost like he was asking her to dance. Steeling herself, Moneva stood up and took his hand.

'Your name?' he asked.

'Moneva.'

'I am Arioc.'

'I know.'

He smiled briefly at that, and led her into the main room and directed her to sit at the table.

'I am very hungry, Moneva. You will join me for supper,' he said, sitting opposite her.

It wasn't phrased as a request, but then Moneva got the feeling that this was a man who didn't need to make requests very often. He seemed to be being polite, though, which was something. A small thing ordinarily, but in this situation Moneva took some reassurance from it.

Arioc was an impressive figure, emanating authority more than anyone she had ever met—and Moneva had met a number of Dalriya's rulers in the last few weeks. His presence filled the room, and Moneva felt like his chambers had reduced in size now that he was here. He had the build and physique of a warrior, and, much like Clarin, didn't seem to be at ease sitting down, as if his body struggled with the inactivity. But in addition, he had the intellect and aura of a sorcerer: like Soren, but more powerful. His dark eyes seemed to possess the power to see everything. Moneva felt like his gaze was a weapon whose full power she had been spared from for now, but that could be turned on her at any time.

As Babak prepared food for them in the background, Arioc made idle conversation. He asked her where she was born, and into what kind of family. Moneva answered with the truth. Even before Arioc had arrived she had concluded that this was the best strategy; but now, she was even surer that she should be totally honest. Arioc had the ability to find out what he wanted from her, one way or another. If she gave him what he wanted freely, she might live. If she lived, there was a chance that Gyrmund and the others might live too.

Babak served the food and then left the chambers. It was a bird of some kind, heavily spiced, with a range of vegetables. Arioc poured a bottle of Cordentine red into two glasses. Despite her predicament, it was the tastiest meal Moneva had eaten in a long time. Arioc didn't seem to want to talk much while he ate. The silence might have been unbearable, but Moneva had barely been fed during the last few days, and this made it easier for her to focus on the food.

When they had finished Arioc walked over to his desk and poured out two more glasses of a rich looking, amber coloured liquid. He handed one over to Moneva.

'Would you like to move into my bedroom, now?' he asked.

Arioc's dark eyes focused on her own, studying her reaction. Moneva didn't trust herself to speak, but nodded her assent.

In the bedroom Arioc gestured for Moneva to sit on the bed before joining her. He took a drink and indicated that she should do the same. Moneva took a sip and rolled her eyes at the strength of it. She swallowed it down and felt it move down her chest into her stomach. Her tongue felt pickled from it. Arioc watched her with some amusement.

'You've never had arak before?' he asked needlessly.

She shook her head.

Arioc's face turned more serious. 'You are not stupid, Moneva, so you must know why you are here. It was a great surprise to find you and your friends in Edeleny. I found you in the Temple. I went there looking for something. A staff. It wasn't there. I need you to tell me everything you know. Don't miss anything out.'

There were no threats and, again, Moneva was grateful for that. But that didn't mean that Moneva was unaware of the consequences if Arioc decided she was lying or holding something back. So she told him everything. She began with the attack on the Temple of Toric in South Magnia, and explained what happened from there. She left out no names or major events along the way. Occasionally Arioc would stop and question her when he wanted more information. When she described the fight between Pentas and Nexodore on the Great Road he got rather childish, and wanted her to recount every tiniest aspect of it. He actually giggled at the ending. When she was trying to explain their run in with Duke Emeric in Coldeberg he grunted and made a face.

'What did you think of him?' he asked.

'I never actually met him, Your Majesty.'

'Oh,' he replied, disappointed. 'Call me Arioc, for fuck's sake.'

When she recounted her rescue of her friends from Coldeberg prison, he didn't hide his respect. His expression and manner towards her changed, as if he suddenly realised he was talking to a different person than he had previously thought.

He whistled when she told him about the death of Nexodore in the lands of the Blood Caladri, but let her carry on with her retelling. He listened intently when she described what went on in Edeleny.

'Well,' he began when she had finished, 'that was more than I could have possibly expected. But at the Temple,' he said, following up on the issue that he most wanted to be solved, 'your friends disappeared. With the Staff. Teleported away somewhere. Where, and by whom?'

Moneva thought about it. She was worried now, that he would insist she answer a question she couldn't.

'Soren was the only sorcerer. He was with us—'

'It wasn't him,' interrupted Arioc. 'The woman, Elana. She is also a magic user.'

'Well,' said Moneva, considering the possibility. 'I suppose she is, but not in the same way as Soren. Maybe she could have done it.'

'But highly unlikely,' conceded Arioc.

He looked at Moneva, measuring her with those dark eyes for a while. He then nodded, as if accepting that she was telling the truth as she knew it.

'Then the most likely agent of their escape was Pentas. With Nexodore's death he escaped and made his own way to Edeleny. But why would he do that?'

Arioc was speaking to himself now, lost in his own musings. 'I have no proof of his involvement,' he continued, then looked at Moneva. 'Nor any idea where your friends are. But at least I know exactly who I'm looking for now,' he added.

The last comment made Moneva feel even worse than she already did. She wondered what the others would think of her, revealing their secrets at the earliest opportunity? What kind of torments were Gyrmund, Soren and the others already suffering now, while she sat on this comfy bed, well fed with a drink in her hand?

She looked up at Arioc to see that he was staring at her now, a new, hungry look on his face. This was the moment, she knew. She had to finish through with her strategy. Give Arioc everything he wanted. He was interested in her more now, she knew. Interested in her as a person, to some extent. She also knew that he had taken a liking to the Haskan woman, Shira, who, like Moneva, had been taught how to fight. He had even made Shira his queen. Moneva had to make sure that he was interested enough in her to want to keep her alive.

Arioc took Moneva's drink from her. He reached down to the floor, putting both glasses down with a clink.

'I've never met anyone quite like you before, Moneva,' he said, moving towards her.

Wanting desperately to recoil away, Moneva instead made up the distance between them. At any moment Arioc could decide he didn't want her, and might make her a prize for his soldiers to enjoy. She had to be strong. Wanting to hit out and run away, she instead let Arioc put his hands on her body. As he leaned over to kiss her, she wanted to scream out for help, but instead she let him touch his lips to hers. Wanting to cry and to sob and to beg him to stop, Moneva parted her lips and let his tongue into her mouth, let it find her own, as the smell of the arak on his breath filled her nostrils.

X

ATOP BURKHARD CASTLE

SITTING BY ASHERE'S BED in his small convalescing room in the Emperor's Hall, it was almost possible for Farred to forget that there was an army thousands strong on its way to kill them all. For some reason, the myriad sounds of a castle garrison barely penetrated this room: rowdy soldier banter became faint whispers, while the clang and scrape of armour and weaponry might have been a bird walking on the roof.

Instead, the sound that dominated the room was Ashere's breathing. It was unnaturally loud—the sound you make when you are struggling to suck in air after heavy exercise. Except that Ashere had been laid up in bed since Farred brought him back to the castle two days ago. His face, once a healthy golden brown, now seemed drained of colour. His black hair hung lank at his sides, and sweat gathered on his brow.

But it was the smell that dominated Farred's senses. Someone had tried their best to mask it by littering the room with rushes, fennel, and other herbs. But the cloying smell of fever, and of the prince's rotting flesh, would not be denied. Farred had spent as much time in the room as anyone, but it was not a smell that you could get used to. Staying in the room was an ordeal, and everyone, Farred included, would soon find a reason to leave.

It was the wizard, Gustav, who had identified that there was poison in Ashere's wound. It was, apparently, common practice amongst the Isharites to lace their crystal swords with a poison. Gustav had also declared that there was no cure that he was aware of. The wizard had done his best to treat the Prince. His apprentice, a slight young woman called Inge, had taken on most of the care. She had cleaned the wound and applied a salve of fennel, mugwort, and various other herbs. But both had made it clear that their magic could not help.

There were mutterings from several quarters, North Magnians and Brasingians, about the role played by the two wizards. But when one of Archbishop Godfrey's priests had barged in to the room insisting that Ashere should be bled, Brock had threatened to gut the man on the spot, and there had been no further attempts to wrest control of the patient away.

'I thought I would hate you, you know?' said Ashere, his voice breathy and weak. It was perfectly audible in this room, but would have got lost in the noise of the castle outside it.

'What do you mean?'

'Before I met you. South Magnians were the enemy as far as I was concerned. How stupid. How stupid that seems now after the horrors that we've seen.'

'Yes, pretty stupid,' answered Farred, pleased to see that this got a smile out of the Prince, 'but understandable.'

'Well, if we've done anything, Farred, you and I, we've proven what a load of horse shit that is. We've proven that North and South can work together. *Should* work together.'

'Agreed.'

There was a brief knock at the door before Walter entered.

'Your Highness,' he said, nodding at Ashere.

'Walter. How are the preparations going?'

'I now have to hope they've gone well enough,' Walter responded.

Farred and Ashere looked at one another and then back to the Marshal.

'You both asked me to let you know when it happened. Well, the army's now in sight, heading this way.'

There was a silence for a moment, simply because there was nothing to say. Farred made eye contact with Ashere.

'Go on, you two,' said the Prince. 'Let me know what happens.'

'You're not coming to skewer a few more Drobax, Your Highness?' enquired Walter with mock solemnity.

Ashere smiled at that. 'I can't be bothered. Maybe tomorrow.'

Farred turned and left the room, hiding a lump in the throat he didn't want Ashere to see. He took a few breaths of fresh air to steady himself. Walter joined him.

'That's a brave man,' commented the Marshal.

Farred nodded. He thought of two or three replies but none of them seemed right. Walter sensed his mood and gestured forwards.

'Come on, there's a viewpoint along here where some of us will watch what happens. We'll witness some more bravery.'

Walter led Farred along the flying bridge that connected the Emperor's Keep on one crag with the Duke's Keep on the other. While Walter must have crossed this bridge countless times by now, and didn't give doing so a second thought, Farred still found it daunting, trying to resist looking at the huge drop to the ground below. Once he was safely across, Farred realised that he could hear the thud of the Drobax army marching towards them.

They arrived at the viewing point, which overlooked the winding path leading up the first crag to the Duke's Keep. A few other spectators had already assembled here. Adalheid, the Duchess of Rotelegen, with a small group from her duchy, peered down with a grim expression. The soldiers who had been asked to defend the path were all in place. Adalheid's son, Jeremias, was down at the bottom of the crag with the Rotelegen soldiers, awaiting the onslaught. Farred wondered at the decision to send him down there. If he was killed, the last son of Ellard would be dead, and the morale amongst the men of Rotelegen would plummet. But at the same time, he understood why she did it. Her son had escaped the duchy and left it in the hands of the enemy. If he was to keep the support of his people, and ever return, he had to prove himself worthy.

In addition to the Rotelegen group, several other high-ranking figures were gathered there, including Godfrey, the Archbishop of Gotbeck, with some of his priests.

'No Baldwin?' Farred asked Walter.

The Marshal shook his head. 'Gustav advised him against it. The Isharites might target him. The Kellish are all on the other side,' he said, gesturing back towards the Emperor's Keep. 'Who knows, they might attack both crags simultaneously.'

It made sense for Baldwin to stay protected. Farred recalled the trap the Isharite wizards had laid for the Magnian forces two days ago, the bank of fog which had hidden their whereabouts. It wouldn't be a surprise if they had similar plans for taking Burkhard Castle.

Walter walked over to talk with Godfrey, leaving Farred to have a good look down at the forces lined up to receive the initial strike from the Drobax. He could make out the slight figure of Jeremias, still a boy really, surrounded by men, presumably the best warriors the Rotelegen had left, whose job would be to protect him at all costs. The Red Rooster standard of his duchy flew at his side, almost an invitation to the horde heading his way.

Farred looked out into the distance, his eyes straining to detect movement. He could hear the army of Drobax coming, knew well enough what to look for. His brain began to fill the hole, telling him that he could see something when he couldn't. At some point in time, when exactly he couldn't be sure, the vision his mind created became reality. He could see them. Farred looked at those around him but no-one else seemed to have noticed. He looked back. Yes, they were definitely in sight.

'There they are!' he shouted, pointing into the distance.

The words seemed to burst from his mouth without being told to, and he had shouted so loud he startled himself. The soldiers on the ramparts looked up at him and then out to where he indicated. Suddenly the whole crag was alive with conversation as the soldiers began to spot the approaching army, or complained that they couldn't. Weapons and shields were readied, buckles tightened, final prayers or swear words muttered under the breath. The nervous energy seemed to make the crag come alive, the air almost crackling around them.

The movement that Farred had detected on the horizon turned into a full army. The noise of thousands upon thousands of feet, clanking weapons and armour, grunts and shouts, wheeled carts and mules to pull them, all mingled with the steady thud of drums banging out a beat to announce the presence of a fearsome horde; maybe the largest army Dalriya had ever seen. The tactic of hiding their presence, which had worked so effectively against the Magnians two days ago, had now changed. Now the Isharites were intimidating the defenders with the sheer size of their army.

Before long Farred could distinguish individual shapes marching towards them. He was not surprised that he saw no Haskans or Isharites. Instead row upon row of Drobax headed their way, stretching as far along the horizon and as far back as one could see. Still they came, a plague of Drobax, as if there were enough of them to fill the whole of Dalriya. They intended to overcome the defenders by force of numbers.

The first lines of Drobax stormed into the remains of the settlement which Walter had finally cleared out yesterday. He had done a good job but, mused Farred, some people just won't be helped. Sure enough, a young woman, flushed out by the Drobax, emerged from the jumble of wooden walls and rafters and came running towards the castle. Farred presumed that she was a prostitute, desperate enough and stupid enough to ignore the warnings, and instead staying close by the castle to ply her trade.

The reaction of some of the soldiers seemed to confirm it. Some men cheered her on as if she had entered a bizarre sporting event. Others laughed hysterically, pointing at the sight and gripping their sides.

Farred didn't share in the humour of the spectacle. But he understood it. The soldiers of the Empire were tense, fearful, and, having seen the enemy army for the first time, doubtless in shock. The sight of the fleeing prostitute allowed some of them to break the tension. However, before long she was run down and speared by the Drobax, who continued their advance on Burkhard Castle.

When the first of the Drobax got within distance of the imperial lines they faltered, waiting for greater numbers to advance. But the Drobax didn't operate in formations or any similar kind of tactics. Once there were enough of them they moved forwards again, relying on their greater weight of numbers. They approached in a disorganised mess of shouts and roars, intending to force their way up the castle. But the narrowness of the path meant that they were funnelled into lines of only half a dozen wide, unable to make their superior numbers count by getting around and behind their enemy.

Farred watched the initial clash from his vantage point atop the crag. The Rotelegen soldiers moved down to meet the Drobax with their spears levelled and a horrendous crunch echoed upwards. There was little to see for a while as the two armies pushed against each other, the great force of the Drobax horde pushing against the Brasingians who had the height advantage. Spears wouldn't be much use down there now: smaller weapons, which could be used in the crush of bodies to stab and rip at the enemy, would be more effective.

The standard of Jeremias, the young Duke of Rotelegen, held firm. After a while his men started to get the upper hand. Their superior armour and weapons, along with the height advantage, began to tell. The bodies of Drobax started to pile up at the bottom of the crag and get in the way of the next line trying to move forward. In the end, they pulled back about fifty metres. The men on the castle cheered, but the Drobax leered back, inviting them to come and fight out in the open.

A flurry of activity at the bottom of the castle ensued, as soldiers from the front lines either made their own way or were helped up the path: presumably those injured in the fighting. Farred quickly noticed the standard of Jeremias was among them. He couldn't help looking over at Adalheid, but she observed stony faced. It would be a disaster for them if the young duke had been killed in the first of the fighting.

Minutes passed and the two armies remained separated by a few feet of ground in front of the castle. As they got closer, Farred could see that amongst the group of men climbing the path was Jeremias, alive but nonetheless being speedily manhandled up by his bodyguards. The small group arrived at the top. Jeremias yanked off his helmet, his face red with exertion, his hair dripping wet with sweat, but he didn't look injured.

'Mother, how dare you order that I be dragged up here? I should be down there with my men,' he demanded, genuinely fuming.

'You've done your job, Jeremias,' Adalheid replied matter-of-factly. 'There's nothing to be gained by risking your life more than is necessary. Are you hurt?' she asked, the mother's concern for her child slipping out at the end despite herself.

Jeremias pulled a face. 'Of course not—' he began, but was interrupted by Walter.

'Well done, Your Grace,' he effused. 'You and your men fought well and hard. It was vital we stopped their momentum at the beginning.'

Everyone else joined in with their own congratulations, which succeeded in mollifying the young duke enough for him to drop his complaints. Of course, the truth was that the Drobax had hardly been defeated, and they were already readying for another assault. Many Rotelegen still occupied the bottom of the castle path, apparently unwilling to give up their position at the front, but they were also being supplemented by the men of Gotbeck, proudly watched over by their Archbishop a few feet from Farred's position. The Drobax charged on in a second assault, a cacophony of drumming, shouts, and the clanging of metal rising to the top of the crag.

As he watched on, Farred had to admit that he had underestimated the Brasingians. He had been all too aware of the terrifying effect the Drobax could have, but had not fully considered the point of view of his allies. They had been waiting for weeks to engage the enemy, their frustration and anger building as the Drobax destroyed their homes, and Baldwin's orders had been to retreat and concede ground. They had witnessed Farred and the other Magnians ride off to take on the enemy, while they could only watch them go. And they had endured weeks of gruesome stories about the ferocious creatures who had invaded the Empire, so that when they finally appeared, the Drobax may even have been an anti-climax.

Because as Farred watched the carnage, he began to recognise that it was the Brasingians who were the more ferocious. They were desperate to spill blood, snarling with rage and fear, releasing the pent-up adrenaline of all the waiting around they had endured. They didn't seem to tire or want to stop. They fought with the desperation of the cornered animal, of the outnumbered.

The Drobax had been force marched all the way to the castle: they tired more quickly, and had less to fight for. They attacked a third time, in just the same way as they had done, and with just as little success. Farred reckoned that each attack lasted for half an hour to an hour. After the third attack, the Drobax, presumably receiving an order, perhaps via the booming drums, made a full retreat. They marched away from the castle, and kept on marching, until they were completely out of sight. It might even have been possible for the defenders of Burkhard Castle to wonder if they had imagined the attack, were it not for the pile of bodies that lay at the bottom of the crag.

Every morning, after breakfast, Emperor Baldwin met with his war council. He was joined by the leaders of the armies stationed at Burkhard Castle. Duke Arne of Luderia, father of the Empress Hannelore, sat on his right. On his left was Godfrey, the vigorous Archbishop of Gotbeck. The young Duke Jeremias of Rotelegen attended with his mother, Adalheid. Due to the sickness of Prince Cerdda, Farred attended, representing the Magnians and Middians. Walter the Marshal, Baldwin's brother, always began the meeting with an account of the defences, supplies, and any other information on the current situation. Finally, Gustav the Hawk, Archmage of the Empire, was usually there. This morning he wasn't. It was never clear to Farred what his role was, though he would occasionally provide information about the enemy forces. No one ever asked how he obtained this information.

After Walter gave his briefing, talk naturally turned to the attack on the castle the night before.

'I must start,' announced Baldwin, 'with my congratulations on the way Duke Jeremias fought and led his troops yesterday. Your father would have been proud.'

The other dukes banged their fists on the table in appreciation, and so Farred joined in. Jeremias nodded sombrely. Whatever emotion he felt, if any, he kept to himself.

'Thank you, Your Majesty,' Jeremias acknowledged. 'The people of my duchy will be ready to fight whenever you ask.'

'Nobly said,' commented Duke Arne.

'Bearing the attack in mind,' continued Baldwin, 'now is a good time to review the disposition of our forces. I don't want people to gain the impression that myself and the Kellish have been put in a safer location than the other imperial forces.'

'Oh,' said Arne, puffing out his cheeks, 'I don't think anyone has that impression at all.'

'We are perfectly content where we are,' added Godfrey.

'I think,' began Walter, 'that the soldiers will not like to be moved about unnecessarily. We don't yet know whether the enemy will always target the Duke's Crag. If the situation arises where one group has done much more of the fighting, then we can think about moving things about.'

Everyone seemed happy with this judgement. The meeting lasted a little longer. It was agreed that Arne's Luderians would defend the bottom of the crag for the next attack. But in truth, they were ready, and there was very little to do. They just had to wait for the next attack to come.

The meeting broke up and Farred made his way to the Emperor's Crag where the Magnian forces had been barracked. He dropped in on Brock and the Middians to pass on the details of the meeting. Farred had now taken over the leadership of the Southern troops and felt responsible for these men, cooped up in some castle miles from their homelands. He spent as much time with them as possible, chatting or playing dice, finding out about their families and lives back home. He was especially careful to spend time with the North Magnians who had effectively lost their prince. Farred took his lunch with them, and in the afternoon, he and Brock went up to the walls of the keep, from where there was an excellent view of the lands surrounding the castle, including the Great Road. He knew that he was avoiding Ashere, but tried to put the thought out of his mind.

'I wonder what they're doing,' Farred said as they gazed out into the distance. 'I've heard some people suggest that the whole army is marching south to Essenberg.'

Brock considered this, screwing up his face in thought.

'If you were them,' said the Middian eventually, in his deep voice, 'would you do that?'

'No—I wouldn't. If I had an army that large, I wouldn't run away from a fight.'

Brock grunted, nodding. 'I agree. They'll be back soon enough.'

There was a pause as the two of them looked out over the landscape.

'When it's time,' Brock said, 'will you ride out with me.'

'What?'

'I can't die on this rock like a cornered animal. When it's time I'm going to ride out against them. Walter says I can have a horse. He'll give you one.'

It was a heroic image, and Farred couldn't help but like the idea of it.

'Very well, Brock. I'll ride out with you.'

They stood in silence for a while, and they were amongst the first to see the return of the Drobax army. From every direction they appeared, a mass of tiny figures closing in on the castle. From mid-afternoon until the evening they came, surrounding the castle, but stopping short of missile range.

The numbers were incredible to see. Men kept shaking their heads in disbelief until it became a general source of humour. They chuckled at the sight and made dark jests about the victory they would enjoy tomorrow. Everyone now realised what Farred and Brock had known for days. This wasn't an army that could be defeated in battle. It wasn't an army at all in the sense that people had understood the word up to now. It was a migration.

The Drobax made their camps. As the sun went down, the light from their fires shone out around the castle. It was a terrifying sight yet somehow beautiful, as if all the night sprites had gathered together for a midnight party. The soldiers in the castle began to get their suppers. The mood seemed to drop. There was no escape now—Ishari had demonstrated that they were all doomed. Few of them would get a good sleep tonight.

Farred rose and said good night to Brock. He took in a deep breath. It was time to see Ashere.

When he entered Ashere's room the smell was worse, and he couldn't help covering his nose. The Prince was lying on his back, and his eyes had been closed, but he opened them when he heard Farred enter.

'Hello,' Farred said quietly, 'How are you?'

What a stupid question, he thought to himself. He looked worse than ever; didn't look like himself any more. His body seemed to have shrunk, except for his bones, which threatened to burst out of his skin.

Ashere made a facial gesture which may have been intended as a smile, but was just a grimace.

'How do I look?' he croaked, as if there was no water left in his mouth.

Farred moved over to the bed, propped him up and put a drink of water to his lips. Ashere gulped some down but it looked like it pained him to swallow. Farred let him back down.

'Have you heard that the army is back again today?'

'Yes, Inge has been in. She told me.'

There was a pause.

'Farred. I'm dying. I'm in agony,' Ashere's voice cracked with emotion when he said these words, as if he was going to break down, but he pulled himself together. He took a deep breath. 'Please end it for me.'

'No!' said Farred in horror. But was he really surprised? Was this why he had avoided visiting Ashere all day?·

'I'm sorry, my friend. I thought I would be much stronger than this. But I can't take it anymore—'

Again, his emotions got the better of him. A tear rolled down his cheek. Farred's heart felt like it would break.

'I don't think I can do it,' Farred said, now struggling to get his own words out.

'It has to be you, Farred. I can't ask anybody else. Please.'

Farred nodded. He knew it had to be him.

'Is there any...message for anyone?'

'If you get out of here alive, tell my brother and sister I love them. I—I hope you do get out of here, Farred.'

There was nothing else to say now. More words would only make the job harder.

Farred gently lifted Ashere's head, pulled out his pillow, and lowered his head back onto the bed. He placed the pillow firmly over Ashere's face and pressed down.

To the Prince's credit it was only at the very end that his arms shot upwards. His hands found Farred's arms but they had no strength in them. Then the struggling stopped. Farred waited a while longer and then stopped. He carefully replaced the pillow.

He bent down and kissed him on the lips.

'Farewell, Prince Ashere,' he murmured. 'Be at peace.'

XI

PRISONS

I T FELT GOOD TO GET AWAY from the High Tower and its claustrophobic atmosphere.

Looking at her riding companions, Belwynn got the impression that they felt the same way. Theron, more than anyone else, had taken responsibility for confronting Galenos: organising his supporters, persuading others that the cause was just. Tomorrow he would achieve his goal, and his uncle, Sebastian, would be sworn in as the new Grand Master of the Order of the Knights of Kalinth.

Sebastian was spending the day fasting and praying in preparation for the ceremony. Theron would have no special role to play, and so could afford an excursion today. His squire, Evander, accompanied them as always.

Rabigar also seemed a changed person today. He had gained a new sense of purpose for the first time since the sickening attack in Coldeberg prison which had left him blind in one eye. Now that he had resolved to return to his homeland, he seemed to be more alive, more in charge of his own destiny.

The four of them rode along at a steady pace, being as kind as they could to their horses on a hot summer's day. The grassland they rode through was scorched dry, with few trees to offer shade. No one felt the need to talk much, but they travelled in an easy, companionable silence.

It was still before midday when they reached the crossroads. Rabigar's journey would take him south, to the mountainous lands of the Krykkers, where humans were forbidden. They all dismounted. Rabigar and Theron gave each other a rough embrace.

'Look after her,' Rabigar growled.

'I will,' said Theron obediently.

Rabigar gave Evander a big slap on the back before turning to Belwynn. She suddenly burst into tears, surprising herself as much as anyone else.

'Don't worry, I'll be fine,' said Rabigar.

Belwynn understood that Rabigar was an exile, and that it was therefore dangerous to return home. But that wasn't why she was crying.

'I'll miss you,' she explained, sobbing, and feeling like a silly little girl.

Rabigar nodded. 'I'll miss you too. But if everything works out the way I want it to, I will see you again soon.'

He climbed back onto his mount, a gift from Sebastian, and continued his journey alone. They waited until Rabigar was out of sight before heading east.

'I'm looking forward to showing you the fortress,' said Theron, smiling like a goofy boy. He had remembered their conversation about the High Tower, and had decided that he had to show Belwynn the fortress at Chalios before they left for the north, and missed the chance. Belwynn had been happy to go along and, though she kept it to herself, pleased that the knight was taking such an interest in her.

It was another hour's ride until they drew within sight. The path Theron led them on grew steeper and rockier; not quite the mountainous terrain that Rabigar was heading for, but part of the same chain. The surrounding area was largely heathland, and while the path towards Chalios was well maintained, the view it afforded was of a sparsely settled landscape, relatively untouched by human habitation.

Chalios was certainly impressive. Not in the same way as the castles of the Empire Belwynn had recently visited, with their carefully designed geometric shapes, and thick walls imposing themselves onto their surroundings. Neither was it like the Knights' High Tower, designed with beauty in mind. This fortress was a huge rock cliff jutting out of the ground with steep sides. As they rode closer, Belwynn could see that it had been cleverly augmented by human engineers. The path up to the entrance was flanked by huge rock walls and towers, allowing defenders to resist an approaching army from almost every angle. The top of the cliff had battlements and some other indefinable structures, too far up for Belwynn to properly make out. But in essence, it was a natural defensive structure rather than man made. It would be a strong place of defence even without any of the modifications. Belwynn felt that it had a sense of ancient history to it, as if peoples had been using it for the same purpose centuries past, before the Knights of Kalinth existed; and would continue to use it long after they disappeared. The thought was a little melancholy but, at the same time, somehow reassuring.

They left Evander with the horses on the path; Theron explained that there was stabling for horses inside, but that it wasn't worth risking injuries to them by leading them in today. As they approached the open gates, Belwynn turned around to wave at Evander. He waved back.

'He looks so tiny sitting there, surrounded by those huge towers,' she said.

'Mmm,' said Theron, attempting to sound interested in the size of his squire. 'The gates are solid but they have to be quite wide to bring horses in and out. That makes them the weakest point of the fortress. That's why we've constructed such a heavily fortified approach to them. Any army would suffer huge losses before they got here.'

'Are his parents alive?' Belwynn asked.

'What?'

'Evander's parents.'

'Yes. They have estates in the north-east. I know his father very well,' answered Theron. He made a face.

'What is it?'

'You're not that interested, are you?'

'Sorry, Theron, I am. Please tell me more.'

'This is the very place where Stephen fought the Green Dragon, you know?'

Belwynn wasn't sure whether Theron really believed the story, but thought it best not to ask.

'Yes, I know. It's in the song.'

He smiled. 'Come on. I'll take you to the top.'

The inside of the fortress couldn't have been a greater contrast with the High Tower. The whole place was deserted. There were no separate rooms, just one huge open space. It was the middle of a bright summer's day but it was still dark and gloomy inside. Much of the inside space had been carved out by hand, and the walls were rough and unfinished. Its purpose as a last place of refuge could hardly have been lost on even the most casual visitor. To Belwynn it felt like a place to die. She mused to herself that, if ghosts truly came out of their graves on certain nights to revisit the lands where they once lived, this must surely be a popular haunt.

Theron led her up a twisting stone stairway to the top of the cliff, and they emerged back into the sunshine. The cliff top was also well fortified. Battlements faced out towards the path while to the rear of the cliff, more stonework protected the area from enemies who had discovered alternative routes to the top.

Belwynn peered over the edge.

'Evander!' she bellowed out.

The squire, now an even tinier figure than before, dutifully waved up towards them.

'Well? What do you think?' asked Theron.

'It's very impressive. I was wondering when was the last time it was used?'

Theron puffed out his cheeks. 'Not for generations. Not since the great wars with the Kharovians.'

Belwynn nodded. 'Because it is a strange place for the Knights of Kalinth to hold.'

'Yes, I understand what you mean. Our strength is as a cavalry force, which is useless here. But this place isn't meant to be just for the Knights. It's for all the people of Kalinth. We maintain it on their behalf.'

'I see.'

'Belwynn,' began Theron, and she immediately caught the change in tone. Butterflies flew about her stomach even before he continued speaking.

'I enjoy spending time with you. I—' he began, but seemed at a loss for words, and walked towards her. Belwynn let him take her hand. He looked into her eyes and shook his head. 'Why can't I get my words out?'

Belwynn felt a sudden, mad urge to kiss him. It felt like, atop this cliff, they were free to do whatever they liked, with no consequences. She took a breath and controlled herself. They weren't free. And she wasn't a wilful child.

'I understand what you are trying to say, Theron,' Belwynn said. 'But you are a Knight of Kalinth and have taken your oaths. You are about to lead a Knights' army against your king. I need to find my brother. If we both get to the other side of all of that— then we can speak about this.'

Theron nodded. He clasped her hand in both of his as if he didn't want to let it go. 'Very well, Belwynn. But I promise you. After I restore my country, I will find and rescue your brother.'

Don't make promises you can't keep, she thought, but didn't say it. Instead she moved forwards and they embraced, not letting go of each other until it was time to leave.

***

He swam from unconsciousness towards consciousness, sliding through the membranes in his path, but being careful not to go too far. A queasy feeling in his stomach made him stop. He peered ahead tentatively, fighting down the natural urge to re-join his body. Pain and fear. That was why he was hesitating. That was his waking life now. Fighting down panic, he tried to force his cloudy thoughts to think clearly, without waking him up.

Who am I?

It sounded like a stupid question but he had to start somewhere.

Soren.

Yes, that was it. Soren the wizard. Not a very clever wizard, though, because he had let himself be captured. He had been captured in Edeleny, by the Isharites. He had been part of a group. Some of them had been captured, but...

Something made Soren wake up. He couldn't see or hear anything. Since being separated from Herin, Clarin, and the others, they had somehow removed his senses. He didn't know what kind of room he was in, or whether there were other people in it. He didn't know if he was lying down, sitting, or standing. He didn't know how long he had been there.

He knew about the pain. The excruciating, agonising pain that He had inflicted on him. It wasn't happening right now, but his nerve endings were so raw it felt like it was. The pain overload would have caused most people to have gone mad or die by now. He hadn't, because his magic powers helped to keep him alive; and, because He still wanted something from him.

Who 'He' was Soren couldn't be sure. He was a powerful wizard and so could have been Arioc, or even Erkindrix himself. Or some other. He had done this many times before. Using the pain, He had gained entry into Soren's mind, finding out all about his life; his magical gifts and knowledge had been forced out of him; all the details of his journey from Magnia to the Grand Caladri. Soren had fought him all the way, protecting and separating information, with the aim of keeping any small secret; but the pain was unbearable, and his torturer already knew all the tricks, shoving a clawed hand around in Soren's brain, scratching and picking out the pieces until his job was done.

And yet his job wasn't done. Because Soren was still alive. There was one thing his torturer didn't know, hadn't fully found out, that he was still looking for. Soren's link with his sister, Belwynn.

Soren had closed this off early on, knowing that if the link was found it could be used to locate and kill Belwynn. His interrogator knew there was something Soren wasn't telling him; that there was something unusual about him. But He didn't know what it was: as far as Soren knew the link was unique, so his interrogator didn't know exactly what he was looking for. The pain had forced Soren to give everything else up—he would have given his life for it to stop a long time ago. But because this involved the life of his sister, he had found the strength to resist. It had surprised and shocked his torturer at first. Soren had got some small sense of satisfaction from that. But he soon realised that it had also sparked an interest, and that He wouldn't let go until he knew everything.

'Soren.'

It was Him. The voice of his tormentor. Smooth and confident, it was the voice of a God, and Soren was an insect squirming on the sole of His shoe. Had He just arrived or had He been there all along? Was He speaking inside Soren's head or was He there in the room?

'Soren, I'm glad you've returned. Because you know we have unfinished business, don't you?'

'Please,' whimpered Soren. His pathetic and purposeless begging made Soren disgust himself, but he pleaded and begged anyway, every single time.

'I've been thinking, since last time. This thing you are hiding from me, and can't tell me about. I've been thinking that maybe you don't know what it is yourself. That maybe someone else has hidden it. That would explain why you haven't been able to tell me so far. Do you think I'm on to something, Soren?'

'Yes,' said Soren. 'Yes, that must be right.'

'Right. Well, let's focus on that this time then. Are you ready?'

'But...but doesn't that mean you don't have to hurt me?'

'Oh, no. The pain still has to be there.'

'Please. If I don't know where it is, maybe there's no need for the pain—'

But the pain came, it coursed through Soren's body, his nerve receptors flaring up until there was nothing but pain, unbearable pain that somehow didn't stop. Soren screamed and screamed. I'm screaming, he thought to himself. I'm screaming, but am I screaming out loud, or just in my head?

***

Cyprian would always be much faster than him, Gyrmund admitted to himself.

Another day in the mines, and Gyrmund's back was aching, his knees were creaking, and his head felt dizzy. His work partner, on the other hand, seemed to be built for this kind of work. Cyprian was small and wiry, able to bend down and stretch back up all day long without getting noticeably tired. It might have been demoralising if they had not started to get along with each other. Occasionally, the Persaleian would shake his head in bemusement at Gyrmund's efforts, and chuck some of the crystals he had excavated himself into Gyrmund's box.

Cyprian was from the busy port of Lumberco in Persala, and the two of them had first hit it off when Gyrmund recounted a visit he had once made to the city, being careful to emphasise his admiration for the place. Cyprian had now taken over the conversation, and was running through all of the jobs he had worked in Lumberco since childhood.

'You can get dock work all the time, once you know who's who and you've got a reputation for doing a full day's graft. You just turn up with your hook early in the morning, and you can work through 'til evening. Tough work that, mind. By the end of the day you're starving and gasping for a drink. I'd end up spending half my wages in the pub on an evening.'

At that moment, the thought of spending all day working outside, and all evening in the pub, sounded like heaven to Gyrmund.

'And did you get any work on ship, Cyprian?' he asked.

'Yes, I did that several times. Local routes, usually up the rivers, to sell on the goods that had arrived in port.'

'And the longer routes—they're all controlled by the Sea Caladri?'

'Yes, that's right,' said Cyprian, hacking away at one side of a clump of crystal he was excavating.

It was said as if it was something he wasn't happy about, but wasn't going to complain about either, so Gyrmund didn't probe any further. He knew that the Caladri control of sea trade was a sore point in many kingdoms, and that one of the reasons the Persaleians had originally constructed the Great Road was to open up an alternative, inland route, which they could control.

Anyway, Gyrmund thought, *I've done enough skirting around the issue.* 'We need to get out of here,' he said in a quiet, low voice.

Cyprian looked over. 'That we do,' said the Persaleian, before resuming his work. Just as Gyrmund thought that might be it, he looked over again, with a slight twinkle in his eyes.

'And you and your two friends are the ones that can do it. I can feel it.'

'Well—the other two maybe.'

Cyprian shrugged. 'Maybe more them. But if they can lead, there's plenty of us who can follow. I've been here as long as most. I know who could be persuaded to help.'

This was exactly what Gyrmund wanted to hear. 'That's great. How many do you think?'

'First of all, though,' said Cyprian, apparently ignoring the question, 'you'll have to deal with Vamak. He has a good relationship with the guards, and if he gets a whiff, he'll tell 'em about any escape plan. Plus, he's feared enough to stop people siding with you. So, like I say, that's your job. In the meantime, I'll be quietly sounding out some of the other miners. But don't worry 'bout that. I'm not going to blab anything to the wrong person. So, to answer your question about numbers, we won't know exactly how many. We'll have a few on side. And we'll have the rest, who we just won't know about for sure until it happens.'

Gyrmund nodded. 'I'll let Herin and Clarin know. When you have some information, you can tell any one of us.'

'Fine. Now, help me along with this, will you?'

Gyrmund hefted his axe and resumed his back-breaking work in the mines, but now with a little more hope that he might make it out alive.

XII

A BLESSING

THE KNIGHTS OF KALINTH were on the move.

Belwynn had mixed emotions as the High Tower of the Knights receded into the distance behind them, and then disappeared. But most of all she was glad to be moving on.

The sun was out as the mounted force made a good pace along a narrow but well used road. They had left the seat of the Knights of Kalinth for Heractus, the seat of its kings. The road was mostly mud, and looked like it got wet and boggy in the winter months, but after several weeks of warm weather it had now been baked dry, leaving big cracks on the surface. There was little shade on the route, the landscape dominated by low lying vegetation like heather and gorse, which allowed the scouts to get a good view of the area around them, in all directions. Nesting birds, disturbed by the armed force passing their homes, would fly or run away, causing the few dogs with them to bark, the handlers to curse, and some of the horses to get jittery. But apart from the wildlife, there seemed little else to worry about, and the mood was relaxed.

The momentous events at the High Tower had culminated yesterday in the formal removal of Galenos as Grand Master of the Order, and the adoption of Sebastian as his replacement. It had been a bloodless revolution, and Galenos was now being held in comfortable conditions in a room in the Tower. But Sebastian and his advisers knew that news of their actions would already be spreading across the country to their enemies. They had to move fast and retain the initiative.

Sebastian already had the makings of an army at his disposal. Almost all the Knights had been in attendance at the High Tower, and most of those who supported Sebastian, who were in the clear majority, now joined him in the march south. Remi, Sebastian's long-time friend, had been left in charge at the Tower, to run things in the new Grand Master's absence, and to coordinate communications and supplies.

Many of the knights had brought with them a sizeable entourage of squires, men at arms, and other followers. In addition, Sebastian now had charge of the Order's servants, which included craftsmen whose expertise lay in working with metal, leather, or wood. These groups swelled the force at Sebastian's disposal to something like three thousand fighters in all. But, as Theron explained to Belwynn as they rode together near the head of the army, many other knights had not brought their soldiers with them. Theron himself only had Evander, his squire.

'My largest estates, in Erisina, are to the west. I've written some letters, and given them to messengers to take to that part of the country. Other messengers are heading to the estates of our supporters all over Kalinth. Enough should get through in time to add to our army by the time we reach Heractus.'

'How many soldiers might come from your estates?' asked Belwynn.

Theron thought about it. 'Probably about fifty men who know how to fight. Not all of them are trained soldiers though. More of them are farmers, or other workers. Blacksmiths are usually pretty good in a fight.'

'How many more might we get altogether?'

'If you include the force that Remi will bring over from the High Tower we might reach five thousand.'

Belwynn thought about that. It wasn't very many, even though the Knights were the best warriors in Kalinth. If they were to enter the capital, Heractus, they would need a superior force, and it didn't seem like they had one.

'And what do we do when we reach Heractus?'

'That depends on the reaction we get. The city is well defended. There is a city guard who patrol the walls, and a royal guard of well-trained soldiers who serve the king. Jonas has many wealthy supporters who can raise soldiers of their own. We can't rule out resistance.'

In the early afternoon, they made a stop by a fast-flowing river. Theron identified it as the Pineos, that travelled west and emptied into the Lantinen Sea.

The squires and other servants quickly got to work giving the horses a drink and a feed. The riders began to dismount so that their animals could get a proper rest, and their own legs could get a stretch after hours in the saddle. Theron went off to speak to Sebastian and the other leaders, and so Belwynn led Elana and Dirk away from the busy atmosphere somewhere quieter. They found a flat piece of rock by the river that was big enough for all three of them to sit on. It had been nicely warmed up by a full morning's sunshine. Belwynn leaned back, enjoying the warm rays of the sun on her skin. Looking over at Dirk, she saw that the ride had done his health little good. His skin still had a white pallor to it, and his hair and face were wet with sweat. Elana began attending to him, working her healing magic by holding his hands inside hers and then pressing her hands onto the back of his neck and his forehead.

It was a routine they had both got used to, but it still made Belwynn feel awkward, as if she were intruding on a private moment. She looked around them, thinking she might go for a short walk by herself, when she saw a group of half a dozen knights making their way towards them. She got to her feet. Elana noticed and stopped attending to Dirk, a quizzical look on her face.

As the knights got nearer, Belwynn recognised a couple of faces as younger knights she had seen here and there at the High Tower, but she didn't think she had been introduced to any of them.

They seemed a bit unsure of themselves and glanced nervously at one another. One of the knights eventually stepped forward. He was a sandy haired young man, whom Belwynn judged had not yet reached twenty years.

'Lady Belwynn, I am Philon, a Knight of Kalinth as are my friends here,' he said, gesturing at the men around him. His friends nodded, one or two staring sheepishly at the ground. 'We apologise for disturbing you all at your rest.'

Philon paused, waiting for a response.

Belwynn was a bit unsure how to proceed, but the group of knights seemed harmless enough.

'Please, there is no need to apologise. What is it you have come for?'

'Well, we all listened to your song...your singing, in the Great Hall, and we all got talking about how inspiring it was for each of us. All of us have said it was a very moving experience, each in our own way...'

Philon's voice drifted off, unable to continue the sentence any further. He turned around to his friends and flapped his hands a little, as if to appeal for help.

The nearest knight cleared his throat and stepped forwards. He suddenly went down on one knee.

'Lady Belwynn,' he began—large brown eyes framed in long, wavy brown hair looked up at her, 'we are all going to war for our first time, and we have a request that—would it be possible for you to bless our swords?'

120

Belwynn was taken aback and looked at Elana for help. The priestess nodded. She could hardly refuse such a request.

'Yes, of course,' she said, without having any idea what was involved in blessing a sword.

The other five knights, including Philon, adopted the same position as the brown eyed knight. They all drew their swords and, gripping the hilt in both hands, placed the sharp end into the ground. When this was done, they bowed their heads, seemingly ready to receive the blessing.

Belwynn turned to look at Elana again, who to her surprise had put one hand to her mouth, and seemed to be trying not to giggle out loud.

She approached the first knight.

'May I ask your name?'

'Leontios.'

'And where are you from, Leontios?'

'From Fyllo, my lady.'

'Leontios of Fyllo, I bless your sword, may it serve its master well in battle.'

She quickly looked at the downturned faces of the knights to see their reaction, but there was no sign that they were disappointed with the choice of words. So, Belwynn moved from Leontios to Philon, and on to the rest of the knights, giving the same blessing to each of them.

Half way through Theron came striding over, the initial look of concern on his face quickly turning to bemusement as he took in the spectacle. Once Belwynn had finished, the knights returned to their feet, evidently pleased with what had passed. They offered their thanks and, giving a final bow, made their way back to the road.

Theron's eyes followed the knights and then turned back to Belwynn, as if studying her closely.

'What, Theron? Was I wrong to do that?'

'No, not at all. I think it was good,' he said, his voice light and breezy.

But he continued to look at Belwynn, as if in some way he were now truly seeing her for the first time.

***

Moneva was finally out of Arioc's apartments. After two more nights with the King of Haskany she was now allowed the freedom of the fortress. He had held her chin in one hand, and agreed to her request as if he were an indulgent father. The memory of it made her stomach twist, but Moneva ruthlessly pushed it aside. She had to learn to banish those memories. She had to use the little time she had to achieve something.

Moneva knew that this meant that Arioc had started to trust her, but that if she did anything to lose his trust there would be no second chances. So, she couldn't stay out for too long. Neither could she ask him about the whereabouts of her friends. This left the chances of her finding out anything of use dismally low, but at least she could get her bearings.

Babak had given her a brooch with Arioc's sigil on it: a serpent, coiled around into a circle and eating its own tail. This allowed her free passage around his tower.

Since virtually all the people she came across in the tower also displayed the same sigil somewhere about their person, on uniforms, or necklaces, or brooches just like hers, Moneva concluded that the whole tower was Arioc's domain in some way, and everyone in it a follower of his. She therefore acted on the assumption that since Gyrmund and the others had been captured by Arioc, they would most likely be here too. But after a couple of hours of fruitless searching, she started to give up on that idea. Presumably, most of the other towers of the fortress were occupied by great Lords of Ishari, just like Arioc. But there was likely to be other areas where prisoners were kept, and it was these she had to locate.

Knowing that she had little time left before raising suspicions, Moneva made her way to the eastern exit of the tower. Two guards stood on duty at the door, mean looking men like the ones who had held her captive on the way here.

Moneva approached them, making sure that the brooch was visible. The guards saw her coming. One of them said a few words to the other and they both laughed in her direction, lips curling in contempt. Steeling herself, Moneva approached the exit, trying to make her expression and body language look as confident as possible.

One of the guards put out an arm, his hand grasping a spear that blocked her from leaving.

'Where are you going?' he asked, speaking Dalriyan in a much more heavily accented voice than Arioc did.

Moneva nodded ahead of her. 'Out there,' she said.

'No, not allowed.'

'Arioc says I *am* allowed.'

Moneva sensed some doubt in them now. These men didn't want to make a mistake and displease their master. Arioc's last lover, Shira, was now on the Council of Seven after all. It wouldn't be wise to insult Moneva if she was going to become his new favourite.

'You can tell him where I went,' she said, looking impassively at both guards.

The guard with the spear looked at his partner who gave a small nod. The arm was withdrawn. The second guard opened the wooden door for Moneva, who wasted no time in passing through it.

The corridor she entered was just the same as the one she had left, tough stone walls on either side, and a wooden ceiling above her, which served as a walkway for the castle defenders above. Torches in the wall made just enough light to see ahead.

But the feeling of this corridor was totally different. Everywhere she had been on the other side of the door, every inch of every room, had resonated with Arioc's presence, as if he were aware of everything that happened there. But once Moneva had passed through the door, beyond his part of the fortress, the feeling vanished. It was powerful magic, admitted Moneva, but even Arioc's magic had boundaries. That thought gave her hope.

Passing through an unguarded door at the end of the new corridor, Moneva found herself in a small courtyard. The wooden walkway above her continued its route around the fortress wall. As she passed under it, she found the courtyard was open to the elements, and she was able to breathe fresh air for the first time in days. The yard narrowed quite sharply ahead of her, making it a wedge shape. The left of the courtyard was being used as a dumping ground for materials: a pile of stones, neatly stacked lengths of timber, and several large canvas sacks tied with rope.

Servants were carrying more of these sacks into the courtyard, and dumping them against the wall with a clatter. A couple of soldiers entered the courtyard from an opening in this wall, and passed through to a similar opening on the other side. Servants and soldiers alike gave Moneva a brief look, but were too busy, or perhaps too disinterested, to do more than that.

A stone bench ran along the far end of the courtyard, the thin end of the wedge. A lone figure, seated on the bench, gestured to Moneva to come over.

Moneva looked around uncertainly but no-one else was watching. She moved over warily. The figure gestured with his arm again, as if she should hurry up. He was wearing a cowl that partially hid his face, but as Moneva moved a step closer she could see a pair of red eyes staring out at her. She stopped with a start. It was Pentas.

Pentas beckoned a third time, looking frustrated. Moneva moved over more quickly, taking a seat next to the sorcerer and trying not to look suspicious.

'Moneva,' he began, turning towards her, his red eyes drawing her in. 'We don't have long. Don't draw attention to our conversation. We don't want anyone to remember us. I am under surveillance and so will you be.'

Moneva nodded. 'How did you find me here?'

'I've known where you were all along. I've been waiting for you to get out of Arioc's Tower.'

Moneva felt anger flare to the surface. 'You knew what was happening to me, and you did nothing?' she let out, trying to stop her whisper from becoming a scream. She felt tears in her eyes.

Pentas stared straight back at her. 'Yes. I hoped you would survive it.'

'You hoped?' said Moneva incredulously, and lashed out, aiming to slap Pentas in the face; but his hand shot out, grabbing her wrist.

'I told you not to draw attention,' he said sternly, pushing her arm down before letting go. He looked around the courtyard before continuing.

'I am sorry for what has happened to you, Moneva. But there are many lives at stake right now.'

It was said with some feeling, but hardly made Moneva feel better. She tried to control her emotions, surprised at how quickly they had come flooding out.

'I have to be very careful,' continued Pentas. 'You are strong, and you have survived. But now I need you to help me. I know where your friends have been taken.'

'Where?' demanded Moneva.

'I will give you full directions. Gyrmund, Herin and Clarin have been sent to a slave mine attached to the fortress, and Soren is being held in one of the towers here. There is only so much help I can give you all. Soon Herin and the others must be ready, somehow, to escape the mines. I want you to find them and give them warning of this. You, too, will have to be ready. But I can't risk seeing you again, Moneva, unless there's a real emergency. I won't be here in the fortress all the time, either. I must give you all your instructions now. Do you understand?'

Moneva understood that she was putting herself completely in the hands of this sorcerer, whom she had no reason to trust. But at least he was offering her a plan and giving her purpose, when she had been hopelessly lost before.

'Yes.'

'Good. And there's one other thing you can do. You don't like it I know, but you are now in a position to influence Arioc. That makes you powerful. There are certain things I would like you to talk about with him. But I need to know now whether you agree to all of it? You will be risking your life if you do.'

Moneva sighed. Did she have any choice?

'I agree, sorcerer. Now tell me where my friends are.'

***

From where they stood, Burkhard Castle looked like the model castle her Uncle Koren owned back home and had, on special occasions, let her play with. The Drobax, on the other hand, didn't resemble the toy soldiers that went with it: Koren just owned brave knights and men at arms, not deformed creatures like these. Shira was only too aware of the irony that the brave soldiers she had imagined in her childhood games were the ones defending the castle from *her* army.

Shira's own people, the Haskans, were stationed two miles away, and weren't being used in the attack. Joined by Koren and Mehrab, she had located a rocky outcrop from where they could observe the attack. But she had no real role to play herself. It was Roshanak and his team of Isharite wizards who were in charge, driving the Drobax forwards and giving them their instructions.

The drums pounded out the beat for an all-out attack, and the creatures charged at the castle like rabid animals. As much as Shira and Koren despised the Drobax for not being true soldiers— and Mehrab despised Roshanak and his associates for not being true magi—the reality was that this army of Drobax was the most powerful force in the land.

As she looked on, they swarmed towards the two outcrops of rock which represented one of the best natural defensive positions in Dalriya. On the left of the scene stood the larger of the two crags with the Emperor's Keep on top. The Drobax approached it from all sides and began to climb. No path had ever been constructed by the Brasingians on this crag, and the Drobax had to negotiate their way up the steep rock surface. They used roughly made wooden ladders, propping them up against the side, but the going was slow.

The crag on the right was the obvious target for the Drobax, and was heavily defended by the castle's soldiers, who had stationed a force right at the bottom where the path began. The narrow path neutralised the numerical superiority of the Drobax, and gave the defenders a height advantage. The Drobax launched their attack at this part of the castle but the defenders held firm. Although she was too far away to see the individual weapons, Shira knew that there would be a wall of shields bristling with spears and pikes waiting for the Drobax. As she watched, a pile of dead bodies began to grow at the bottom of the path.

'Whose banner is that?' asked Mehrab, pointing at the device of the green tree which was being flown over the heads of the defenders who were engaging the Drobax.

'The duchy of Luderia,' replied Shira. 'Arne is their leader; the Emperor's father-in-law. A fat waste of space, so I am told.'

'Well, his men are doing alright,' said Koren sharply. 'I'm going for a piss,' he added, heading off back down the outcrop.

'Your uncle isn't enjoying this?' asked Mehrab when Koren was out of earshot.

'Not his idea of how wars should be fought,' said Shira. 'Nor mine, but I guess I'm more philosophical about it.'

'You mean that you understand that this is the last war humans will ever fight.'

Shira shrugged. She didn't like the comment. But then she didn't like Mehrab.

The hours went by and little changed. Koren never reappeared, and Shira didn't blame him.

The Luderians retreated up the path. Not far, but it represented some progress. They moved behind a gate which blocked the path up the crag. The Drobax attacked, hacking and ripping at the gate. From a ledge above them, the defenders threw missiles down. It was hard to make out what, but there would be rocks, spears, arrows. Maybe hot oil, which was commonly used by castle defenders in Haskany. It would be carnage, and the Drobax retreated under the onslaught.

At the same time the Drobax on the other crag were finally encountering the defenders. About half way up a small wall had been built which encircled the whole crag. The Brasingians manned this wall so that they had a common point of defence, and as the Drobax struggled up towards it, the imperial soldiers could thrust with their spears or fire missiles down, with the wall to protect them. It was easy work for the defenders. The Drobax arrived at the wall in small, irregular numbers rather than all at once, and could be picked off at will. Shira had no faith that any of them would get through.

The attack continued for the rest of the day. Towards the end, the Drobax on the path managed to rip down the gate, but were then counter-attacked by the Luderians who had been able to conserve their strength. The Drobax were driven right down to the bottom of the path. Finally, the drums ordered a retreat, and the Drobax made their way back to the pathetic camps that encircled the castle. Thousands of them were dead, and Shira knew that some of the bodies would be collected and cannibalised tonight.

She sighed. 'We're not getting anywhere like this.'

Mehrab nodded. 'We might as well not bother, and just starve them into surrender. Can't your Haskans do a better job?'

'I'm not sending them into this death trap! No, it's time for you to contribute something now. Arioc sent you Isharites to overcome problems like this.'

Mehrab grunted. But he didn't disagree. 'Like what? There's no point getting ourselves killed in the fighting. We're not expendable like the Drobax.'

Shira thought about it. 'The leaders,' she said finally. 'The soldiers up there fight for their leaders. If we can kill Baldwin and the others, their morale will collapse. But Baldwin most of all.'

'That's easier said than done, Shira.'

Shira stared at him. 'You don't address a member of the Council of the Seven by their first name.'

Mehrab looked a little disconcerted. 'Apologies, Lord,' he muttered.

'I didn't say it would be easy, but that's your job. I want the Emperor dead, Mehrab. Find a way. Find a way, and then we can smash Burkhard and finish off the Empire.'

XIII

A GREAT MOOT

RABIGAR URGED HIS HORSE ON, guiding it along the uphill track. They were now entering the impenetrable mountainous terrain that was the heartland of the Krykker realm. He had made good time since leaving Belwynn behind in Kalinth four days ago, and it had been good to spend a few days on his own, travelling in the open air. Since his exile from his homeland, when he had still been a young man, he had been forced to spend a lot of time in his own company. He had settled in various places and made acquaintances, but had always moved on eventually. Whereas in his youth he had been surrounded by family and friends, Rabigar had now grown used to being alone.

The few days of light travelling had done his health good. It had given him time to think, too, especially about the injury he had received in the dungeons of Coldeberg Castle. With only one eye left, he knew his sight would never again be what it was. But he also had reason to be thankful that it hadn't been worse: that Moneva and the others had rescued him before more damage was done. He had survived his exile with no kin to support him, and he had lived to an age that most people never saw.

As he had crossed from the borderlands of Kalinth into the lands of his people, a sense of peace had fallen on Rabigar. He was coming home. His life had come full circle. If his homecoming wasn't accepted and he was to die— well, then so be it.

Rabigar decided it was time to dismount and walk the rest of the way. He gave the mare a pat and some food and water. Sebastian had given him a good mount. When she was ready, he led the beast along, studying the rocky terrain closely with his one good eye for familiar features.

After a while Rabigar found what he was looking for. To his left was a cave entrance, mostly hidden by scrub, a few metres away from the path. Gently encouraging the horse, he got it to climb up the rocks and into the darkness of the cave. The roof of the cave was only a foot higher than the horse. It wasn't very deep either, but there was enough space for Rabigar to walk in his mount. He tied it up on a hook carved into the cave. He unloaded his carrying bag, took off the saddle, and laid out the remainder of the fodder and water.

'Here you go,' he murmured reassuringly. 'You'll be safe here until someone collects you.'

Rabigar moved over to the wall of the cave, touching the rock for the first time in over twenty years. Tears came to his eyes as he did so. This rock could not be found elsewhere in Dalriya. It belonged only to the Krykker, and the Krykker belonged to it. It would last forever. And so would the Krykker, the first people of Dalriya. Before the Isharites, Humans, Caladri, before even the Lippers had come, the Krykkers had been in Dalriya. They would outlast them all, too.

He concentrated now, focusing on his hands and on the rock, emptying his mind of any other thoughts. He stood like that for a while, he was not sure for how long, as he entered a trance like state. It had, after all, been a long time since he had last done this. Then, slowly, his hands began to disperse the particles of rock. Pushing forwards, they began to submerge into the rock as if he was sticking them into a vat of butter. As they did so, the rock shifted around him to make room. Rabigar pushed further, using his thighs to force his arms into the rock. The mare whinnied nervously as his limbs began to disappear.

The critical moment came as Rabigar's face and shoulders met the wall. The temptation, especially when a Krykker was learning this technique at first, was to panic as the face entered the rock, due to the natural fear of asphyxiation. Krykker rock walkers had to train themselves to ignore this natural reaction, and have faith in their ability. Rabigar pushed head first, holding his breath as if he were diving through water rather than rock. Gathering speed, he pushed until his whole body was inside the rock, and he had left the cave behind. He kept moving, secure in the knowledge that this was a safe area to pass through. Nevertheless, when Rabigar's head emerged on the other side of the rock, he took a relieved breath of air.

He had passed into an underground tunnel. It was pitch black. Rabigar knew where he was going, but he gave himself some time to let his eyes adjust to the lack of light. Turning right, he began walking towards the nearest Krykker settlement.

Rabigar's plan was to keep walking until challenged, arrested, and taken before the local chieftain. The clan in these parts were the Dramsen. Rabigar remembered the local Dramsen chieftain as being young and fair minded. He hoped that he was still alive, and that age hadn't soured him.

It didn't turn out quite as Rabigar had foreseen it. Instead of being challenged while making his way along the tunnel he caught up with a young Dramsen. The youth had a flat, open wheeled cart attached around his shoulders with rope, and was steadily pulling it up the tunnel. It was filled with timber. Rabigar remembered being given the same job many times when he was the same age, no longer a child but not yet an adult warrior. The Krykker blacksmiths had an insatiable appetite for timber, and young men were sent out with these carts and an axe to cut down and strip trees. They would not be allowed to return until their carts were full.

The rumble of the wheels on the floor of the tunnel meant that the young man didn't hear Rabigar catching up to him, and so in the end he had to holler out for him to stop. The young man turned and peered at Rabigar, trying to place him; his puzzled expression indicated that he couldn't.

Rabigar approached steadily and held out a hand.

'My name is Din.'

'Stenk,' came the reply.

The young man was friendly enough and willingly shook hands. However, his puzzled expression returned as he stood looking Rabigar up and down.

'Din?' he repeated, eyeing Rabigar carefully. 'But—you're not—Rabigar Din? Are you?'

Rabigar held up his hands. 'Yes, I am. But I'm not here to harm you.'

Stenk looked back with a strange mix of awe, fear and uncertainty.

'I will surrender to you, and you can take me to your chieftain. Is Torinac still in charge here?'

'Wow—' said Stenk, ignoring the question. 'I never thought I would meet Rabigar Din. I thought you would be dead by now. Everyone knows about you,' he informed Rabigar.

Rabigar wasn't sure how to respond. 'Torinac?'

'Oh, yes, sorry. I'll take you to him.'

'You had better take my sword from me,' said Rabigar.

'Right. Yes.'

Rabigar unbuckled his sword from his belt and passed it over. Stenk took a good grip and gave it a couple of swishes.

'That's a good weapon,' he commented, before carefully placing it into his cart.

They set off up the tunnel to find Torinac. Rabigar was under arrest. Though the process hadn't been as formal as he had expected.

'Are you sure you want to do this?' asked Torinac. 'This is your last chance. I could say you escaped in the night.'

It was the next day. Rabigar had been treated with great respect by the chieftain of the Dramsen. Stenk had led him up a series of tunnels to the outside, where Torinac had his stone hall. Rabigar had been given pride of place by the fire as if he were a guest, and there was no guard set over him.

Torinac had sent out messengers to the other chieftains of the Krykker clans, advising them of Rabigar's presence and calling for a Great Moot, a meeting of the clans. This is what Rabigar had wanted, for it would give him a chance to explain his presence, and warn his people of the threat posed by Ishari.

'No. I need to address the Great Moot about something very important. More important than my life.'

Torinac shrugged. He looked interested in what Rabigar had said, but didn't pursue it. He was a powerful looking warrior. His great grey fur coat, made from raccoon, made him look twice as big as he really was. He turned around to the score of other fur clad warriors who had gathered in the hall.

'On!' he bellowed, in a booming voice which was used to being obeyed. 'Clan Dramsen has called a Great Moot!'

A cheer rose up, and before Rabigar knew it, the group was barging its way to the doors of the hall. He readied himself to follow, when he caught sight of Stenk watching on from the side.

'Torinac?' he said.

'What is it, Rabigar Din?'

'You may think it highly presumptuous. I would request your man Stenk to be my man for the duration of the moot.'

'Stenk!' bellowed Torinac.

Stenk sidled over.

'You will serve Rabigar Din.'

'Yes, lord!' replied Stenk, nodding excitedly. He hurried off in the opposite direction.

'Stenk! Where are you going?'

'To get a weapon, lord.'

'Hurry up!'

Rabigar waited for Stenk to fetch an axe, and then they hurried after the Dramsen warriors. It all felt rather madcap and disorganised to Rabigar. He sighed. He had been away from his homeland for so long that his people seemed strange to him. It was an uncomfortable feeling.

Torinac's men scrambled down the mountainside at pace. What would be considered a dangerous climb down to most humans was a daily journey for them. Rabigar and Stenk caught up with them half way down, where the group had stopped in front of a sheer drop to a rocky area below. Two of the warriors were pulling on a rope which seemed to be operating a pulley system below. Rabigar peered over the edge. He could see two sets of metal rails running down a smooth slope into the shadows. It wasn't possible to see how far they went.

Torinac came over, grinning.

'You're about to see that times have moved on since you were last here, Rabigar Din.'

His grin became rather manic looking, and Rabigar looked down the slope again with alarm. He could hear a scraping sound of metal on metal, which didn't make him feel any better.

Eventually the item which the two warriors were pulling up the slope came into view. It was a very large, open, rectangular shaped metal box. The scraping sound was the metal wheels at the bottom of the box which were passing between the two sets of metal rails on the floor.

'Well, what do you think?' asked Torinac, as the closest edge of the box was attached to the rock face with a giant metal hook. 'I call it a rail way.'

One of the warriors clambered into the box.

'You don't expect me to get in that?' asked Rabigar, as the other warriors began jumping in.

'I'm ordering you to get into it. You're my prisoner, remember?' said Torinac, pleasantly enough.

'We'll all die.'

Torinac seemed very disappointed. 'Don't worry. We've tested it plenty of times.'

'How many?'

'Just get in.'

Rabigar got in, heading for one of the sides of the box which he gripped tightly.

Torinac and Stenk followed him in. It was now a very tight squeeze inside the box. The final warrior joined them. Using the handle of his axe, the warrior knocked the hook out of the rock. Rabigar watched him, aghast. One moment they were being held in place, next, over twenty Krykkers inside a giant metal box began rolling down a mountain slope.

As the box gathered pace the warriors began screaming and whooping in delight. The noise nearly masked the scraping of the metal wheels on the rails. Rabigar closed his eyes. He could hear Torinac laughing hysterically. He felt the box getting faster and faster. The shouting got louder and then, suddenly, with no warning or reduction of speed, the box hit the bottom. Rabigar fell onto his back from the impact, and some of the Krykkers fell on top of him. The box had become a mass of flailing arms and legs. The box lurched forwards back up the rails a few feet, causing everyone to roll over to the other end of the box. It then slid back down to the bottom again, causing further mayhem as elbows and knees struck people in the face, where at last it came to a rest.

Dizzily, Rabigar made his way to the end of the box and hauled himself out, moving away a few feet. His head was spinning and he sank down to his knees. Torinac appeared.

'What do you think?' asked the chieftain.

Rabigar felt like he was going to vomit.

'Very good. I guess that's saved us a lot of time.'

'Certainly has. It's a very popular invention. A lot of the other clans are starting to build their own. We haven't quite perfected the landing yet, though.'

Thousands of years ago, the Great Meeting Chamber of the Krykkers was carved out of the mountain Kerejus. Only accessible via underground tunnels, it represented neutral ground, where all the clans could meet on equal terms.

It was a dramatic setting. Great pillars, made of the original mountain rock, had been left in place, supporting the rough ceiling of the cavern. They had been intricately carved, some in arresting patterns, others depicting the collective stories and heroes of the Krykkers' past. These heroes were also depicted in over-sized statues that lined the walls of the hall. Warriors abounded, but also justice givers, like Chief Huderam the Righteous, who dispensed justice on behalf of the oppressed against the mighty.

In the middle of the chamber stood the circular arena. Tiered stone seats looked down on the central stage, where the chief speakers of a Great Moot would address their audience. The representatives of each clan could be seated and heard, and the circular shape meant that no clan was given more status than another.

It was here that Rabigar had been tried and sentenced to exile. He had been a different man, then. Young and arrogant, he had revelled in his status as one of the best warriors of the Grendal clan, and as a rock walker. Popular and respected amongst his peers, he was talked of as a future clan leader.

But that had all ended one night. Rabigar and his friends had drunk far too much, feasting in the hall of their chieftain, Lidimas. Rabigar had long held a fancy for the chieftain's daughter, Maragin. He couldn't remember exactly what he had done to upset Lidimas that night. It was more than the usual flirting, certainly. He had not behaved with respect. Lidimas had come storming over, demanding an apology. Ordinarily, Rabigar would have backed down, understanding the rules that governed clan life, and recognising the danger of the situation. But the drink made him behave differently. Maybe the presence of his friends, or of Maragin, affected his behaviour too. But in failing to back away from Lidimas he was challenging his chieftain's authority.

Before Rabigar knew what was happening, both men had weapons in their hands. It was over quickly. Narrowly avoiding a swing from Lidimas, Rabigar had lashed out violently, all of his angry, beer-fuelled strength in the strike. His sword connected with the side of Lidimas's neck. His chieftain collapsed to the floor. He didn't die immediately; but in the last few days of his life, he never regained consciousness.

Rabigar had suddenly sobered up. Then came the screams. It was the screams that stayed with Rabigar, visiting him even now when he slept. Maragin's screams as she knelt by Lidimas, looking accusingly up at Rabigar, and back to her father.

Rabigar's memory of the trial was hazy, as if he had been asleep at key moments. Many favoured death, but some, like Torinac, had accepted that Rabigar struck in self-defence. Still, he had killed his own chieftain. The sentence was reduced to exile for life. Many Krykkers in Rabigar's position would have preferred death to such a punishment. But, guilt ridden, he accepted the verdict as his penance. One final judgement was made. Rabigar was a noble, warrior's name among the Krykker. He was no longer entitled to it. He would thereafter be referred to as Din, a low born name. Rabigar who was, now no longer existed.

Torinac and his men filed into the chamber, quietly taking their places. Rabigar sat next to the Dramsen chieftain on the front row of seats. Some of the other clans had already arrived, and taken their seats in the arena. Their chieftains also took positions at the front, so that if needed they could enter the circle and speak for their clan. There were murmurs from some of the other clans, but they respected the rules of the Great Moot, and did not challenge Torinac or Rabigar before proceedings had formally started. They had to wait for the remaining clans to arrive first. Rabigar kept his eyes fixed to the floor, not talking, aware that he was the centre of attention. Time went slowly. Stenk had to go and empty his bladder against the far wall of the chamber. Finally, the last clan to arrive settled into position.

Torinac stood. He walked slowly into the centre of the space in the middle of the arena, turning around in a full circle so that he was addressing everyone gathered. Rabigar lifted his head up, looking out at the faces, his eyes naturally searching out his own clan, the Grendals. When he found them, he got a shock that twisted his insides. Staring back at him was Maragin, seated as the chieftain of the Grendals. They made eye contact briefly. Her face was expressionless and composed. It was Rabigar who turned away, unable to hold the gaze. As Torinac began to speak, Rabigar could barely concentrate on what he was saying. A feeling of desperation came over him. Things had gone well to this point. But with the daughter of the murdered Lidimas speaking for the Grendals, it would surely be impossible to persuade the Moot of his case.

'I am Torinac, chieftain of the Dramsen and I have called this Moot,' began Torinac in a booming voice. 'Yesterday, unknown to me and uninvited, the exile, Din, came into the lands of the Dramsen clan. It is fair to say, I believe, that we all know who Din is, and that we all know the penalty for breaking his exile is death?'

Shouts of 'agreed', 'yes', and other affirmatives met this question.

'Din explained to me that he had come back to warn our people of a dire threat, to the peoples of Dalriya including our own. He argued that instead of killing him, I should allow him to pass on this warning. This is what I bring before the Great Moot today.'

Torinac fell silent, waiting for a response. After a pause one of the chieftains, Guremar of clan Plengas, raised an arm.

'Guremar,' said Torinac, indicating that he gave way to the chieftain.

Torinac returned to his seat, and Guremar made his way to the central stage. He was one of the oldest chieftains, stern-faced, with grey, bushy eyebrows, that seemed to be set in a permanent frown.

'I understand why Torinac has brought this matter before the Moot. But my verdict is clear. When Din murdered his own chieftain over twenty years ago, my clan demanded the death penalty, but others, such as Torinac, disagreed. Now that Din has returned; I propose that the sentence be carried out.'

Guremar now fell silent. Rabigar sneaked a look over towards Maragin but she remained still. Instead another chieftain, of clan Swarten, had raised an arm.

'Hakonin.'

Rabigar did not recognise the name Hakonin, and so didn't know what to expect from the next speaker. When he walked to the centre of the stage, Rabigar saw why. He was a young man, and must have been a child on the day of Rabigar's exile.

'No one can disagree that our laws say that Din's punishment should be death. But I propose that first we hear what he has to say. It would be foolish of us not to listen to him in case his warning is genuine. I would add that Din has not attempted to return since his exile, and so something serious may have motivated his arrival now.'

Two more chieftains stood to agree that Rabigar should be heard. Heads turned towards Maragin, wondering what she had to say, but still she sat unmoved, stony faced.

'Din.'

He had been called. This had been his objective, to speak to the Moot. He had prepared himself to accept whatever came afterwards. Rabigar stood and walked to the circle. He took a final glance at his old clan. He detected a mixture of expressions. Some, naturally, were hostile. Others, those who had been his close friends, nodded solemnly; some even smiled. At the front Maragin remained expressionless; unreadable.

'I, Din, have spent these last years living as an exile in the lands of men. I accepted my punishment, but I have returned to speak these words, and I swear they are true. In the service of Prince Edgar of Magnia I was ordered, with other warriors, to retrieve a dagger that had been stolen from his lands by agents of Ishari. Here,' he said, indicating the patch that covered the hole where his eye had been, 'is where the agents of Ishari took my eye.'

He hoped, not for sympathy, but for a sense that he had received a suitable punishment for his former crime. 'I am now sure that this dagger which we retrieved is one of the seven sacred weapons from the Battle of Alta, when our greatest hero, Bolivar the Bold, defeated the dread lord of Ishari.'

Rabigar paused here, stretching his arm out and gesturing to the statue of Bolivar in the Meeting Chamber, who held his great sword across his chest. He waited until his audience had turned to look at Bolivar before continuing.

'Not only this, but we entered the lands of the Grand Caladri moments before their destruction by the forces of Arioc, retrieving a wizard's staff, which I am sure is a second sacred weapon.'

There were gasps at this statement, but Rabigar continued.

'Both weapons are now in Kalinth. As I speak, the Knights of Kalinth are moving to take control of their kingdom. You must know that an army of Drobax entered the Empire about two weeks past. Torinac said I came to warn you, and there is some truth to this. The Krykkers are in danger from Ishari, just like everyone else in Dalriya. But you already know that. No, I come, humbly, to summon the clans to war. A second great battle is coming. Bolivar's Sword is needed to fight Ishari again. The Krykkers are needed to fight for Dalriya once more.'

Rabigar nodded to indicate that he had finished speaking.

Whispering broke out amongst the Krykkers seated in the chamber. The chieftains turned around in their seats, glaring at their followers to keep quiet. Several hands shot into the air. Rabigar looked around. Maragin's hand was not one of them. By custom, he chose a chieftain who was likely to present a counter argument.

'Guremar.'

'Clan Plengas observes the arrogance of Din who dares to come here, a criminal and exile, and call the Krykkers to war. The Krykkers are under no threat and this is not our war. As for Din's stories of sacred weapons, does he bring us any proof of this? No. Just the word of a murderer,' finished Guremar, pointing directly at Rabigar.

'Hakonin.'

'We cannot close our eyes to the threat posed by Ishari. Who amongst us would have thought that the Grand Caladri could have been destroyed in a matter of days? Do not forget the conquest of Persala, or the invasion of the Empire. We Krykkers do not have such short memories as the other peoples of Dalriya. We know we are not safe from Ishari, even here in our mountains. The arrival of the sacred weapons cannot be ignored. That the messenger we hear this from is Din is irrelevant; it is the message itself that we must all heed.'

Hakonin looked around the chamber.

'Porimin.'

Next to stand was not a chieftain but an old man, seated on one of the stone benches half way up the arena. Porimin made his way slowly down to the floor. He was well known as a historian of the Krykker people.

'Hundreds of years ago,' he began, his voice more fragile than those who had gone before, but still strong enough to carry to those listening. 'Our ancestors helped to defeat Ishari at the battle of Alta. But they knew that the enemy wasn't vanquished, and they recorded for us their accounts, and their warnings that the threat would need to be faced once more. We have kept these safe for generations, as we have kept Bolivar's Sword, knowing that it would need to be used again. Given what we now know, it is hard to do anything but come to the conclusion that we are facing the very same threat they faced. The Krykkers must face it with courage, just as we did once before.'

The old man looked around the arena.

'Torinac.'

Torinac took the floor.

'I would like to remind those gathered of a messenger I received, sent from a Lord of the Grand Caladri, named Kelemen. He wanted to request safe haven in our lands for his people. If we agree to act, we should also consider our response to him. My clan has always defended the southern border of our lands. My view is that we should stand shoulder to shoulder with the Kalinthians and the Caladri in this war. I also believe that Din has shown bravery in coming here, and that his life should be spared.'

Torinac looked about the arena. His eyes widened somewhat. Rabigar followed his gaze. Maragin's hand was raised.

'Maragin,' said Torinac softly.

Maragin stood slowly and walked to the centre of the arena. A hush fell over the moot. She looked around, looking the men about her in the eye. She

138

was a formidable figure, and the longer she waited to speak, the more the tension in the chamber rose.

'Din killed my chieftain and my father,' she began. 'He was rightly exiled from our lands but has returned nonetheless. On the other hand, we as a people must respond swiftly to a vicious enemy that would kill us, kill our children, stop our children's children from coming into the world. To do this, we must be united. I propose we raise an army, just as Din has suggested. Further, Din's punishment for breaking his exile is death: and this punishment must be carried out.'

Murmurs of agreement could be heard. There was little sign of dissent, such was Maragin's moral authority on the issue.

'However, to maintain unity I propose a solution. Din will lead us south to Kalinth, and serve the Krykkers one last time. His punishment of death will be postponed until he has done this.'

Rabigar looked around the assembly. Everywhere, from chieftains to followers, from one clan to the next, the Krykkers nodded in agreement. Hakonin raised his sword in the air.

'War!' he cried.

Guremar and Torinac raised their swords. Maragin, still in the centre of the arena, did the same. The other chieftains followed suit. The warriors of every clan raised their weapons.

'War!' they cried.

Rabigar breathed a sigh of relief. He had achieved his purpose in returning home. And, for a while at least, he had kept his life.

XIV

A CLOTH OF GOLD

THERE WERE STRONG WINDS ON THE steppe, hurrying the clouds across the sky, but the sun still shone down. Edgar's army, four thousand strong, and made up equally of men from South and North Magnia, was making good progress; but there was no shade to be found. The soil underfoot was bone dry, and the long grass was being blown about by the wind. It had been a couple of days since they had passed a stream safe enough to drink from, and the soldiers had been given strict orders to conserve the water in their skins.

The Middian Steppes were good land for husbandry. The tribes who lived here were used to roaming the landscape with their animals, mainly cattle and sheep, locating good pasture before moving on to a fresh area when the land had been used up. The tribes had lived this way for hundreds of years, and the presence of their big herds prevented trees and bushes from growing in most places. Edgar could look in every direction and see grassland for miles and miles.

The nomadic lifestyle of the Middians meant that they were in the saddle all day, and they were known for being amongst the best horsemen in Dalriya. It also meant that they were not rich, with far fewer towns than in Magnia, and no great cities such as they had in Brasingia or Persala. This combination meant that they were often recruited as mercenaries by merchants or warlords. On this occasion, the men of Frayne's tribe had been recruited by the kingdom of Cordence, and would join with the Magnians under Edgar's command. The rendezvous was supposed to be happening today, but so far there had been no sign of them.

'Where are we?' asked Edgar irritably.

Wilchard, Edgar's chief steward, made a sighing sound, and pulled out a piece of parchment from a leather bag he carried around his shoulder. As he continued to ride, he laid the parchment down on his mount's withers, and began to study his map of the area. The wind frustrated his efforts, flapping at the edges of the parchment. He persevered a bit longer, squinting his eyes at the lines and spidery writing which denoted the internal and external borders of the Steppe. He looked about him in a vain search for landmarks that might help his task, before turning back to Edgar.

'I don't know where we are,' he said, equally irritated.

Edgar kept his face straight as he watched Wilchard fold up the parchment and put it back in his bag. It was about a week ago, in a treaty signed at Wincandon in North Magnia, that Edgar had volunteered to lead a Southern army to Brasingia in support of Emperor Baldwin. Initially, he had decided to leave Wilchard behind in South Magnia to act as his regent, since he was Edgar's most trusted and most able adviser. However, once the preparations for the army got under way, he changed his mind. The logistical complexities of raising an army, and keeping it fed and properly equipped, were a full-time job, and he needed Wilchard with him. The maintenance of this army had to be Edgar's priority.

He turned to his left, where his chancellor, the wizard Ealdnoth, rode to one side of them, seemingly oblivious to the conversation. Edgar had noticed that it was a trait of wizards to spend a lot of time in their own private world. His cousin, Soren, was just the same. His thoughts turned to Soren and Belwynn who had retrieved Toric's Dagger from the Empire; only to head north into the lands of the Blood Caladri and disappear. Another situation he had no control over. He had to focus on the here and now.

'Ealdnoth?'

'Yes, Your Highness?'

'We've just been wondering where we are?'

Ealdnoth frowned and looked around, as if such a troublesome question had never occurred to him before.

'Well, I would think we hardly have to worry about finding the Middians, Your Highness. Surely they will find us?'

It was not an entirely satisfactory answer, and yet was sufficient to end the conversation.

In the end, Ealdnoth was proved to be correct. It was two hours later when a small group of riders could be seen heading towards them, coming from the northwest. As they approached, Edgar could see that it was a group of six men. They wore leather boots, and wraps around their waists, and little else. They were bare-chested, with the dark-skinned bodies and the long hair of the Middians, pulled back and tied behind them. Most carried spears. They came

141

at quite a pace, and pulled up when they reached the front of the army. Frayne was not amongst them, but Edgar nudged his horse forwards, expecting there to be a message or discussion.

Instead one of the men raised his spear.

'Follow!' he shouted, before turning his horse around with one hand on the reins and kicking it forwards.

Edgar looked back and forth amongst his advisers.

'I guess we follow them,' he said, slightly bemused, and no one disagreed.

Two of the riders headed back in the direction they had come at some pace. The other four continued at a slower pace, but still too fast for Edgar's army to keep up with, which had to travel at the speed of the carts which carried their supplies. Their carts were pulled by big strong horses, but they had heavy loads and had been walking all day. Their four guides turned around and rode back to the front of the Magnian forces, muttering and shaking their heads, before riding on at the same pace. This happened several times, on each occasion the Middians seemingly incapable of adjusting to the speed of Edgar's army.

Eventually, the Magnians were led to the site where Frayne's forces had made camp. Dotted around were the tents of the Middians, conical shaped and covered with animal skins. Soldiers lounged around in the grass and the smell of cooking meat made Edgar feel suddenly hungry. He was satisfied that the size of the Middian army looked equal to Edgar's force of Magnians, which had been the original agreement made in Wincandon. To the south side of the camp, Edgar could see and hear a vast number of sheep and cattle which had been paddocked, giving it the feel of an outdoor market as much as a military camp.

One of the Middians had moved over to Edgar.

'Frayne!' he stated, jutting his spear in the direction of a large tent close by.

Edgar dismounted. Wilchard ordered the officers of the army to make camp, leaving an appropriate space between the Magnians and Middians to reduce the chances of conflict between the two groups. Together with Ealdnoth and Edgar's ever-present bodyguards, Leofwin and Brictwin, they walked over towards the tent to meet with Frayne, the chieftain. As they approached, Frayne saw them coming—he bounded out to greet Edgar, giving him a great hug.

'You remember Ealdnoth, Wilchard—' Edgar began.

'Of course, of course,' said Frayne, patting them all on the shoulder and gesturing that they should enter the tent. He clapped his hands and two girls ran off. Edgar hoped that they would be bringing food.

Two men stood up to greet Edgar as he entered the tent. Lord Emmett was a Thessian nobleman, representing Duke Coen. Lord Rosmont performed the same role for King Glanna of Cordence. Both men had signed the Treaty of Wincandon on behalf of their leaders, and had now been sent to accompany the army.

Edgar took a seat on the floor where cushions had been laid out. The other men did the same. There was not much room, so Leofwin and Brictwin remained outside the tent, keeping watch.

'So, how have things gone since we last met?' asked Edgar, primarily addressing Emmett, since he had been back to the Empire.

'Things are more serious,' began Emmett, and the grim faces of Rosmont and Frayne confirmed it.

'Emeric has become more aggressive: our local forces on the border have fought several skirmishes. The Barissians have been coming off better. Emeric has committed more troops than Coen, and he's taken several of our castles. Duke Coen has been waiting for you to arrive before pushing his main army north. But the Barissians are getting bolder, and look likely to invade in force any day now.

'Duke Coen asks that we change our earlier meeting point of Lindhafen. Instead, he requests that you head north-east, and he will rendezvous with his army. Our joint forces will then be able to intercept Emeric's army before it does further damage.'

Edgar shared a glance with Wilchard and Ealdnoth. Emmett made it sound like they would be in battle any day now.

'How long do you think it will take us to reach the new rendezvous point?' asked Wilchard.

'Two days,' said Frayne.

Emmett nodded in agreement.

Two days. Edgar felt his stomach tighten with anxiety. He let out a deep breath. He could be leading his troops into battle in two days' time.

The serving girls returned to the tent, carrying dishes of spiced lamb. Edgar looked at the food. His appetite had disappeared.

***

Arioc was in a talkative mood this night. Some nights he would return to his chambers in a foul mood and he would use Moneva's body, barely talking to her, before falling asleep. Those nights she feared for her life all over again. Other nights he was all charm and smiles, taking an interest in her, holding her close in the night.

'What is Erkindrix like?' began Moneva, feeling her way into the conversation. Pentas had asked her to use her position to influence Arioc. She knew she had to try.

Arioc was lying next to her on the bed, leaning back on his elbows. He laughed; it was a short, humourless sound. 'I'll have to introduce you to him. It's an experience, believe me.'

'Well?'

Arioc considered it. 'The closest thing you can get to raw power. It both attracts and repels you at the same time...it's hard to explain.'

Moneva studied Arioc carefully. He seemed partly in awe of his leader, partly greedy for that kind of power himself.

'How old is he?'

'He's ancient. Centuries old. The magic has kept him alive.'

'That's not natural.'

Arioc smiled. 'It's not natural. Not natural at all. But then I can't complain about my father living a long life, can I?'

'Your father?' asked Moneva, genuinely shocked.

'So they say. No-one knows for sure. You've never heard the rumour?'

Moneva shook her head. 'Why don't you know? Has he never spoken to you about it?'

'No. There is no reason to. I doubt whether he would remember.'

'But—he's never been a father to you?'

'Ah, well now you are learning about the differences between Isharites and humans, Moneva. Your father cared for you as a child but that's not how we do things. I have several sons but I don't owe them anything. I've brought them into the world; that is enough.'

'Your mother?'

Arioc gave Moneva a strange look.

'Do you know why I only have sons, Moneva?'

Moneva shook her head again.

'It still amazes me how little your people know about us. In Ishari we have a saying, 'know your enemy'. But you humans like to forget we exist. If you close your eyes for long enough, we will disappear. Like a bad dream.'

Moneva felt troubled by the conversation. There was some truth on the edge of her understanding.

'You don't have...' she began, uncertainly. 'There are no women, are there?'

'You've got it,' said Arioc, condescension clear in his voice. 'Isharites are aliens here, in Dalriya. We should not be here. In your own words: it is not natural. One side effect of this is that when the first Isharites arrived in Dalriya, our women conceived no girls, only boys. Our womenfolk died out a long time ago. So, we now breed with humans like you. Human women make our babies, but still, they don't conceive girls, only more boys.

'My mother was a human slave. Erkindrix could have been the father. People gossip about it, but it doesn't matter. He is one of the last of the pure blood Isharites. The rest of us are half-castes, or worse. That is one of the reasons he has been kept alive for so long.'

'But even he must die sometime?'

Arioc shrugged. 'Yes—he is half dead now.'

'So what happens when he dies? Who will be the leader then? You?'

Arioc's dry laugh returned. 'It should be me—don't you think? I'm the son. That's how it works in your kingdoms, isn't it?'

'But not in Ishari?'

'In Ishari the next person to sit on the throne will be the one who takes it.'

'So, who will take it?'

It was Arioc's turn to look troubled by the conversation now.

'Erkindrix will not die. He is too powerful.'

Arioc rolled on to his side away from Moneva. She felt a sense of relief. Moneva knew that Pentas would want her to try to pursue the subject. But she had learned more than enough for one night.

**

Belwynn and Theron sat contentedly outside his tent, sharing a quiet moment after breakfast.

On previous mornings, they would be packing up by now, orders passed around to make ready to march. But today, Sebastian and Theron had agreed to wait awhile. They were in striking distance of the capital of Kalinth, Heractus—and they were sure that King Jonas and his court were still there. What they weren't so sure of was the kind of response they were going to get.

Sebastian's army had swollen to about five thousand fighting men, half of whom were fully trained knights. The rest were squires, men-at-arms, armed labourers and the like.

'Will they know we are here?' asked Belwynn.

'Yes. Jonas will know about Sebastian replacing Galenos, and he'll have been told by his scouts exactly where we are.'

'What do you think he'll do?'

'Well,' answered Theron, 'if I were king and the Grand Master of the Knights led a rebellion against me, I would fight. But then I would also have fought if Ishari had threatened my kingdom. So who knows what a coward like Jonas will do?'

'A rebellion? Is that what this is?'

Theron shrugged. 'That depends on your point of view. We can sweeten the words we use, and we will when we speak to him. But essentially, we are trying to take over his government and give it to Sebastian. I don't think we're rebels—I think we're trying to free our country.'

Tycho strolled over towards them, winding his way around the tents and campfires, which were crammed together on the large expanse of moorland.

'Morning,' he called.

Theron and Belwynn got to their feet. Theron and Tycho hugged each other.

'My lady,' Tycho addressed Belwynn.

'Lord Tycho,' she greeted him.

'Sebastian wants to see you. Seems like a royal army has left Heractus and is heading our way.'

'How big?'

'The scout's in with Sebastian. He'll tell you what he's seen.'

Belwynn turned to return to the tent she shared with Elana and Dirk.

'Come,' said Theron.

She followed the two knights, who strode the short distance to their leader's tent. Sebastian hurried all three of them inside, eager to get on with it.

146

There was no-one else inside except for the scout, a young knight who stood nervously in the far corner of the tent. Belwynn recognised him as Philon, the young, sandy haired knight who had asked for her blessing a few days before. With all eyes on him, the young man went a little red.

'Right,' began Sebastian, looking at Philon. 'Take us through what you have seen.'

'We were keeping a lookout on a ridge that overlooks the city. We had seen two different groups of soldiers already this morning. Both seemed like scouts for the king. Then the gates of the city opened, and a royal army passed through them. We waited until we thought the whole army was through the gates, then I set off to report it. The others are still there and will send a message with more news when it is clear where the army is headed.'

'How many?' asked Theron.

'We reckoned about the same size as ours, five thousand. Mostly foot soldiers, but some horsemen.'

'Well I say we get going and head straight for them. That gives us the most options,' suggested Theron.

Sebastian was frowning. 'Why send out a force that seems to be inferior to ours? They could have just stayed in the city.'

'Could be a trap?' suggested Tycho.

'Could be,' said Theron, but he didn't sound convinced. 'Could just be a poor decision. They can't have gathered many more than five thousand in the time we've given them. Once we get a bit closer, we can decide what to do. I'd like to go ahead now with Philon, and take a look for myself.'

'I'll come with you,' offered Tycho.

The three knights made a quick exit from the tent.

'Excuse me, Belwynn,' said Sebastian. 'I'll have to get this army moving.'

Sebastian left the tent and Belwynn could hear him barking out orders. The new Grand Master was getting ready for battle.

It took over an hour before the army was ready to go. Horses' hooves were checked and rechecked; the giant warhorses bred by the knights were the crucial component of their army, and gave them a clear advantage over the king's forces. Weapons were sharpened; squires helped knights into their mail armour, tightening and adjusting straps until everything was perfect. Once they were on the move, battle might come at any time, and they needed to be ready.

In contrast, it had taken Belwynn, Elana and Dirk only a few minutes to get ready. They were used, now, to packing up their possessions into a sack and moving on. At last, the army got going. It was organised into several fighting units, each one made up of knights, squires, and usually some men-at-arms or other infantry. All combatants travelled on horseback. Belwynn and the others travelled with the baggage towards the back of the army, along with any other hangers on who were not preparing to fight. Evander had offered to accompany them, but Belwynn knew that he belonged with Theron, so she declined.

They headed in an easterly direction. After an hour, Theron came trotting down the line to find her.

'The army's heading in our direction. Philon was right, they've got about the same numbers as us.'

'But are they as good fighters?'

'Few of them are as well trained or equipped as a Knight of Kalinth. But some of them will be from noble households and will be our equals. Of course, we have a lot of untrained fighters with us as well as knights; but then I suspect that will be the same for them as well.'

'What's the plan?'

'I've told Sebastian I think we should keep going as fast as possible. We're all mounted, and it's not far. The terrain around the city is flat. If we catch them quickly they will not have time to find a defensive position that could cause our horses problems.'

'They'll have less time to retreat back to the city too?'

'Yes, exactly. We need to capitalise on this. I think it's an opportunity for a quick victory over Jonas. That's what we need. Not a civil war.'

Theron was excited and speaking fast. His nervous energy was contagious. But Belwynn also noted how focused he was on his objectives. It reminded her more of her brother, Soren, than most of the soldiers she had met before. Men like Clarin, who in her experience was typical, tended to be easy going, almost childlike in their approach. Theron was different—more of a general than a soldier.

Theron returned to the front of the army and the pace picked up noticeably for the rest of the morning. The baggage train fell behind, unable to keep up with the mounted soldiers.

Approaching midday, they caught up with the soldiers. Word passed down that the enemy was in sight.

Belwynn pulled to the side of the column and looked ahead, but she couldn't see the royal army from her position. She shared the nervous anticipation of everyone else as they waited. Then, more orders came. The soldiers were being lined up in formation. From being a long column on the march, Belwynn watched as the army slowly transformed itself into battle formation. They faced the enemy in a semi-circular or arc shape, the cavalry on each end of the formation pushed furthest forwards, as if they were the pincers of a crab ready to snap.

The baggage train, made up of horse drawn carriages that carried the supplies, was positioned behind the army. Belwynn, Elana and Dirk were asked to carry water bottles over to the soldiers. Belwynn took hers to a group of mounted knights on the left wing of the army.

'Thank you, my lady,' the first knight said graciously, taking a glug of water, and then passing it on to a comrade. Belwynn still found it rather strange that she had become so well known—most of these knights had been in the Great Hall of the High Tower on the night when she had sung of Stephen and the Green Dragon.

'Can you see the enemy?' she asked.

'Over there, my lady,' said one of the knights, pointing eastwards in the direction they were facing. 'If your eyesight is good you can make them out.'

Belwynn looked in the direction indicated. Seeing nothing, she moved forward a few feet. She was nearly ready to give up when she finally saw a smudge on the horizon. It was moving slightly and she realised it was a long row of infantry assembling. To each side, she could see smaller groups of soldiers—presumably cavalry forces positioned on the wings. It was the first time she had been on a battlefield, and it held a grim fascination. So much so, that she didn't realise her name was being called until Theron was nearly on top of her.

'Lady Belwynn!' he shouted again, sounding exasperated.

He pulled up his mount. Behind him came Evander, also mounted, who was leading a spare mount.

'What are you doing here?' he asked. 'I've been looking for you everywhere. I thought you would be with the baggage.'

'I was, but they asked us to give out water.'

'Who did?' demanded Theron, sounding angry.

'Oh, Theron! No one in particular. What is it?'

'Sorry. I just got worried,' he said, dismounting. 'We're going to try to talk to the leaders of the royal army under a truce flag. I would like you to come with us.'

'Me?' asked Belwynn. 'What good will I be? You don't want me to sing again, do you?'

Theron forced a smile out. 'Well, that would be lovely, but no.'

He helped Belwynn into the saddle of the spare horse. Evander then had to clamber off his horse, and help Theron get back up, because of the weight of mail the knight was wearing. Belwynn shook her head in disbelief, wondering what the rest of the army made of the spectacle; they were surely all staring at them by now.

'You've become very popular with the knights, Belwynn,' said Theron. 'We need that because, after all, we're asking them to fight against the king they've sworn oaths to defend. You can help to persuade them that they're doing the right thing. Evander, do you have it?'

'Yes, my lord,' answered the young man brightly. From his saddlebag, he drew out a lavish cloth of gold. Theron took it from him before presenting it to Belwynn.

Taking it, she could see that it was a robe made of silk, with the yarn wrapped in strips of gold. It was a magnificent piece of clothing.

'You can't be serious? You want me to wear this? Now?'

'It's one of the most precious items belonging to the Order. I know you think it's ridiculous and in one sense you're right. But it would mean a lot to the men to see you wear it. Things like this matter when you're about to go into battle.'

'Well, I can hardly say 'no' to that, can I?'

Belwynn put her arms into the robe. The right side of the robe was wider than the other and Theron and Evander helped her to wrap it around her chest, pulling it tight before tying it up at the back. A cheer could be heard on the battlefield. Theron looked her up and down, a big smile appearing on his face.

'You look amazing,' said Evander, going a little red but grinning nonetheless.

'Come on then,' said Theron. 'Let's try to talk some sense into these people.'

150

Theron trotted forwards and Belwynn and Evander followed on. Waiting for them was Sebastian and his squire, Alpin, who held a white flag of truce on a long pole. Sebastian stared at Belwynn for a moment, then nodded, but said nothing.

'Are you ready, uncle?' asked Theron.

'Yes. Let's just hope they've got someone sensible in charge.'

'Will Jonas not be there?' Belwynn asked.

'Very doubtful,' said Theron, 'but not impossible.'

Sebastian led them on. As they got closer, Belwynn could make out the royal forces ranged against them more clearly.

'Who are they?' she asked Theron, indicating a group wearing red cloaks who had been positioned near the centre of the infantry line.

'They're the city guard of Heractus, used to defend the walls and the castle. They're reasonably well equipped, but not trained for pitched battles. Most of the rest of them are individual noblemen and their retinues. A bit like us, they'll be a mix of soldiers and extra men pressed into service. The best fighters will probably be mounted.'

'To counter your cavalry?'

'Yes, but they simply don't have the numbers for it. We *are* the cavalry of Kalinth, after all.'

Sebastian raised his arm and they stopped, approximately half way between the two armies. Then they waited. It was a bit unnerving for Belwynn, but she supposed that if the enemy ignored the flag of truce and tried to attack, they should be able to turn around and ride back to their own lines without fear of being caught.

'There,' said Evander, pointing.

A small group of riders could be seen making their way towards them. As they got closer Belwynn could count four in all.

'Can you see who's there?' asked Sebastian.

'Not quite,' answered Theron, waiting. 'I think that's—yes, it's Diodorus. Count of Korenandi. Looks like he's in charge. He's not an idiot.'

'It could have been a lot worse,' agreed Sebastian.

The four riders continued to approach before one of them raised a hand, indicating that the other three should wait where they were. It was a gesture which emphasised his authority and lack of fear in approaching the knights alone. He moved his horse on a few paces before stopping in front of them.

'Diodorus,' acknowledged Sebastian.

'Sebastian. Theron.'

Diodorus looked at Belwynn and appeared to be about to say something, but then seemed to think better of it. He was a big man, with huge shoulders, a thick neck and a large head. His hair was shaved short and Belwynn thought he had something of a sad, or at least world weary, expression.

'I presume King Jonas has made you general of this army?' asked Sebastian.

'That's right. And I understand that you have taken control of the Order of the Knights of Kalinth. But what is your army doing here?'

'The Order has come to restore strength to our country. Kalinth must stand up to Ishari. I am here to make sure it does.'

'By starting a war with your king?'

'Come on, Diodorus,' interjected Theron. 'We could go on like this all day, but it isn't the time or place. We've come to speak to you to avoid bloodshed.'

Diodorus shrugged. 'I'm listening.'

'You must have had an idea about what you were trying to achieve with this force of yours—but you've ended up in the open, facing our army which has a cavalry force far superior to yours, and is capable of inflicting heavy losses. You must also know that it was never our intention to spill Kalinthian blood.'

Diodorus turned behind him to look at the other three riders before turning back. When he spoke again it was in a low, quiet voice.

'Jonas ordered me to go and destroy your army. Of course, we tried to reason with him, but he got hysterical, wouldn't listen. Started throwing wild accusations at everyone. So, I obeyed his orders. But I'm not stupid, Theron. I know I'm in a heavily compromised position. And I would be happy to avoid a battle if possible.'

'If possible?' repeated Sebastian.

'I've been asked to defend my king. If I don't fight you, what will you do with him?'

'I swear a knight's oath,' began Sebastian, 'that if you surrender now, no-one in your army will be harmed, no-one in Heractus will be harmed, I will not harm Jonas, and he will remain king. What I *will* do is wrest control over the government of his kingdom, and restore some direction and dignity to it. I admire your loyalty to your king, Diodorus. Believe me—I have tried my best to be loyal to him too. But that must be weighed against loyalty to Kalinth and its people.'

'Alright, Sebastian,' Diodorus said quietly. 'I regard you as an honourable man. I will take your word.'

'However,' added Theron, 'if you do surrender you must ensure that everyone in your army disperses immediately, that none of them will be allowed to return to the city, and if any try to return, our offer of protection will be withdrawn and they will be killed.'

Diodorus seemed taken aback at first, but then nodded. His gaze turned to Belwynn again, a puzzled look, as if he wondered who she was and what she was doing here. She looked away, embarrassed by her presence and her golden robe.

'There's one more thing,' said Diodorus. 'If I surrender you must also make an oath to protect me. Many men will call me traitor, and want me dead after today.'

'I offer you my protection,' confirmed Sebastian.

'Then it is agreed,' said Diodorus. 'I will order my army to disperse.'

He turned his horse around and began to return to his three companions.

'But don't disappear,' called Theron. 'We'll need your help to get into the city.'

Diodorus looked back, a pained expression on his face.

'Very well,' he said finally.

'No battle after all,' commented Sebastian as they began to make their way back to their own lines. 'So far, so good.'

Belwynn turned around to look at the retreating figure of Count Diodorus, and wondered how many lives the melancholy looking man had saved today.

XV

IN THE PRESENCE OF ROYALTY

THE MEN OF KELLAND MANNED the Emperor's Keep for another day.

From its walls, Farred watched the Drobax climb the steep sides of the crag—tiny figures inching their way up to meet the spears of Baldwin's men. On the other crag, he could see the Mace flying, as the men of Gotbeck took their turn to defend the path up to the Duke's Keep.

Prince Ashere's death lay heavy on him. They had buried him yesterday, deep inside the bowels of the Emperor's Crag, where dark caverns seemed to stretch on interminably. Walter had stored all sorts down there—barrels of drink and food, even horses, that had somehow been winched down. It seemed to Farred a desolate sort of resting place, and he feared that Ashere's soul might be unhappy. But at least the prince was far from the monsters who were tormenting the living.

Despite the fighting going on around him, Farred couldn't shake off a strange feeling of disinterest. Maybe, he wondered, this is what all of us will be like by the end. Maybe when they finish us off, we won't care very much anymore.

'Farred!' a voice interrupted his thoughts, and he was glad of it.

'Thought I'd find you up here,' said Walter.

They clasped hands. Walter looked at Farred for a while, perhaps judging whether further words on the Prince were required, and instead slapped Farred on the shoulder.

'We've found something very interesting up in the keep, Farred. And I know you'll want to be one of the first to see it.'

Walter had the face of a child torn between blurting out some exciting news and keeping it to themselves.

'Well, I'm in suspense already. Lead on, Lord Walter.'

Walter led Farred to the top floor of the Emperor's Keep, and into the corridor off which Baldwin, Walter, and the other key members of the imperial entourage had their rooms.

'Notice anything...unusual?' asked Walter, that childish expression still on his face.

Farred had a look. There was nothing in the corridor to see. Castle corridors were dark by nature, but this one had plenty of wall sconces on each side, with torches throwing up light. There. Towards the far end of the corridor, shadows flickered off an irregular shape. He looked over at Walter. Walter made a 'what could that be?' facial expression.

Farred walked over to investigate. At first, he didn't quite believe what his eyes were telling him. Poking out of the wall was half a forearm, a wrist, and a hand flopping downwards at the end. Farred gave it a long hard look. He gave it a touch. It was a human hand. A man's hand. He turned around to Walter with a quizzical expression.

'Quite,' came the reply. 'How does one respond to that? I decided to tour the keep, checking the walls, floors, ceilings. I won't drag you down there to see, but in the granary, behind a sack of flour, one of my men found the edge of a shoe. I cut into it and sure enough, there was an inch of someone's foot poking out.'

'So—you think it's Ishari?'

'Who else? Haskan soldiers. Their sorcerers beamed them up here, presumably in the night. Almost certainly more than these two, who knows where the others ended up? Mid-air, presumably, some of them. And there's more.'

Walter reached under his cloak and retrieved a dagger.

'This is what our friend here was holding when he got beamed up. It was on the floor. That's what I saw first, actually.'

'Assassins, then.'

'Yes. Sent to kill my brother.'

Farred nodded. All things considered, it wasn't so much of a surprise.

'You've told Gustav?' he asked, thinking it was something a wizard could perhaps protect against.

'Yes. He knows. He says he's working on a response, and Inge has been added to Baldwin's bodyguard.'

'Can I do anything?'

Walter smiled. He clearly hadn't confided in him just for the sake of it.

'Oh, I see.'

The Marshal put his hands up.

'It's not a big deal, Farred, really. Baldwin's pretty set on not ordering your men into battle for the foreseeable future.'

Farred nodded. He wasn't about to disagree with the Emperor—the Magnians and Middians had given a lot already.

'But I haven't got many spare men to reassign. If you could give me some trusted men to stand guard at certain points around the keep? It would need to be day and night, in shifts. I'm thinking thirty at a time, eight hours on?'

'That's not a problem, I'll get them for you. Starting tonight?'

'If you can do it.'

'We can do it. Anything else?'

Walter hesitated. Farred raised an eyebrow.

'Something else just for you, Farred. But completely optional. I am led to believe that, in Magnia, people are often...less bothered by sorcerers than they are in our country?'

Walter seemed surprisingly uncomfortable with this topic.

'In Brasingia,' he continued, 'there is a great deal of animosity. Especially from the Church. Baldwin can get away with having them: he's the Emperor. But that's the exception.'

'Well, I suppose it's more accepted in Magnia. My prince, Edgar, has a wizard. His relative is a wizard too.'

'What about you, Farred?'

Farred thought about it. 'I don't know much about it. I guess I'm not particularly bothered.'

'The reason I ask. Inge is with Baldwin now, and no longer assisting Gustav. But the Archmage needs some help. I don't know what it involves. Frankly, I don't want to. You're trustworthy, discrete; not too involved elsewhere. If you can do it, it would be a big help. If not, that's fine too.'

'I'll think about it, Walter. How about that?'

'That's as much as I hoped for.'

***

The Isharite jailers ushered them over to the pits. Another day in the mines, another man hanged at the end of it, and now another night spent underground.

Gyrmund took in his last breaths of fresh air. He gulped it in, as if that would help him last until morning. He felt the now familiar sense of panic as they approached the pits. His breathing grew more rapid, his heart beat fast, his palms began to sweat. His feet stopped, refusing to get any closer.

He felt a hand grasp him tightly round the arm. He turned his head around. It was Clarin. The big man held him in an iron grip and, without words, forced him towards the edge of the pit, then forced him down into it.

'There,' said the warrior, 'you did it.'

Gyrmund nodded.

But he knew that one day soon Clarin wouldn't be able to get him down here.

He moved over to the far wall and stood for a while, letting his eyes adjust to the darkness, hoping that his nose might adjust to the fetid smell.

He began to pick out the other figures in the pit. He noticed Cyprian, the small Persaleian he had befriended, signalling him over. He was standing with some other prisoners, and as Gyrmund approached them, Cyprian gathered him into a small huddle of half a dozen men.

'Gyrmund, meet Zared,' he said quietly, indicating the youngest member of the group. He was strong looking, wearing what once must have been fine clothes. He was already starting to lose his hair on the top, but still had boyish looking facial features.

Zared offered his hand and Gyrmund took it.

'I wanted to meet,' said Zared, his voice confident but tired sounding. 'Cyprian has told me that you plan to escape. I speak for the Persaleians in here. We are ready to support you when the time is right.'

'Thank you,' said Gyrmund. 'I will pass that on to my two friends.'

'There are others, too,' continued Zared. 'This is Tamir.'

Before he knew it Gyrmund was shaking hands with the tallest and oldest man in the group, who had an iron strong grip.

'I am a chieftain,' said Tamir, with a strong eastern accent. 'My people, whom you know as Barbarians, have suffered more than anyone from the Isharites and have been in this hell for the longest time. I can speak for them. We too are ready to give our lives.'

Gyrmund nodded his appreciation.

'Rudy.'

'I'm Jurgen.'

The last two men introduced themselves, with Brasingian accents. They looked similar, both slight of build and smaller than average height.

'We're cousins, from Rotelegen. Both of us were at the battle in Grienna where our army was butchered,' Rudy explained. 'We were among the few to survive, and they brought us back here. We haven't been here much longer than yourself. We've still got enough energy to fight.'

'I can't stand it no more,' added Jurgen. 'I'll do anything you ask.'

'I met Duke Ellard, briefly,' replied Gyrmund, remembering the journey they had taken with the Duke and his men, north from Essenberg. Messengers from Rotelegen had found them and informed Ellard that the Haskan army had arrived on his northern border. He had rushed ahead to meet the threat. 'I'm sorry to hear about what happened to your people.'

Rudy gave him a piercing look. 'We'd like a chance for revenge.'

'Do you have a plan?' asked Zared.

'Not a complete one,' Gyrmund answered uncomfortably, mindful of the needy stares of the other men. 'We need to get rid of Vamak first,' he said, looking around for the Dog-men, but they were in their usual place at the far end of the pit. 'Then we will be free to organise as many of us as we can. Then we get over the fence outside. But after that—'

'After that there's the biggest fortress in Dalriya, full of Isharite soldiers and magi, in the middle of nowhere,' Zared finished for him.

They were in a desperate position, it was true. But what did these men want him to say?

'Will your friends be able to get us out?' asked Jurgen hopefully.

Gyrmund looked over to Herin and Clarin, stood not far away from the Dog-men, talking quietly together. There was something about them, a sense of confidence they exuded in the middle of this horror, that these men looked to. Just like Gyrmund, they were desperate and needed hope. He understood what they wanted from him.

'Yes, give them a few more days,' he said, doing his best to look and sound confident. 'Hold on a bit longer. Then we're getting out of here.'

Gyrmund made his farewells and shuffled over to stand next to Clarin. He hoped that he had done enough to keep up the spirits of the other men in the pit. They would need their support if they were going to make a successful escape bid.

Exhausted, Gyrmund dropped down to sit on the floor, his back resting against the wall behind him. He felt like offering hope to the other men in the pit had somehow drained it from him. He put his head in his hands. He experienced a sudden certainty that they weren't going to escape from this alive. None of them—not even Moneva, wherever she was. If she wasn't dead already. From out of nowhere, he felt the urge to cry. He hadn't cried since he was a kid.

He turned at movement to his right. Clarin had sat down next to him.

'Want to tell me about it?' asked the big man.

'About what?'

Clarin gave a half shrug.

'About whatever is making you suffer in here, and in the mine. You're not the same man you were in the Wilderness. Tell me. It might make you feel better.'

Gyrmund looked Clarin in the eyes. There was an intelligence, an empathy there, that he hadn't seen before. Perhaps he'd just ignored it, assumed that he was all brute strength, no brains. And perhaps Clarin played up to that.

'I've never told anyone before.'

'Then perhaps it's time you did.'

Perhaps so, Gyrmund considered. *And in all honesty, what is there to lose now?*

'It's from my childhood. We got ill. My whole family, my parents and sisters and me. One of the things I found hardest to accept, for a long time, was that my father was the one who brought it into the home. I idolised him when I was a child. He was strong, resourceful—I thought he was invincible. Do you understand that?'

'Yes. My father was a tough man, too. A soldier. He trained me and Herin as fighters from when we were mere lads through to adults. Every lesson I had worth learning was down to him. Ain't that right, Herin?'

'Yes, that's right. If I've done anything well in this life, it's down to him.'

So, Herin has elected to stay standing, but he is listening in too. So be it.

'No-one knew where he got it from. He was a huntsman, so perhaps he picked it up from the forest—a poisonous plant, or diseased animal of some kind. He came home and fell sick. In a few hours we all had it. His landlord—his friend—decided it best to quarantine us, to stop the disease from spreading. We had to stay in our tiny little house, with no fresh air or sunlight, and they posted food and water under our door.

'We lay there, too ill to move, for days. Dying. My mother and sisters passed away. Then my father died. I had thought he would last the longest, but it was me who was left alone at the end. Then, I started to get better. For some reason, I fought off the illness. They made me stay in there, with my family, 'til they were sure I was better. My father's landlord raised me as part of his family afterwards.

'Since then, I've had a dread of enclosed spaces. Cowardly, I know.'

'Not a bit,' said Clarin quietly. 'Understandable.'

'No,' Gyrmund replied firmly. 'I'm a coward. I was the one who lived, and what have I done with my life? I've been running away from that memory, like a scared child, ever since.'

***

When the army had reached the outskirts of Heractus, Theron went to the gates of the city. With him went Count Diodorus, the general of the king's disbanded army. Evander accompanied them with the white flag of truce. Theron's role at the gates was to speak for Sebastian and the Order—to calm fears about their objectives in taking the city, but also to demand peaceful entry. Diodorus was there to make it plain that there was no longer a royal army, and that no help would be forthcoming.

Belwynn wasn't required to appear in her golden robe on this occasion, for which she was grateful. Sebastian wasn't required either, so they stood around and waited while the army made camp.

She was a bit underwhelmed by the city of Heractus from this distance. There was no extravagance like the Knights' High Tower. No defensive structures that came close to the fortress of Chalios. It didn't seem to be half the size of Essenberg in the Empire. What it did have was a lot of grey. There were grey stone walls defending the city, and she could make out more grey walls inside, presumably the royal castle. The walls looked strong enough, but there was nothing to give the Knights much cause to have doubts, and, she thought, nothing to give those inside the city much hope.

'Do you think they'll open the gates?' Belwynn asked Sebastian, as she waited impatiently for Theron to return. Her fear was that the Kalinthians inside the city would turn on him while he was negotiating.

'It would be best if they did. Jonas won't want to do it, and his eldest son, Straton, is a bit of a hothead. But we must hope that other voices in the city put their foot down. A siege would lead to misery for everyone concerned.'

Eventually they spied Theron and the others returning, at a leisurely pace, which indicated that at least they weren't in any danger. In fact, Belwynn became frustrated at their speed, desperate as she was to hear their news.

When they made it to the camp, Evander had to help Theron from his horse before he was ready to share his news.

'They're opening the gates for us,' he declared with a grin. 'Diodorus played his part in persuading them that was the better option.'

'Thank you both,' said Sebastian.

Diodorus nodded in acknowledgement, but still had the slightly sad expression Belwynn noticed when they had first met him.

'What do you think our approach should be now?' asked Sebastian.

'I still think we need to be careful,' replied Theron. 'Tycho and I will bring some troops in first, I reckon about two thousand. Take some into the castle, find quarters for the rest, and set up a new city guard. When I'm happy the whole place is secure, we'll send for you. The rest of the army will have to stay out here for the night, unless you want them all in. But that would mean turfing people out of their homes.'

'No, that's fine,' said Sebastian. 'We want to get people on our side as soon as possible, not upset them.'

'I'll get started straight away,' said Theron. 'We want to get control before nightfall.'

Theron and Tycho rounded up the units they needed and marched them to the city gates. There was a pause of some minutes before they were slowly opened and the Knights of Kalinth entered Heractus, to the cheers of the men left behind.

Sebastian's tent had been erected for him. Belwynn, Elana and Dirk sat inside with the new Grand Master, while his squire Alpin came and went on errands. Sebastian suddenly seemed very alone, with only the three of them for company. Time crept slowly as they waited for the news that Theron had the city under enough control for him to enter.

'Waiting is hard,' Sebastian commented, perhaps noticing Belwynn's tension. 'But such is war. Endless waiting, interrupted by brief moments of terror. Theron will have the city secured soon,' he said reassuringly.

'How does being a Grand Master suit you?' asked Elana.

Sebastian thought about it. 'Not so well. I'd rather be in Theron's position. Doing something instead of sitting here like a precious relic that needs protection. But that's the way it has to be, so there's no point in moaning about it.'

Indeed, Theron was playing the role of the villain in the capital, using force to exert his authority over Heractus. This allowed Sebastian to be disassociated from any unpleasant measures and, hopefully, to retain his popularity.

'But you're still the one in charge, in control of the situation,' said Belwynn. 'Theron and the knights are only doing what you want them to.'

'True enough,' Sebastian replied, 'to a point. You would think I should feel in control of things. Leader of the Order, in charge of an army. But I don't— not fully. I wonder if that's how Jonas has had it all these years. King of Kalinth, but not even in control of his own country.'

Belwynn thought it was a gloomy reply in the circumstances and she wondered why. Sebastian was perhaps looking ahead to his meeting with Jonas, and the daunting tasks ahead of him now that he had secured power. Standing up to Ishari being first among them. Indeed, she considered, taking power away from Jonas was all very well. But it didn't, by itself, solve the problems that the Kalinthians faced.

Sebastian was studying her.

'Of course, here I am dwelling on my position when your own situation regarding the fate of your brother is far worse. But rest assured, Belwynn. Once we get inside the capital we are another step on the road to rescuing him. And I should take this chance to thank you all. In your own ways, you have strengthened the faith of my supporters. It doesn't feel like chance that our paths crossed at this very moment.'

'Indeed,' agreed Elana, 'it is not.'

The priestess said no more, but everyone understood what she meant.

A rap at the door. Theron.

'Come in,' said Belwynn, seated on her bed in her room in Heractus Castle. Though really, she didn't want him to. She wanted to be left out of this.

Theron slowly entered with an expression grim enough to match her own. They looked at each other for a while.

'This is going to be the worst dinner of my life,' said Belwynn eventually. 'Why are you making *me* go? Elana and Dirk have been allowed to escape from here into the city.'

Theron shrugged, without much sympathy. 'They invited you.'

'But they don't know me!'

'The Lady of the Knights. That's who they asked for. That's what people are calling you now.'

'Ridiculous,' said Belwynn, standing up and smoothing down the white linen tunic that had been put out for her to wear.

Theron, who was wearing a man's version of the tunic, put out his arm and when Belwynn took it, led her out into the castle corridor.

She suddenly wondered who Theron had forced out of the room for her to have it. They were making a lot of enemies in Heractus, and top of the list was the royal family, who had invited them to what was surely going to be an excruciating dinner. It summed up the uneasy situation they were now in. Jonas was still king; but Sebastian had taken over the capital and the government. No-one in Heractus quite knew what was going to happen next.

Theron knocked at Sebastian's door and they waited outside for him to come out. Alpin opened it and Sebastian walked briskly out, before getting straight to business.

'Right. Jonas's queen is Irina,' he began, speaking to Belwynn. 'It is tradition here that she hosts the dinner. The only other guests at the table will be their two sons. Straton is the eldest. He tends to speak before he thinks. The younger, Dorian, is quieter and a bit brighter. Now,' he continued, turning his attention to Theron. 'They are all going to be upset. That is understandable and we shall let them be. Belwynn and I will control ourselves, so you must as well, Theron. Now is not the time to throw our weight around or argue, so save it for another time, even if Straton gets in your face. The fact that they have decided to be civil, and invited us to a meal, is a good sign for the future, so let's not spoil it.'

'I will be cool as ice, uncle. Don't worry.'

With a sinking feeling in her stomach, Belwynn let them lead her down to the king's hall. A small table on the dais was being laid by servants, while at the fire stood the royal family, just as Sebastian had described them.

Jonas had long, iron grey hair that matched the colour of his capital city. He had a strong looking physique, but nonetheless looked like a man past his best years, his skin pallid looking and wrinkled. His wife, too, had gone grey, and to Belwynn the pair of them looked like someone's grandparents rather than a king and queen. Straton, a big looking ox of a man, looked kinglier, with brown, shaggy hair on his head and his face. Dorian was slimmer and clean-shaven.

As they approached, the family turned to look at them, a mix of emotions playing on their faces. Jonas himself looked at them impassively enough, but his wife Irina didn't disguise her hatred. Straton's face flushed red with anger.

'Sebastian,' said the king, 'welcome, it's been too long.'

The two men crossed the distance between them and embraced.

'Your Majesty,' responded Sebastian.

He turned to Irina, who gave him a filthy look. But, after a glare from her husband, she held out her hand and allowed Sebastian to kiss it. Sebastian moved on to speak to the two princes, while Theron led Belwynn over.

'Count Theron,' Jonas got out through gritted teeth, his dislike overcoming his manners.

'Your Majesty,' replied Theron neutrally.

The king turned to Belwynn.

'This is the Lady Belwynn, Your Majesty,' introduced Theron.

Jonas stared at her until it became uncomfortable. Belwynn looked at Theron, who nodded that she should offer her hand. She did so, but the staring continued.

'Jonas,' whispered his wife.

The king seemed to come out of his reverie and took her hand, briefly putting it to his lips. The skin of his hand and lips felt rough to the touch, and Belwynn was relieved when it was over.

'So,' said Irina, an icy expression on her face, 'you are the one who calls herself the Lady of the Knights?'

'I—no, I don't call myself that,' answered Belwynn, feeling herself blush.

'I see. Your idea, was it, Theron? I should have known. Very clever.'

'No, not me, Your Majesty,' replied Theron smoothly. 'That is the name the people have given her.'

'The people? Ha!' snorted Irina. 'And I hear,' she continued, 'that you have the gift of healing?'

164

'No,' said Belwynn, startled by the question. 'That's not me—'

'I see. What *have* you done to earn this name then, I wonder?'

Belwynn didn't know what to say. She saw Sebastian looking at her with concern and knew that she had to keep control.

'Nothing, I'm sure.'

'Oh, not nothing,' persisted Irina, her voice full of sarcasm. 'You sang to the Knights, didn't you?'

Belwynn looked at Theron and Sebastian. This had started just as badly as she thought it was going to.

'Come,' said Jonas, rescuing her. 'Let's dine.'

The group of seven walked over to the dais, Irina smiling at her as if she had won a victory.

Once seated, they were served with vegetable barley soup, a hearty dish that Belwynn enjoyed after what already felt like a long day. She noted that they were all served from the same tureen which reassured her. She didn't know how paranoid she was being, but she wondered if it wouldn't be in the interests of the king to have the three of them poisoned. Then again, it wouldn't have surprised her if Theron had installed his own people in the kitchens. His occupation of the city had been nothing if not thorough.

The king sat with his wife on one side and Sebastian on the other, while opposite them were Belwynn and the three younger men. She felt as if she was a member of a dysfunctional family, with three parents sternly staring over at their unruly offspring.

'What are your plans for the government, Grand Master?' asked Jonas mildly, looking at his spoon as he brought it to his lips. 'I understand you are not happy with current policies.'

To her left Belwynn heard Straton snort, though she couldn't tell if it was with humour or anger. She didn't turn to look, but kept her attention on her soup, waiting for Sebastian to reply.

'Well I thank you for the opportunity to discuss this so soon, Your Majesty,' replied Sebastian. 'I am not sure how familiar you are with recent developments abroad. Ishari has not only invaded the Empire, but conquered the lands of the Grand Caladri.'

Belwynn took a peak at the king. He looked upset enough and nodded along. Whether he already knew about Ishari's aggression or not, she couldn't tell.

'In these circumstances,' continued Sebastian, 'I believe the current policy of...peace,' he cleared his throat, 'while well intentioned...must now change.'

'Ah,' said Jonas, nodding along. 'And a king's duty is to defend his people, am I right Sebastian?'

'Agreed.'

'Then I ask you this,' began the king, his voice getting slightly more animated. 'If the Isharites have destroyed Persala, the Grand Caladri, and the Brasingian Empire, what makes you think that Kalinth can stop them? And if we try and fail, what will happen to my people?'

'It is the duty of Kalinth to fight in such a war,' responded Sebastian. 'Not to stand by and do nothing.'

'Answer my question!' demanded Jonas, his voice suddenly full of aggression. 'What will happen to my people if you fail!'

'You talk as if Kalinth has escaped the war,' interjected Theron, coming to the rescue of his uncle. 'But war has come already. Raids in the east from Haskany, in the west from Kharovia. Your people have suffered murder, seen their property destroyed and stolen, and countless other crimes. And your government did nothing!'

'Not your noble League, though, Theron.' Now it was Straton's turn to get involved, his voice dripping with sarcasm. 'Riding about with your friends, undermining royal policy, so that you can play the hero. You've broken every oath to your Order and betrayed your king, but you're still as self-righteous as you've ever been. This crusade against Ishari is going to drag the whole country to hell!'

'We've been sleepwalking into hell these past years,' said Theron, his voice measured despite Straton's taunts. 'Now it's time to make a stand. The honour of the country demands it.'

'Don't talk to me of honour,' Straton shouted back down the table, the two men wisely positioned at opposite ends. 'Not you.'

'Then join us,' Theron asked, his voice almost pleading. 'You can be the one to rouse the country to defend itself!'

Belwynn looked at Straton, seething with anger. But did his face show some doubt, was he tempted to take up Theron's challenge? She looked over at the king and queen, concern visible on their faces lest their son should join up with the Knights; Sebastian, equally keen that he did.

'What's more,' began Straton, 'I demand the release of Count Ampelios, who is at this moment languishing in the dungeons of this very castle! You have no authority to imprison the man, who has been a faithful servant of the crown for years!'

'I warned him several times that if he tried to impede the Knights' business I would have to arrest him. It was his own foolish actions that got him there.'

The moment had gone. Theron and Straton continued to argue across the table as the servants came to take away the soup bowls and brought in hot steaming pies. Belwynn could smell spiced mutton and pear but couldn't help a small sigh, as her appetite had now disappeared.

'Are you alright, my lady?' Prince Dorian whispered to her while the raised voices to either side continued, his face looking genuinely concerned.

Belwynn looked around the table, but no-one was looking in her direction.

'I was wondering,' she replied, keeping her voice down. 'How many more courses are there likely to be?'

XVI

GUSTAV THE HAWK

D UKE COEN WAS A VIGOROUS MAN, and had set off at quite a pace. Lord Emmett and Frayne followed close behind, while Edgar found himself bringing up the rear, unfamiliar with the Thessian terrain. Prematurely bald, Coen's head glinted in the sunshine, otherwise Edgar would have lost sight of him altogether.

Coen's route began to take them uphill, allowing Edgar to fall in behind Emmett as their mounts slowed down a touch. As they made their way up Herne's Hill, Edgar began to get glimpses of more of the Thessian countryside, stretching out in all directions. Looking behind them, he could see the army camp, where a sea of tents had been erected.

Emmett stopped ahead and dismounted, so Edgar did the same. Coen had already left his horse chewing at a clump of grass, and had begun marching up the final few feet to the top of the rise.

Edgar followed on. It was windy up here, and the breeze cooled him down after the brisk ride.

Coen had asked that just the four of them should come to Herne's Hill alone. He had decided that they were to be the four commanders of the army, and should come and look at the terrain for themselves. Perhaps, also, to bond, since apart from Coen and Emmett, they hardly knew each other.

Coen pointed off in a north-easterly direction as they gathered round. 'The Thessian-Barissian border is mostly a porous one. Walk a mile or so from one village to the next and you've crossed it. The Barissians have been in my territory for a few days now. It's been hard, letting them destroy homes, take castles, kill our people. Hard not to go right after the bastards. But instead we've been harrying, making life difficult, without committing to a fight we'd likely lose. But the numbers you've brought can tip the balance, and I thank you. Sincerely thank you.'

Coen certainly looked sincere as he looked Edgar and then Frayne straight in the eye. The duke paused briefly, the first time Edgar had seen him stop. It suddenly hit Edgar how much this campaign meant to the Thessians. Their lives, and those of their families, hung in the balance.

'You're welcome, of course,' replied Edgar. 'Can we see potential battle sites from here?'

Coen nodded. 'I've got a good idea where the battle will be, though in truth my duchy is as flat as your hand; this hill we're on is as high as it gets.'

The duke pointed off into the distance again.

'Salvinus has been pushing south, trying to draw us into a pitched battle.'

'Salvinus?' Edgar blurted out. 'That's the man who attacked our temple.'

'Well, sounds like your men might have even more reason to fight,' commented Emmett.

Edgar nodded. He would be happy to take some revenge. He remembered them studying each other in the temple complex at Ecgworth, before Salvinus had retreated, with Toric's Dagger in his possession. Brictwin had lurched out and knocked one of his riders off his horse. Ealdnoth and Soren had interrogated the man, and that was how they'd been able to put a name to the face.

'He's Emeric's general,' Coen informed him. 'I assume that Emeric allows him to make most of the military decisions. Either way, I've been forced to give ground and head west, so that we could meet up with your forces. The Barissians have driven further south, cutting off the road to Lindhafen. They're now free to march on my capital. Tactically sound on their part, but of course they didn't know I was getting reinforcements!'

At this, Coen's eyes sparkled a little. 'If we march straight on them now they'll be keen for a battle. Defeat us and they can take Lindhafen quickly, before heading north for Essenberg, which is Emeric's real goal. I can't delay engaging any longer, even if I wanted to. I would lose too much, and my soldiers are fed up of retreating as it is. Are you ready?' he asked pointedly.

'Yes,' replied Edgar, hoping he sounded surer than he felt. 'How do you envisage deploying the forces?'

'Three main divisions,' said Coen. 'Myself in the centre with most of the Thessians, the rest under Emmett on the right. You and the Magnians on the left. The Middians are the best horsemen, so Frayne, I would ask your men to act as the reserve.'

Frayne nodded, his face impassive. 'We will fight wherever we are put.'

It all sounded so simple. Edgar, still unsure of the geography, looked out over Thesse to where he guessed the road to Lindhafen was. Two armies, now roughly equal in numbers, fighting it out in the open.

'How long will it take us to get there?' he asked.

'Two days.'

***

Why do I agree to things? Farred lectured himself as he slowly made his way up the steps to the top room of the tallest tower in the Emperor's Keep. *What am I, a child?* he berated himself, *as if walking slowly will somehow prevent it happening?*

Despite the telling off, he found his legs moved just as slowly as before. In the end, though, they took him to the room of Gustav, Emperor Baldwin's Archmage.

He rapped on the door.

'Enter' came the reply.

Taking a deep breath, Farred swung the door open.

The room was one of the biggest in the keep, but it was less alien than his imagination had led him to believe. No magic potions bubbling away; no body parts kept in jars. A long table dominated the central part of the room, and it was completely bare. A large window let in the fresh air from outside. Gustav stepped forwards and offered his hand which Farred took.

'Farred, I'm much obliged that you've agreed to help me out,' said the wizard, ushering him into the room.

'You're welcome.'

Gustav, Farred had to admit, wasn't much like the wizards from the stories that had been told around the fire back home. He didn't have a large scraggly beard, didn't display unconventional behaviour, didn't have a wild animal of some kind sharing his living quarters. He was business-like, broad shouldered, and healthy looking for a man of older years.

'I'm not going to ask you to do much at all, you'll be relieved to hear,' Gustav began. 'Walter has explained to you about the Isharites teleporting killers into the keep?'

'Yes. He showed me.'

'Mmm. Well, I have agreed that my apprentice, Inge, should stay with the Emperor for the time being, until we can be more relaxed about his safety.

Not that we can ever guarantee it, of course. Baldwin has asked me to respond to the attacks in some way. So, I'm asking you to fill in for her when I need some help. Right. I'm about to turn into a hawk,' the wizard explained.

Farred's jaw dropped open. Had he just heard Gustav correctly?

'I could just do it myself, but to be on the safe side, I need to be restrained while the transformation occurs,' continued Gustav matter-of-factly. 'When I become a bird physically, my mind doesn't change; I can still think perfectly clearly. So, I will just want to be moved over to the window so that I can fly off.'

He opened a box by the window and pulled out three lengths of rope. 'It's best if I lie down on my chest. Tie me to the table, as tight as you can. You'll need to hold me down as well. And take care of my head, I don't want to bash it too much.'

Gustav handed Farred the ropes, undressed himself, and proceeded to climb onto the table.

I take it back, Farred thought to himself. *I'm tying up a grown man—naked, by the way—onto a table.*

Farred looped the rope around the wizard and the table, pulling hard on each before tying them off.

Gustav didn't waste any time. He began muttering to himself, and then his whole body began to shake, seemingly uncontrollably. Farred turned Gustav's head to one side, and with one hand held it down onto the table so that he didn't bang himself. He used his other hand to put weight onto the wizard's back.

Gustav then let out a loud, throaty cry of pain, and Farred could see the change happen right before his eyes.

The wizard's legs sprouted talons where his toes had been. Feathers sprouted all over his body, countless shades of brown, grey and cream, including a tail that reached out beyond his legs. A sharp beak extended out of his face where his nose had been, pushing his eyes out to the sides. All the while this was happening, his body shrunk in size, so that the ropes, which had been tight moments before, loosened until they weren't holding him at all.

Farred released his hold and backed away a couple of paces, alarmed at what he had witnessed. Gustav the Hawk, for now his nickname made perfect, dreadful sense, stood up and looked at Farred. The bird's eyes that stared at him were the same colour as the man's had been before the transformation.

For some reason, that was one of the things that disturbed him most, and it would be those hawk eyes that haunted his dreams over the next few nights.

Farred remembered that Gustav had wanted him to help him to the window. He looked cautiously at the wicked, curved talons of the hawk, sharp enough to slash through clothes and skin, strong enough to mangle his arm. Gustav had said his mind would be intact. But still...

Tentatively, Farred held out his arm. Slowly, Gustav walked towards it and climbed on, holding onto Farred with only the gentlest pressure. Carefully, Farred turned around and took him to the window. Gustav stared at him again with those large, brown eyes. Farred leaned his arm out of the window and the hawk was gone in an instant, it's powerful wings beating fast as it developed the speed required to fly. Farred followed its flight until he lost sight of it.

He turned and looked around at the empty room. What was he supposed to do now? He decided quickly. Gustav had said nothing about waiting for him, and Farred made straight for the door.

***

'How many days have we been here now?' asked Shira, her bored tone an attempt to hide her increasing frustration and anger.

Every day seemed to be identical to the last. She watched as the Kellish defended their wall on the large crag. The flags of Gotbeck and Rotelegen, the Mace and the Rooster, flew on the opposite crag. Hadn't the Gotbeckers manned the path yesterday? Maybe it had been the Luderians—she couldn't remember, and didn't care.

'It's been a week,' replied her uncle, Koren, to what Shira had largely meant as a rhetorical question.

A week. Arioc had conquered the Grand Caladri in a day, and she couldn't take one fortress in a week. Like every other day, Shira, Koren, and the Isharite wizard, Mehrab, had travelled from their camp to the castle, to observe the siege. Not that they had intervened once. Roshanak and his wizards were in control, sending the Drobax against the Brasingian defences in one mindless attack after another.

'What about Baldwin?' she demanded of Mehrab. She had ordered him to use his Isharite wizards to kill the Emperor, and thereby crush the morale of the enemy.

She heard Koren sign, letting her know his displeasure at the idea, but chose to ignore him.

'We have sent soldiers into the Emperor's Keep two nights running,' replied the Isharite.

'And?'

'Well, I can't confirm any success, Your Majesty.'

'Huh,' sneered Shira. 'I think we would know if it had been a success.'

'Maybe so,' the Isharite replied.

'What we know,' interjected Koren, 'is that brave soldiers have been sent up there to their death in a pointless exercise.'

'Pointless?' Shira retorted, turning to face her uncle. She'd had enough of his patronising attitude. '*This* is pointless!' she shouted, waving her arms at the gory spectacle of Burkhard Castle.

Koren reached over and grabbed the front of her coat. Her uncle had never manhandled her before, and Shira was shocked that he would do so now. She tried to twist away to the side, but Koren pulled at her with all his weight and they both stumbled over to the ground. As they did, Shira felt a searing pain along the side of her head.

Koren released her and pointed up at the sky. 'Get it!' he shouted.

Shira looked up and saw a hawk wheeling away from them. An orange coloured blast of magic flew into the sky after it, as Mehrab tried to down the bird. But the hawk soared away from the path of the bolt, and was gone.

Shira staggered to her feet.

'Their wizard, Gustav,' said Mehrab bitterly, looking up at the sky.

Shira followed his gaze but the hawk was out of sight, and was unlikely to return now that the element of surprise had gone.

'Let that be an end to it,' demanded Koren harshly, looking from Shira to Mehrab and back again. 'No more magic tricks and quick fixes. We have brought the Drobax all the way here to take the fortress. Let them do it.'

Shira put a hand to her head. It came back wet and sticky with blood where the talons of the bird had raked along her scalp. If her uncle hadn't yanked her out of the way, it could have been much worse.

Mehrab was looking at her for confirmation.

'Very well,' Shira said, giving in. 'No more attacks on the Emperor.'

She gazed over at the Drobax slithering up Baldwin's crag like a swarm of insects.

'He can live, and watch us destroy his Empire.'

***

The waiting tied her stomach in knots. Each moment that passed, Arioc or his servant, Babak, were more likely to notice that Moneva had been gone longer than usual, raising their suspicions. At the best, her movements would be restricted. She needed the freedom of movement Arioc had granted her, or her hopes of escape would be over.

Moneva crouched behind some bushes. She hoped the evening darkness would conceal her position. She had spied on the prison camp at Samir Durg at this time last night. She had seen Gyrmund and the others with her own eyes. When the guards released them into the open area they had made straight for the stretch of fence she was now hiding near. It seemed like this might be a routine they had developed, looking out towards the fortress and talking amongst themselves, before they were herded, along with the other prisoners, into the underground pits where they were kept overnight.

It was risky, but she had to try to talk to them if she could. She was sure they had been out of the mines by this time last night. Perhaps they had been brought in early, and were already in those miserable looking pits.

A noise on the other side of the site interrupted her thoughts. Gates were being opened. Orders shouted. Then, she could make out the tired looking figures of the prisoners entering the fenced area. Gyrmund, Herin and Clarin made their way over to the same part of the fence they had occupied last night. Gyrmund put his hands onto it, as if he needed to hold himself up. He looked awful. Moneva hadn't been close enough to make out their faces last night. Gyrmund looked tired and lined, big bags under his eyes. He was a lot thinner. Herin and Clarin didn't look quite so bad, though they too had lost weight.

She couldn't waste time.

'Hey!' she whispered. 'It's Moneva!'

Herin's eyes narrowed, and he looked over in her direction.

'Did you hear that?' he asked the other two.

'What?' asked Clarin.

'Shush.'

'It's Moneva,' she repeated.

'I see you,' replied Herin, looking around to make sure that no-one else was in earshot.

Clarin and Gyrmund also seemed to pick her out from behind the bush. Gyrmund's eyes filled with tears but he said nothing.

'I've got to be quick,' began Moneva. 'I'm going to free you one night soon. Not tonight and not tomorrow. But from then on you need to be ready each night. I'll let you out of the pits. You need to be as ready as possible. We've got to go back to the fortress to free Soren.'

'Is he alright?' whispered Clarin.

'I haven't seen him. But I think he's still alive. How are you?'

'Well, we've just come back from a double hanging, but otherwise we're doing fine,' said Herin drily.

Gyrmund looked like he was about to say something, but he couldn't get any words out. Now wasn't the time anyway.

'I've got to go,' said Moneva. She didn't wait for a reply and didn't give them a final look. She turned around and headed back to Arioc's chambers.

XVII

THE BATTLE OF LINDHAFEN

'**E**DGAR!'
IT WAS WILCHARD, looking excited as he hurried over.

'Coen's scouts have located Emeric's army. Only a mile away.'

Edgar's heart hammered in his chest. He felt his hands go clammy. This was what they had been hoping for, and yet the news made his guts twist with anxiety. He found himself following Wilchard to the front of the camp.

Coen was already there, talking hurriedly with Lord Emmett and a group of Thessian noblemen. A mood of anticipation hung in the air. Coen was one of the smaller men in the group, but his bald pate made him stand out, and he had an air of authority which Edgar found reassuring. The duke noticed him and welcomed him over. Edgar offered his hand and Coen grasped it wordlessly. They would need to work closely together today and, more importantly, so would their soldiers. It was important for them to be seen to be united.

'The Barissians are more or less where I expected them to be. My scouts are sure that Emeric's whole force is there. They're on the road to Lindhafen, but haven't gone too far east; no doubt suspecting that I would double back on them. It means that we can approach them from the south.'

'Why do you want to do that, Your Grace?' asked Wilchard. 'Is the terrain better this side of the road?'

'Not particularly, Lord Wilchard. No, it's nothing to do with that—this whole region is mostly flat and featureless. I'd prefer to approach from the south because I don't want his soldiers to feel trapped when we engage them. A large proportion of his army is made up of mercenaries. When the going gets tough, I want them to feel free to retreat north. Our numbers are going to be similar. I'm relying on the fact that our men will be stauncher today.'

Edgar had never fought in a real battle. He had trained for it plenty enough, since he was a young boy. Hours of physical exercise and weapon training, every day. He had even read up on tactics. But Coen's description of what was going to happen this morning suddenly sounded very real, and not very appealing. Two sides hacking at each other until one couldn't stand it anymore, and vacated the field. The Thessians were fighting to defend their homeland. He had to make sure that the Magnians, with less to lose, also stood firm.

'I say we march towards them now, and when we're within sight get into formation. Are we still agreed on deployment?' Coen asked.

'Yes,' replied Edgar.

On tactics, at least, he was clear. The Magnians would form the left division and mostly fight on foot. Edgar would stand with his men on the left, the North Magnians to his right. A small detachment of cavalry, led by Wilchard, would protect the left flank.

'And Frayne?' asked the Duke.

'He's fine.'

Frayne and the Middians would act as the main cavalry force and stay in reserve, to intervene where and when needed. The middle and right divisions would be commanded by Coen and Emmett, respectively. Everyone understood their roles.

'Then let's crush the bastards!' declared Coen, with real malice.

Leofwin and Brictwin finished tightening off Edgar's straps. The chain mail was heavy, but it was a weight he was used to, his father stressing more than once the importance of accustoming oneself to movement in armour. Uncle and nephew then checked each other, while all about them men helped each other into armour.

Ulf the smith, who until a week ago had worked under Rabigar the Krykker, was bright red in the face, as he ran from one emergency to the next, making small adjustments to armour and weaponry.

Edgar had a sword strapped to his waist and a dagger in his belt. It had been agreed with his advisers that he would not stand in the very front row, with spear and shield. There he would be too much of a target for the enemy. But he had insisted that he wouldn't position himself so far away as to be considered a coward. Supporting the front lines, he knew he would see his fair share of the battle once it started.

He looked around. The men of Magnia were ready to fight. He would lead them, and he prayed to Toric that he wouldn't let them down.

The combined army of Magnia and Thesse was soon moving into position. Coen placed them in open grassland which ran gently down to the Lindhafen

Road. Emeric's full army wasn't in sight, but it was clear that the Barissians knew they were there. Their scouts came and went on the north side of the road, reporting their numbers and deployment back to Emeric and his commanders.

Once he was happy with the arrangement, Coen had his soldiers place caltrops to each side of the army. These metal spikes were particularly good at defending areas from cavalry advances. Coen was keen to constrict the space on the battlefield, and to protect the infantry from the Barissian cavalry.

Edgar began organising the Magnian forces, nearly four thousand men, subdivided into smaller units who would fight together. They were formed into a rectangle, with the long end facing the road. He angled it away from the road slightly, making it harder for the Barissians to force their way around. Here, at the front, the most experienced and ablest soldiers were placed. Quite a few of them were older men who had fought in the Magnian Civil War—on both sides. All Magnians now fought together, and Edgar was proud of that.

He walked down the line, exchanging words with the men under his command. Some were eager to talk, boasting to their Prince about what they would do in the upcoming battle. Others preferred to nod and greet their Prince but keep their thoughts private. Some drank, using it to stiffen their courage before the fight. Others prayed to Toric or other gods. Edgar showed equal respect to all.

The front row was heavily armoured and all carried shields which they would hold together to form a defensive wall. The second row stood a few feet back, spears driven into the ground point first beside them. When the Barissians came, the spearmen would poke their spears over or under the shields of the first row, trying to find gaps in the enemy's shield wall.

The ranks at the back were taken by those who were less experienced and less well armed. If they had been placed at the front they were likely to break and allow the enemy through. Here they could play a support role, and fill in at the front when required. Some had bows. These archers would be able to move through the ranks to get the best shot at the enemy. Edgar's job with the rear ranks was to reassure and encourage, reminding them of what was expected of them. It wasn't complicated, and Edgar found himself repeating the same two words.

Stand firm.

Ealdnoth approached.

'Do they look ready?' asked the wizard.

'Yes, they do. I feel like I want it to start now.'

Ealdnoth harrumphed at that idea in displeasure.

'Where will you be during the battle?' Edgar asked him.

'Everywhere,' replied Ealdnoth. 'In her letter, Belwynn made it clear that Emeric has an Isharite wizard as an adviser. He will be here. My job will be to nullify anything he tries.'

'Well, be careful.'

'Oh, it can be done quite safely. I won't be in any danger. It's you who are putting your life on the line.' Ealdnoth was far from happy with Edgar's decision to fight near the front. 'Listen to me. No heroics, Edgar. Just get through the day alive, that's your job.'

'Right,' Edgar agreed. Getting through this alive sounded like very sensible advice.

Finally, the Prince met up with Wilchard. The steward was already mounted, along with two hundred of the best Magnian cavalry to the left of Edgar's infantry. Wilchard knew that his job was to protect the flank of Edgar's infantry and, if possible, to outmanoeuvre the enemy.

'Any news?' Edgar asked.

'No. Still can't see the Barissians. Do you think they'll come to us?'

'Coen seems to think so. Be careful, Wilchard. There aren't many of you. Don't get caught up in a fight you can't win.'

Wilchard nodded. 'I will do my best not to get anyone killed, Your Highness.'

They clasped hands, and Wilchard then turned his horse around to join up with his cavalry. It was time. Edgar moved into his position in the third rank of his infantry. His bodyguards stood to either side of him. On Leofwin's left stood Ragulf, a young nobleman who had been given the honour of holding the Prince's standard. The flag of the Sun in Glory stood tall, symbol for all Magnians.

The Magnians were ready. The Thessians were ready also. Their flag, a six-spoked wheel above two crossed ears of corn, could be seen in the central division, indicating Coen's presence there. The army was ready, but the Barissians did not come.

Soldiers sat down and rested. Those with the stomach for it had their lunch, making sure that they had enough energy to last as long as would be required.

'Will we have to go and meet them?' murmured Brictwin, as the initial excitement of the preparations began to turn to boredom.

'Coen seems pretty convinced that Emeric wants to bring him to a fight,' replied Edgar, who had been starting to think the same thing as the younger man. 'He's been trying to for days, apparently.'

'Maybe they don't like the odds any more,' said Leofwin.

There was that. Coen was about eight thousand fighting men stronger with the Magnian and Middian forces. The outcome was far from a foregone conclusion for either side.

Then, noise spread back from the front ranks in a wave. Edgar made his way forwards. There they were. Coming over a rise and into view were rank upon rank of Barissian soldiers.

The noise became shouts of anger and howls of derision from the Thessians. The Thessians had suffered their homeland being ravaged for the last few days. They weren't about to forget or forgive. They sounded ready for the fight. The Magnians began to join in, letting out tension by shouting at the approaching army. Some hurled abuse, some just let out wordless, animal noises.

The Barissians stopped just before the road, only a few hundred feet away. Edgar could get a good view of them.

'About the same numbers of infantry as we have,' suggested Leofwin, peering over Edgar's shoulder.

Edgar nodded. 'More cavalry than we do, though. And they'll be holding a force in reserve, too.'

The enemy were organised into three divisions in the same way as Coen had done with their forces. The boar of Barissia was held aloft in the central division. A second flag was displayed there too, a golden crown on a red background.

'Of course,' Edgar murmured to himself. 'He's a king now.'

Would Emeric himself be there? If so, the two dukes would fight in the centre of the battlefield. However, Edgar thought it more likely that Emeric was seated on a horse some distance from the front line.

They watched on as the Barissians organised themselves into their formations. It was tempting to order a charge now. But the plan they had all agreed to was for the Barissians to come to them.

It seemed, however, like they would be disappointed. The Barissians got themselves ready and then waited. The battlefield went quiet. Neither side seemed willing to make the first move.

'Gods, let's just get this done,' Edgar heard one of his soldiers say, almost in despair.

The waiting was excruciating. But no doubt better than what was to come.

Then, finally, sound and movement. Brass instruments were blown. Drums were pounded.

The Barissians began to shuffle forwards.

Edgar moved back into position. In amongst his men, he lost a clear view of the whole battlefield, but he could still see down to the road. The infantry division opposite his own, the Barissian right wing, was now crossing it. The Barissian drums beat out a steady rhythm, so that the ranks could march at the same pace and keep their order.

All the Magnian soldiers were now on their feet, weapons ready. The front rank locked their shields together, presenting an intimidating wall to the enemy. Shouts began to roar out again as the moment of impact drew close.

They heard the clash over to their right as the Barissians engaged with the Thessian units. Shouts and grunts filled the air, followed by screams.

A roar erupted from the Barissian infantry ahead of them, and they began to charge the remaining distance towards the Magnian shields, intent on smashing their way through. A few feet to go and the Magnians responded, running to meet them. An enormous thud filled the air as shield after shield smacked against each other in a long line.

In some places along the line Magnians had been pushed over, in others Barissians had fallen backwards. As the two sides heaved against each other, those in the front rank who had a free hand stabbed with short swords, or hacked with hand axes. The spearmen in the row in front of Edgar began their deadly work. One of them leaped high into the air, thrusting his spear downwards over the shoulder of the man in front, trying to find an undefended spot. Again and again he did it, the wicked iron tip thrusting down at different angles. Next to him a second spearman used a different technique. He was crouched down on one knee and he thrust his spear in between the legs of the men ahead of him, hoping to connect with the shin or ankle of the enemy, either to wound or to knock them off balance. Meanwhile, the Barissians were doing the same. Ear splitting screams rang out from both sides as metal plunged into limbs, weapons of all kinds found exposed faces, necks and groins.

The ranks ahead of Edgar had succeeded in stabbing and maiming several enemy soldiers. It looked like there might be potential to open a gap in the enemy line. Edgar and Leofwin shared a look and nodded in agreement.

'Push!' shouted Edgar at the top of his voice, though he wasn't optimistic about how many of his men heard the instruction above the shouts and screams around them. He had to lead by example. Edgar, Leofwin and Brictwin moved forwards together, adding their weight to the front rank. At the same time, Edgar had to beware Barissian thrusts coming over from their side of the wall. He bent his legs somewhat so that the top of his head wasn't too exposed. The rest of the Magnians, to the side and behind, joined in, so that Edgar was now himself being pushed forwards by those in the ranks behind him.

He stuck his head up to grab a quick look at the enemy. The Barissians had been quick to react and were now pushing back, the two armies involved in a massive scrum. The Magnians had gained a little ground at first, but the contest had become even. He looked along the line in both directions. The same pushing match was taking wherever the two armies had met. But the Magnians had made better progress in some places than others, so that while Edgar's section of the line was ahead, off to the sides the line bent back behind him.

A Barissian short sword jabbed down, inches from Edgar's head. Its owner had leaned over the shoulder of the man in front of Edgar and was driving down with the blade. Edgar tried to move out of the way, but he was so squashed in now he didn't have much wriggle room. He knew that he needed to act.

He struggled to release his right arm which still gripped his own sword. He did so by pushing himself backwards with his left hand, allowing enough of a gap for him to jerk his right arm free. The Barissian sword came down again. This time the tip of the blade hit the back of the soldier in front of Edgar, but didn't come down with enough force to puncture his armour. Edgar reacted quickly, chopping at the wrist of the Barissian with quick, brutal hacks. The enemy was forced to release his sword and drew his arm away before Edgar could do serious damage.

Edgar followed the retreating arm, standing up tall to take a good look at his enemy. He took in a sea of squashed soldiers, red faces groaning amid the crush of bodies. Ahead and slightly to the left was the man he had clashed with, shouting in his direction, spittle erupting from his mouth. Edgar crouched down a little, pulled his arm back, then launched up and forwards, thrusting his sword towards the Barissian's face. The man reacted, gripping Edgar's forearm just in time to stop the blow. Edgar didn't stop, though. He yanked his arm backwards and forwards until it broke free. He shoved his sword into the neck of his enemy, drew it out, shoved it in again. Again, and again. Making sure that he was dead. When he was sure, he looked. The man was dead alright, his head lolling to one side. But the crush of bodies meant that his body was still upright, with no room for it to fall to the floor.

Then, something gave. Edgar found himself stumbling forwards as the resistance of the Barissians collapsed. He just managed to keep his feet and looked around him. The clear lines of the two armies had disappeared and Edgar was unsure which direction he was facing. The shield walls had collapsed into a chaotic melee. Leofwin and Brictwin were soon by his side.

'Back off!' Leofwin shouted in his ear.

But Edgar didn't want to back away from the fight now, not when they had broken through the enemy's line.

Leofwin grabbed him by the arm.

'We need you alive!' he demanded.

Edgar nodded. He had to control himself. He let Leofwin lead him back a few yards, to where young Ragulf held the Magnian flag.

He took the opportunity to look around the battlefield. While the Barissian shield wall had given way at this point, it had stood firm elsewhere along the line, and the Magnians hadn't been able to take advantage of it, getting caught up in hand to hand fighting with the rear ranks of the Barissians who had moved to block the hole. Even now, Barissians and Magnians were backing away from each other as the first few frantic minutes of battle led to a pause. The Barissians continued to retreat, leaving a space between the two sides, and allowing everyone to catch their breath.

Edgar could hear the sound of fighting from his right, suggesting that the Thessians and Barissians in the centre were still going at it, but he was too far away to see. Ahead, though, he could quite clearly see the bodies of the dead littering the ground between the two armies. It hadn't taken long for the two sides to have killed so many. Some of the badly wounded took the chance to leave the front line, helped along by their comrades. Their fight was over already.

The Barissians were on the move again, but instead of renewing the attack they retreated further backwards. Edgar looked down after them. He was about to ask Leofwin whether they should order an attack, then he closed his mouth again. The infantry was withdrawing to allow the Barissian cavalry to advance.

'Spearmen!' Edgar shouted, and others joined in the call, as the Magnians reorganised themselves. The long spears were the best defence against cavalry, a bristling line of wood and iron that deterred a charge. The Magnian spearmen readied themselves, some of them planting the shaft against the ground to give the weapon greater resistance.

The Barissian cavalry also carried spears. They had now organised themselves into a straight line and advanced towards the waiting Magnians. Not a charge, but intimidating nonetheless. Their warhorses were bred for the battlefield and could reach sixteen hands in height.

The Barissian cavalry came at the Magnian position. Some of them hurled spears, standing in the stirrups to give them extra force. But all had to be mindful of the Magnian spearmen, who could cripple their horses if they got too close. Unlike the brutal shoving and thrusting of the infantry clash, this was more a test of discipline. The horsemen started to approach the Magnian line, looking for any weaknesses, before retreating away. Some of the Magnian spearmen gave chase but those who went too far found that the horses could quickly be turned around and were cut off, isolated, and brought down. Meanwhile, those spearmen who worked together could approach an isolated horseman from several angles and get in a strike on a horse, bringing the rider to the ground and skewering them.

This game of cat and mouse went on for some time, before the Barissian cavalry retreated down to the road. They had made little impact in terms of casualties, but had tied up the Magnian spearmen, forcing them to concentrate while their own infantry could rest. The Barissian infantry, though, now returned for a second time—the drums behind them beating out a marching rhythm.

Once more, the Magnian shield wall set itself in place to meet the attack. Once more, Edgar placed himself in the third rank. His army needed him to stay alive. Even at the best of times it was common for soldiers' morale to break if their leader died. Here, in a battle that Edgar knew not all his men thought necessary, that was even more likely.

Those archers who still had arrows left fired them at the enemy. Those with shields raised them in defence. Then, the Barissians came at them again, the shield walls clashing against each other. The Magnian spearmen in front of Edgar resumed their deadly work, reaching out to strike the enemy where they could. The Barissians forced the Magnians a few paces backwards. The spearmen, unable to use their weapons effectively in the more confined space, gave way for Edgar's rank to move in, pushing back against the Barissians and chopping and thrusting with their shorter weapons.

The grunts and screams of pain returned as men on both sides suffered injuries. The stink of sweat and piss assailed Edgar as he supported the man in front, while looking to attack the Barissian wall. Their shields were packed tight. He thought about crouching down to look for an opening, but with the press of bodies feared that he might lose his footing. He found that he was shouting: mindless, animal roars. *Madness*, he thought to himself. *Why do men do this? Utter madness.*

Eventually the two walls broke apart, nothing gained by either side. Again, it was the Barissians who withdrew. Were their efforts getting more half-hearted, Edgar wondered? He remembered Duke Coen's thoughts about Emeric's army. Many of them were mercenaries, and mercenaries weren't keen on getting themselves killed or maimed. But that was what everyone faced here. Neither side was gaining an advantage, and the longer it went on, the more the casualties would pile up.

The front rank was battered and bruised. Some had huge gashes inflicted on them. Others had broken ribs. Fresher soldiers came in to replace those who couldn't remain. But the new arrivals were generally younger and less experienced. Edgar was getting increasingly keen for this to end, but Coen's tactics were to hold their position, and so that was what they must do.

There followed a lull in the battle as the Barissians seemed in no hurry to renew their attack. Some of the soldiers sat down to rest. From somewhere Brictwin had been given a flask of ale which he passed on to Edgar. Edgar took a swig before passing it on to Leofwin.

'Your Highness!' came a shout.

Edgar walked to the front of his army, and looked into the distance, where some of his soldiers were pointing. Onto the road came a new cavalry force.

185

It took Edgar a while to register what it was. The Barissian reserves. A large force of mounted men was heading their way. Emeric had played his last card. The intention was clear. His reserves had been sent to drive the Magnians from the battlefield, and then turn on the Thessians.

'Ready yourselves!' shouted Edgar. 'Get a message to our cavalry!'

He wanted to make sure that Wilchard had seen the danger—though in truth, his steward's small force could have little impact on the numbers heading their way.

The Barissian reserves joined up with the cavalry of their right division and swung around, aiming for the far corner of the Magnian line. They were constrained from manoeuvring much farther to their right by the caltrops laid by Coen's men.

They were coming at speed, much faster than the first cavalry attack of the day. His men had their line of spears ready for impact. Edgar got a glimpse of Wilchard's force making a feint towards the Barissians, before turning their mounts around and retreating. A good portion of the Barissian cavalry chased after them.

Well, considered Edgar, *that was all Wilchard could have done. If he had tried to engage he would have been swept aside.*

Meanwhile, the main part of the Barissian cavalry came crashing into Edgar's infantry, only a few yards from where the Prince himself was standing. Some of the horses were speared and came crashing down to the ground, thrashing in agony. The Magnian line was disrupted, with more horsemen riding through and engaging the defenders. The far corner of Edgar's division started to bend out of shape, as the impact of the attack pushed people out of place.

Edgar was quick to see the danger. If he didn't shore up the Magnian position it could quickly be overrun.

'Come on!' he instructed his two bodyguards and, for once, Leofwin didn't argue.

'The Prince! The Prince!' Leofwin shouted, letting those in front know that Edgar was coming.

Men saw Edgar arrive and redoubled their efforts, organising a line around him. Edgar pressed onwards, taking the fight to the Barissians. The battle line was now a mess of bodies, both man and horse. The Magnians could move in and out of the obstacles more easily than the mounted Barissians, who had to take care where they took their horses.

Edgar knocked away a lunged spear with his sword and then slashed it across the face of the rider's horse. The beast backed away, its rider struggling to stay on. Edgar then moved to support Brictwin, who was being pushed back by two riders. He drew one of the riders towards him.

Looking up, Edgar got a shock. It was a face he recognised. It took a split second for him to work out why he would recognise one of the Barissians. It was Gervase Salvinus, the man who had led the attack on Toric's Temple. Edgar remembered their eyes meeting across the yard of the temple complex, before Salvinus had led his men away. This time, they were a lot closer. They locked eyes again. Recognition flared on Salvinus's face. Maybe only now did he realise that the man he had encountered at Ecgworth was the Prince of South Magnia.

'To me!' shouted Salvinus, his voice carrying across the battlefield. 'Kill their Prince!'

Salvinus trotted forwards, raising his spear above his head as if Edgar were a fish he was about to skewer. Leofwin appeared to Edgar's left, threatening the mercenary leader. Outnumbered, Salvinus was in a dangerous position. If he made a lunge at Edgar, he would expose himself to an attack from Leofwin. Instead, he backed away from them.

'To the Prince!' shouted Leofwin.

Magnian soldiers began to congregate around them. Ragulf arrived with the standard. At the same time, Edgar could see Salvinus organising his mercenaries for another attack. These were the men who had served under him for years. Experienced, ruthless men. No doubt many of the soldiers who had raided Toric's Temple were here. So be it. It seemed to Edgar that the next few minutes would decide the outcome of the battle.

After being protected back in the third rank for most of the battle, Edgar now stood in the centre of his front line. Leofwin had found him a shield to use. If the Barissians were in any doubt, Ragulf's flag flew above him, indicating exactly where he was. But he needed to be there. His men needed to see him fighting for them, if they were to fight for him.

Salvinus and the Barissians came for them. Their objective was clear: kill Edgar, force the Magnians off the battlefield, and then encircle Coen and the Thessians.

187

Salvinus wanted the kill for himself. He shoved his spear straight at Edgar. Edgar blocked it with his shield. The force of the strike made him stagger backwards, but someone behind propped him up and kept him on his feet. Someone sent a spear in Salvinus's direction, but he casually swerved out of the way. He sent his spear back towards Edgar, but somehow Leofwin was waiting for the move. Edgar's bodyguard lashed out with his sword, and cut the wooden shaft in two. Salvinus let out a roar of frustration, throwing the useless half of the weapon in Leofwin's direction, and drawing his sword.

A few of Salvinus's men came for them, trying to take Leofwin down as much as Edgar. Edgar fought with desperation. For the first time, he felt the battle rage that men talked about around the fire, as adrenaline pumped through his body. He shoved forward with his shield arm, blocking strikes, aiming for the nose of any horse that got too close. He swung his right arm down, raining down blows with his sword, forcing the enemy to keep their distance. Again, and again, he hammered his weapon down, his fury seemingly giving him limitless energy. Beside him, Brictwin was doing the same. As Brictwin moved forwards so too did the soldiers to his right, so that the whole Magnian line shifted around.

Salvinus was now out of sight, the to and fro of battle pulling him one way, and Edgar another.

The Magnian aggression had seen off the Barissian attacks for now. Cavalry were used for speed and manoeuvrability, for chasing down enemies. They could be used for a mass charge. But against an organised shield wall equipped with spears and swords, they were less effective.

Edgar could see some of them circling around, trying to get behind the Magnian line. This was dangerous. If they got into the softer rear of the Magnian forces, the Barissians could break up his division and isolate his men. Edgar looked over to where Frayne's Middian reserves had been kept for such an eventuality, but there was no sign of them. If they didn't come and help soon, his division might be lost.

Shouting from behind grabbed his attention. Turning to look, Edgar could see his worst fears being realised. A large group of Barissian cavalry were engaging with the rear of his force.

'Shit,' he said out loud.

'It's the force that chased off Wilchard's cavalry,' commented Leofwin, who had turned to look in the same direction. 'They've double backed on us.'

'We'll have to deal with them,' said Edgar. It was part statement, part question.

Leofwin nodded grimly. 'I think so.'

Ordering some of his men to hold the front line, Edgar led another group towards the new threat. Again, Leofwin and Brictwin shouted and pushed men out of the way, so that Edgar could march straight towards the enemy. Ragulf followed on, bringing a stream of soldiers who would fight under the Magnian flag. Edgar wasted no time in getting stuck into the enemy, reinforcing the resolve of the more inexperienced and poorly equipped soldiers in his army. Brictwin leapt into the air, crashing his sword against a mounted Barissian with the full force of his bodyweight and armour behind the blow. The Barissian toppled off the back of his horse which turned and bolted, straight into a group of riders, causing their horses to fret and dance away. A cheer rose from the Magnians who ran at the enemy while they were still disoriented, grabbing at reins and pulling more men from their horses.

Any attempt at creating a shield wall now seemed hopeless. Instead Edgar and his band of men began to roam the battlefield, looking for the most dangerous looking Barissians. They intercepted a group of Barissian infantry who had marched into the melee with some degree of discipline, and had begun to pick off stranded Magnians. Edgar attacked, swinging his sword at the tallest of them, who blocked it with a shield, the impact sending a vibration up Edgar's arm. The man returned the favour, launching a massive axe in his direction. Edgar got his shield in front of it just in time, but was still stunned by the force of the blow, which sent him down to one knee. It also gave him a dead shield arm, making him unable to clench his left hand. Still on one knee, Edgar swung his sword at the axeman, hoping to catch his legs. But the Barissian jumped back to avoid the stroke.

The battle fury of a few minutes before was now dissipating. Edgar was getting tired from his exertions in full armour, and every muscle in his body seemed to ache.

The Barissian infantry came at them, but Leofwin was at his most dangerous when he could counterattack. He avoided a wild spear thrust and lunged forwards, smashing his shield into the face of the spearman with a massive crack that floored the Barissian. With lightning speed, he crashed the hilt of his sword into the face of another soldier, before thrusting it into the side of the axeman who had tangled with Edgar, penetrating his armour. He struggled to pull it free, but by then Edgar and Brictwin were falling on the enemy, forcing them on the defensive until those that could, turned and ran back the way they had come.

Suddenly, Edgar couldn't move.

It was the strangest feeling. His feet couldn't lift from the floor, his fingers were stuck in place, holding his sword and shield. He couldn't turn his head to look around. Then, he heard and felt horsemen approaching.

Something clattered into him, dragging him to the floor. He felt, rather than saw, riders whistle past him. He found that he could move freely once more.

Brictwin quickly helped him to his feet. Edgar looked around to get his bearings.

The disintegration of the Magnian shield wall was allowing the Barissian cavalry to manoeuvre around the battlefield at will, and this group had come at Edgar from behind, while he had been pinned in place by some force. Brictwin had pushed him out of the way just in time. Others hadn't been so fortunate. Ragulf, his standard bearer, lay dead on the floor, the Magnian banner of the Sun in Glory trampled into the ground.

'Get them!' shouted Leofwin off to the side, keen to engage the Barissians before they could wheel away and do it again. They had ridden into a second group of Magnians, and were trying to extricate themselves.

Edgar, suspecting magic, looked about the battlefield, but couldn't see any signs of a wizard. He had to assume that Ealdnoth was protecting him.

Edgar wasn't sure if he had the energy to move anymore, but when Leofwin ran after the Barissians he made himself follow. His lungs burned with the effort, and his legs felt like jelly. How could he swing his sword when he was this exhausted? At that moment, he wished that he had fought on horseback instead of on foot. But when he got to the enemy he somehow found the strength to raise his sword and fight once more.

One of the horsemen had dismounted and came for Edgar, perhaps keen to win the glory of taking down the Magnian Prince. Edgar had lost his shield, probably when Brictwin had bundled him over. When the Barissian swung his sword at him, Edgar blocked it in a two-handed stroke. The clash of steel rang out and Edgar's arms shuddered with the impact.

He was tiring, he knew. He could no longer raise his arms up high enough anymore, his shoulders aching with each effort. He blocked another swing. Self-preservation was the only reason he could keep doing it. If his life wasn't in immediate danger, he would have collapsed onto the floor by now. The Barissian came at him again. This time, Edgar used footwork to avoid the swinging sword. There was an opening in his opponent's defence, but Edgar was too tired to take it, preferring to circle around. Just gripping the hilt of his sword and moving was hard enough now. His opponent smiled at him, sensing his weakness. Then, Brictwin approached from behind, striking down on the top of his head like he was cracking a nut. The skull caved in and the body collapsed to the floor.

Edgar put the tip of his sword into the ground to keep himself standing. His head was spinning. He vomited, too tired to lean over, instead letting the fluid dribble down his chest. He looked around the battlefield but struggled to make much sense of it. For the moment, there weren't any Barissians in the immediate vicinity.

Another group of horsemen approached them. But they were wearing Magnian colours. The lead rider removed his helmet. It was Wilchard.

'We've done it!' he crowed, a big beaming smile on his face.

Could it be true? Edgar took a second look over the battlefield, trying to focus. The Barissian cavalry had mostly departed. A few skirmishes continued, but the fighting had almost stopped. He looked down towards the road. Barissian infantry could be seen heading north the way they had come. His Magnians stood or slumped all over the battlefield. Any sense of organisation had all but gone. But they had won.

He looked at Brictwin and Leofwin, both wearing grins of their own. For some reason, Edgar couldn't bring himself to smile back.

'What happened?' he asked Wilchard, his voice coming out as an unrecognisable croak. His throat was parched dry.

'Emeric threw his reserves at you,' said Wilchard.

This, Edgar already knew.

'When Frayne saw that you were withstanding them, he took the Middians around and attacked the Barissian left. He fought off their cavalry and then got into their infantry. The Barissian left collapsed, and then their central division was hit.

'Meanwhile, the reserves who chased us off the battlefield came back and hit you hard. But we came back to hit them from behind. When they realised what was happening on the rest of the battlefield, they knew they had lost.'

'So,' said Edgar, 'the Magnians took the brunt of the damage when Salvinus brought his reserves against us.'

'True,' said Leofwin, 'it sounds like we suffered the most. But we won, Edgar! And you led us to victory. I know that your father would have been very proud to see you today. Today you became a different kind of leader to the one you were yesterday. The men who fought here won't forget it.'

Edgar had rarely seen Leofwin get so emotional. It brought a lump to his own throat, and he reached out to grab the older man's shoulder, who hugged him back.

'Thank you both,' he said to Leofwin and Brictwin. 'Brictwin? Would you mind recovering our standard?'

'Of course, Your Highness.'

Brictwin carefully picked up the standard, still cradled by Ragulf's broken body. He took it to Edgar who passed it up to Wilchard. When his steward held it aloft, it elicited a cheer from those men gathered about. It was dirty and damaged in places. But it had survived.

XVIII

THE SECOND DISCIPLE

BELWYNN WAS LOOKING FORWARD TO getting out of Heractus Castle. The atmosphere remained awkward, with a King and a Grand Master occupying the same building, and nobody quite sure who was in charge of what.

Yesterday's news made her even more eager to leave. A Krykker army was marching to Heractus to ally with the Knights. Belwynn could only assume that Rabigar had worked some miracle there, and persuaded those who had exiled him to join in the fight against Ishari. But the result was that the castle had become a hive of manic activity, as Theron and Sebastian worked day and night to prepare for another military expedition—this time into Haskany. Food and other supplies had to be found. Maps of enemy territory needed to be carefully studied. Belwynn was delighted that things were suddenly moving so fast, but she knew that she wasn't needed.

Prince Dorian had offered to take her down into the city. Unlike the rest of his family, he seemed to bear her no ill will. As they left the castle gatehouse, Belwynn wondered whether it was all an elaborate sham, and she was about to be killed and dumped somewhere. But she doubted it.

As Dorian began to point out the sights in Heractus, Belwynn warmed to the city a little. The morning sunshine helped to dispel the poor first impression she had received. There was still a lot of grey, it was true. But she realised that Heractus wasn't trying to impress her, as was the case with the greater cities of Dalriya. The Kalinthian people seemed reserved, yet dignified; and Belwynn didn't mind that.

'The building where your friends are staying is just up here,' said Dorian, taking them along one of the central city streets.

'I have to ask,' said Belwynn. 'You've been very welcoming, Dorian, under the circumstances. Is there a reason why you don't hate me, like the rest of your family?'

'Hate you?' Dorian responded. 'I'm not sure that anyone in my family hates *you*. Count Theron is another story, maybe,' he said, with a grin. 'The way I see things is, Grand Master Sebastian wants the best for the country. So does my father.' He shrugged. 'I'm hopeful that they can work things out. Here we are.'

It was a large town house, built from grey stone and wood. It suggested that some of Elana's supporters had been willing to spend a considerable amount of money.

The door was open and she knocked before entering. Several people were sitting or standing in the front room, mostly women and children. Elana was there, talking with a middle-aged woman. She looked around to see Belwynn come in and smiled at her. Belwynn and Dorian waited near the door. With a few words Elana extricated herself and came over to greet them.

'Belwynn, it's good to see you. How are things?'

'Good. It's busy up at the castle. We've got word that a Krykker army has been raised and is heading here. I'm hoping that Rabigar will be with them. This is Prince Dorian, the son of King Jonas.'

Dorian took Elana's hand and pressed his lips to it.

'You are a healer?' asked the Prince.

'Yes. Word's got around a bit,' Elana said wryly, indicating the group of people congregating in the room.

'Thank you for ministering to our citizens. Please let me know how I can help. Any provisions you need, or anything else—'

Elana smiled. 'Well, there are a few things.'

'Write me a list before we leave. I will see to it.'

'Thank you, Your Highness. Was there anything in particular you wanted, Belwynn?'

'Yes, I wanted to speak to you and Dirk. Is he in?'

'Yes, he's upstairs resting. Come up.'

Dorian waited downstairs while Elana led Belwynn up to the next storey.

'Are there many people staying here?'

'Oh, yes. Theron has filled the house with his knights. I think the whole city is full to bursting. The Prince seems nice.'

'Yes. The rest of his family are a bit of a nightmare, but he seems different.'

'How are Sebastian and Theron?'

'Fine. Just busy with army stuff.'

Elana stopped and knocked on the door of one of the upstairs rooms. After a pause Belwynn heard Dirk's voice.

'Come in.'

Belwynn followed in behind Elana, to the sound of Dirk coughing. He was sat up in bed, looking no better than the last time Belwynn had seen him.

'How are you feeling?' she asked.

Dirk pulled a face. 'The honest version is, not great. I think the last week has taken a lot out of me.'

'I wanted to talk to you both,' Belwynn began nervously. Now that she was here and ready to talk, she felt a bit foolish.

'Go on,' said Elana encouragingly.

'I've been doing a lot of thinking lately. About all kinds of things. Not just Soren, but what we've all been through—what we still must do. I've changed my mind about a lot of things.'

Belwynn was still struggling to get her words out.

'Elana. I would like to become a disciple of Madria. If you think it's not a good idea, I totally understand—'

'Oh, Belwynn!' Elana interrupted her, smiling. 'Of course! It feels perfect!'

The two women embraced. Dirk struggled out of his bed and gave Belwynn a hug.

'It just feels like the right thing to do,' said Belwynn, wiping her eyes which had become wet with tears. 'Thank you for saying yes.'

'I know that you've made the right decision,' said Dirk, settling back onto his bed. 'I've been doing a lot of thinking myself. For some reason this feels like the right place for Elana to settle and work. I'm so grateful that you've made this decision now. Because it helps me with my own. I've decided to ask Elana to stop healing me. She's kept me alive for this long, but she can't do any more.'

'No, Dirk!' said Belwynn.

Dirk raised a hand, asking her to let him finish.

'I'm in a lot of pain, and...I feel like my work is done, now.'

'You can't mean that.'

Belwynn looked to Elana, but the priestess had a resigned look on her face, as if Dirk had already discussed this with her.

'I am at peace with the decision, Belwynn,' Dirk explained. 'I protected Elana from Nexodore. I travelled with her to safety here. My responsibility as first disciple is complete. I now pass it on to you. But first, let me witness the moment.'

At first Belwynn didn't understand what Dirk meant by 'the moment'. Then she recalled how he had become Elana's first disciple back in Vitugia. The image of it was somehow burned onto Belwynn's memory. She went down onto her knees.

'Elana, I submit my soul to Madria's keeping, and ask that I become your disciple.'

'This is what Madria wishes,' replied Elana. 'Belwynn of Beckford, you shall be my second disciple.'

Elana reached over to touch Belwynn's forehead. Belwynn stood. She felt like something very important had just happened—maybe the most important moment of her life. At the same time, she had the feeling that a great weight had been lifted from her.

***

'We'll need your support,' Gyrmund said to Zared, the young man who seemed to be the leader of the Persaleian prisoners.

'It's tonight?' Zared asked.

The poor light inside the pit flickered on his features, emphasising the look of manic excitement that briefly flitted across his face.

'Phase one,' replied Gyrmund, before moving on to his usual position with Herin and Clarin towards the far end of the pit.

They looked as calm as ever, but their insides had to be churning as much as Gyrmund's. They were taking their first step towards escape.

Vamak and the other four Dog-men began their nightly tour of the pit.

'Mind where you tread,' demanded Clarin as they walked past. The Dog-men turned their heads to look at him, disbelief showing on all their faces. Clarin's challenge had come from nothing, and Gyrmund could see that, for a moment, it had put them on the back foot.

Vamak slowly approached, his muzzle widening into an unpleasant grin.

'So, it's time for us to play, is it?' he asked, his eyes lighting up in anticipation.

The other Dog-men backed him up. One of them stared straight at Gyrmund, as if he was challenging him to their own, separate fight.

Herin moved forwards. Gyrmund did the same.

'This is between the two of them,' Herin demanded, indicating Clarin and Vamak. 'You four can back off,' he added.

'Is that right?' asked Vamak.

'Yes,' said Zared, moving towards the confrontation with Cyprian and about another dozen Persaleians. Rudy and Jurgen were there too, the cousins from Rotelegen who had fought with Ellard. They began to form a circle around Clarin and Vamak. Gyrmund and Herin joined it, Herin pointing to the Dog-men, to indicate that they should do the same.

They looked to Vamak for leadership, who angrily shoved a clawed hand in their direction, directing them to join the circle. He clearly wasn't happy at this show of strength against him, but he was trying to look in control.

Now that the circle was complete, Vamak and Clarin paced around it, eyeing each other up. Vamak's dark eyes glittered in the half-light of the pit, and his muscles rippled as he moved. Some of the others in the pit scurried over to watch.

Vamak came for Clarin, clawed hands going for his neck. Clarin met him, grabbing Vamak's arms around the biceps. The dog-man snapped his jaws but Clarin kept him at arm's length. Vamak lifted one leg and aimed a kick, but Clarin blocked it with his knee. Each now had a firm grip on the other's arms and they pushed and pulled at each other, twisting one way and then another. Neither gained an advantage. Gyrmund could see blood where the dog-man's claws gripped Clarin arms. Clarin let go, banged Vamak's arms away and punched him hard in the stomach. Vamak let out a bark of pain and jumped backwards.

'Finish him!' shouted Herin in a bloodthirsty voice.

The Dog-men barked across the circle, baring their fangs.

Clarin moved towards Vamak but the Dog-man sprang out of the way, then unleashed a vicious swing, his claws scraping down Clarin's forearm, drawing more blood. Clarin grabbed his arm in pain and Vamak was on him, claws flashing. Clarin tried to move out of the way, but Vamak launched himself at him, sinking his teeth into Clarin's shoulder. Now Clarin cried out in pain, smashing his elbow onto Vamak's head to dislodge him. Vamak kicked out, and sent Clarin sprawling backwards towards Gyrmund.

Gyrmund quickly reached down and picked the big man up before Vamak could do more damage. Clarin fumbled around with one hand behind him. Gyrmund looked down just in time to see Herin passing something into his hand. He caught a glimpse of something glinting in the darkness before Clarin staggered off to the side.

His movements looked tired and clumsy. A cruel smile spread over Vamak's face as the Dog-man took his time to move in for the kill.

Gyrmund looked to Herin in concern. Herin winked at him.

Vamak leapt towards his prey. Clarin sidestepped the attack and brought one hand down on top of Vamak's head, holding him still in an iron grip. With the other hand, he punched hard into Vamak's neck. From his place in the circle Gyrmund could see a piece of crystal, with a strip of leather wrapped around it to make a grip, poking out of Clarin's fist as he punctured a blood vessel.

Clarin punched again, tearing into Vamak's neck. Blood gushed out, soaking Clarin, and spilling onto the floor of the pit. Clarin let Vamak drop to the floor, blood still pumping out of the lifeless body.

A cheer rose around the circle.

'We're in charge now!' shouted Herin, striding into the circle to stand with his brother. He pointed at the Dog-men. 'Either you accept that or you die.'

Gyrmund looked at the men of Persala, blood lust showing on their faces. They seemed more than ready to finish the job, and the Dog-men saw it too. They scurried over to Clarin and Herin, heads down in submission, tails tucked between their legs.

'You do what we tell you, now,' Herin informed them.

The Dog-man on the far end was grabbed by a couple of Persaleians and dragged away. One of them punched him to the floor, the creature yelping in pain. Others then joined in, punching and kicking at their victim. Gyrmund moved to intervene but Herin put an arm to his chest, shaking his head. They made short work of it, leaving a bloody corpse. Emboldened, a group of them came back for another one. It whined in fear.

'No,' said Herin, holding out an arm. 'They might be useful.'

'That's enough,' said Zared, coming over to add his authority. 'Back to your places.'

The men shuffled off, obedient enough.

'You do what we tell you or die,' said Herin to the remaining Dog-men. Their eyes already filled with terror, they nodded at him.

'Yes, sir,' one of them said.

'Go to your old places for now,' said Herin. 'It's the safest place for you.'

They backed away to the far end of the pit.

'Well done,' said Zared, shaking Clarin by the hand. 'Are you badly hurt?'

'I don't think so,' said Clarin with a little grin. 'I was faking the injury. He gave me a good bite on the shoulder, mind.'

Herin took a look. 'I don't think it's too bad. I'll do my best to clean it.'

'What now?' asked Zared.

'We need to be ready to escape any night from now,' said Herin. 'But we can't give anything away to the guards. What do you think they'll make of them?' he asked Zared, nodding at the two corpses.

'They're not going to care about two dead prisoners. Fights happen all the time in this place. So long as there are enough of us for the mines, they don't give a shit about anything else. My concern is over them,' he said, gesturing at the Dog-men who had been spared.

'Let us deal with that,' said Herin. 'They don't know anything about the escape plan, after all. But when it comes to it, they might just be useful. We're going to the need all the fighters we can get if we're going to break out of here.'

Zared nodded, conceding the point. 'I can't believe we're going to do it.'

'It won't be easy,' warned Gyrmund.

Zared looked at him. 'We're all ready to get out of this hell or die trying. Don't worry about that.'

***

Rabigar looked about him as thousands of Krykkers began to shout at each other in the fields outside Heractus.

There was already a camp owned by the Knights of Kalinth outside the city—Heractus itself was too full to house all the Knights, never mind being able to find room for the biggest Krykker army that had been raised in generations. It looked like a logistical nightmare. But it wasn't Rabigar's problem. Three clan chiefs—Torinac, Maragin, and Guremar, had joint control of the army. No. Rabigar was quite happy to leave things to them, and wandered over towards the Kalinthian camp, leaving the noise and aggravation behind him.

He wasn't used to being with so many people for so long. Torinac had allowed him to serve with the soldiers of clan Dramsen—it wouldn't be possible to fight with his old clan, the Grendals. To many of them, he would always be a chieftain killer. Rabigar was extremely grateful to the Dramsens for accepting him, and was keen to pull his weight. But as the days passed, his patience wore thin. Long days marching in the heat of summer; inane conversations and pointless banter; shouting, snoring and farting; boasting, posturing and bullying. It all got too much after a while. His younger self would have loved the experience. But Din the exile was too used to his own company. In other words, he had become a miserable, old git.

'Rabigar!' called a voice.

Looking up he saw Belwynn, half running towards him from the direction of the Kalinthian camp. Rabigar smiled. He had missed the girl; he hadn't realised how much until now. She looked as beautiful as ever—though there was sadness in her eyes too.

'I can't believe it was that easy!' she said in greeting, slightly out of breath. 'I thought I was going to have to search through the whole army to find you.'

They gave each other a hug.

'Well, it's good to see you,' said Rabigar. 'How is everyone else?'

'That's why I came to find you. Dirk is dying.'

They didn't talk much on the way to Elana's house. Belwynn spoke a little of her decision to become Elana's disciple, a move that surprised Rabigar. But it didn't feel right to discuss other things before seeing Dirk.

'Here it is,' said Belwynn.

The front door of the house was open, and she led Rabigar in, then up the stairs to Dirk's room. He was sitting up in bed, but his eyes were closed. Rabigar had only once seen him look so ill, in the immediate aftermath of the attack by Nexodore in the lands of the Blood Caladri. At that time, they had all assumed he would die, but Elana had somehow kept him alive all this time. He was emaciated, his skin thin and translucent looking, his bones more pronounced. Elana sat in a chair by his bed. She rose to greet Rabigar. He gave her a hug.

'How is the patient?' he asked.

Dirk opened his eyes.

'Rabigar?' he said. 'It's good to see you again.'

'You too, my friend,' said Rabigar, gripping his hand.

'And you've brought an army with you?'

'Yes. The Krykkers and the Knights of Kalinth fighting together. Things should get interesting over the next few days.'

Rabigar took a couple of paces back to stand next to Belwynn.

'I'm sorry I'll miss it,' Dirk said quietly.

'Me too. Is there nothing Elana can do?'

'Yes. She could keep me alive a while longer, I'm sure. But I don't want that any more, Rabigar. I'm at peace with it.'

Dirk turned awkwardly in the bed. 'Belwynn has become Elana's disciple. I won't be leaving her alone, now.'

'Yes,' said Rabigar. 'So I've heard.'

'I'm glad you're all here,' Dirk continued. 'Elana?'

'Yes,' replied the priestess. She opened a chest located in the corner of the room, taking out Toric's Dagger. She silently passed it on to him. They had obviously discussed the weapon between themselves before.

'I will no longer be the keeper of Toric's Dagger,' said Dirk. 'I used it once, to kill Nexodore. Now someone else may have need of it. I think it should be you, Belwynn. In this also, you are my successor.'

'Are you sure?' asked Belwynn, hesitant to accept the weapon. 'I already look after Onella's Staff.'

'True,' replied Dirk. 'But the staff will be Soren's eventually.'

Belwynn smiled. 'I hadn't thought of that. I hope you are right.'

'I have a sense that he will take ownership of the Staff. As for the Dagger, I feel it still has more work to do. Will you accept it, Belwynn?'

'Of course.'

Belwynn moved to Dirk's bed. He handed her the weapon, and they held hands for a while.

Dirk closed his eyes and leaned back in the bed. It looked like he had been freed of the responsibility and could finally rest. They stayed with him for his last moments until he passed away. Rabigar and Belwynn left the room so that Elana could have some time alone. Wordlessly, they both headed downstairs, keen to get outside and take some fresh air.

'So, in the end Nexodore *did* kill him,' commented Rabigar, unable to avoid a feeling of bitterness.

'He died at peace, Rabigar,' said Belwynn. 'Most people don't get that.'

'True. And I can understand the timing.'

'You mean my becoming a disciple? It makes me feel a little like I killed him.'

'I wasn't thinking about that, though I expect it helped him to make his decision. I mean the war ahead of us. Elana's powers will be needed when the fighting starts. Who knows how much it cost her to keep Dirk alive all this time?'

'I hadn't considered that,' said Belwynn. 'I'm not even sure that Elana's powers work like that—in the same way as Soren's magic.'

'It's exactly the same,' said Rabigar.

He seemed so sure that Belwynn didn't see the point of discussing it further.

'Have you heard from Soren?' Rabigar asked.

'No, not in the whole time since you left. I fear for him, and for Clarin and the others too, of course. But I sense that he still lives. Maybe you don't understand, Rabigar, but finding my faith in Madria has helped me to deal with it. I feel like their fate is in Her hands. It's a comfort.'

'I understand well,' replied Rabigar. *After all, I know much about loss.* 'I take Elana's message from Madria seriously. I mentioned to you before, after we left Edeleny, that the Krykkers have one of Madria's weapons. Bolivar's Great Sword, that he used to defeat the Isharites at the Battle of Alta. It is here. We have brought it with us. So, we now have three of the seven weapons in the same place. Maybe that is enough to destroy Ishari.'

'Elana believes that we need all seven to do that.'

The Krykker legends implied that Bolivar won his victory single-handed. But Rabigar had learned enough of the world to think that Elana's version was probably correct.

'Then maybe it is enough for us to win a victory. A victory big enough to see your brother go free.'

'I pray that it will be.'

XIX

SIEGE

THE WALLS OF COLDEBERG LOOMED large. Edgar could see the southern wall ahead of him, but also the far northern wall which rose much higher. The city was situated on a hill, on the summit of which the dukes of Barissia had built their mighty castle. *Nothing in Magnia comes close to being so well defended*, Edgar reflected. None of this deterred Duke Coen, however, who along with his troops had carted huge siege engines to the capital city of his enemy, Emeric.

Inside somewhere was Emeric and the remnants of his army. It had been defeated at the Battle of Lindhafen, but not destroyed. Frayne's Middian cavalry force had given chase to the Barissians, but a substantial part of Emeric's army had been on horseback, and they had successfully fought a rearguard action, allowing his soldiers to make an orderly retreat, and thereby avoiding a massacre.

Edgar's Magnians had seen the worst of the fighting on the left wing of the army. Many had died. Many more had serious injuries, and Coen had ensured that this group were sent with haste to his capital, Lindhafen, for treatment. The rest of the Magnians, who could be described as the walking wounded, had travelled on to Coldeberg to see the campaign to the end.

Edgar put himself firmly in the camp of the walking wounded. After the battle was over, he noticed injuries that he hadn't even known he'd sustained. They had celebrated with barrels of Thessian wine which did a good job of keeping the pain at bay. But it came back with a vengeance the next morning. He felt like he had been thrown off a castle's battlements onto the ground below. His shoulders, arms and legs were a constant dull ache, muscles too stiff to move after his exertions the day before. His back and neck were agony, the slightest movement flaring sharp jolts of pain up and down his spine. He had a headache that wouldn't go away, and a ringing in his ears.

Leofwin and Brictwin had picked him up and forced him to walk around while they supported him on each side. They insisted it did him good to loosen up his muscles, though all they received from him for their help was a string of curse words. Edgar was by no means the only one in such bad shape, and Coen had gone out of his way to ensure that all Magnians had avoided any physical duties since the battle. Edgar still had aches and pains today. He was quite happy to take an observer's role in the siege, while the Thessians prepared camp defences, and began the task of constructing siege equipment.

Edgar had one job to do, though. Coen insisted on the formality of offering the besieged army terms. To Edgar's mind, Emeric's association with Erkindrix of Ishari made such an approach unnecessary and dangerous. But Coen saw it as important, and Edgar had agreed to go with him as the representative of the Southern Alliance. He had insisted that Ealdnoth accompany them, though. Emeric had his own wizard within the walls, and Edgar had no doubt that he would love to see Edgar and Coen dead.

Edgar and Ealdnoth rode ahead to meet Coen, who had come with only one man, holding up a white flag of parley. They made their way to the main gate of the city.

It was a still summer's day, and the flags on the battlements hung limply. The Boar of Barissia could be seen, along with Emeric's newest banner, the Golden Crown. Emeric's decision to claim a crown for himself was starting to cost him dear. Edgar had no sympathy.

The walls were heavily manned by soldiers, confirming their intelligence that Emeric retained a large portion of his army within the city. Coen looked over at Ealdnoth with poorly concealed distaste.

'This wizard of Emeric's. He was at the battle, then?' Coen asked.

'He was, Your Grace,' replied Ealdnoth. 'He was working against the Magnian division and targeted Prince Edgar.'

'Hmm. Is he likely to pose us problems during the siege?'

'He is a powerful wizard. He could pose several threats. Setting fire to siege weapons, targeting individuals on our side. I will need to be vigilant.'

Coen nodded, seemingly willing to let Ealdnoth deal with that issue. He held a hand up indicating that they should stop. They were still some distance from the walls, and Edgar noted that some of his own suspicions about Barissian honour had rubbed off a little on the duke.

They waited a while for someone in authority to arrive. Eventually, a man's head appeared atop the main gate.

'You are safe to approach,' he shouted at them, noting the distance at which they had stopped.

Coen looked at Edgar, who nodded his acceptance. They moved a few feet closer.

'This is Coen of Thesse, and Edgar of Magnia. With whom do we speak?'

'I am Curtis, an officer in the king's army. I recognise a truce for parley and will take your words direct to the king.'

'Nobly said, Curtis. Our message is simple. After our victory at Lindhafen, and with a superior force, we intend to take this city and to arrest the traitor, Emeric. If Duke Emeric surrenders his person to us and the city is opened to us, everyone else here will be free to leave with their possessions and will be unharmed. If there is no surrender, we will take the city by siege, and the lives of those inside will be forfeit. Is that message clear, Curtis?'

'It is, Your Grace. I will pass your terms on to the king.'

'Thank you. Then we are done.'

Edgar turned his horse around, keen to be on his way. The others came with him.

'Do you have any hope of a surrender?' asked Edgar.

'We will see,' replied Coen. 'But never underestimate the willingness of men to save their own skins.'

***

Whilst Ashere's death still haunted him, especially at night, Farred found that his days had become busy enough for him to put it to the back of his mind.

He would, at any odd time of the day, be summoned to Gustav's room. Almost always, it was to help with the wizard's transformation into a hawk. The strangeness of it didn't disappear, but each time it happened he got a little bit more used to it. Brock had noticed these comings and goings, but Farred had made it clear it wasn't something he wanted to discuss. After his first experience, he had made the decision that it would be much easier to keep it to himself.

In addition, he was responsible for supervising the watch in the Emperor's Keep. All the Kellish soldiers were deployed in the defence of the Crag, and so Walter had asked Farred to use his Magnians to keep a permanent guard, especially outside the imperial bedchamber. He made sure that that his men did their duty, and rotated them regularly. But since Walter had first made him aware of the Isharite attempt to send assassins into the keep with magic, it had not happened again.

Farred was carrying out one of his checks with his men when the door to Baldwin's room slowly opened. Turning towards it, he saw a figure emerge. It was Inge, Gustav's young apprentice. She had been given the job of staying at Baldwin's side, in case there was another attempt on his life. She looked straight at Farred, as if expecting him to be here.

'Will you come in?' she asked.

Farred crossed the few feet of floor space and arrived at the door.

'Is everything alright?'

'Yes,' she replied, smiling at him. He wasn't sure that he liked this witch's smile. 'Will you come in?' she repeated.

'Isn't His Majesty inside?'

'Yes.'

She tugged at his arm, pulling him inside the room before closing the door behind him.

'There,' she said, pointing at the bed.

Farred got a glimpse of Baldwin and quickly looked away. The Emperor was spread-eagled on the bed, completely naked. Concerned, Farred took a second glance, but could see his chest rising and falling. He was asleep.

He looked at Inge. She was studying his face, enjoying his reaction.

'I'm afraid I've tired him out,' she said.

Farred could feel his cheeks go red despite himself. There was Inge's smile again. She was smiling at him, not with him.

Farred took a second look at the witch. He had not paid her much mind, until now. When they had first met he had been too concerned about Prince Ashere's injuries to notice her very much.

There was no doubt she was pretty. Very slim, with more of a girl's body than a woman's. Her face, too, was thin and young-looking, framed by braided, long blonde hair. Her bright blue eyes were fixed on his: sparkling at him, and mocking him at the same time. He could understand why some men might find her attractive. She was making it perfectly plain that Baldwin did.

Why had she brought him in here? To toy with him? Because she wanted to show off that she had bedded the Emperor?

'You seem surprised,' she whispered at him, her voice sounding huskier. 'What would you do if you shared a room with me day and night?'

Again, that mocking smile.

Farred felt a burst of anger. He grabbed the door handle.

'What the Emperor does is his business.'

At the same time as he said it, a contrary train of thought ran through his mind. Should he tell someone? Should he tell Walter that his brother, the Emperor, was fornicating with a witch? While his men fought for him outside on the Crag?

He pulled open the door and left the room, closing it behind him to the sound of tinkling laughter.

In the corridor, he was met with knowing smiles and winks from his men.

His mind raced with paranoia. *What, exactly, are they smiling about? Does the sound of Baldwin and Inge screwing carry through the walls?*

'Not a word,' he said, keeping the warning suitably vague.

Turning, he stomped off down the corridor.

More secrets, he said to himself. *More secrets I don't want.*

***

Until Theron had shown her a map, Belwynn hadn't fully appreciated how precarious Kalinth's position was.

To the north lay three enemies: Kharovia, the lands of the Drobax, and Haskany. All were under the control of Ishari. To the east lay conquered Persala. To the south, the newly conquered lands of the Grand Caladri. The only friendly border the kingdom had left was with the Krykkers. Thanks to Rabigar's intervention, they had now provided a formidable army to bolster the Kalinthian forces. But the odds seemed stacked against them, nonetheless. It made her wonder to herself whether King Jonas's policy of peace was so wrong after all. But she wasn't about to express that thought out loud. Not when Sebastian, Theron, and the rest of the Knights were risking so much on this venture.

Sebastian's close friend, Remigius, had come down with his force of knights from the High Tower, where the old Grand Master, Galenos, was still held captive. Sebastian added these knights to his army, but appointed Remi to take control of Heractus until they returned.

Prince Dorian had agreed to join the army, bringing with him a few hundred Kalinthians willing to fight for wages or advancement. When

Belwynn had asked him about it, he admitted that his father was unhappy with the decision—a comment which she was sure must be a massive understatement. Even if the force under Dorian's control was small, his presence lent a legitimacy to the army, for which Sebastian was extremely grateful.

After a Council of War with the Krykker chieftains, Theron had got agreement for his invasion of Haskany. There were various strategic reasons behind the decision, which Theron had explained to her, and which Belwynn only half understood. Of course, the fact that the main Haskan army was besieging Burkhard Castle in the Empire, and had therefore left the country only lightly defended, was easy enough to comprehend. But it was also felt that the move would put the greatest pressure on Ishari, and for Belwynn that was all that really mattered. It meant that it held the greatest chance of a rescue of Soren, Clarin and the others. However remote that chance might be.

They marched at a slower pace than the army of the Knights had done on its way to Heractus. While the Krykkers kept up a mean walking pace, they travelled on foot rather than horseback. The Knights of Kalinth scouted the route ahead, but otherwise were restricted to the pace set by the Krykker infantry.

In addition, both the Knights and the Krykkers had brought many carts, filled with siege equipment and other supplies. These carts trundled along at the rear of the army, and acted as another break on the pace they could set. The Kalinthians used draft horses, specially bred for their size and strength. They were larger but slower than the horses used for war. The Krykkers, meanwhile, pulled their carts with buffalo. The biggest of these reached the height of a horse. They had wicked looking curved horns, that sprouted from a solid bone base which covered the top of their heads. This bone shield made them even more formidable looking, and Rabigar had warned Belwynn not to get too close to any of them.

The weather was fine. Belwynn rode next to Elana, with Dorian on the other side of the priestess. The Prince's force of Kalinthians followed behind them, positioned between the Knights and the Krykkers.

To the east, the Dardelles mountain range knifed out of the ground, serving as a natural boundary between the lands of Kalinth, Persala and Haskany. Their route took them to the far north of Kalinth, from where they could cross east into Haskany. It was rough, hilly land compared to most of Magnia. The

Krykkers, however, referred to it dismissively as flatlands, and it proved no obstacle either to them or to their buffalo drawn carts.

A feeling of exhilaration swept over the force as they crossed from Kalinth into Haskany. Belwynn was no exception. It felt daring to be in the lands controlled by Erkindrix of Ishari. There was also a sense of relief, that they were no longer cowering in fear from the threat, but instead acting to deal with it. Belwynn was sure that nobody present doubted that the odds were stacked against them. For now, though, they could almost feel like they were winning.

It wasn't long afterwards that the Kalinthians came to a halt. Dorian ordered his men to wait, too. Behind them, the stragglers from Dorian's unit and the Krykkers would take a while to catch up. Belwynn and Elana dismounted to stretch their legs.

A group of riders came down the line from the front. One of them was Evander, Theron's squire, and he stopped when he saw them.

'The Grand Master asks that you attend the War Council,' he said, addressing Dorian. 'He also invites you to come too,' he said, turning to Belwynn and Elana.

'You two go,' said Elana. 'If we're stopping for a while it's a good time for me to attend to the soldiers.'

'Are you sure you don't want me to accompany you?' asked Belwynn.

'No, I'll be fine.'

'Moris, please accompany the Lady Elana while I'm away,' Dorian asked one of his men.

'Of course, Your Highness.'

The soldier immediately dismounted and attended on Elana.

'Thank you,' said Elana.

Belwynn remounted her horse, and she followed Evander and Dorian up the line to the front of the army. Evander turned to the left and took them off the track. A group of sheep moved out of their way as the squire led them up a slope to the top of a rise. Here, Sebastian, Theron and Tycho were waiting for them. Evander helped Belwynn to dismount, and she and Dorian joined the three knights. Theron pointed ahead of them. The terrain sloped downhill and then back up. On the far rise lay a large Haskan fortress. It was a square shape, and had good views over the surrounding area.

'Masada,' said Theron. 'Built to control this route into Haskany. Our two countries have been at peace for a century, but nonetheless it's been upgraded recently.'

It looked a formidable structure to Belwynn, with thick walls all the way around.

'I believe that we still have the element of surprise,' Theron continued, 'and that there will only be a skeleton garrison inside. But that doesn't mean it's easy to break in.'

'What about ignoring it and carrying on past?' asked Dorian.

'It's an option,' agreed Theron. 'But at some point, if he has not already, Erkindrix will get news of our army. If that fortress gets reinforced, and we find ourselves wanting to retreat, we could get trapped.'

Dorian nodded, acknowledging the dilemma.

'What's up?' demanded a gruff voice, as Sebastian's squire, Alpin, led four Krykkers up the slope to join them.

The voice belonged to Torinac, one of the Krykker chieftains. He carried Madria's weapon, Bolivar's Great Sword, tucked into his belt wherever he went, and acted like he was in charge of the Krykker army. But, in fact, the other two chieftains held equal weight. Maragin, a female chief, was much quieter, but Belwynn suspected had a sharper mind. Guremar was the third. He tended to scowl a lot, especially at Rabigar, who had accompanied them. He clearly didn't like the fact that Rabigar attended these meetings, but Sebastian always made a point of inviting Belwynn's friend along, and Guremar had stopped short of directly complaining about it.

'Greetings,' said Sebastian, shaking each of them by the hand. 'We have a good view of the fort of Masada from here,' he explained, indicating the view. 'We were just saying it's an impressive structure, but probably lightly defended. We need to decide what to do about it.'

'Take it,' said Torinac immediately. 'Between us we have all the necessary siege equipment.'

'The trouble is,' said Tycho, 'a conventional siege may last days. That would give the Haskans and any other Isharite forces time to get an army together and attempt to raise the siege. We may end up facing superior forces here with very little achieved.'

'I take your point,' said Torinac. 'But we can't leave it in enemy hands behind our lines either. That could lead to disaster. We'll have to leave a force here to carry out the siege while the main part of the army moves on.'

'That might be the most sensible move,' agreed Theron. 'I was thinking of trying a ruse of some kind. Moving our army past the fort as if we are gone, but staying hidden. Then allowing a small force to get close to their gates, see if we can draw them out into the open.'

Torinac shrugged. 'It's worth a try, Count Theron. Why not? I would say the chances of them opening the gates are small, though. They must know that their best chance of survival is to hold tight and wait for support.'

'You're sure there's only a small force inside?' asked Rabigar.

'I can't be completely certain,' said Theron. 'But we know that the main Haskan army is in Brasingia under Queen Shira. Until a few days ago Kalinth was a neutral neighbour. There would be no reason to leave a significant force here. Why do you ask?'

'I have an idea of a ruse that may work and save us some time. I would have to put it to the three chieftains first, in private. They may well disregard it.'

The three Krykker chieftains looked at him, their faces showing varying amounts of interest and suspicion. The four of them walked down the slope for their private conversation, dispersing a group of sheep who had dared to venture half way up.

Belwynn looked over at the fortress. In a matter of minutes, this war had become very real, and rather complicated.

***

It was pitch black. Even with his superior eyesight, Kaved had to tread carefully. One false move and the whole Magnian army might wake. The Magnians had the exact same tents as the Middians, which made it hard to determine if he was in the right spot.

Every tent had soldiers inside, with guy ropes pegged into the ground. They were invisible in the darkness, and Kaved had to move cautiously to avoid tripping over them. Despite his care, more than once he walked into a rope, some down at his ankles, others at chest or waist height.

He positioned himself in what seemed to be the right spot, and waited. Out there in the darkness somewhere were Salvinus and Tirano. The tent they were all aiming for belonged to Prince Edgar's wizard. Tirano had insisted that they had to kill him first, if their assassination of the prince was to be a success. The wizard had frustrated Tirano's attempts to kill Edgar at the Battle of Lindhafen. That had probably been enough to turn the tide of the battle from victory to defeat.

Well. Now it was time for revenge.

An owl hooted. That was the signal. Tirano must have somehow determined that the wizard was in the tent.

Kaved moved towards their victim, treading carefully once more. He took his hand axe from his belt, the perfect weapon for close quarter butchering. To his left his eyes just made out the form of someone else heading for the tent. Tirano. So, he was in the right place.

'Go.'

The wizard's voice, drifting through the night, was so quiet you could make yourself believe that you had imagined it.

Kaved got to the tent. A last-minute change of mind. He swapped his axe for his sword, since it would be easier to get in with the piercing blade. Holding the canvas taut, he punctured it with the sharp tip of his sword blade, then sliced down, making an opening big enough to get through. He dived in, keen to be as quick as possible.

Someone entered from the opposite side of the tent. Salvinus. Kaved looked around. There. The wizard was sitting up, but held immobile by Tirano's magic. He had one arm outstretched towards the front of the tent as if he were trying to combat the spell. Kaved moved in for the kill. The wizard caught the movement, his eyes turning in his head to look at Kaved. But the rest of his body still couldn't move. Kaved plunged his sword into the wizard's chest from the side. Salvinus had now caught up with the action, and he finished the job, repeatedly stabbing the wizard, to make sure that he was really dead.

Kaved gave a shudder. He relived the eyes of the wizard turning towards him, looking at his killer but unable to move. Not a good way to die.

'Come on, let's go,' whispered Salvinus in the dark. 'We need to kill the prince as quickly as possible.'

XX

THE ROCK WALKERS

I T WAS STILL NIGHT-TIME. WHAT had woken him?

It took a moment for Edgar's mind to break through the fog of sleep. He was in a tent outside the city of Coldeberg. He always slept lightly in a new place. Maybe that was all it was. Still, some instinct made him sit up and reach over for his sword.

His movement stirred his ever-watchful bodyguards, Leofwin and Brictwin. Then, black forms could be seen: out in the darkness, outside the tent. Edgar tried to call out a warning, but he found that his voice didn't work. His muscles couldn't move. The same thing that had happened to him in the Battle of Lindhafen. He pushed against the restriction, trying to move his body, but it was no good.

From three different directions, the tent was suddenly invaded by the black forms. Edgar could see Leofwin and Brictwin stumble to their feet. To Edgar's right, a Krykker, heavy-set and carrying a sword and axe, burst in. Brictwin reacted first. As the Krykker spotted Edgar, Brictwin slashed at the creature with his sword, forcing it to block the strike.

To Edgar's left, the second figure to enter the tent was familiar. Gervase Salvinus. So—they had come to kill him. Perhaps he should have expected this. Salvinus walked towards him but Leofwin blocked his path.

From the front of the tent a third figure emerged, the whites of its eyes focused on Edgar in the darkness. Edgar instantly knew that this was the Ishari wizard who served Emeric, and that his immobility was caused by the wizard's magic. With the wizard's focus fully fixed on him, he had no chance of escaping the spell.

Where was Ealdnoth?

Leofwin feinted towards Salvinus, who blocked at a strike that never came. Instead, Leofwin launched himself towards the wizard.

'Stop him!' the wizard screamed, turning his attention from Edgar to Leofwin.

Edgar struggled to move, but somehow the wizard's spell still kept him pinned down.

The Ishari put out a hand towards Leofwin, and a bolt of magic leapt from his outstretched hand towards Edgar's bodyguard.

Leofwin cried out in pain, but forced himself to push through the bolt at the wizard. Salvinus had now caught up with Leofwin, and ran him through from behind.

Edgar let out a silent scream as he watched his enemy slay the man who had been by his side since youth.

Somehow, with whatever strength he had left, Leofwin kept his momentum going forwards. Edgar could see the wizard's eyes open in fear, as Leofwin plunged his blade into the man's chest, before collapsing to the ground.

Suddenly, Edgar was freed. Rising, he raised the sword still clutched in his hand, and charged at Salvinus, who leapt out of the way.

'It's lost,' shouted the mercenary leader, backing out of the tent.

The Krykker, who had been contained by Brictwin, followed suit, exiting through the slit he had cut in the tent's side. Brictwin rushed over to his uncle, stabbing down into the neck of the wizard to make sure he was dead.

Edgar glanced down at Leofwin's prone body before following Salvinus out of the tent. He could just see the mercenary ahead, making his way in between two tents.

'Awake! Awake!' shouted Edgar at the top of his voice. 'Enemies!'

He chased after Salvinus, determined not to let him out of his sight. Suddenly, his face had slammed into the dirt floor.

'Shit!'

He'd tripped over a damned tent rope. Pushing himself up, he looked for Salvinus. But he was out of sight, swallowed by the darkness.

His men were beginning to emerge from their tents.

'Two of them,' Edgar yelled at them. 'One of them was Salvinus, the other a Krykker.'

Bleary eyed, the Magnian soldiers began their search, but Edgar knew that he had lost his best chance of catching Salvinus.

With a heavy heart, he returned to his tent. Brictwin was kneeling next to his uncle's body. He had turned Leofwin over onto his back, but there was no life left in him.

'I'm sorry,' said Edgar, sinking down to his knees on Leofwin's other side.

214

'Don't be, Your Highness,' said Brictwin. The younger man's face was grave, but there were no tears. 'He died to save your life. He wouldn't have wanted it any other way.'

A rustle of noise made Edgar look up.

Wilchard entered the tent, blanching at the sight of Leofwin's corpse. He locked eyes with Edgar.

'I'm sorry, Your Highness. It's Ealdnoth. They killed him first.'

'No,' Edgar moaned.

Too much. The price he'd paid for this war. Too much.

***

Shira walked gingerly towards the great doors of the Council Chamber of Samir Durg. She had been forced to endure a teleportation from the siege of Burkhard Castle all the way to the Isharite fortress. Her stomach roiled as if she was going to be sick.

Waiting for her outside the room, as was his custom, was her husband. With Arioc stood Rostam, one of his lieutenants. Shira was surprised to see him here. As she neared she noticed a strange expression on Arioc's face. She couldn't quite identify what it was, but decided it was probably bad news.

'Husband,' she said to Arioc, nodding at Rostam as well.

'Wife,' said Arioc, with equal irony.

Rostam had his usual smirk on his face. He was favoured by Arioc, useful as both a military commander and as a magus, though Shira was unsure how powerful his magic was. He was certainly an intimidating man, who wore only black and carried a black crystal sword, matching his dark hair and eyes. There were also the rumours that he was Arioc's son. It was nothing Arioc had ever commented on, but it added to Rostam's sense of self-importance, that was for sure.

What a twisted little family we are, thought Shira.

'Well, we have *some* good news,' said Arioc. 'Rostam has been promoted to the Council.'

Shira couldn't hide her surprise. Rostam's smirk grew bigger.

'Congratulations. But how?'

'Nexodore is dead,' replied Arioc. 'I informed Erkindrix of this some time ago, but it took him this long to believe me. Rostam was appointed in a small meeting of the Council yesterday.'

Arioc openly voicing frustration with Erkindrix was unusual. There was a strange tension in the air, something Shira couldn't quite put her finger on. Arioc should have been happy. He now had both herself and Rostam, essentially two puppets, on the Council. Nexodore, one of his biggest rivals, had somehow been removed. Yet he still looked troubled.

There was no time to find out more. Without further comment, Arioc moved to the doors to the Council Chamber and pushed them open.

Everyone else was waiting for them. At the head of the table sat Erkindrix. Shira tried to avoid looking directly at him. To his left was Siavash, High Priest of Ishari, Erkindrix's shadow. Next to Siavash sat Pentas, the haughty red-eyed wizard. To the right of Erkindrix was Ardashir, an Isharite said to equal Erkindrix in age, and who had been a loyalist for centuries. Sat next to him was a strange looking creature Shira had never met before. Logic said it must be Dorjan, King of the Shadow Caladri. He was a thin, wizened man—his limbs looked like they might snap if put to too much use. Yet at the same time he carried an aura of power that matched the others at the table.

The full Council was here, for the first time since Shira had been made a member.

Shira, Arioc and Rostam took their places at the opposite end of the table to Erkindrix. Shira was glad to be as far away from him as possible.

'We *should* have had a victory by now,' said Erkindrix with no preamble, his voice wet with saliva. 'Diis is not pleased.'

Diis, Arioc had once explained to Shira, was the being that inhabited Erkindrix. She hadn't wanted to know more than that, and the mention of its name put her on edge.

'Shira,' continued Erkindrix, his grey eyes turning to her and the black eyes beneath burning like hot coals in her direction. 'Why have you failed to conquer the Brasingians?'

Shira swallowed. She was to feel the wrath of the dread lord, and neither Arioc nor anyone else on the Council would offer her the tiniest amount of support.

'They have put up a stern resistance at Burkhard Castle,' she explained, only too aware of how pathetic she sounded. 'Even the Drobax have not yet been

216

able to break through. When we take Burkhard, the rest of the Empire will fall.'

'The Empire is proving tougher than we expected, Arioc?' continued Erkindrix, his voice full of sarcasm.

'Indeed. We have a setback to report. The forces of Duke Emeric have been defeated by a mixed force of Thessians, Magnians and Middians. I had not anticipated the intervention of the Southerners, for which I apologise. However, Rostam and I have completed clearing the Grand Caladri from their lands. The remnants of their race have been given sanctuary by the Krykkers. I am now free to deal with the Empire.'

Shira went hot with anger, struggling to hold it in. Rather than backing her, Arioc had implied that he should take over the invasion of Brasingia.

'*I* will decide who goes where,' said Erkindrix, letting vent to his own anger. He pointed a finger at Pentas. 'The weapons of Madria are still at large. They have found their way to Kalinth.'

'Then he spirited them there himself,' accused Arioc.

'That is a lie,' responded Pentas, remaining calm but defending himself. 'Arioc had the chance to get the dagger and staff in Edeleny and bungled it. I have only just traced them to Kalinth. It would now seem that the Krykkers have raised an army and joined the Knights of Kalinth. I suspect they have their sword with them. They intend to go on the offensive.'

'How could you have let this happen?' demanded Siavash, looking around the table. Shira had never heard him speak before. He had a quiet but deadly sounding voice. 'We have committed our forces to gain a quick victory. The longer the enemy resists, the more they could become a threat to us. The weapons should have been taken by now.'

'Don't forget,' said Pentas, 'that it was Nexodore who was tasked with finding Madria's weapons, something he singularly failed to do. But this turn of events should be seen as an opportunity, rather than something to fear. Now that I know where they are, I can put my hands on three of the weapons at once. That will end the threat from Madria for good.'

'I'll get the weapons,' snarled Arioc.

'You just said you would deal with the Empire,' Pentas pointed out smugly.

'Enough,' said Erkindrix. 'Siavash is correct. We must deal with these threats quickly. A new army must be raised to confront the Kalinthians and Krykkers. All remaining forces in the north, including the Drobax, will be deployed. Rostam, you will raise this army and defeat the enemy. You will take some of the forces based here, and supplement them as best you can. Pentas, you will liaise with him, but your focus will be on bringing me the three weapons, as soon as possible. Arioc and Shira, you will destroy the Brasingians. Use Emeric's forces or ignore them, but either way I must see this done. No more excuses. Ardashir and Dorjan, your campaigns have stalled. I need to see them concluded so that your armies can be redeployed. Anyone who fails me will be killed and replaced.' Erkindrix looked around the table. '*Anyone.*'

They left the Council Chamber. Arioc was quiet but Shira could tell that he was fuming. Rostam's smirk had gone.

'I'd better get straight to it,' said the younger man. Shira knew what he was feeling. The exhilaration of commanding his own army for the first time, mixed with the responsibility. 'Good luck in Brasingia,' he added.

Arioc and Shira nodded at him and he marched off.

'How *dare* he threaten me?' whispered Arioc hoarsely.

Shira hadn't seen him this angry before. She was unsure what to say. Caught between the hostility of Erkindrix and Arioc, she felt out of her depth.

'I should have been put in charge of dealing with the Krykkers,' he continued. 'My record is flawless.'

'Well, for what it's worth, I agree.'

And she did. Arioc's presence could offer little to speed up the siege of Burkhard Castle. While Rostam and Pentas hardly inspired confidence as a team.

'Greetings,' said a smooth voice. Pentas, a sardonic smile playing on his lips. Shira got a creepy feeling, as if he had been reading her thoughts.

'What do you want?' snapped Arioc, full of hostility.

'I will get the weapons,' said Pentas confidently. 'But still, all is not well. Erkindrix is getting weaker; his decision making less sound. This whole campaign has been poorly managed.'

Arioc's eyes opened wide. 'Disloyalty. You play a dangerous game, Pentas. I should kill you where you stand.'

'I could be an ally, Arioc,' replied Pentas, sounding serious for once, looking him in the eye, doing the same to Shira. Those red eyes, repulsive and inscrutable. His gaze turned back to Arioc. 'How long can we let this go on for?'

With that, he turned and walked away.

Shira raised her eyebrows, waiting for some comment from Arioc. But there was none. Instead, that unfamiliar expression had returned to his face. Then she realised what it was. A state of mind she had never witnessed in him before. Indecision.

***

The Dramsen clan were a hive of activity: assembling, testing, and then firing their great siege weapons in the direction of the Haskan fortress of Masada. Making his voice heard above all the noise was their chief, Torinac. Instructions, advice, admonitions—all were hurled in a torrent of words at his hardworking soldiers. Whether he was any help; whether his men were actually paying any attention to him, Belwynn couldn't be sure. But she admired his energy, nonetheless.

She watched, fascinated, as the men working on the machines made their modifications. Each time, they got a bit closer to their target.

Rabigar's plan had asked for a lot. He wanted the biggest boulders that the Krykkers had carted with them from their homeland to be fired, not at the walls of Masada, but over them. That required such a huge amount of force that only their largest weapons, the trebuchets, could be used. The Knights had nothing as large as this, and so had been deployed to defend the army's position, preventing any attempt by the defenders to destroy the great weapons.

The Krykker machinists had to move slowly and carefully. The pressure on the wooden frame was immense, and if the beam holding the ammunition were to snap, those standing close by could be seriously injured. In addition, a massive counterweight had to be deployed to create enough force to send the boulders over the walls, and there was a danger that this could pull the whole contraption over.

By the end of the day, the Krykkers had built two trebuchets that could successfully and reliably fire the required weight over the walls. Rabigar had wanted the boulders fired at night time, and so, in the gathering darkness, they were laboriously and carefully nestled into the trebuchet's sling.

The first weight was released, and everyone's hearts were in their mouths as the boulder soared high up into the sky. Once it reached the top of its arc, the boulder descended quickly, but Belwynn could clearly see it come down

219

on the other side of the wall. A thud could be heard as it hit, suggesting that it had landed on the ground within the fort's walls.

Everyone looked at each other for a while. They had done exactly what Rabigar had requested. Only time would tell whether his plan would work. Torinac gave the command, and the next boulder was loaded on.

***

Rabigar waited. It had been a long time since he had stayed in rock for this long. He had to rely on the training from his youth, to make his mind ignore the feelings of claustrophobia and suffocation. If he let himself panic, he would die.

Suddenly there was a massive crack above him, and Rabigar felt the impact as another boulder landed on top of his. He heard it roll off onto the floor. *That's a good sign*, he told himself. *It shows the targeting of the trebuchets is accurate.* He waited until the noise of boulders thudding into the fort had stopped, and then he waited some more, just in case.

It was time to move. He began to push his way out of the boulder. It wasn't easy to get started from his position: fully encased in stone, lying all ends up. He pushed hard with his legs, pulled with his arms, until he forced his head out of the rock. He took a long, deep breath of air. The dirt floor of the fort was just a few inches beneath him. He wriggled free of the massive boulder, taking great care with his movements. He had the cover of darkness in his favour, but the fort's defenders could be close by.

Once Rabigar was out, he lay prone for a while, avoiding any further suspicious movement. He began to scan the area. It was difficult in the darkness, in an unknown environment, to get his bearings. He could see the outline of half a dozen other boulders around him. At one, then a second, he saw Krykkers slithering out. But he still wasn't sure about their location. Slowly, he crawled around to the other side of the boulder. Here, he could see the outline of two walls. Where they met, at one corner of the fort, he could see a tower. So, they had made it, then. They had been thrown inside the fort.

How many had survived? He crawled back around his boulder. He could see a group of Krykker meeting up in the darkness and joined them. He was relieved to see that one of them was Maragin. When he had first come up with the idea of using Krykker rock walkers to get into the fort, he knew that it was

Maragin who would have to be convinced. Guremar had been against the idea of course, because it was Rabigar's. Torinac was easy enough to persuade. It was Maragin, as a rock walker herself, and as the leader of the best trained rock walkers from the Grendal clan, who would have the decisive say.

Krykkers couldn't move through just any rock, or they could have pushed their way through the fort walls. They could only move through Krykker rock, from their homeland. The fact that they had brought with them four carts full of massive boulders had given Rabigar the idea in the first place. But the only way for the plan to work was for them to enter the boulders and get catapulted over the walls while inside them. Rabigar had thought they would be relatively safe inside the rock, but he couldn't be sure. Maragin had thought about it for some time before agreeing.

'How many?' Rabigar whispered to her.

'Seven of us here,' Maragin replied. 'Seven still out there somewhere. It's too dark to see where all the boulders landed. We'll have to look for them.'

Rabigar hadn't fully thought through this part of the plan. In his mind's eye, they would quickly leave the boulders and head for the fort's gate. It wasn't quite as easy as that.

'We can't afford to be seen,' he warned Maragin. 'We'd be better off going straight for the gate.'

'Give me two minutes,' she said.

'Alright,' Rabigar acquiesced.

It had been more of an order than a request anyway. The other rock walkers were *her* soldiers, and would do what she said. They were all younger than Rabigar, and still had two eyes each, so he let them head off around the courtyard of Masada to locate their comrades. It didn't take long. As he watched them move about, other figures emerged from the darkness to join up with them. The only delay occurred around one boulder. Rabigar could see two Krykkers push into it and drag out a body. They left it on the ground. So, one of them hadn't made it: killed by the initial impact as they had landed on the ground, or perhaps by suffocation inside.

Maragin led her soldiers back to Rabigar's position.

'Thirteen,' she whispered.

Thirteen of the fourteen rock walkers were here. They had suffered the first casualty of the war. War, when lives suddenly became assets which leaders traded for advantage. If they lost just the one life in exchange for opening the gates of the fort, it would be considered a good trade.

'Are we ready to go then?' he asked her.

'Ready.'

They moved off, the plan of attack agreed before they had climbed into the boulders. They all headed to the left, away from the tower, before moving ahead. Rabigar, along with most of the Krykkers, aimed straight for the main gate.

'Who goes there?' came a call, from the walkway along the wall above them.

It was quickly followed by warning shouts.

'Invaders!' went the cry.

They had been seen. No great surprise, but they had to act fast. Rabigar ran faster, hoping to make the gate before he was shot down in the open. He sensed an object flash past him in the darkness, but kept on moving.

Two other groups, each made up of three rock walkers, had peeled off to the sides: heading for two rooms located either side of the gate. Beyond the gate was a portcullis. One of the rooms would contain the lever mechanism that raised it. The gate and portcullis had been built a few feet apart, creating an area known as a killing field. The two rooms would have murder holes facing this area, used to kill an enemy that got trapped between the gate and portcullis. The two smaller groups had to neutralise these rooms. It was risky, because they didn't know whether Haskan soldiers would be stationed there; and if they were, how many there would be.

Rabigar and the main group of Krykkers got to the main gate. It was made of solid wood, shod with iron. Their first job was to lift off the heavy iron locking bar that ran horizontally across the full width of the gate. They heaved together, lifting it up from the hooks it rested on. They walked back with it a few steps, before dumping it on the ground. The other Krykkers got to work on the locks on the gate, fumbling in the dark. Rabigar got to his knees and took out the torch he had brought with him on his belt. Holding it between his knees he then reached inside his pockets for flint and steel. Scraping the steel along the flint, Rabigar got a spark to land on his char cloth. He carefully coaxed it into a flame until the tinder of his torch caught alight.

Without warning, a blow on his chest nearly knocked him over. He put one hand out to break his fall, only just managing to keep hold of his newly lit torch. Quickly getting to his feet, he saw an arrow lying on the floor. Luckily, it had deflected off the tough scales on his chest, and he was unharmed.

The other Krykkers had got the gate open. Rabigar rushed forwards. Ahead, he could see the portcullis being raised. That meant that the other rock walkers had successfully cleared at least one of the rooms. There could still be Haskan soldiers in the other room, plus there were the soldiers manning the walls. But he had to risk it.

Rabigar sprinted through the gate and kept going. Before he knew it, he was ducking under the portcullis, still only half way up, and then outside the fort. He waved his torch from side to side, and hoped that he could be seen.

XXI

PENTAS THE WIZARD

A FTER THE EXCITEMENT OF THE TREBUCHETS, Belwynn rushed over to the forward position of the assault squads. They were located as close to the fort as they could get, without the risk of being seen. Here, a jut of rock emerged from the ground that provided sufficient cover. If Rabigar and the rest of his Krykkers managed to open the gate, it was a relatively short dash to get inside the fort. Sebastian wanted both the Knights and the Krykkers to gain credit for a victory, so there were two units. On the right side of the rock, Guremar led a force of Krykkers. On the left, Theron led a force of Knights, all on foot. Both units were fully armoured, to give them maximum protection when they approached the walls.

There was a nervous tension in the air as the soldiers waited in silence. It began to affect Belwynn. She started to worry about Rabigar—had his gamble worked or not? It had taken her aback when she had first heard his plan. The idea that some Krykkers could immerse themselves inside rock was something she had never heard of. Moreover, the news that Rabigar was one of those with the power surprised her further. It wasn't just that he had never mentioned it before. She remembered, more than once, the Krykker expressing a hostile attitude towards magic. If walking through rock wasn't magic, she didn't know what was. But it appeared that the Krykkers didn't see it that way.

Excited murmurs rose amongst the Krykkers, suggesting that they had seen something. Belwynn peered in the direction of the fort, but couldn't make anything out in the darkness. The Knights hadn't reacted either—perhaps the Krykkers had better eyesight in the dark.

Guremar moved his forces out, around the jut of rock towards the fort.

'It's open,' he shouted gruffly across to Theron and his knights.

Belwynn could see Theron's Knights hesitate, before they too began to move out from their hiding place. She peered towards the fort a second time. Yes—perhaps she did see a flicker of light at the bottom of the fort, where the gate would be.

Once they were out in the open, the Krykkers and Knights picked up speed, running for the fort as fast as they could in their heavy armour. The Krykkers moved faster, since they only required armour for their limbs and heads; the thick scales on their torsos negating the need for the heavy coats of mail that weighed down the Knights. There was no time to waste. Rabigar's team may have got the gate open, but the fort's defenders would be desperate to get it closed again as soon as possible.

Belwynn watched on anxiously, as the assault squads disappeared into the night. Part of her wanted to chase after them, but she stayed where she was. She peered into the darkness, and listened out for the sounds of fighting.

The rising sun shed its light over the newly captured fortress of Masada. The generals of the army, led by Sebastian and Prince Dorian, made their way through the gate that Rabigar's team had forced open. Sebastian's knights now manned it, as they did the high walls of the fort, which had been left undamaged by the trebuchet attack.

Belwynn had spent the night inside the fort. She had helped Elana tend to the injured. There were mercifully few of them: only four fatalities in all, and the priestess had been able to carry out her healing on those with serious wounds. Elana was confident that there would be no more deaths, though some of the soldiers would survive with permanent disabilities. The priestess had healed the injured Haskan soldiers with equal attention. There had been some grumbling at this, but they had been allowed to complete their work.

Sebastian and Dorian inspected the courtyard of the fort. While the walls of the fort had been avoided, the same could not be said for this area. Great boulders, that had once contained Krykkers, still lay scattered about where they had landed the night before. It was a strange sight, and Belwynn had to smile at Sebastian's slightly baffled expression. He noticed Belwynn at the far side of the courtyard, and he and Dorian walked over to join her.

'Lady Belwynn,' Dorian said, formally.

'Your Highness,' she replied. 'Theron is in the main hall. I can take you both there, if you wish.'

'Yes,' said Sebastian. 'We need to be on our way this morning.'

Belwynn led them to the far end of the courtyard, where the fort buildings were located. She passed the barracks, where some of the soldiers still slept, and led them to the hall of the fort commander. It was a simple affair, with an open space for public meeting, and some private quarters. Inside Theron was alone, standing over a table. On it was a map he was carefully studying, but he stopped when he noticed his visitors.

'Congratulations!' said Dorian as they entered.

'I can hardly take much credit, Your Highness,' said Theron, moving over to shake the Prince and then his uncle by the hand. 'That should go to Rabigar and the Krykkers, for getting inside and opening the gate. Once we got inside, the Haskans couldn't put up much resistance, they were too small in numbers. When we forced our way onto the walls it was over.'

'Well,' said Dorian, 'I shall make sure that I find Rabigar and offer my thanks.'

'We have about fifty of them altogether as prisoners,' continued Theron. 'I wasn't sure whether we should keep them alive—'

'Theron!' said Belwynn, shocked.

'I should think so,' said Dorian. 'The Haskans aren't our real enemy, after all. They are following the orders of Arioc and Erkindrix.'

Theron shrugged. 'If we keep them alive here it will mean leaving a larger force behind to guard them. Otherwise we should just let them go.'

Sebastian nodded. 'Letting them go may be the best option. Have you any thoughts about today?'

'It gets difficult from here. We need to head north-east so that we threaten the Ishari fortress of Samir Durg. That is likely to have the biggest impact. But we need to scout carefully about us. The Dardelles mountains become a forest to our east, and it's a perfect place to hide an army. To the west lie the lands of the Drobax. If he doesn't know already, Erkindrix will soon learn about our invasion. We're in very dangerous territory from now on.'

'At least we have the fort here to fall back on,' commented Dorian.

Theron looked at him. 'I've been thinking about that. We need to leave a garrison behind here, and I think your Kalinthian force is the perfect size. It would also mean we don't lose any Knights or Krykkers from the army. We'll need every one of them should we come to battle. Would you be willing to stay as the commander?'

Dorian looked taken aback by Theron's suggestion, glancing first at Sebastian, then at Belwynn.

'It makes sense,' Sebastian added. 'We need a strong presence here. It's strategically vital.'

226

'Then of course I will stay at the fort,' said Dorian, regaining some composure. 'I will organise my men at once. If you will excuse me?'

Sebastian nodded and Dorian turned about, leaving the hall at pace.

'Was that necessary?' Belwynn asked Theron when the Prince had left.

'His force is perfect for the job,' said Theron. 'Able enough to defend the fort, but not so big a loss from the army.'

'Yes, but someone else could have stayed behind to lead them,' Belwynn pointed out.

'Well, I don't trust him,' Theron admitted. 'He's only here to gain the glory from the campaign for himself.'

'That's unfair,' said Belwynn, angry that Dorian was being done a disservice.

'Maybe so,' said Sebastian. 'But this way at least he stands a better chance of living through it. I don't particularly want to get an heir to the throne killed. Those of us who carry on need to be aware that their chances aren't good.' He paused, looking her in the eyes. 'I think you should stay here too, Belwynn. I know you want to get your brother freed. But there's no point in getting killed in the process.'

'No way,' she insisted immediately.

'It will be dangerous,' commented Theron. 'But the Knights...many of them will fight better if she comes. They've come to see her as a fortune bringer.'

A fortune bringer. It was a stupid idea, and Theron had played it for all it was worth. But Belwynn wanted to go, so she kept her thoughts to herself.

Sebastian sighed. 'I've noticed. Warriors are superstitious by nature. We have no king to inspire them, and now we are leaving our Prince behind. But if you come with us, Belwynn, you can't expect any special protection. We can't spare a single soldier.'

'I understand that. And should there be a battle I hope that I will be of some help to Elana.'

The Grand Master of the Knights nodded, his expression grim. 'So be it.'

After days of sunshine, grey clouds covered the skies above Haskany and the temperature cooled. On the ground, the combined army of Krykkers and Knights left the fortress of Masada far behind, heading out into the featureless landscape of the far north.

Dry scrub dominated the terrain, making it seem, to Belwynn's eyes, an inhospitable land. It certainly wasn't farming land, and they didn't pass near a single settlement as they trudged along. Despite the cloud cover above, it didn't rain, and the land looked like it rarely got watered. Instead, Belwynn could see evidence of fire damage on the tinder dry landscape, as the army marched along a dirt track that would take them to the lands of the Ishari. The Dardelles mountain range receded behind them, but nothing of interest replaced it. As the hours dragged by it felt like the scrubland would stretch on forever. It reminded Belwynn of their visit to the forests of the Caladri. The Grand Caladri had used magic to make it seem like they were making progress, when in fact they were walking in circles, getting nowhere. Was it possible that the Isharites were doing the same thing?

The army's march came to a mid-morning halt. Evander and Alpin, the squires to Theron and Sebastian, came riding down the line. Evander stopped when he found Belwynn and Elana, while Alpin continued going; presumably on his way to find Rabigar and the Krykker chieftains. Something was going on.

'What is it?' she asked the squire, as she and Elana nudged their horses over to join him.

'A man...a magus has arrived,' replied Evander, sounding slightly troubled. 'He says he knows you. Count Theron asked me to fetch you.'

For a moment Belwynn's heart leapt, imagining that Soren had somehow escaped and met them. Then her logic kicked in and told her that she was being ridiculous.

'What does he look like?' asked Elana.

'He...,' Evander paused, frowning. 'He has red eyes.'

Belwynn and Elana shared a look.

'You'd better take us to see him,' said the priestess.

'He was just standing in the road. Waiting for us,' Theron whispered to her.

Belwynn allowed herself a grim smile. Pentas was just as Belwynn remembered him. Friendly; seemingly oblivious of the reaction his sudden arrival had caused. But Belwynn knew that it was all an act. She recalled his magical fight with Nexodore on the Great Road. She recalled too their brief meeting in Onella's Temple in Edeleny, before he had spirited them away. The corpse of Dorottya, the Caladri elder, had lain dead on the floor. *We had an argument*, he had said. She knew that they were dealing with a powerful and ruthless individual.

They were standing in a patch of scrub by the side of the road. There was Belwynn, Elana and Rabigar, who had all confirmed the identity of the wizard; Sebastian and Theron, representing the Knights of Kalinth; Torinac and Maragin, representing the Krykkers.

'Your brother lives,' said Pentas casually, as if it were something he had almost forgotten to mention.

The information provoked a flood of emotions and questions in Belwynn. All she could get out, though, was a brief question, in a croaky voice.

'Where?'

'In Samir Durg.'

'And the others? Clarin, Herin...'

'All alive for now.'

'For now? What do you mean?'

Pentas looked at her with his unreadable red eyes.

'None of them are *safe*,' he replied, as if it were such an obvious point it shouldn't have needed saying. 'You've done well getting this far, the three of you. Much better than I had hoped. Though I was hoping the fourth member of your party would be here. The dagger wielder.'

'Dirk died a few days ago,' said Elana. 'He didn't recover from his injuries.'

'I see,' said Pentas, sounding disappointed. 'I am genuinely sorry. I owed him my life.'

'Why are you here?' asked Belwynn.

Pentas looked around the group. 'As I say, you have done well; enough to create some doubts on the Council of Seven. Erkindrix has ordered an army to be raised to defeat you. As we speak, Isharite magi, Haskan soldiers, and Drobax, are being gathered just south of the Ishari border. The army is under the command of Rostam, Nexodore's successor on the Council. It is a hastily assembled force. Militarily, you stand a chance. But Rostam will also command magic users. You will need my help.'

'Who are you?' asked Elana, in her direct manner.

Pentas looked at her thoughtfully, as if weighing up what to say. He nodded, whether to himself or at Elana, Belwynn couldn't tell.

'I am a servant of Madria, Elana. Just like you. Unlike you, I was born into it. My job has been to halt the rise of Ishari—as much as possible. To undermine them, I have served Erkindrix. More accurately, I have served Diis: the being who sent the Isharites to Dalriya, to take control of our world from Madria. Most of the peoples of Dalriya have let themselves forget about this foul creature. But he hungers for control as much as he ever did.'

Maragin spat on the floor. 'You're a member of the Council of Seven; no doubt responsible for countless atrocities. Are we supposed to believe that all this time you've really been on our side?'

'You may doubt what I say,' responded Pentas, 'but twice in the last few weeks I have stopped Madria's weapons from falling into their hands and you three,' he said, pointing at Belwynn, Elana and Rabigar, 'have witnessed that. Some in Ishari have their suspicions of me, but I have evaded them so far. Now, if your army does meet theirs, I must again ensure that the three weapons you carry are not lost.'

Torinac put his hand to the hilt of Bolivar's Sword, frowning at the idea.

'What of my brother?' asked Belwynn, desperate to know more. 'Is he well?'

'I have not seen him personally. But no, he will be far from well.'

Belwynn put a hand to her mouth.

The wizard watched her impassively. 'I have a plan that will give your brother and his friends a chance of escape. A chance, mind you—and a small one at that. But that is the best you can hope for. To give them the best chance possible, we must hurt Erkindrix. Even if we don't win, we need to land a blow. We need to hurt the Isharites and shake their confidence.'

'That's why we're here,' said Sebastian.

'You said,' began Theron, 'that, militarily, we had a chance. Can you tell us anything about the forces this Rostam will have? What kind of man is he?'

The two Knights and the three Krykkers began to talk tactics with Pentas. Elana put a reassuring arm around Belwynn.

'Are you alright?' asked the priestess.

'Yes,' she replied. 'It is the best news I could have expected.'

'We can do this, you know,' said Elana, with the easy confidence that had become familiar to Belwynn—the confidence she had come to rely on.

'Yes,' Belwynn replied. 'I believe we can.'

***

The funeral pyres for Ealdnoth and Leofwin were still smoking when the gates of Coldeberg were opened.

The men of Thesse, Magnia, and of the Midder Steppe, were armed, just in case. Edgar, standing at the head of his men, looked across as the Barissian army filed out of the city. Next to him were Wilchard, his steward, and his surviving bodyguard, Brictwin. Few men jeered, or even talked much. The Barissians were largely met with silence as they approached the besieging army.

Most of the Barissians left on foot, but a group at the front were on horseback. Edgar recognised Gervase Salvinus, leading his mercenaries. He had a smirk on his face as he approached the waiting army.

'It's him,' Edgar hissed.

'Control yourself,' said Wilchard. 'Don't give him the satisfaction of seeing you hurt. That goes for you too, Brictwin,' he added, trying to dissuade the young warrior from doing anything rash in revenge for the death of his uncle.

Salvinus's troop passed them and stopped in front of Duke Coen. Salvinus reached into a cloth sack that was tied to his saddle. Holding it by the hair, he pulled out a decapitated head. Emeric. No doubt Salvinus had ordered the killing himself, so that he and the rest of his men could escape unharmed. It was no more than Emeric deserved. But it made Edgar sick to his stomach that Salvinus would get away completely free. Free to sell his services to some other lord.

Coen nodded. 'You have met the terms I offered,' he shouted, loud enough to carry to most of the men present outside Coldeberg. 'You are therefore free to go. But I warn you against raising a sword against the Emperor ever again. He would not be as lenient as I.'

Salvinus gave Emeric's hair a swing and let go, so that the head landed on the floor a few feet from Coen. He then led his men away. The rest followed, many probably ordinary Barissians recruited into a false king's army, and glad to be going home alive.

'No sign of the Krykker you fought with, Brictwin?' Edgar asked.

'No, Your Highness. I can't see him.'

'He's no doubt found his way out of the city by now,' Edgar said. 'By Toric, how I want those two dead.'

'We defeated Emeric,' said Wilchard, trying to lift Edgar's spirits. 'The Empire can be united again. We achieved what we set out to do.'

'Yes. I know. At too high a price, though.'

'You've heard,' said Wilchard, 'that Coen is talking about taking his army to Essenberg next? Baldwin had to leave it virtually undefended when he took the Kellish army north.'

'I've heard,' Edgar replied. 'But we've shed enough blood here. It's time to go home.'

***

The prisoners in the pits started to wake up. Men shared whispers in the darkness. There it was again. A scrabbling sound on the metal grates above them.

Dare I believe, thought Gyrmund. *Dare I believe that Moneva has come to rescue us all?*

Then, one of the grates swung open. Gyrmund stood up, and peered out to see the night sky above them. A figure loomed above the pit opening.

'Well? Let's get a move on, then!'

Moneva's voice drifted down, incongruous sounding in the circumstances. Some of the prisoners rushed to the opening.

'Wait!' demanded Herin.

It seemed strangely cruel to Gyrmund, to make these desperate prisoners wait a moment longer. He felt his own desperation to escape so keenly. But Herin wanted to assert his authority, and Gyrmund understood why. If any of them were going to make it out alive, they had to work together, not go charging off in all directions.

Herin ushered Clarin, the hero of the pit fight with Vamak, over to the opening. He was to be the first to leave. Clarin reached up to the edge of the pit with one hand, while Moneva grasped the other. Between them, they pulled his body up and over the edge. Herin was next, then Gyrmund. He gave Moneva a brief embrace, holding her tight, because he had thought he would never get to hold her again.

Then, it was back to work. Working in pairs, they began to haul the rest of the prisoners out of the pit, keeping as quiet as they could. First out were the Persaleians: Zared helped up by his men; Cyprian so light and wiry that Gyrmund hardly felt any weight. Once out, the Persaleians took over, giving Gyrmund and the others a rest. Out came Rudy and Jurgen, the two cousins from Rotelegen; Tamir and his Barbarians, the biggest group, were next. Zared looked to Clarin when it was the turn of the three Dog-men; but when Clarin gave the nod, he told his men to lift them out as well. Finally, the great Bear-man staggered over to the pit entrance, sniffing the air. Clarin and Herin took a huge clawed hand each and, bracing themselves, heaved backwards, dragging it up and out.

Moneva took Gyrmund, Cyprian, and a few other Persaleians to a small pile of bodies she had dumped to one side; the guards she had killed to get inside the camp. The pile was invisible in the darkness, but would be all too revealing when the sun came up. Gyrmund and the others took a body each, holding them under the armpits. They dragged them over to the pit opening and dropped them inside. Rudy and Jurgen took great pleasure in closing the metal grate with a soft clang.

For a few moments, everyone stood around, looking at each other. Gyrmund studied the faces. Some had looks of exhilaration, some fear. Many looked tired and bemused. He disliked the way some of the men stared at Moneva, but at the same time understood it. These were men who had not seen a woman in months, and perhaps never expected to again.

'Well?' asked Herin, as the four of them stood to one side. 'What's the plan?'

'I've been told where they are keeping Soren,' Moneva replied. 'It will involve getting into the fortress.'

'Told by whom?'

Moneva made a face. 'By Pentas.'

'The wizard?' exclaimed Gyrmund. 'What's he doing here?'

'I don't know exactly. He told me where to find you three. I have to assume he's telling me the truth about Soren.' She looked at them. 'So, what do we do?'

Gyrmund understood the question well enough. Moneva was asking whether, having rescued them, they really wanted her to lead them back into danger. A big part of Gyrmund wanted very much to turn around and get as far away from Samir Durg, as quickly as possible.

'We go and get him,' said Clarin decisively.

Gyrmund accepted the decision. Soren had helped to rescue him from Coldeberg prison—he owed the wizard.

'What about them?' Herin asked, indicating the thirty or so men waiting to one side. There was no doubt that some of them would be very useful if it came to a fight.

'Would they come with us?' asked Moneva.

'Yes; some of them will.'

'Then I think we should take them.'

Clarin moved back to speak to the prisoners, who gathered round.

'We are going to the fortress to rescue our friend,' he said plainly. 'We will have most success if we all stay together.'

Some, such as Rudy and Jurgen, nodded along enthusiastically. Others looked less convinced.

'Breaking into that fortress is virtual suicide,' said Zared, the leader of the Persaleian group.

Gyrmund could see that he was mentally weighing up the options for himself and his men. Going it alone might be safer for them. But although they had escaped their prison, they were still behind the massive walls of Samir Durg, with no obvious way of escape. Gyrmund knew that the Persaleians saw something special in Clarin and Herin. Trying to get out of Ishari territory by themselves wasn't going to be easy. Despite his youth, Zared was a shrewd man, and would follow the option with the best chance of success.

'Our friend is a wizard,' said Herin. 'He's going to be our best chance of getting out of here alive.'

That seemed to be enough to swing it, and Zared nodded his acceptance.

'I will come with you,' said Tamir, the tall leader of the Barbarians. 'But some of my people want to stay, to free the men kept in the other pits here. They have family.'

'That is understandable,' conceded Clarin.

'How many?' asked Herin.

The Barbarians briefly talked amongst themselves.

'Five to stay,' said Tamir.

'If they do,' said Gyrmund, keeping his voice quiet, 'it could be a useful distraction for us.'

Herin nodded. 'Agreed. But ask them to wait for one hour to give us time to get to the fortress.'

Tamir relayed the order.

'What about him?' Gyrmund asked, indicating the Bear-man.

The Bear-man stood, looking around as if somehow confused by what he saw. Down in the pit he had been a sad looking creature, kept in the corner. But out here, as he stretched his limbs, it was possible to see the sheer physical strength he possessed.

'I think he will come with us,' said Tamir.

'As will you,' said Clarin, addressing the three Dog-men.

'Yes, master,' one of them agreed, bowing its head. The other two copied the motion.

Everyone looked about again, until all eyes fell on Moneva.

'Follow me.'

She had managed to collect a small pile of weapons from the guards she had killed, mainly short spears and knives. Gyrmund grabbed a knife and shoved it in his belt. There weren't enough weapons to go around yet, and they would have to rectify that as soon as possible.

Moneva led them away from the pits and out through the fence gates, which she had already contrived to open. The path to the crystal mine led off to the right, and Gyrmund felt a powerful sense of relief that he would not have to travel that way ever again. He promised himself that he would not be captured this time. If he was to die in the next few hours, then so be it.

Instead, Moneva took them in the opposite direction, through a no-man's land that led to the eastern walls of the main fortress. Huge towers had been built at regular intervals along its length, and Moneva made for one of these, before stopping a few hundred feet away.

'That's where I came out,' she explained, indicating a wooden door. 'I had to kill some of the guards to make sure that I wasn't seen. I think a few of us need to go first to make sure that it's still safe.'

Clarin told the other prisoners to wait, while the four of them crept over to the tower. It was an unnerving feeling for Gyrmund, knowing that soldiers patrolled the wall walks above them, with only the darkness of night to hide their approach. He wondered at Moneva's ability to do all this on her own.

They reached the door, weapons at the ready. With one hand Moneva slowly reached out to it.

Behind her Gyrmund tensed, ready to fight or run depending on what waited for them. It was so quiet that he could hear the others breathing.

Slowly, slowly, she pulled on the door with her fingertips, peering inside for any signs of movement. The door opened wider and wider, giving her a full look inside.

Then she was in. Gyrmund moved to the door, holding it open as he looked inside. It was dark, and it took a moment for his eyes to take in the main features. The ground floor room of the tower was a rough, semi-circular shape. There were no other exits except for a set of winding steps to the right that led up to the next floor. To the left was a table and chairs but other than that it was bare. It reminded Gyrmund of the room that he, Herin and Clarin had been kept in on their first night at Samir Durg.

Moneva was already creeping up the steps to look at the next floor. Gyrmund entered the room, followed in by Herin and Clarin. He spotted something in the shadows under the stairs. Three bodies had been dumped there, no doubt by Moneva.

'Good,' whispered Herin next to him, peering at them. 'More weapons.'

Moneva had now gone out of sight, but Gyrmund didn't think it was wise to follow her up, in case she had to quickly retreat down the narrow steps.

'How come,' Herin whispered, 'she has been given the run of the fortress?'

It was a question that had also been in the back of Gyrmund's mind. She seemed able to move around Samir Durg at will: two visits to the pits; a conversation with Pentas. Clearly, there was something she wasn't telling them. He sensed that now wasn't the right time to ask, however.

Moneva returned down the steps, fast yet silent.

'We're fine for now,' she whispered. 'The tower's empty.'

'I'll get the others,' said Clarin, exiting via the door they had come in through.

'What next?' asked Herin.

'I'm not sure,' replied Moneva. 'I wasn't convinced that we'd get this far,' she added, a tense half-smile playing on her lips.

Gyrmund could see her hands shaking. She looked pale and drawn. No doubt he looked worse; but she had doubtless been through a lot since Arioc's Isharite soldiers had separated them.

'Pentas told you where Soren is being held?' asked Herin.

Moneva nodded. 'The Tower of Diis. It's on the north side of the fortress.'

'To my mind,' Herin began, casting a quick glance outside to where his brother was rounding up the rest of the escaped prisoners, 'we have two objectives. One, get Soren. Two, get the hell out of here. Objective one requires as few people as possible. We don't want all thirty of us wandering about this fortress, we won't last five minutes. Objective two is where the numbers are needed, to break out. Any idea how we do that?'

'When it's time to leave,' said Moneva, 'we need to head south to the external towers. The wall walk links every tower. We'll reach another tower just like this one to the south,' she said, indicating the direction with a hand. 'Keep going, and the next tower along is an external one: a corner tower much bigger and better defended than this one. But it has a southern exit. That's our best hope of getting out.'

'So,' replied Herin. 'I think it's best if you two go for Soren. Clarin and I will control things here. We'll hold on until you get back.'

An idea occurred to Gyrmund. 'I could put on a guard's uniform, and act as if I'm taking Moneva to this Tower of Diis. It worked for us back in Coldeberg Castle.'

Moneva nodded. She didn't look enthusiastic. The truth was, there was little hope of success. Moneva and Gyrmund were more than likely to get stopped. The force here was bound to be discovered soon—when new guards arrived, or the dead ones were noticed missing.

'Look,' said Gyrmund, speaking to Herin. 'We need to be honest. We're not likely to get back. You can't wait here for us forever. What if you give us two hours before you go?'

Gyrmund looked at Moneva for agreement. She shrugged her acceptance.

'I understand what you're saying,' said Herin. 'But I think we'd be better playing it by ear than fixing a time. If we're going to be brutally honest, the chances are that we'll get discovered here well before two hours are up. We'll wait for you for as long as we can. Who knows, if there is a disturbance here, maybe it will help you three to escape.'

Gyrmund nodded. He and Herin had never got along. But he admired the man's courage. He offered his hand and Herin took it. Gyrmund got a strange feeling—some would call it a premonition—that they would not meet again.

XXII

BOLIVAR'S SWORD

CLARIN INSISTED ON ACCOMPANYING Gyrmund and Moneva to the third floor of the tower, where they would exit onto Samir Durg's battlements. He had helped Gyrmund put on the armour of one of the dead tower guards. It wasn't going to bear close scrutiny, but it might work at a distance.

Moneva opened the northern door and they peered out. A walkway led along the walls to the next tower along. Clarin took a look down into the inner courtyard. A maze of further walls led off towards a central structure with a domed roof. Everything seemed still in the dark of the night, but it was clear that the fortress, with its walls that stretched off as far as the eye could see, and its many towers, would barrack hundreds of soldiers. It was perhaps best not to dwell too long on that.

He said his farewells, and watched as the two figures crept off into the night. Both were quiet and agile—they were the right people for the task. He hoped that they could get Soren out of here and back to Belwynn. He hoped that he would see them again.

Clarin looked out to the east, where the mine and the pits lay. It had been a place of horror and hardship, of course. But it was also a place where he had stayed strong, and become a leader. He felt different. Responsible. More clear-minded.

On the horizon, he detected the first light of sunrise. A new morning. That, probably, would mean a change of guard, as those on night watch would be relieved by a new set of soldiers. There wasn't much time left. They had to be ready.

***

Belwynn wore the cloth of gold, and played her role as Lady of the Knights. Her outfit caught the light of dawn, and drew all men to her. Knight after knight came for their weapons to be blessed before the battle. The younger knights: Philon, Leontios, and their friends came first. But so too did the older knights—so too did knights she had never met before. The biggest surprise came at the end of the queue, when Theron appeared with his friend Tycho.

'Are you serious?' she demanded, raising an eyebrow.

'I would receive your blessing before the fight, my lady,' said Tycho plainly.

Belwynn understood a soldier's need for magic charms before they went into battle, and didn't argue further. She gave her blessing to Tycho, and then turned to Theron. She felt a lump in her throat but said the words despite it.

'Theron of Erisina, I bless your sword, may it serve its master well in battle.'

She embraced them both. No more words were spoken, and the two knights left to make their way to the field of battle.

Belwynn walked a little way towards the lines of soldiers forming up into position. Just visible in the distance was the enemy. Rostam of Ishari had gathered an army of tens of thousands to block their path to Samir Durg, and then drive them from Haskany.

His force, so the Kalinthian scouts had reported, was predominantly made up of Drobax. Thousands upon thousands had left their northern homeland, and travelled south down the Great Road to invade the Brasingian Empire. But there had still been plenty available to fill the ranks of the Isharite army here. They weren't the only ones fighting under Rostam's command, however. Some Haskan soldiers remained to defend their homeland. A Kharovian force had been spotted too—the dread rovers of the sea were more used to raiding than fighting pitched battles, but they had heeded the call of their masters nonetheless. The barks of the Dog-men, also loyal to Ishari, could be heard from time to time, the wicked sound crossing the distance between the two armies and making Belwynn's blood run cold. Finally, of course, there were the Isharites themselves. They were few in number, but a good proportion of them would be wizards, and this made them the most dangerous enemy of all.

In contrast, their own army had only one wizard, and not one that Belwynn totally trusted either. As if reading her thoughts, Pentas strolled over towards her.

'I see that the Knights have made you their mystic,' he commented.

Belwynn shrugged. She saw no reason to feel any embarrassment about it in front of him.

'Not necessarily a bad thing,' he added, perhaps aware that she had taken it as a criticism.

'What can be gained today?' she asked him, changing the subject.

'Win or lose, you are making those on the Council feel very uncomfortable right now,' he replied. 'After the destruction of Edeleny, the Isharites thought that they had won Dalriya. Now there is an enemy army not so very far from Samir Durg itself.'

'And what chance that we might do more than make them feel uncomfortable?' Belwynn asked him.

She tried to keep bitterness from her voice, but it would be a sorry waste of lives if that was all they achieved.

It was Pentas's turn to shrug. 'We shall see.'

Belwynn returned her gaze to the battlefield. Between the two armies was a few hundred yards of flat scrubland, nothing to offer protection to either side. Although it had been a chill night, the sun had risen in a cloudless sky, and Belwynn knew that the conditions would be hot and dry. In front of her was a simple formation. The Krykkers stood in the middle, all on foot, a few ranks deep. They fought in their clan groups, and their job was to hold position against the enemy. Some distance behind them, to each side of the Krykkers, were two units of Kalinthian Knights. One was commanded by Theron, the other by Sebastian. They would have an offensive role, threatening to outflank and encircle the enemy. Whilst it was vital that the Krykkers withstand the enemy, the Knights had to find a way to win.

Trumpet calls blasted out ahead of her. The Krykkers and the Knights were signalling their readiness for battle. It was about to start.

'Time for me to get ready,' murmured Pentas.

Belwynn turned to him. 'There are people here very important to me,' she said. 'I don't want to lose them.'

Pentas nodded, his red eyes gleaming. 'There are people here who are very important to Madria, too. There is a priestess of hers. A Krykker man wielding her sword. A human woman carrying her dagger and her staff. In the bigger picture, all others are expendable.'

He turned and left. Belwynn turned her back on the battlefield and began to make her way to the camp, about a mile behind the front line. There she would find Elana, whose healing skills would be needed today more than they ever had before.

***

Trumpets rang out from the infantry ranks of the Krykkers, answered by the massed cavalry of the Knights.

Rabigar hefted his polearm, readying himself. He stood in the middle of the front line, with Torinac and the Dramsen clan. The other clans were positioned in separate rectangular units to either side. These units were known as buffalos amongst the Krykkers, since they shared the defensive strength and offensive reach of the horned creatures. On the left, Maragin led the Grendals; Guremar and the Plengas clan were on the right. Next to Rabigar stood Stenk, holding a great, long, two handed pike. Rabigar was keen to keep his eye on the lad, in his first real battle.

A few feet away, Torinac held aloft Bolivar's Great Sword, symbol of their people's defiance against the forces of Ishari. He pointed it ahead, towards the enemy. The Krykker army began to move.

The first two ranks of their army all held pole-arms of various descriptions. Those fighters situated on the two short edges of their rectangle also carried the same weapons, so that they could engage with any enemy who tried to attack from the side. Most common were the long, straight pikes that Stenk carried. But other warriors had variations on this basic design, often crafting their own weapons. Some had added an axe head to the long blade of the pike, so that their weapons could be used for chopping as well as thrusting. Rabigar himself favoured a weapon with a crossbar across the end of the pike. It prevented the blade sliding too far into an enemy and getting stuck, and he anticipated that his blade would see a lot of action today.

Despite these minor variations, the Krykkers were still able to present a long line of bristling metal points to the enemy. Holding the deadly points of their weapons up in the air in front of them, they picked up the pace of their march. The knights who had scouted out the Ishari position had done a good job. They identified that forces had been arriving at the enemy camp from various directions. But they were not yet well organised, and Rostam was most likely waiting for more to arrive before moving against them. His location had been chosen as a place for his forces to meet up, rather than as a location for a battle. But if he had been expecting the Krykkers to sit and wait for him, he had made a serious mistake. Now was the time to fight, before the superior forces of Ishari were ready.

Drums began to pound as the enemy realised that the Krykkers were on the march. Rabigar could see enemy units beginning to move in their direction. Unsurprisingly, the Drobax were being sent to intercept them. Rostam's plan would be for his most expendable troops to soften them up, before sending in his elite soldiers.

Rabigar looked along the line with pride. Despite marching at pace, the Krykkers held their positions, presenting a long, impenetrable forest of steel-tipped wooden shafts. The Krykkers didn't have horsemen like the Knights. They didn't have archers like the Caladri. They lacked the sheer numbers that the Brasingian Empire could field. But Rabigar knew that they had the best infantry in Dalriya. They were the best equipped and the best drilled, learning iron discipline from youth. They fought, not as individuals, but as one whole. It had not been witnessed by the rest of Dalriya for generations. But here and now, it would be.

The Drobax were now close enough to pick out individually. Most went semi-naked, their hairy grey bodies rarely protected by anything resembling armour. Their weapons were rudimentary, made from wood or stone. They had been sent to fight in rough units, but they were already disintegrating. Some of the creatures came at a faster pace than others. The different units began to merge together so that the Krykkers faced an undulating sea of creatures bearing down on them.

Torinac called the halt. The first two rows gathered themselves, making sure that there was the correct space between each other. Rabigar's front row put their left knees to the ground, bracing their weapons for impact. The Drobax charged. When they came into missile range, stones and spears were hurled at them from the rear rows. Many of the Drobax went down. Others tripped over the fallen bodies. Still more had stopped, in an effort to avoid the flying missiles. The Drobax advance stuttered.

'Charge!' bellowed Torinac.

Rising to their feet, pikes now pointing straight ahead, Rabigar's line went for the enemy. He could see the fear on the faces of the Drobax as the wall of pikes bore down on them. Some of them carried spears and held them out in front of themselves, but they were barely half the length of the pikes, and no real competition. Still others carried short clubs. They would have to avoid the pikes and get in close to do any damage.

Rabigar fixed his weapon on a Drobax spearman. As he approached he saw the whites of its eyes. It lurched to its left at the last minute, in an attempt to avoid his strike. But Rabigar simply pulled his arms into his body and then thrust forwards, going down on one knee, skewering it through the chest. He checked on Stenk, who had also struck a target, through the thigh. Rabigar pulled his pike free and sent it into the chest of Stenk's Drobax, to make sure that it was killed. With a shout, the second rank of Krykkers levelled their pikes over the heads of Rabigar's rank and thrust forwards, finding more targets in some cases; in others, dissuading the Drobax from counterattacking.

Rabigar's line moved forwards and thrust again, killing the next rank. A Drobax holding a club ran in-between Rabigar and Stenk's pikes, making for the younger man. Rabigar let go of his pike and moved to intercept it, but a pike emerged from the rank behind, and skewered the creature before it got close.

Again, the Krykkers moved forwards to strike at the Drobax, and once more. Rabigar found himself having to kneel on a corpse as he kept his position in the line. Pools of dark blood lay across the parched ground.

In the end, the inevitable happened, and the Drobax broke. Unable to halt the Krykker war machine's progress and facing certain death, self-preservation took over, and the horde of Drobax turned and fled back the way they had come.

The Dramsen clan paused briefly to draw breath. A few injured soldiers were being guided through to the back of the unit, but Rabigar couldn't see any fatalities. He looked to his left and right. The Drobax had been broken right across the battlefield, meaning that the other two buffalos were also free. Seeing this, Torinac wasted no more time and ordered an advance.

They followed the retreating Drobax across the dusty ground. Rabigar began to make out the beginnings of the Isharite camp, where tents had been pitched, and wagons parked. Moving out to challenge them were a dozen smaller units of Haskan infantry. The Drobax ran through the gaps between the Haskan units and on into their camp. Hopefully they would keep on running.

Rabigar could see that they were now dealing with a different, more superior threat. The Haskan soldiers were well armed and their smaller units were fast—faster than the Krykker buffalos, with their long pole-arms that had to be held aloft as they moved.

Some of the Haskan units were moving to the sides, outflanking the buffalos of the Grendal and Plengas clans without getting too close. Looking across to his left, Rabigar could see Maragin's dilemma. If she moved her unit across to deal with the threat, the Grendals would become detached from the Dramsens and potentially encircled. If she kept moving ahead, the Haskans would be able to attack from the rear. Both the Grendal and Plengas buffalos came to a halt, pikes facing outwards at all angles. Still, the Haskans manoeuvred around them without engaging.

Rabigar could see Torinac looking around nervously. Their advance had come to a halt. If the Isharites were able to regroup the Drobax, they could be in real trouble.

Rabigar felt the ground tremble. Everyone turned around to look.

'The Knights!' declared Stenk enthusiastically.

Two streams of cavalry were arriving on the battlefield in a wide arc. As Rabigar watched, they quickly outflanked the Haskan units and turned around to face them from the sides. In a matter of minutes, the dynamic on the battlefield had changed. The Haskans found themselves caught between the Krykkers and the Kalinthian cavalry with no means of escape—the Knights were too fast. Sebastian and Theron had arrived at just the right time.

Trumpets sounded from both groups of cavalry. They formed into a long line, levelling their lances so that they pointed ahead. Another blast from the trumpets gave the order to charge. It was an imposing sight, watching the armoured horses gathering pace. The Haskan soldiers would be terrified. Meanwhile, Maragin had taken advantage of the situation to order the Grendals to attack. The Haskans would be crushed between the two forces.

Rabigar looked to Torinac. He saw the chieftain looking ahead. Rabigar could make out Haskan cavalry forces leaving the enemy camp and heading to engage the Kalinthians. But surely, they would be no match for the Knights? Ahead of the Dramsens were two of the Haskan units. They had kept a safe distance away from the Krykkers, but now seemed unsure of what to do. Rabigar knew what Torinac's order would be before it was given. Torinac wanted to win the battle right now. He raised Bolivar's Sword again, and gave the order to attack.

Pole-arms raised, the Dramsen clan marched forwards, leaving the rest of the battle to their allies. The two units of Haskan soldiers reacted, looking to trap them in a pincer. Torinac ordered an attack on the Haskan unit to their right. The Krykkers turned in that direction, held their pikes aloft, and ran towards them. The Krykkers could be surprisingly fast when they picked up speed. The Haskans dithered and that was their downfall. They seemed to be unsure whether they should retreat, or attack the Krykkers in order to implement their pincer. In the end, they did neither, merely holding their ground.

As the Dramsens approached, the Haskan front line locked shields together. They wore mail armour and presented a formidable defence. Rabigar's rank dove to their knees and thrust their pikes at the legs of the shield men. The second rank thrust forwards at head level. No shield was big enough to defend against pikes at both ankle and face level, and many Haskans fell. Those that survived counterattacked with shield and spear. Rabigar was quick to drop his pike, drawing the sword that he favoured in close combat.

With neither the wall of shields or pikes intact any more, it quickly became a vicious melee. Rabigar hacked and sliced with his sword. He swung at a Haskan spearman who took the blow on his shield, and then thrust forwards with his spear. Rabigar stepped back out of range. The spearman poked at him, creeping forwards. He then launched his attack, thrusting forwards. Rabigar sidestepped and grabbed the wooden shaft of the spear. He yanked at it, pulling the spearman off balance, before thrusting with his sword into the neck area, between hauberk and helmet. He pulled his sword free with a gush of blood.

Rabigar looked around for Stenk and spotted him, keeping an enemy at bay with his pike. Rabigar joined him but didn't press the attack. The longer line of the Krykker buffalo was now curling around the Haskans, who found themselves being attacked from the sides. Rabigar waited until the odds were fully in his favour before joining in with the slaughter. The red mist rose as he strode around, looking for enemies to kill. Assailed from all sides, the Haskans had no chance. Many begged for mercy, but the Krykkers cut them all down.

When the job was done, it was time to turn around to deal with the second Haskan unit. As they had been drilled countless times, the pikemen at the rear end of the Dramsen buffalo had formed a defensive line to stop the oncoming Haskans. This kind of defensive formation was three ranks deep, with pikes facing the enemy from three different heights, like the quills of a porcupine. Rabigar and the other Krykkers moved around it to face the enemy, who had been unable to break through. Without waiting for an order, the Krykkers now charged the second Haskan unit. The pikemen who had been on the defence now thrust forwards. Rabigar and the men around him outflanked the Haskans and attacked from the side. The Haskans put up a stout resistance, but their defences were inevitably breached, and a second slaughter, just like the first, ensued.

When it was done, the Dramsen clan paused to take breath. Soldiers looked at each other, grim smiles for comrades covered in blood and gore. The stench of it was overpowering. Rabigar wiped his sword clean on a corpse.

He took a look at the rest of the battle. Things were still in flux. The Haskan cavalry had engaged with the Kalinthians, and some of their infantry units were still active. None were close to the Dramsen's position, however, and the way was now clear to the enemy camp.

'Forwards!' bellowed Torinac, Bolivar's Sword now dripping red.

They marched for the camp where Rostam and the other leaders were based. If they could drive them off now, there was little chance of the Isharites regrouping from such a defeat any time soon. Those who still had their pole-arms moved to the front ranks. Rabigar found Stenk and persuaded him to stand with him in the third rank. Stenk passed his pike over to another soldier and took an axe from his belt.

No-one was there to prevent them from entering the outskirts of the camp. They looked around. Tents lay empty. Horse-pulled wagons and carts with food and other supplies sat undefended. Rabigar spied a forge wagon, fitted up to carry the furnace, bellows and other tools required by a blacksmith to make running repairs to weapons and armour. But the craftsmen to go with it were nowhere to be seen. The camp was deserted.

Torinac led his clan into the centre of the camp, a feeling of slight unease spreading amongst them. Something didn't feel right.

Then, from out of nowhere, words were being shouted in an alien tongue. The Krykkers turned to look for the source in all directions, but there was nothing to see. Suddenly, an enemy force appeared in front of them. It was the strangest sensation. Part of Rabigar realised that they had been there all along, but they had somehow been hidden from sight. By magic.

But there was no more time to think about it. Charging straight at them, howling and barking, were the most fearsome creatures in the Isharite army. Dog-men. The Krykkers turned to face the threat, quickly trying to get their pikes ready to face the attack. A force buffeted them, like a strong gust of wind.

It caused men to stumble and lose their footing. Polearms were blown about, difficult to hold onto; more than one soldier got a crack on the head or arm from their neighbour's weapon.

Then, the Dog-men were on them. They bounded up to the row of pikes and leapt high in the air. Some were caught before they landed. In front of Rabigar, a Dog-man failed to avoid a pike and was skewered, the force of its descent making its body slide all the way down the length of the pole. But others leapt powerfully over the pikes and crashed into the ranks behind. More of them came, recklessly throwing themselves into the Dramsen buffalo.

Before he knew it, a Dog-man was descending on top of Rabigar. He braced his sword arm, ready to thrust through its middle. But the creature somehow pushed his blade aside with its hind leg and crashed on top of him. Rabigar went down like a sack of oats, the wind knocked out of him. On top of him, the Dog-man grabbed his forearms with its sharp claws and pushed itself up into a seated position, its weight on his chest keeping him pinned to the floor. It opened its muzzle, revealing two rows of vicious teeth, and aimed for Rabigar's jugular, which he knew it could rip out in one go. Before it got the chance, however, Rabigar could see Stenk's axe coming down from behind the creature. The blow was true, the blade of the axe smacking down straight into the back of the Dog-man's skull, killing it instantly. It collapsed on top of Rabigar, who shoved the creature off.

Stenk had his axe blade stuck, and planted his foot on the creature's head to help him yank it free. Just as he did so, the whole rank of soldiers in front of them collapsed backwards as more Dog-men leapt into the fray. Stenk collapsed under a mound of kicking arms, legs and claws.

Rabigar quickly grasped for his sword which was lying on the ground next to him, and forced himself up. He knew he had to act quickly. The wicked claws and powerful jaws of the Dog-men gave them a distinct advantage in a scrum like this. Meanwhile, the pole-arms carried by the Krykker soldiers were now useless, and they had to be given time to get their hands on their shorter weapons.

He thrust down into the sprawling mass in front of him, being careful to avoid his comrades, and finding the exposed flesh of the poorly armoured Dog-men.

Reaching down with his left hand, he grabbed Stenk around the chest and pulled him out, all the while keeping his sword in front of him to deflect any attack. Stenk picked himself up, looking none the worse: he had even managed to keep hold of his axe. They both returned to the fray, helping the surviving Krykkers up, and fending off the Dog-men, who backed off.

Then, Rabigar saw him. Torinac lay dead amongst the bodies, his arms spread wide and his eyes staring up at the sky. His throat had been torn out. Rabigar looked around the body of the fallen chieftain. Much as he regretted Torinac's death, far more important was the whereabouts of Bolivar's Sword.

He turned bodies over, getting more desperate by the second. Stenk began to help him. There! Buried in the body of a Dog-man, perhaps the same creature that had killed Torinac, was the Sword. Rabigar grasped the hilt and pulled the blade free. He could feel the power of the weapon coursing through him, from his grip, along his arm, and into his chest. He held the sword aloft, marvelling at it. Now it belonged to him.

A blast hit them again, this time accompanied by a blinding light. It seemed to strike the Dog-men as much as the Krykkers. Rabigar sank to one knee, holding Bolivar's Sword close to his body in an effort not to lose his grip on it. He looked down at the ground to avoid looking at the light. Just as he thought he would be forced to close his eye and topple over, the magic stopped again. Looking up, patches of light still obscuring his vision, he saw just in time that a new enemy had appeared. Striding past the sprawled Dog-men came the Isharites themselves.

They made straight for Rabigar, since he was the only Krykker nearby who had not collapsed from the blast of magic. A crystal sword came swinging down at him. Still on one knee, Rabigar blocked it. The Isharite pushed down on him with all of his weight, his thin, dark features snarling with hatred; but Rabigar resisted, matching his strength. Pulling back, the Isharite took a quick swing at Rabigar from the side but he was ready for it, blocking the strike again, and then regaining his feet. Another blow came for him, but he managed to block it, as if the Sword he held guided his hands.

He danced backwards, out of the reach of the Isharites who outnumbered him. Now he felt the presence of the other Krykkers, who joined him to face down the new threat.

The Isharites and the remaining Dog-men stood for a moment, staring at the Krykkers. *No*, thought Rabigar, *they are staring behind us*. Then suddenly, without warning, all of them turned and ran. They ran as fast as they could, to the far side of the camp, and kept running.

Looking behind him, Rabigar could see a group of Kalinthian Knights heading in their direction. It took the Knights seconds to reach them, and Rabigar just got a glimpse of Theron in the lead of the mounted force before they shot past, chasing down the enemy. This was when a cavalry force such as this really came into their own. The Knights would be able to chase down and harass the departing Isharite army for miles if they needed to. There would be no chance for the Drobax forces to regroup and come back at them now. They had won.

The others felt it too and a wave of relief came over them all. Stenk appeared next to Rabigar, and he gave the young man a great hug.

Some shouting ahead of them caused them to break their embrace. The Dramsens had found their fallen chieftain. Rabigar turned in the direction where the noise was coming from and strode over.

The clan gathered around in shock at the sight of Torinac lying lifeless on the ground. A strange feeling came over Rabigar.

'Your chieftain died as a hero today,' he intoned. 'Now the duty and honour of wielding Bolivar's Sword falls to me.'

The Krykkers of the Dramsen clan looked at Rabigar with blank expressions. But no-one challenged him. And that was as it should be. For this sword sang to Rabigar, and told him that he was meant to have it.

XXIII

SAMIR DURG

MONEVA LED GYRMUND ALONG THE WALLS of Samir Durg, always on the lookout for sentries. She kept a fast pace, keen to make as much progress as possible while the last hour or so of night afforded them protection. When she spotted a guard, she would indicate for Gyrmund to wait while she investigated. Sometimes they were able to detour around them, or wait until they moved. Invariably, the safest and quickest way to deal with them was a knife through the base of the skull; before moving on as fast as possible.

Gyrmund needed minimal attention; he knew how to conceal himself, and was content to leave the decisions to her. What did concern Moneva, however, was his pale, drawn face, and lack of energy. It was only after they had been going for a while that she realised he must be half starved and dehydrated. While she had been eating Arioc's rich, spiced food since she had arrived in his chambers, Gyrmund must have been on the meanest of rations, while at the same time working all day.

Moneva took more care to secure food and drink on the way. She then led Gyrmund to the top room of a tower. She had learned that these rooms were mostly deserted, sometimes serving as storage. Occasionally, Isharite soldiers used them as places to rest up or sleep.

She handed Gyrmund a pile of dry crackers, which seemed to be the staple rations of the Isharite soldiers. She also pulled out a pot of something strong smelling. She thought it might be similar to the arak that she had drunk in Arioc's chambers. She took a sip and scrunched up her face. The alcohol in it wasn't as strong as the arak, but it tasted of sour milk. Gyrmund took it to go with his crackers. He didn't seem to mind the taste, and a bit of colour returned to his face once he had finished it.

They sat for a moment, looking at each other.

'If we get out of here—' whispered Gyrmund.

'If we get out of here we can talk then,' said Moneva.

She hadn't meant to be so abrupt. It was the stress she was under. But she couldn't do emotions—not now. It was a distraction, and Gyrmund should have known better.

It looked like he was about to reply, and then he stopped, perhaps thinking better of it. He cocked his head, as if listening to something. Moneva tuned in. It was the sound of soldiers moving.

She got to her feet, drawing a knife. Gyrmund's eyes widened and he grabbed his knife too.

She could hear footsteps, getting louder. If they tried to leave the room now, they were likely to run straight into the soldiers. She surveyed the room quickly, imagining a soldier coming up the stairs and looking in. Pointing at a straw mattress, she indicated that Gyrmund should lie on it. He didn't try to argue, again trusting her judgement, which she was grateful for. She draped a blanket over him. Perhaps, just perhaps, they might mistake him for a lazy soldier and not investigate further. She chose the corner of the room that lay in shadow for herself. She draped her hair over her face and put her hands behind her back, so that her skin could not be seen. Then, they waited.

Moneva heard the soldiers entering their tower, arriving from the north of the fortress. *Have we been spotted?* She fingered the blade of the knife. If the soldiers were after them, they would be in the room in seconds. She knew that a fight in this chamber wouldn't last very long. But a part of her still hoped that the soldiers were heading somewhere else.

They were moving fast. She could now hear them directly underneath the room. She listened to the hurried conversation that drifted up the stairs, but while she had got somewhat used to the Isharite language during her time at the fortress, picking up a few words, she couldn't process anything she heard now. And then, they were gone, heading south along the fortress walls. She stayed still for a while longer, not yet daring to believe it. The sound of footsteps disappeared. Then, just as Moneva began to relax a little, a second group came past, passing directly underneath them and heading in the same direction. She detected a slight movement in the room and looked to see Gyrmund's head poking out of his blanket.

Moneva indicated that he should remain where he was. She forced herself forwards, willing her muscles to move and peel her body away from the wall against which she had flattened herself. She was used to operating with fear swirling around her body, and steadily, if jerkily, her limbs did as she commanded. She approached the stairs down to the third floor of the tower on her belly and, edging over the gap, peered down to have a look. The room below seemed empty. Pulling herself up into a crouching position, she made herself creep down to make sure.

It was empty. She could smell the sweat and the leather of the soldiers who had passed through. She glanced outside. A new day's dawn was throwing its light on the walls of Samir Durg. She quickly made her way back up to the top chamber.

Gyrmund had come out from under the blanket.

'It's empty now,' Moneva whispered.

'They're going for Clarin and Herin, aren't they?' he asked.

Moneva shrugged. 'I don't know for sure, but...'

But it was the most obvious explanation.

Gyrmund nodded. 'What now?'

Moneva sighed. 'The sun's up. No more night to hide us. I think we need to take a risk now. Leave this tower and head into the centre of the fortress. Go straight for the Tower of Diis. I'll lead us, but you need to act as if you're taking me there. Look people in the eye but don't stare at anyone. Everyone in the fortress may be preoccupied with taking Herin and Clarin's tower, and we can slip past unnoticed.'

For Gyrmund's sake, she sounded as confident as she could. He nodded his acceptance of the plan.

'What about getting in?' he asked.

'Here,' she said, producing the brooch with Arioc's sigil on it. 'It's the symbol of Arioc and his men. Tell them he's sent me to the prisons there. He's the King of Haskany—he has humans working for him.'

Wordlessly, Gyrmund took the brooch and studied it, tracing a finger along the circular shape of the serpent. She knew he wanted to ask how she had got it; about her time with Arioc. Instead, he did as she had asked, and pinned it to his cloak.

They slipped down the tower stairs unchallenged, all the way to the ground floor. Moneva nodded at the door that opened into the central part of the fortress. Gyrmund moved over and opened it, taking one step outside. He then reached inside and grabbed her arm, pulling her with him.

***

They had taken care of the change of guard when it came.

Six soldiers had arrived as the sun began to rise in the sky above. Clarin asked Zared and a few of his men to help with the ambush. The Isharite soldiers were surprised as they entered the tower from the walkway. They were attacked from all angles: Herin cutting off their retreat; the agile Cyprian even jumping down on top of them from the chamber above. None of them could escape, and Clarin and his men avoided injury. But killing six men isn't easy. During the desperate fighting in the enclosed space, there was many a shout and scream, and Clarin knew that it was now only a matter of time before more soldiers came. Next time, there would be more of them, and the element of surprise would be gone.

The Persaleians busied themselves stripping the Isharite bodies of their armour and taking it for themselves. All the Persaleians, and most of the Barbarians, were now armed with a weapon of some kind.

'What now?' asked Zared.

Clarin was still getting used to the fact that he was in charge. Even more strangely, Herin looked at him, as if waiting for orders. He considered their situation. There was little more they could do for Gyrmund and Moneva now. He had to think of their own predicament, and the last thing he wanted was to get everyone trapped in this little tower. The Isharites would be able to approach from both directions and take their time digging them out. They would be able to use fire and smoke, and Toric only knew what else. That was no way to die.

'We'll close off the northern door with whatever we can find,' he decided. He looked south along the wall. The next tower was identical to the one they were in, and would be lightly defended.

He pointed. 'Then head for the next tower.'

Clarin looked at the Persaleians in their Isharite armour. 'Those of you who can pass off as Isharites should go first. If they shut the door on us, we'll be trapped. Get as close as you can until they realise something's up and then charge it. We'll be right behind you.'

Apart from a table and chairs, there was little else but dead bodies to prop against the north door of the tower. The young Rotelegen cousins, Rudy and Jurgen, each armed with short spears, insisted on staying back to defend the position while the rest of them went ahead.

'Don't hesitate to retreat when the position is lost,' instructed Clarin, and they nodded obediently.

As Clarin watched from the doorway of their tower, armed with a spear of his own, Zared and four of his best men left the tower and moved along the walkway. To their left, crenellations had been constructed to protect the defenders of the fortress, while to the right was a sheer drop down to the inner courtyard. Two Isharites manned the wall on the far side of the walkway, and turned at Zared's approach. They shouted over, unintelligible words in the Isharite tongue.

'Shit,' commented Herin, crouched next to Clarin in the shadows. His brother gripped a knife, ready to charge down the walkway.

Zared called back. Clarin couldn't tell if the Persaleian had picked up a bit of the Isharite language, or was simply bluffing. But it seemed to work. The two Isharite soldiers waited and let Zared and his men approach. Then, suddenly, they began shouting. Herin didn't waste any time, shooting off down the walkway. Clarin followed close behind.

Ahead, the Persaleians ran at the two Isharite soldiers. It was a narrow walkway, and for a moment the Persaleians found their path blocked. The two Isharites continued to shout out their warning. The impasse continued until they contrived to throw one of the Isharites from the wall down to the courtyard below. The second Isharite was bundled to the floor, while Zared and two of his men managed to sidestep past and run for the tower door.

Clarin edged carefully past the prone, struggling figures on the walkway, wary of falling off into the courtyard below. Then, picking up some speed, he made it through the door of the next tower. His brother was already grappling with an Isharite on the floor, while Zared and one of his men were fighting two more soldiers in the confined space of the chamber. Unable to use his spear effectively, Clarin dropped it and grabbed a soldier around the head, twisting his neck until it broke. The two Persaleians finished off the other soldier. Clarin stamped on the head of Herin's adversary, allowing Herin to pull his knife hand free, and stab into the Isharite's exposed neck. One of Zared's men was seated on the floor, his lifeblood ebbing away from a stab wound in his chest. But he was the only casualty.

Clarin helped Herin up. Wordlessly, his brother headed down the stairs to make sure that the rest of the tower was empty. Looking behind him, Clarin could see that the second Isharite soldier on the walkway had been disposed of, and that Tamir was leading the Barbarians across towards them.

Shouts came from the courtyard down below. It was no surprise that their assault had been witnessed. Clarin moved over to the southern door of the chamber and looked out. As Moneva had described, beyond the next stretch of walkway was a huge corner tower. It guarded the southern wall of Samir Durg, and was a massive piece of construction, the size of a castle keep. It would have many rooms inside it, with more soldiers posted there. Indeed, as Clarin thought about it, it was quite likely that it represented the living quarters of a substantial number of Isharite soldiers.

He moved back from the door, as the rest of the escaped prisoners began filing into the tower. Herin was telling them to head down into the lower floors. A few feet away, Zared was kneeling by his dying friend's side, whose face had gone deathly white, but whose eyes continued to stare forwards. Zared looked up at him.

'What now?'

**

It was impossible for Shira to deny that they were making better progress than before. To be fair to herself, Arioc hadn't changed the basic strategy. He had just added an extra layer of ruthlessness to the tactics.

They were standing a mile or so away from the looming presence of Burkhard Castle. Ahead was the path up the nearest crag. The Drobax were hurling themselves up this steep track, pushing the Brasingian defenders back. They had already smashed their way through three of the wooden gates that had been constructed to stop their ascent. The Brasingians continued to enjoy a height advantage, and the losses were still far heavier on the Drobax side. But any Brasingian slow enough to get caught by the monsters was immediately overwhelmed and torn apart; or else simply thrown off the crag to meet the same fate down below.

At the bottom of the path was Arioc's innovation. A group of armed Drobax waited for any of their kind to descend from the crag. Here, retreating Drobax would be butchered. They had been given a stark choice: force your way up to the top of the crag, and live; fail, and die. It had provided the extra motivation needed for the progress to be made.

Arioc stood watching the attack impassively. Shira's uncle, Koren, always deferential to her husband, waited on him attentively. The Isharite wizard, Mehrab, was also present. Since Arioc's success he wore a permanent smirk on his smug face.

An arrival from further behind them interrupted the silence. An Isharite strode forwards and sank to one knee in front of Arioc. His long black hair was plastered with sweat, and he looked pale and ill. He physically shook as he spoke.

'Your Majesty, I have come from Lord Rostam with haste. Our army engaged with the Krykkers and Kalinthians. We were driven from the field by their forces, and our own soldiers are in full retreat.'

A wordless shout of fury erupted from Arioc's mouth. Shira felt something close to relief. Her own lack of success in Brasingia suddenly didn't seem so bad compared to such an utter disaster.

'I need to get to Samir Durg immediately,' said Arioc, fighting to control his anger. 'Mehrab, get your men ready.'

With that, Arioc marched off, accompanied by Mehrab. As an afterthought, he turned back to Shira.

'You're in charge here,' he said curtly, before departing for good.

Shira met eyes with her uncle.

'That's one Council meeting I might have enjoyed attending.'

XXIV

THE TOWER OF DIIS

G YRMUND HELD MONEVA AS IF SHE were a captured prisoner, while she led him through a maze of corridors and courtyards towards the Tower of Diis. On their left a domed central building loomed over them; on their right were the high walls and towers of Samir Durg, the diatine crystals within them glinting in the morning sun.

Moneva had been right. The whole fortress seemed to be alive with energy and tension, soldiers and servants rushing in every direction. It was hard to believe that Herin and Clarin's small force, in one small tower, could have caused such disruption. Of course, Gyrmund considered, some of the Barbarians had chosen to stay behind, and release their kin from the other slave pits. Maybe they had succeeded in raising a second force which had been discovered? Whatever the reason, everyone they passed seemed to have an urgent job to do, and few gave them a second glance.

Ahead of them, the Tower of Diis came into view. It was by far the largest of the towers Gyrmund had seen, situated in the central section of the northern wall of the fortress, and dominating its surroundings. He could see two guards on duty outside the main entrance. This was it. Ignoring the tightening in his gut and chest, he steered Moneva towards the entrance, doing his best to look nonchalant.

The Isharite guards were tall and well built, each holding a spear that crossed each other to bar entrance to the Tower. As Gyrmund approached, they caught sight of the brooch with Arioc's sigil, and pulled their spears in. Even here, Arioc's power counted.

'She's for the prisons,' said Gyrmund. He did his best to put on a Haskan accent, just in case the guards could notice the difference.

The guards nodded in a disinterested way.

'Why's Arioc got a human running his errands?' asked one of them pointedly.

'*King* Arioc,' said Gyrmund, as if taking offence, 'rates me very highly. My family is very important in Haskany.'

The guards laughed at him, pulling open the doors.

'Very important in Haskany,' repeated the second guard, imitating Gyrmund's accent. 'That don't mean shit in Samir Durg. You're just an errand boy, here.'

Gyrmund guided Moneva through the doors.

'Where do I go?' he asked.

'Down,' said one of the guards unhelpfully, before they closed the doors on them.

The entrance corridor was only dimly lit, and they took care as they walked. Neither spoke. They had to assume that they could be heard; someone might even be watching them. It was therefore vital that they keep up the pretence of prisoner and soldier.

After a short distance, the corridor branched off to the left and right. It looked like the left path led to a guard room, so they headed to the right, into the main part of the Tower. They arrived in a large, slightly better lit, irregular shaped ground floor chamber. It was empty of people. Various dimly lit passages led off it, at all angles. On the far wall, a set of stairs led upwards to the next floor—but the guards had said 'down'.

Turning to the left, they began circling the chamber, looking for a route down. It didn't take long. The second passage they came to was very short, and ended with a set of stone steps heading down into the dungeons. Gyrmund could smell the damp coming from the underground rooms below.

Warily, Gyrmund began the journey down, still holding Moneva by the arm. Below ground level, the Tower of Diis was even more poorly lit. Gyrmund, his eyes not yet fully adjusted to the gloom, could barely make out the next step in front of him as he slowly negotiated his way, his footsteps sounding heavy in the silent and oppressive atmosphere. Gingerly stretching his front foot forwards, he finally found himself on the dungeon floor, and helped Moneva down to join him.

Their descent must have alerted someone. Gyrmund could hear quick footsteps coming in their direction. As they got nearer, he made out a cowled figure approaching them. The figure looked Gyrmund up and down, taking in the brooch still attached to his cloak. As he did so, Gyrmund got a glimpse of the face under the hood: a man with a thin, mottled face, surrounded with lank, greasy hair.

'You have someone for us?' he asked in a croaky voice.

258

'King Arioc has sent his prisoner here. She's to go with the wizard he captured.'

The cowled jailer, if jailer he was, turned his attention to Moneva.

'Ah,' he said, with an unpleasant grin. 'Arioc's whore. Had enough of you, has he?'

Gyrmund went cold. *Arioc's whore?* His eyes flicked to Moneva, but she had turned her face away to the side. So, that was how she had been allowed to move around the fortress so freely. He knew he shouldn't have been surprised. He knew she had done it to save herself, and had risked her life to save him and the others. Nonetheless, emotions swirled around his head—anger, hatred, jealousy, and every other kind of pain threatened to overwhelm him.

The jailer was watching them both.

'Didn't think I'd know about the goings on up there, did you?' he asked, misreading both of their reactions. 'I know plenty.'

Gyrmund didn't reply. He took a deep breath, trying to regain a sense of control.

'Well, anyway, I'll take her from here,' said the jailer coldly, perhaps offended by Gyrmund's lack of response.

Gyrmund was reminded of his own journey to the dungeons of Coldeberg Castle. He remembered being accompanied by Salvinus's soldier, who had taken him all the way to the cell, making sure that Gyrmund was in chains before he left. Curtis was his name. Gyrmund wasn't likely to ever forget it. 'Have fun' were the last words Curtis had said to him before leaving.

'I need to see her to the cell,' he said to the jailer.

The jailer frowned with displeasure, looking at Gyrmund with suspicion. Gyrmund stared back, and something in his expression dissuaded the jailer from making an argument of it.

'Very well,' he conceded, retreating up the corridor.

Gyrmund led Moneva after him. They followed the jailer down the dark corridor. Gyrmund's eyes had adjusted somewhat to the light, now. The walls of the corridor were made from rough stone. They passed through a wooden door. Now Gyrmund could see doors leading off the corridor, regularly spaced along each wall. These must be the prison cells. He looked about. No other jailers or guards could be seen. Was Soren in one of these cells?

The jailer stopped at one of the doors, fumbling at his side for a set of keys. Gyrmund tried to remain relaxed. It hadn't crossed his mind before, but he wondered what kind of state Soren would be in after all this time.

The jailer unlocked the door and swung it inwards. The door shuddered along the floor as he did so, making a loud scraping noise. Gyrmund peered inside. At first, he thought it was a trick, and eyed the jailer nervously. Then, he returned his gaze to the inside of the cell. There was nothing in there but a large wooden box. But now he recognised it as the box in which the Isharites had transported Soren from Edeleny to Samir Durg. Had he been kept in there all this time?

He swung his gaze to the jailer, his mouth open in mute shock.

The jailer gave him a toothy grin. Then, before either of them could react, Moneva was shoving the blade of her dagger into the base of the jailer's skull. He shuddered—a throaty breath escaped from his mouth—and then Moneva was catching his limp body, and carefully lying it down onto the floor of the cell.

As he watched her, Gyrmund wondered how many people she had killed in her short life.

'Can we just lift it off?' she asked him, nodding at the box as she wiped the blade clean on the jailer's robes and sheathed it.

Gyrmund moved over to the box to examine it. It had a heavy lid but no locks or chains on it.

'Yes. Come on.'

Standing on each side of the box, they lifted the handles and heaved the lid off. An appalling smell assaulted Gyrmund's nostrils as they did so.

'Get him out,' said Moneva, gagging at the smell.

Gyrmund peered in. Soren was in the box, sitting with his knees hunched up and his head resting against the side. His eyes were closed and he looked dead. He had soiled himself many times, and the stench inside the box was horrendous.

Gyrmund reached in carefully, trying not to injure him. He grasped the wizard under the arms and lifted him up into a standing position. He had lost a lot of weight, and his thin limbs dangled in the air.

Soren groaned; he was alive. But he seemed unable to put any weight on his legs as Gyrmund held him. Moneva grabbed his legs, and they lifted him gently out of the box onto the stone floor of the cell.

'Strip him,' said Moneva.

Gyrmund pulled at Soren's trousers, as Moneva moved over to remove the jailer's clothes. He looked worriedly at the cell's open door, dreading it slamming shut on them. But so far, no-one else had come to interfere with their rescue.

Soren lay with his eyes closed, barely moving as they did their best to wipe him clean, then dressed him in the robes of the dead jailer. Gyrmund sat him up, holding onto him, while Moneva got out her pot of fermented mare's milk.

'Soren, I'm going to give you a drink,' she said gently, putting the pot to his lips. 'Don't drink too much.'

His lips were cracked and bloody, but he took a sip and swallowed. He took some more. Gyrmund felt his body relax somewhat.

'Where am I?' he managed to say.

'You're in the Tower of Diis, in Samir Durg. This is Moneva. I've come with Gyrmund to rescue you, so you need to keep quiet. Your eyes are closed. Can you try to open them?'

Soren scrunched up his eyes and forced them open, blinking in the paltry light of his prison cell.

'We need to go, Soren,' said Moneva.

Gyrmund lifted him up, but Soren couldn't make his legs stand.

'Put him down' whispered Moneva. 'Rub his legs.'

They worked on a leg each, rubbing the wizard's muscles back into life. As the blood flowed back into his legs Soren screwed his face up in pain, but resisted crying out.

Again, Gyrmund pulled him up to his feet. This time, Soren was able to stay on his feet. But his back was bent double, and he looked to be in considerable pain. If he had spent the last three weeks constricted in that box, it was no surprise. He had clearly been starved in that time too, but his captors must have been feeding him something, or he would be dead by now.

'I can't see,' said Soren, his voice croaky, as if he had been doing a lot of shouting.

'What?' asked Gyrmund.

'It's all a blur,' added the wizard, waving a hand in front of his eyes.

Moneva and Gyrmund shared a look. This was proving to be far more difficult than they had anticipated.

'Rest on me,' said Gyrmund, putting Soren's hand on his arm. 'I'm sorry, but we have no more time. We have to go.'

They exited the cell. Gyrmund was relieved to be leading them back up the dungeon corridor without having been noticed by anyone else. He took the stone steps up to the ground floor slowly and carefully, guiding the frail wizard, reaching the large, irregular chamber of the Tower of Diis. It was still empty.

Gyrmund and Moneva looked around uncertainly. They didn't have an escape plan. The two guards outside the main entrance would be virtually impossible to remove in broad daylight. Gyrmund could see Moneva looking around for alternative exits. Maybe she could somehow sneak her way out of the Tower, but not with Soren in tow.

'What is it?' asked the wizard, frowning at them.

'There are two guards outside the main door of the Tower,' explained Gyrmund.

'Take me,' Soren commanded.

Shrugging at each other, they led him down the corridor to the entrance. Gyrmund was uneasy. Soren sounded sure of himself—but he wasn't convinced that the wizard was in full control of his faculties after his prolonged confinement in the box.

'Go on,' said Soren, his voice sounding irritable.

After exchanging glances with Moneva, who seemed willing to trust Soren, Gyrmund rapped on the door. It was opened and the two guards raised their eyebrows at the sight of Gyrmund, not only still accompanied by Moneva, but also by a strange new figure in a hooded robe.

Soren walked slowly forward, looking in the direction of the guards. There was something about the wizard's eyes, as they stared, unseeing, at the two Isharites, that disturbed Gyrmund.

'I will need an escort,' Soren said, in a voice that was both his and not his.

Nodding in agreement, the two guards turned around and walked forward a few paces, each holding their spear out in front of them.

Gyrmund understood that magic was being used. He had seen it used often enough over the last few weeks, both by Soren and other wizards. But he had not seen anything quite like this. He cast his mind back to the events in Edeleny. Soren, who had lost his magical powers when using them in the Wilderness, had regained them in the Temenos in Edeleny. Gyrmund had witnessed with his own eyes Soren draining the magic from a Caladri wizard,

Agoston—and restoring his own. He recognised that, somehow, in ways he didn't understand, Soren was a different wizard to the one he had been before.

Soren put a hand on Gyrmund's shoulder to steady himself, and they followed the two guards out into the daylight. Soren took a deep breath of fresh air, closing his eyes and smiling with pleasure. Gyrmund understood the feeling.

'We escaped with Herin and Clarin,' he informed Soren, only just realising that they had yet to explain this to him. 'They have a small force of escaped prisoners in a tower in the south-east corner of the fortress,' he added, pointing in the approximate direction, before realising that Soren probably couldn't see this gesture.

Soren nodded. 'I am glad they're alive,' he said. 'But we need to go there.'

He pointed instead to the domed structure in the centre of the fortress. 'What is that?' the wizard asked the two guards.

'That is the Great Hall of Lord Erkindrix,' one of them replied.

Soren nodded. 'Take us there.'

'We can't go there!' said Moneva in a shocked voice. 'We need to escape!'

'Herin and Clarin need us,' Gyrmund added. 'You need to help them.'

Soren looked from Moneva to Gyrmund. 'Herin and Clarin don't stand a chance. Not unless we strike at Erkindrix now. We need to finish this.'

He shuffled off after the two Isharite guards.

'Wait!' said Gyrmund angrily, grabbing Soren and spinning him around. 'What makes you think we stand a chance of defeating Erkindrix? What makes you think Erkindrix is even there?'

Soren looked at him. He had changed again: the powerful wizard was gone, and all Gyrmund could see was a frail and vulnerable looking man.

'Belwynn told me.'

***

'Can you tell him,' Clarin murmured to Tamir, 'that is the way out of here.'

Tamir pointed to the large corner tower of Samir Durg, and made a series of gestures and grunts at the Bear-man. The Bear-man waved his hands in the air, vicious claws threatening to cut those around him. He roared. Clarin sighed. There seemed to be no way of telling the creature to keep quiet. Meanwhile, time was running out.

'Well?' he asked, trying to keep the frustration out of his voice.

'I think he understands,' replied Tamir.

'That will have to do,' Clarin replied. 'Can you tell your men it's time to go?'

The longer they lingered, the worse their situation got.

Clarin was gambling that they had persuaded the Bear-man to lead a charge on the entrance to the corner tower. Clarin and Herin would lead Tamir's Barbarians and follow up the charge, in an attempt to secure the tower for themselves. If they did, they would have a much stronger tower to defend. They would also, according to Moneva at least, control an exit out of the fortress. If they didn't—well, the gamble will have failed.

'We've got to go,' came Herin's voice, who had been keeping an eye on the tower. 'They're coming.'

Clarin rushed over to see. A group of spear-wielding Isharite soldiers were walking in double file towards them, along the walkway that connected the corner tower with their own. It was now or never.

He signalled the Bear-man over and they looked into each other's eyes. They made a connection—an understanding, of sorts. Beneath the fur and the protruding jaw, this creature was probably no less intelligent than he was. Clarin was asking it, almost certainly, to go to its death. But then, they were all likely to die anyway.

The Isharite soldiers marched along the walkway, looking confident. Then, they set eyes upon a great beast emerging from the tower. The Bear-man roared its defiance at them, and Clarin could see them quail, momentarily, before they regained their composure. Then, it charged. Clarin ran behind, gripping a spear, ready to assist with the attack.

No doubt, Clarin considered to himself as he ran, being charged by a Bear-man would be terrifying. Commendably, the two Isharites who found themselves at the front of their line held their ground, spears at the ready. But, as the creature hurtled towards them, jaws open and teeth out, they thrust their spears forwards too soon. Understandable. Understandable, but a fatal mistake.

The Bear-man stopped in time. It grabbed hold of the top of each spear and pushed them to the side. Then, before the Isharites could react, it was in amongst them. Its clawed hands struck at armour, grabbed at weapons. When the claws found purchase, they pulled the Isharites off their feet, throwing them from the wall. Even if the claws didn't connect, the Bear-man's powerful limbs battered them to the ground. The Isharites still thrust their spears forwards to defend themselves. One of them found their target, the blade skewering the flesh of the creature's thigh.

The Bear-man was so big that there was no room for Clarin to fight alongside it; but, by leaning against the crenellations, he could thrust his own spear forwards. He found the groin of a soldier who had, understandably, been focused on the wild swings of the monster.

Despite its injury, the Bear-man continued to slice and crush, until the neat line of soldiers had disintegrated. Not stopping, it charged forwards once more.

Clarin followed, leaving the sprawled Isharites on the walkway for those behind him to deal with.

A small group of soldiers stood by the door and hurriedly tried to close it before the Bear-man arrived. All too late. The first through tried to shut it on those still on the walkway, who shoved it open, trying to escape. The creature hurled itself at them before they could defend themselves. It crashed into the door, trapping a soldier against the wall, who screamed in agony.

The Bear-man had pushed the door wide open. The Isharites stabbed at it, with spears and swords. The Bear-man fell on them, swinging its arms and snapping its jaws.

Clarin followed it through, thrusting overarm with his spear into the midriff of a swordsman. The blade of the spear didn't get through the soldier's chain mail, but the force of the blow caused the Isharite to double over in pain.

Dropping his spear, Clarin knelt down and grabbed the sword out of his enemy's hands. It was made from crystal—the very crystal he had been mining this time yesterday. He felt a certain sense of justice as he chopped into the Isharite's neck, driving him to the ground—chopping twice more to make sure he was dead. The sword seemed like a decent weapon—surprisingly light, and easy to use in the confines of the tower.

Clarin got a quick view of the interior of the tower. As elsewhere in the fortress, the third floor connected one section of walkway to the next. This room was open plan like the others they had been in, but much larger. The Isharites were arriving from all directions: from the walkway opposite, and from the floors both below and above them.

Herin and Tamir joined them, with the rest of the Barbarians. A desperate struggled ensued as they tried to force their way into the tower, and the Isharites tried to force them out.

The Isharite soldiers were well fed and stronger. They were better armed. The Barbarians, however, knew that they were fighting for their lives. A wild kind of fury overtook them, as they sought revenge for the weeks of captivity and brutality. Clarin joined in with it, glorying in having a sword in his hands; revelling in the chance to fight one last time, when it had looked like his life would be snuffed out in a slave pit.

Several Barbarians fell to Isharite crystal in those brutal minutes of hacking and thrusting. The Bear-man, whose path of destruction had given them the momentum they needed, was finally driven to the ground from multiple wounds, the Isharites desperately spearing its exhausted corpse to make sure it was dead.

But more Barbarians took the place of their fallen kin. Behind them were the Persaleians and the Dog-men. And it seemed to Clarin that it was the Dog-men who finally turned things decisively in their favour. He had been wary of them, unsure whether they would fight with the other prisoners or betray them. But they seemed to understand that if the Isharites won, they would be killed too. Their agility and strength was superior to anyone else's, as they leapt at the enemy. Their barks, and the vicious snaps of their jaws, were somehow more terrifying than spears and swords.

The Isharite soldiers, who had seen many of their comrades killed, now decided that they had suffered enough. They didn't turn and run though. It was an orderly retreat, and Clarin and Herin were obliged to continue to harry them, as they turned the corner and made for the walkway at the front of the fortress.

'Secure the ground floor,' Clarin shouted at Zared, turning his neck and shouting as loud as he could. With relief, he saw the Persaleians following the command, heading down the steps to the lower rooms, where there would be other entrances into the tower.

The Isharites ahead of Clarin backed off further, until Herin was able to shut the door on them. Clarin slammed home the wrought iron bolt. It would hold for a while, but they would have to try to shore it up further. For now, though, the priority was securing all the other entrances into the tower.

As fast as he could, his legs now trembling from the exertion, he made his way back to the third-floor room. He hadn't seen such a bloody massacre before in his life. The walls were painted with blood. Some of the Barbarians were lying or sitting in the gore, too injured or exhausted to move. Wordlessly, he moved through them to the stairs, and headed down to the next floor. Here, he found himself in a small hallway with doors to three separate rooms off it. It seemed deserted, and he moved to head down the next flight of stairs to the ground floor.

Hurrying back up the stairs was Cyprian, the small Persaleian that Gyrmund had befriended.

'Ah, Clarin. The ground floor is secure,' he said seriously, as if he was reporting to a general in an army. 'Just in time, though. Soldiers are gathering down in the courtyard. We've also located a small larder and a small armoury.'

A wave of relief crashed over Clarin. No more soldiers, for a while at least. Food and weapons as well.

'Well done,' he said, giving Cyprian an embrace.

There was one more entrance to secure: the door which they had entered from. Forcing his tired body to move again, Clarin slogged his way back up the stairs to the third floor. He moved gingerly to the door of the tower, the floor slick with blood.

'Wait!' came a shout.

Ahead of him, running at full speed along the walkway, came Jurgen and Rudy. Not far behind them was a group of Isharite soldiers. Clarin had forgotten about the two cousins, and had come close to locking them out. They skidded into the room, slipping over on the wet floor, eyes wide at the sight of the carnage that had taken place there. Clarin slammed the door shut and locked the bolt, breathing a sigh of relief.

'We held them off for as long as we could,' said Jurgen, his breathing ragged from his exertions.

'Well done,' said Clarin.

Herin emerged from the top floor, followed by the Dog-men.

'The Persaleians have secured everything on the ground floor,' Clarin told his brother. 'What's up there?'

'Two bedrooms on the next floor,' said Herin. 'One of them has a set of stairs leading up to the tower roof. You get quite a good view from up there. Not a bad place for a last stand.'

XXV

THE KILL

'PUT HIM HERE,' BELWYNN SAID TO two Krykker soldiers, who had walked a third man into camp, his arms wrapped around their shoulders.

They laid him down gently, looking exhausted from the effort it had taken to get him there. They showed her where the injury was: a heavy weapon of some kind had hit the top of their friend's thigh, leaving a massive dent in his armour. There was very little to see without removing the armour, and a broken bone was unlikely: but Belwynn understood that it could be a serious injury nonetheless. She would get Elana to see to him sooner rather than later.

Belwynn's job, in the aftermath of the battle, was to organise the injured: directing where they should be laid down, providing water and other necessities. She made the initial assessment of their injuries. She would then explain this to Belwynn, and help the priestess prioritise who she should see.

The injured were, mercifully, far fewer than she had feared. The battle had gone as well as anyone could have expected, with Rostam's forces chased from the field. Groups of Krykkers were already making their way back to camp, whereas the Knights were still out there somewhere, harrying the enemy to ensure that it was as complete a victory as possible. She was yet to see the return of any familiar faces, but one of the Krykkers had assured her that Rabigar was alive and well.

Pentas appeared. Belwynn and Elana stopped what they were doing as he approached, his red eyes drifting over the injured soldiers, wearing his laconic smile.

'Victory!' he declared, his smile getting broader, though Belwynn was still unsure of its sincerity.

'What happens next?' Belwynn demanded, keen to get some straight answers. 'Can we reach Samir Durg from here?'

Pentas raised one eyebrow. 'This army cannot reach Samir Durg. It barely has enough supplies to get there, never mind to conduct a siege. Meanwhile, the Isharites will simply raise another army against it. I would say that you have achieved all you could have hoped for.'

'What, then?' asked Elana, sounding angry. 'What of Belwynn's brother and friends?'

'This army cannot reach Samir Durg,' Pentas replied, 'but I can. I will be going back presently. It will be an interesting visit, if nothing else.' He looked at Belwynn. 'Although it will tax my powers, I can take you there if you wish. Who knows? That staff, or the dagger you carry, may come in handy. Of course, I would be taking you into a highly dangerous environment, one that I myself may not escape from alive. I can't guarantee your safety.'

'Will we be able to rescue Soren?' she asked.

Pentas made a face. 'That, I cannot promise. With a lot of luck, your friends may rescue him. Have you tried speaking to him recently?'

She hadn't. She tried, opening that channel of communication that had been so natural since childhood, but that had barely been used in the past weeks.

Soren?

She was met with silence again. But then, was she? This time felt different, as if her brother was there, even if he wasn't speaking.

Soren?

Belwynn?

He sounded distant; confused. But this was the first time that he had answered her in two weeks.

'What is it?' interrupted Pentas, who was studying her closely.

'He's there. He replied,' Belwynn said, her voice shaking.

Where are you? she asked Soren.

I don't know...

His voice had that same, groggy quality to it.

I'm in a prison.

How are you? Are you well? Belwynn asked, trying to keep the sound of panic from her voice.

Gyrmund is here. Gyrmund and Moneva. They're helping me.

'He says that Gyrmund and Moneva are with him.'

Elana beamed at the news. Pentas pursed his lips thoughtfully.

'What about the other two?' the wizard asked.

What about Herin and Clarin? Belwynn asked Soren.

No. Not here.

Belwynn shook her head.

'Listen, Belwynn,' said Pentas. 'You need to tell him to make his way to the Great Hall. It's the large building, right in the centre of the complex, with a domed roof.'

Belwynn passed on the instructions.

'I need to leave as soon as possible,' said Pentas.

'I'm coming,' said Belwynn.

She ran over to her small pile of possessions to grab Onella's Staff. Toric's Dagger was already tucked inside her belt.

'Are you sure that's wise?' asked Elana as Belwynn returned. 'What if the weapons fall into the hands of Erkindrix?'

Belwynn looked to Pentas. He didn't seem sure himself.

'What do you think?' the wizard asked Elana, returning the question.

Elana considered it. Was she having a private conversation with Madria? Was it all intuition? Belwynn wished she knew. The priestess sighed.

'Take them,' she said.

'I don't see any gain in bringing you,' Pentas said to Elana. 'You are more use here, I think,' he said, gesturing at the wounded soldiers she still had to treat.

Elana nodded. 'Agreed. Good luck to you both. Madria goes with you.'

Pentas offered Belwynn his hand. When she took it, he placed his other hand onto Onella's Staff. He began the spell of teleportation immediately. As before, when the wizard had transported her out of Edeleny, into Kalinth, Belwynn felt her stomach drop. Her mouth filled with the taste of bile. Then came the sensation of moving, the air on her face and arms; but her vision was too blurred and indistinct to make sense of where she was going.

For a while they travelled in this way, though it was hard to say how long the journey took. When they stopped, they were inside a building. Belwynn stood bent double, waiting for the room to stop spinning as she slowly regained her senses.

She looked at her surroundings. The room was expensively furnished and lightly scented. Belwynn presumed they were in Pentas's personal chambers. A stone fireplace was the centrepiece. It had a wooden surround that had been decorated in swirling red and green colours. Tapestries hung on the walls, and rugs adorned the floor. Wooden chests lined the room. In the middle was a table, with red velvet covered chairs adding yet more luxury.

'Very nice,' she commented, standing up straight as her body recovered from the journey.

'Yes, well. I have to keep up appearances.'

'So, your appearance is that of a mighty sorcerer of Ishari. But in reality, you are a humble servant of Madria?'

Pentas smiled his enigmatic smile. 'Yes, in essence. I've never claimed to be an Isharite, though. I was born in Persala, as I believe I mentioned when we first met.'

He had, Belwynn recalled.

'The Isharites don't mind?'

'Oh, they mind. Many of them mind very much. But I am a very powerful wizard, you see. And power matters the most to Erkindrix—and to Diis. So, while I have never been fully trusted, I have made myself very useful to them over the years. My behaviour has raised some suspicions from time to time, but never enough to see me removed.'

'And what dark deeds have you done to make yourself useful?' Belwynn asked him.

'What choice did I have?' Pentas answered passionately. His cool demeanour began to slip, at last. 'When the stakes are so high, how else should I have dealt with such a threat to Dalriya? A heroic stand, destroyed by the combined wizardry of the Isharites? What good would that have done? No, I have swallowed my pride—ignored my conscience. For this moment. To engineer a situation where maybe, just maybe, Erkindrix is vulnerable.'

He looked at her with those inscrutable red eyes. Was he looking for praise? Waiting for her to condemn him further? Belwynn had nothing else to say. Right now, she just wanted to find her brother.

'If you are ready,' he said, 'it is time to act.'

Pentas's apartments were in a tower in the north-west corner of the fortress of Samir Durg. From here, he led Belwynn out to the massive compound that lay inside the high walls of the fortress. She hadn't really known what to expect of the place: her mind had pictured, in a vague way, some dark lair where the Isharites hid and plotted their conquests. She hadn't expected this. The walls were crenelated, and sparkled with crystals that had been embedded amongst the stone. They were punctuated by countless towers, of different shapes and sizes: some large and military looking; some with turrets; some slim ones ending in tall spires. In the middle of the space stood a great stone building, topped with a golden dome.

'It's beautiful,' she said. 'Why would anyone who owned this need to conquer more?'

Pentas looked around him, as if examining the site for the first time.

'No,' he said. 'If there is beauty here, I can't see it.'

They walked to the stone building in the middle of the fortress, passing some soldiers and other officials who seemed busy with their own business. Some of them took surreptitious, interested glances at Belwynn. Clearly, however, none had the authority to ask questions of Pentas, who strode to his destination with authority. The guards stationed by the entrance respectfully gave way, and he led Belwynn into the building. They walked down a stone corridor, Belwynn's fear growing as they did. Pentas stopped.

'Around this corner,' he said, 'are the doors to Erkindrix's Throne Room.'

He studied her face, his own becoming almost gentle.

'Once we're inside, I cannot control what will happen, Belwynn. You must follow my lead. I want you to talk to Soren now. I need you to explain to him what he needs to do.'

***

'Down here,' muttered Soren, his mouth nearly too dry for words to escape.

Starved of food and water, his body was beginning to give up. Gyrmund was having to half carry him along the corridor, Soren's legs no longer willing to move. All he wanted to do was lie down to rest. But the reason he had stayed alive was the same reason he kept going now. Belwynn. Somehow, she had found her way to Samir Durg—to rescue him. He couldn't let her down.

They stopped at a door. Soren had to take a few breaths before he could speak again.

'I think this is it,' he gasped. 'But there may be servants in there.'

'Leave it to me.'

Moneva's voice.

'You're not going in there by yourself,' said Gyrmund.

'You'll just get in the way,' she replied. 'Here, give him some of this.'

272

Gyrmund didn't argue further. He lowered Soren down against a wall. Soren felt Gyrmund putting the clay jug of kumis to his lips, and he took a sip. His dehydrated body wanted him to gulp it down, but he knew that would make things worse. He took a second drink and then a third. He felt the liquid fire up and revive his body. The desperate need for sleep was banished, but instead he became more aware of the sharp pain in his back.

He looked up as the door opened. A figure emerged. He still couldn't see clearly, but he somehow knew it was Moneva.

'Well?' asked Gyrmund.

'There were three of them. All clear now. Looks like the right place,' she added.

Belwynn had told Soren to try to find the rear entrance to the Throne Room, accessed via the private rooms of Erkindrix. If they had found it, they were only a few feet away from Erkindrix and his Council. And Belwynn.

Gyrmund and Moneva both bent down to lift Soren back up to his feet. He bit hard on his lower lip to stop himself from shouting out as pain lanced down his spine. They guided him through the door into the room.

It was small and dimly lit, with a musty smell. One of Erkindrix's servants lay sprawled dead on the floor opposite them. Soren could make out items, probably wooden chests, dotted around the room; but he had no interest in his surroundings. He made out an open door to the right, and gestured for Gyrmund to take him there. A soft rug underfoot muffled the sound of their footsteps. As they approached the door, he could hear raised voices.

Gyrmund guided him into a second, larger room, with the paraphernalia of living quarters. But now Soren took even less interest in his surroundings. Directly ahead was a stone archway. Beyond it, he could hear the voices as if they were in the room with him.

'They hit us hard,' someone was saying. 'The Drobax broke like a pack of cowardly animals. After that, it was impossible to regroup.'

Soren dropped to his hands and knees as he approached the archway, moving carefully to avoid being seen. Gyrmund and Moneva joined him, dropping to their haunches. Soren peered through.

They were behind the throne: on which, presumably, Erkindrix was seated. Two figures stood either side of him. Above, the vaulted walls of the Throne Room rose impossibly high. With his limited vision, Soren couldn't properly make out the ceiling, though he could see a golden shimmer at the very top.

A palpable sense of tension filled the atmosphere. In front of the throne, Soren could make out four figures, stood in pairs. He heard Moneva gasp to his right.

'Belwynn!' she whispered.

A chill ran through Soren's body. What was his sister doing here? He focused on the four figures, and picked out the one that was smaller and slimmer than the others. He had thought he would never see Belwynn again. Here she was, so close, yet he was not able to see her clearly, never mind go to her.

Perhaps seeing Soren squinting into the room, Gyrmund leaned over and quietly filled in the details that Soren couldn't make out.

'She's standing next to Pentas. She's holding Onella's Staff. Across from them is Arioc, with one of his men.'

Soren struggled to take in the information. Arioc? It was Arioc who had ordered that Soren be transported in a box to Samir Durg. Was it also Arioc who had tortured him here? Delving into his brain, picking out all his secrets? All but one: his special bond with Belwynn. His torturer had been unable to unlock that puzzle. That was why, Soren was sure, he had been kept alive. But now Belwynn was standing only a few feet away from him, with Madria's weapons. Why had she brought them here, of all places?

Soren felt his mind reeling. Starved and tortured, he couldn't think clearly. He couldn't see what was happening in the throne room, and even after Gyrmund had told him, he couldn't understand it.

He recognised the voice of the next to speak. Smooth and self-controlled, despite the tension in the air. Pentas, the red-eyed wizard they had first encountered on the road to Coldeberg. According to Belwynn, he had rescued her from Edeleny, spiriting her and Madria's weapons away from Arioc. Why do that, and then bring them here, to Erkindrix?

'I have recovered two of Madria's weapons,' he was saying, as if defending himself from some accusation. 'That was the priority. It means that we are now safe from Madria's threat. The fate of one army is inconsequential compared to this. We can simply raise another one to deal with the Krykkers.'

'True enough,' came a voice, a voice that grabbed at Soren's throat and nearly made him choke. The voice of his tormentor. It was coming from the throne, so close to him that Soren could almost reach out and touch its owner. So, not Arioc after all. Some other.

'The weapons are more important to Diis than a defeat,' the voice continued. It wasn't coming from the throne itself, Soren realised, but from a cowled figure, all in black, who seemed to stand in shadow even where there should be none. Soren's mind, assaulted by a slew of emotions, slowly worked it out. Siavash, the leader of the Order of Diis. Arioc had passed him on to this man for interrogation.

'Nevertheless,' Siavash continued, the sound of his voice grating on Soren's nerve endings, reminding him of the agony he had suffered at his hands. 'A defeat such as this is unacceptable.'

Soren's first instinct was to escape. He wanted nothing more than to run and hide from his tormentor. But other instincts prevented him. Anger came to the fore. A savage desire for revenge. Ambition, still there despite the weeks of torture. And a brother's love for his sister. These instincts won out over fear, and Soren took to his feet. Gyrmund laid a restraining arm on him, but he shook it off and took a step through the arch into the Throne Room.

'Indeed,' replied Pentas, as Soren emerged behind the throne.

He must be able to see me, Soren considered. *Did those red eyes flicker,* he wondered, *and give me away? Or did Pentas keep his composure?*

'It would have been much sounder,' Pentas continued, his voice giving no indication that anything had changed, 'to have given the command of the army to Arioc.'

'Treason!' said the figure on the other side of the throne to Siavash.

Soren considered what he knew of the leaders of Ishari. This one must be Ardashir, long-time ally of Erkindrix. His voice sounded like the dry crackle of parchment paper, but it was alive with surprise and pleasure at having caught Pentas out. 'Those were the orders of Lord Erkindrix!'

Ardashir stopped, puzzled perhaps by the reactions of those who stood before the throne. Ignoring him, their eyes had drifted to Soren who now emerged, shuffling, onto the scene. It took what felt like an age to manoeuvre his broken body around the throne, as the eyes of the greatest wizards of Dalriya studied him. They could have destroyed him in an instant. But they didn't. No-one seemed quite sure how to react.

This gave him a chance. Ignoring everyone, even Erkindrix himself, even his own sister—Soren moved in front of the throne until he could look Siavash in the face. The stink of rotting flesh from the throne assailed him, but he stared into the dark eyes of his torturer. Siavash looked back, but there was no sign of recognition.

'What—' began Ardashir, but Soren suddenly unleashed a bolt of magic at Siavash. In his mind's eye, his attack would blast Siavash into pieces, but the High Priest casually negated the bolt as if it were nothing. He smiled then, a thin smile of wicked pleasure.

'Soren!' shouted Belwynn.

Then, things suddenly happened very fast.

Belwynn threw Onella's Staff towards him. He reached out, using his magic to draw the weapon into his grip. On contact, he felt the magic within the stave funnel into him. He understood—instantly, instinctively—its power to enhance and channel his magic.

Immediately, he used its help to address his greatest weakness: his vision. He constructed a picture of the room and the people in it. This was a picture that his mind, and his magic, told his eyes they could see. His eyes returned an image, wonderfully clear and detailed, of his surroundings. The crystal throne sparkled in a range of red hues. The crumpled figure of Erkindrix who sat there had a grey tinge to his skin, interrupted by crusty, yellow scabs. Eyes like black coals stared out from behind the face of the Lord of Ishari. The whole throne room was bathed in a golden light that came streaming through the dome above. It was a version of reality that he could see and react to.

Just in time.

Siavash launched a counterattack at him, blasting a scorching flame in his direction. Holding the staff out in front of him, Soren put up a shield to resist the High Priest's magic. The flames were diverted either side of him, though he only just managed to stay on his feet from the force of the blast.

Belwynn continued to move forwards, Toric's Dagger now in her hand. But the Isharite next to Arioc reacted quickly, throwing a punch which connected with the side of her head, sending her to the ground like a sack of potatoes. The Dagger dropped from her limp hand as she hit the floor, skittering a few feet away. She lay unmoving—unconscious, or worse.

From behind Soren, Gyrmund came storming out from their hiding place. He launched himself at the Isharite, a flash of steel in his hand as he stabbed at him. His opponent, however, was quick. He grabbed Gyrmund's wrist, stopping the blow. They struggled for control of the weapon.

'No you don't!' shouted Pentas, launching an attack on Ardashir.

Soren turned to see the old wizard's outstretched palm facing him, ready to fire a surprise blast. Instead, Ardashir had to quickly change direction, hurling a bolt of magic towards Pentas. The room crackled with energy as the two attacks met. Both wizards visibly strained against each other, but neither seemed able to get the upper hand.

Soren had no time to watch further as a second attack from Siavash came his way. He blocked it, redirecting the blast of magic to the side where it hit the wall of the Throne Room, scorching the stone black. Using Onella's Staff to strengthen his wasted muscles, he backed away, recognising the trouble that they were in. He and Pentas were both fully engaged in defending themselves, while Arioc and Erkindrix remained free to act.

From the corner of his eye he saw Erkindrix slowly rise from his throne. He walked forwards. His was a frail body, centuries old—it looked like it was held together by sheer force of will. Then, Arioc finally moved too, to meet his master. He was the opposite: strong and powerful looking, full of vigour.

'Finish them,' Erkindrix commanded Arioc.

Arioc raised a hand, but to Soren's utter astonishment, instead of turning on himself or Pentas, Arioc fired at Erkindrix. The blast sent Erkindrix flying backwards until he crashed into his throne.

Siavash, rage spread across his face, prepared to strike at Arioc, but Soren got in an attack first. Siavash saw it coming and blocked it easily enough. But Soren knew that he had to keep the High Priest pinned down, so that he couldn't come to the aid of his master. For whatever reason, Arioc had turned on Erkindrix, and this gave them all a chance of survival.

'You are too old now, Erkindrix,' said Arioc matter-of-factly. 'No-one can live forever. It is time for new leadership.'

A bitter laugh escaped from the old wizard. Despite looking like a crumpled bag of bones, Erkindrix regained his feet, seemingly unharmed.

'You think to replace me, Arioc? For so many years you have served me, and yet, it seems you have learned nothing.'

Erkindrix shrieked and bolts of white light emerged from his outstretched fingers to shoot at Arioc. Drawing a sword, Arioc swatted them aside and marched forwards, an implacable look on his face.

Soren, trying to concentrate on his own task, fired another bolt at Siavash. But he was growing tired, and his attack was predictable. Siavash had been waiting for it, and somehow turned it back on him. Soren dived out of the way, narrowly avoiding being hit by his own magic. As he fell to the floor he lost his grip on the staff. His recently regained eyesight vanished. His back spasmed in agony. He would have been killed there and then, if Siavash had not had another priority.

Scrabbling on the floor, his fingers clutched around the staff. A burst of light erupted as his eyesight was restored.

Looking up, he saw that Siavash was using his magic to tug on Arioc's crystal sword. Arioc was concentrating on pulling it back. The interruption allowed Erkindrix to fire his bolts of white light a second time. This time, they hit home, enveloping Arioc's body in white light, forcing it into spasms, and finally driving him to the floor.

Using Onella's Staff, Soren fired a shot at Erkindrix, but Siavash was ready for him. The thin smile had returned to the High Priest's face, and he easily blocked Soren's attempt, before forcing him back onto the defensive with a blast of his own. Soren blocked it, but he was now running on empty. Without the Staff, he couldn't have kept going this long. He had failed to keep Siavash occupied, and despair crept into his thoughts, as he saw the fight going the wrong way.

Then, Erkindrix screamed out—a deafening, unnatural sound unlike anything that had gone before. Soren looked over, and there was Moneva.

She was holding Toric's Dagger, and had plunged it through Erkindrix's chest, into his heart. She withdrew the weapon. Erkindrix howled once more in agony. No blood could be seen where the Dagger had punctured his body. Instead, Soren could make out dark vapours escaping. Erkindrix's howling stopped. His body collapsed and sank to the floor—a dried-out husk that could no longer be kept alive.

Everyone in the Throne Room stopped and stared for a moment, in shock. None of them, it seemed, had quite thought it possible. But the evidence was there for them all to see. Erkindrix had been killed.

Ardashir was the first to react. With a snarl, he raised his hand in Moneva's direction. A shield of magic appeared in front of her.

'I think not,' said Arioc from a kneeling position, his voice calm. 'Moneva has done me a service, today. I am the new Lord of Ishari. Your allegiance now goes to me.'

Ardashir sneered at him. 'You think this makes you Lord of Ishari? Your treachery today has sealed your doom, Arioc.'

The two wizards faced off, ignoring everyone else. Soren quickly looked around. The remaining threat was from Siavash. The High Priest and Pentas had turned to each other, ready to fight.

Soren limped towards Siavash, Onella's Staff raised. It was a bluff—a desperate bluff. He didn't think he had anything left to give now. But Siavash didn't know that.

The High Priest looked from Pentas to Soren. He was outnumbered. It seemed that it was a risk he wasn't prepared to take. He turned and ran a few steps, before leaping into the air. One moment there was a man. The next, a crow was flapping its wings in his place. It flew around the empty throne, and headed for the arch from where Soren had entered the room moments ago. Pentas unleashed a blast of magic in Siavash's direction, but the crow flew to the side avoiding it. Then, it was gone, through the arch and away.

The duel between Arioc and Ardashir had begun. Ignoring them, Soren made for the prone form of Belwynn, but two figures blocked his path.

Rostam and Gyrmund's fight was over now. They had separated, neither seriously injured by the other. The Isharite backed away from them warily, drawing a crystal sword from his scabbard.

'I serve Arioc,' he said.

'Go serve your master, then,' said Pentas.

Rostam's withdrawal allowed Soren to reach his sister. He crouched down by her side.

Moneva arrived. Her hands were shaking, but she still gripped Toric's Dagger tightly. She leaned over Belwynn, as did Gyrmund and Pentas.

Soren wanted to check his sister but suddenly, an enormous fatigue descended on him, and he fell to his hands and knees. He felt like he was going to faint, and had to fight to stay conscious. He watched Gyrmund put a hand to Belwynn's neck.

'There is still a pulse,' he said.

A huge feeling of relief flooded Soren. Was it possible that they would all escape with their lives?

'We need to get them out of here,' said Moneva, looking at Belwynn and Soren, who was still too tired to get up from his hands and knees. He gripped Onella's Staff tightly, using its power to keep his senses working.

'Indeed,' said Pentas. 'Siavash will return with his followers soon. I can't let these weapons fall into his hands. I think I have enough energy to teleport us away to relative safety. If I can get us to her, your friend Elana will be able to treat them.'

'What about Herin and Clarin?' asked Gyrmund.

Pentas shook his head.

'If we try to get to them, Siavash will track us down. If not him, Arioc or Ardashir,' he said, looking over at the struggle between the two wizards which continued unabated. 'If your friends are still alive, they will have to make their own escape.'

Soren wanted to protest. He wanted to get Herin and Clarin out of this place too.

A crashing sound behind him made him turn to see Ardashir pinned against the wall of the room by Arioc's magic. Rostam closed in on the old wizard, sword in hand.

'Alright,' he said, accepting the reality of their situation.

He reached over and took one of Belwynn's hands.

Gyrmund looked at him for a moment, before conceding, and reaching out for Moneva's hand. Pentas put a hand on the staff. Once they had formed a circle, Pentas began his spell.

Soren took a last look at the Throne Room of Samir Durg.

The dried husk that had been the body of the dreaded Erkindrix lay, ignored, by his throne.

They had killed the Lord of Ishari. He was reunited with Belwynn. And they might just escape with their lives. It was almost too much to comprehend.

And then Soren's vision left him, his mind gave out, and his body began to move.

XXVI

LAST STAND

THE SMALL ARMOURY IN THE TOWER turned out to be a treasure trove. Clarin did his best to supervise the distribution of weapons and armour, to ensure that everyone was at least adequately armed. The last thing he wanted was a dispute between the Persaleians and Barbarians over who got what.

He was helped in his task by their different sizes. The Barbarians were taller, and claimed the largest pieces of armour, because they were the only ones that would fit. The Persaleians, many of whom were already well armed, favoured the smaller weapons. For himself, Clarin acquired a quilted linen jacket, on top of which he had shrugged on a riveted chain mail hauberk big enough to fit him. He decided to keep the crystal sword he had acquired in the fight earlier, enjoying the feel and weight of it.

Cyprian had organised the distribution of food and drink from the larder, ensuring that everyone, even the Dog-men, received an equal share.

With everybody fed and getting a chance to rest, Clarin got to work on planning the defence of their position.

He began by exploring the ground floor of the tower. A door to the west led out into the courtyard of the fortress beyond. It was here that the largest group of Isharites were being readied for an assault. Clarin ensured that any spare item was shoved against it, to hold them off for as long as possible. A second door, cleverly built into the curved south wall of the tower, was an exit from the fortress. If they attempted to use it now, they would be cut down by Isharite horsemen in a matter of minutes. Nonetheless, it still represented a chance that they might somehow escape. Even if any realistic assessment of their situation would suggest that wasn't going to happen.

Clarin decided that he would take charge of the defence of the ground floor, along with Zared and the Persaleians, the three Dog-men, and the two Rotelegen cousins, Rudy and Jurgen. Up on the third floor, which the Isharites could access from both the southern and eastern walls, Herin led the defence, along with Tamir and the Barbarians. Herin had taken a liking to the open roof on top of the tower. He had acquired a bow and a quiver of arrows from the armoury, and was keen to make use of the height that the position afforded.

When the Isharite assault came, it hadn't been what Clarin had expected. With all his military planning, he had forgotten that Samir Durg would be crawling with wizards. Not that he could have done anything about it anyway.

The door to the courtyard suddenly engulfed in flames. The Dog-men yipped in panic as the fire took hold immediately. Clarin sent them into the armoury so that they were out of the way. With a whoosh of air, the flames spread onto the furniture that Clarin had ordered should be stacked against the door. Smoke blew at the defenders, forcing the Persaleians back a few paces. Clarin could feel the heat from the fire on his face as the smell of wood smoke hit his nostrils.

There was a crack and the door crashed down into the tower, resting precariously on the burning furniture underneath. Clarin could just about see through the smoke to the courtyard outside. A mass of Isharite spearmen stood waiting for the order to attack. In front of them, he could make out what must be some of the wizards. They raised their hands and another blast of air surged into the tower, scattering hot ash at the defenders. Clarin covered his mouth, his eyes watering from the black smoke that roiled around them, making the Persaleians cough and splutter. The courtyard outside was no longer visible but Clarin could hear the sudden shouting that told him the soldiers had been ordered to attack.

He found Rudy and Jurgen.

'Go and tell Herin what's happening,' he shouted at them, grabbing them and pushing them away when they hesitated. They headed for the stairs up to the next floor, which were now barely visible as the thick smoke continued to spread.

Zared had found him.

'What do we do?' asked the young man, his voice dry and strained.

'Retreat slowly to the second floor,' Clarin ordered. 'Don't make it easy for them, but give ground when you have to.'

Clarin moved into the armoury with the Dog-men. There was more air here, and he took a chance to get his breath back.

'Fight with me,' he told them.

'Yes, master,' said one of the creatures, bowing its head. They had eschewed the weapons that had been available to them, and were instead ready to fight with tooth and claw.

Clarin peered out of the room, waiting. He heard the shouts of battle and, slowly, the sounds grew louder as the melee drew closer. The Isharites would have had to get through the flames, negotiate the debris in their path, and then fight in a very enclosed space. The Persaleians were in a good position to hold them off, but he knew that the superior numbers would tell in the end.

Eventually, he could see them being pushed back, and he ducked back into the room, out of sight. He nodded at the Dog-men to be ready, and then waited for a while longer. Finally, gripping his sword, he ran out of the room.

Clarin got to the Isharites before they knew what was happening. Concentrating on the Persaleians ahead of them, they had ignored the rooms on the ground floor. He raised his sword above his head and slashed down with it, doing as much damage as he could while he had the advantage. The Dog-men joined him, slashing out with their sharp claws in all directions, as the Isharite progress came to an abrupt halt. The Isharites were heavily armoured, but the claws of the Dog-men were still able to find exposed throats and faces.

Clarin took a strong blow on the shoulder that nearly knocked him over. He tottered backwards but managed to stay on his feet. One of the Dog-men was hit with the full force of a spear thrust, the weapon sinking into its belly. It scrabbled at the shaft of the weapon but there was nothing it could do.

'Back!' Clarin shouted, recognising that they were in trouble. Fortunately, the Persaleians had supported his attack, giving him a retreat route. He took it, the two remaining Dog-men following close behind.

The Isharite advance paused and the two groups backed away from each other. The floor between them was covered with mangled corpses and injured soldiers. The Isharites were being ordered into the rooms on the ground floor to make sure that there were no more defenders hiding there.

'Defenders,' shouted Clarin, his eyes kept firmly ahead of him on the Isharites. 'Back up to the stairs.'

They took advantage of the pause in the fighting to make it to the stairs that led to the second floor. Here, they not only had a height advantage, but the narrow, twisting stone steps negated the superior numbers of the Isharites. If done properly, it was a position that could be held for a long time.

'Zared!' Clarin shouted.

'Out of the way!' came the Persaleian's voice, as he tried to reach Clarin through the bodies on the stairs.

'You need to defend this position,' Clarin told him when he got there. 'Two men with spears or other long weapons are needed to keep them back. They need to be given space behind them to retreat into: don't get too bunched up. Rotate the men at the front so that they don't get too tired. I'm going to check on what's happening upstairs.'

'Understood,' agreed Zared. 'Pass me a spear,' he yelled to his men, and began to relay Clarin's orders.

'You two,' Clarin said to the two remaining Dog-men, 'with me. Cyprian, you too.'

Clarin marched up to the second floor. It was deserted, but he could already hear fighting on the third floor above them. This came as no surprise; he had expected the Isharites to coordinate their attacks. His worry was that his group of defenders could get trapped between the two Isharite forces coming from below and above.

Taking the stairs up to the third floor, a quick glance confirmed his fears. Rudy and Jurgen were just about managing to fend off the attackers from the east wall, the defences that had been placed there still holding. The Isharites from the south wall, however, had managed to break into the room, leaving the Barbarians dangerously divided. Half a dozen of them had their backs to Clarin, trying to stop the Isharites getting further into the room. The rest had been pushed back to the stairs that led up to the tower roof.

Clarin turned around to Cyprian.

'Go back and get the rest of them up here as soon as possible,' he told him. 'There's no time to waste.'

Cyprian immediately disappeared back down the stairs.

'Clarin!' said Jurgen, relief in his voice. 'Can you help?'

Clarin could see that Jurgen had a nasty wound across his calf where a spear had sliced into his leg, gouging out muscle, and probably cutting tendons. Blood was pooling in his shoe, and he could barely stand. Clarin quickly moved over and took his weight, manoeuvring him out of the way. The Dog-men replaced him, standing next to Rudy, and snapping menacingly at the Isharites who were trying to force their way in.

Clarin then moved over to help the Barbarians, who were hard pressed to keep their positions against the Isharites who had poured into the room.

'Have you seen Herin?' he shouted at the Barbarians.

One of them nodded a head in the direction of the stairs. Herin was probably using his bow and arrow up on the roof while he still had the chance.

When the Persaleians arrived, he moved back to meet them. Their faces had dropped at the situation.

'We're going to force our way up to the roof,' he told them. 'Zared, you will lead the attack. Join up with the Barbarians. Then start feeding your men up to the roof. I'll hold things here.'

Zared nodded, though it was the dull kind of agreement of a man who couldn't think of anything better. To their credit, though, the Persaleians wasted no time, and ran at the Isharites.

'Rudy,' said Clarin, moving over to the far side of the room. 'Take Jurgen up to the roof. I'll replace you here.'

The young Rotelegen man looked like he was going to argue, but instead nodded his assent and put his arm around the back of his cousin. Together, they hobbled towards the steps that led up to the roof.

Clarin took a glance nervously down the steps to the second floor, checking to see if the Isharites from below had followed the Persaleians up yet. It was still clear, so he joined the two remaining Dog-men. Although they lacked the reach of the Isharite spearmen, their snarling presence seemed to have done enough to keep them at bay.

A spearman jabbed at him through the door, going for his legs. Clarin knocked the strike away with his sword. He waited to see if he would try the same thing again. He did. This time, Clarin stamped down on the shaft of the spear. Before the Isharite could withdraw it, Clarin reached down and pulled at it with all his strength. He won the tug of war, pulling the Isharite along before wrenching it out of his hands. One of the Dog-men leaned over and sunk its claws into the head of the Isharite and somehow pulled him out further, before sinking its teeth into his neck, its face coming up bloody and triumphant.

Gripping his newly won spear, Clarin moved back over to the steps leading down to the second floor. There they were. The Isharites were marching quickly up the stairs. In a matter of moments, they would find themselves stuck between the two forces. He launched his spear down the steps. The soldier in front tried to move out of the way, but there was nowhere for him to go, and the spear lodged in his shoulder, sending him tumbling over.

Clarin looked across. The momentum of the Persaleian attack had now stalled. They had to move. He went back to get his sword.

'Come,' said Clarin to the two Dog-men.

Leaving the entrance to the east wall undefended, they rushed for the set of steps leading upwards.

'Go!' Clarin thundered as he arrived.

The Barbarians went first, running up the steps after Rudy and Jurgen, who had only just hobbled their way to the roof above. Next went the Persaleians, fighting a desperate rearguard action as the Isharites swelled around them. That left Clarin and the Dog-men. They backed up to the steps. Clarin held his sword out in front of him, daring the Isharites to attack. The two Dog-men snarled, crouching down low, ready to leap at the enemy.

The Isharites now seemed reluctant to make a move. Clarin, moving backwards, put a foot on the first step and then his other foot on the second. Still the Isharites didn't come, content to let them take the stairs. There were shouts from amongst them, and he could see that some of them now looked confused, as if they had been ordered to hold their position.

Glancing behind him, Clarin could see empty stairs, and he quickly made his way up before the Isharites changed their mind. He took in the scene. Jurgen and Rudy sat together a few feet away, leaning against the circular wall of the tower roof. Rudy was wrapping a rag around his cousin's calf. Persaleians and Barbarians alike lay or sat on the tower roof, utterly spent. Only a few still stood around the stairwell exit with weapons in hand, ready to continue the fight when the Isharites arrived.

The two Dog-men appeared on the roof, but still the Isharites waited below.

'Clarin!' called Cyprian. He was looking over the edge of the roof at the courtyard below. Smoke from the fire on the ground below swirled past him.

Ordering the Dog-men to defend the stairs, Clarin went to see what he wanted. Cyprian pointed down. The Isharite soldiers were now leaving the tower and heading away. For a while Clarin watched in disbelief as they kept moving—heading, it seemed, for the circular building in the centre of the fortress. He tried to understand what was happening. They had been all but defeated, with nowhere else to run; and yet the Isharites had left without finishing the job. He frowned, thinking.

'Soren?' he croaked to himself.

'What?' asked Cyprian.

Clarin shook his head. 'Gyrmund and Moneva went to rescue Soren. Maybe they found him...'

Cyprian looked far from convinced. 'I hope so.'

Clarin turned away. Zared approached him, offering his hand.

'Thank you,' said the young Persaleian.

Clarin took his hand, though he didn't feel like self-congratulation.

'Have you seen Herin?' he asked.

Zared shook his head.

'Herin?' shouted Clarin, staggering into the middle of the roof. His shoulder had gone numb and his sword hand ached. He had to concentrate on opening his fingers, they were gripping the hilt so tightly. As he did, the sword dropped to the ground with a clatter.

What was left of their sorry group had all collapsed onto the ground. None of them had escaped without an injury of some kind. He spied Tamir, the Barbarian chieftain, who was sitting down in the centre of the roof, nursing one of his hands. As Clarin approached he saw that he had lost two of his fingers from the hand, and a third was barely attached.

'Where's Herin?' he asked him.

Tamir frowned and turned around. With his good hand, he pointed to the far wall of the tower. 'He was fighting over there.'

He wasn't there now. Then, something made Clarin's heart quicken with fear. A bow and a quiver of arrows lay where Tamir had gestured. He moved over to look. Herin had perhaps used the position to fire on the Isharites approaching from the south wall. Clarin peered down. You could get a good shot in from here, and stay well protected by the wall that ran around the roof. But then what had happened? Maybe Herin had drawn his sword and left the roof to fight the Isharites? That would make sense.

Clarin scanned the roof once more. He then peered down at the walls below: all the way down to the courtyard, though it was hard to see clearly down there. He walked right around the roof, looking to see if Herin had fallen off, and landed over on the other side of the fortress. There was no sign of him.

Wearily, he headed for the stairs.

'Where are you going?' asked Zared, as Clarin walked past him.

'I have to find my brother.'

***

'What do you make of it?' asked Walter.

Farred looked out from their vantage point atop Burkhard Castle.

'It's like our prayers have been answered,' he said.

Beyond them, the horde of Drobax had turned around, and were marching away from the castle. They left a trail of devastation behind them.

The last few days had taken their toll. The Drobax had attacked the Duke's Crag night and day, and had nearly reached the summit. All but two of Walter's wooden gates had been torn down.

It was a scene from a nightmare. They had been unable to remove the bodies that littered the path up the crag. The crumpled bodies of Drobax had lain rotting in the sun for days. The stench was unbearable, and many of the men had started coming down with maladies: vomiting and diarrhoea were rife, and they spread yet more disease. Even the bodies of the Brasingians lay where they had fallen: some of them defiled by the Drobax, who had gnawed on the corpses of men who had died defending their country.

Footsteps behind them made Farred turn around. Emperor Baldwin had arrived to see for himself.

'We did it,' he said, so quietly that Farred wasn't sure whether he was speaking to himself or to them.

'It could be a ruse,' warned his brother.

'I think not,' Baldwin replied, pointing out to the east of the castle, in the direction of the Great Road. Here too, the Drobax, who had surrounded the castle for the last two weeks, in numbers so overwhelming that it had made any chance of survival seem impossible, had disappeared.

'What kind of ruse would it be?' continued Baldwin. 'To make us believe they had left, only to return and crush our spirits? We were fighting for our lives anyway.'

'Maybe so,' acknowledged Walter warily, seemingly unwilling to accept what he was seeing at face value. 'But why leave now? It doesn't make any sense.'

'Because they failed,' replied Baldwin. 'They failed to take this castle.'

Hardly, thought Farred. He doubted it had much to do with the siege. Hour by hour, the Drobax had been gaining the upper hand.

'Whatever the reason,' he said, 'the Isharites didn't lose this war. I fear they will return.'

Three weapons found, four still to go.

The Weapon Takers will return in Book Three, *The Jalakh Bow*.

Many thanks to everyone who has supported me.

Special thanks to Marcus Nilsson for beta reading (and sorry about the spelling of Inge).

CONNECT WITH THE AUTHOR

Website:

jamieedmundson.com

Twitter:

@jamie_edmundson

Newsletter:

http://eepurl.com/cvEqgP

'The best way to thank an author is to write a review.'

Please consider writing a review for this book.

Turn over for a sneak preview of the sequel to
Bolivar's Sword...

THE JALAKH
BOW

Prologue

'**E**RKINDRIX IS DEAD,' SHIRA said, keeping her voice steady. 'Arioc and the other members of the Council are at each other's throats. Now is the perfect time.'

The men in the hall didn't look convinced. Many of the most powerful noblemen in Haskany had made the journey to Shira's estate. She had fed them all, and plied them with arak to drink. But evidently, none of that meant they were going to commit to her cause.

These were hard looking men. Wrapped in furs that made them look twice as big as they were, they had agreed to come despite a cold snap that signalled late autumn was turning to winter.

They had served Arioc since he had become king. They would continue to serve him if necessary. But Shira knew, at the same time, that their country's servitude to Ishari chafed at each and every one of them. They were proud Haskans, who would see their country become independent. But they were careful. A failed rebellion could see them and their families destroyed.

'Together we could raise a reasonably strong and well provisioned army,' suggested Etan, a widely respected figure. 'I have no doubts over your leadership of it, or that of your uncle,' he said, nodding at Koren, who was standing to one side of Shira, arms folded. 'But the Isharites have magi. They have the Drobax. While that remains the case, we are not in a position to act against them.'

'*They* are not in a position to act against *us*,' she retorted, not willing to give in. 'Arioc, Ardashir and Siavash all fight each other to succeed Erkindrix. Not one of them has the resources to take on a united Haskany, and who knows how long their conflict may take? Even if one of them should emerge victorious, how likely is it that they will have the same power and reach as Erkindrix did? Would you cower in your halls, year after year, waiting until the Isharites return to claim our throne?'

There was anger at that—murmurs and whispers filled the hall. Maybe she had pushed them too far. But she knew that she needed to win these men over *now*. Should they drift aimlessly into the spring and summer months, divided and purposeless, a year would go by and they would have done nothing.

She looked at the faces in front of her. As many were against her as with her. And most weren't in either camp, unpersuaded and reluctant to commit to any path.

A knock at the door to the hall. Koren walked over to investigate. A whispered conversation followed. The attention of Shira's guests shifted in that direction. Uncertain, Shira turned to look.

Koren pulled the door wide open.

'Lord Pentas,' he announced in a strong voice, that gripped the attention of those in the hall.

Pentas sauntered in. It was the first time that Shira had ever been pleased to see him. He surveyed the hall, his red eyes fixing on the key figures in the room, making eye contact, a half-smile playing on his lips.

The atmosphere in the hall switched instantly. Pentas possessed powers that none of these men could understand or measure. Shira was their Queen, a member of the Council of Seven, yet Pentas exuded an authority she could never possess. It galled her, and yet she knew it might make the difference between success and failure.

'So,' Pentas said, drawing out the syllable, and raising his arms to encompass everyone who had gathered in the hall. 'Here are the new rulers of Haskany.'

And that, Shira knew, as she observed her countrymen, *is that.*

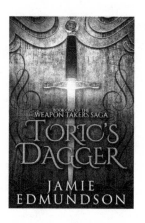

TORIC'S
DAGGER

Find out how it all started in the first instalment of
The Weapon Takers Saga.

'Outstanding...Quite simply, this is the most fun I've had reading
since the *Kingkiller Chronicles*' - *readper*